START SHOOTING

Also by Charlie Newton

Calumet City

START SHOOTING

A NOVEL

CHARLIE NEWTON

DOUBLEDAY
NEW YORK LONDON TORONTO
SYDNEY AUCKLAND

 Published in the United States by Doubleday, a division of Random House, Inc., New York, and in Canada by Random House of Canada Limited, Toronto.

www.doubleday.com

Lyrics from "Mornin' Ain't Comin' " by Kenny Herbert (www.kennyherbertmusic.co.uk).

Grateful acknowledgment is made to New Directions Publishing Corp. and Georges Borchardt, Inc. on behalf of the Estate of Tennessee Williams for permission to reprint excerpts from *A Streetcar Named Desire* by Tennessee Williams, copyright © 1947 by The University of the South. All rights reserved.

Jacket design by Emily Mahon
Jacket photograph © Grove Pashley / Photographer's Choice / Getty Images

Library of Congress Cataloging-in-Publication Data
Newton, Charlie.
Start shooting : a novel / Charlie Newton. — 1st ed.
p. cm.
1. Police—Fiction. 2. Corruption—Fiction. 3. Crime—Fiction. 4. Race relations—Fiction.
5. Brothers—Fiction. 6. Chicago (Ill.)—Fiction. I. Title.
PS3614.E73S73 2011
813'.6—dc22
2011002844

ISBN 978-0-385-53469-7

MANUFACTURED IN THE UNITED STATES OF AMERICA

1 3 5 7 9 10 8 6 4 2

First Edition

ACKNOWLEDGMENTS

Bobby and Arleen's novel is about hopes and dreams, the bet-it-all contracts that either propel you through the fire or burn you to death. If not for the backstage, to-the-bone candor of several remarkable individuals, the pages that follow couldn't go where they go.

ON BEING AN ACTRESS
Anne Johns and Kaaren Ochoa

ON BEING THE POLICE
Denny "Ten-Inch" Banahan, Bobby Vargas, Jason Cowin, Bob Anderson, and Patti Black

THE THEATER
Kevin Nance

THE EDITORS (HARD, SOULLESS MEN WHO TORTURED INSECTS AS CHILDREN)
Easy Ed Stackler and Don McQuinn

THE READERS (COUSINS OF THE HARD, SOULLESS MEN WHO TORTURED INSECTS AS CHILDREN)
F1 & F2: Sharon & Doug Bennett, Brian Rodgers, Big Jean Viallet, Catriona Kennedy, and Billy Thompson

AND MY PAL
Bill Owens

START SHOOTING

CHICAGO

The girl was thirteen and Irish, and fashioned out of sunlight so bright she made you believe in angels. The box was older, made from the same steel that armored battleships. It held momentous sins; the dark, grisly legacy of a terrified empire in ruin.

Seven thousand miles and thirty-seven years separated their burials, the box in a reinforced granite cave on the east end of Hokkaido Island, Japan; the girl in a velveteen-lined coffin at 111th and Central.

Give a Nobel laureate this year's NASA budget and every witch in New England and there's no way he could marry the two. Maybe the tarot readers in Chinatown saw Pandora coming—God knows they love that mystical shit more than money—but I didn't. I didn't see the murders of my friends. I didn't see the stacks of life-out blood money. I didn't see people I loved forcing me into a box so dark your soul melts.

Nineteen years I've been a ghetto cop and thought I'd worked every heartbreaking, horror combination possible. But I hadn't. I wasn't *marginally* prepared for how bad six days could get. And neither was anyone else.

1 SIX DAYS AGO

OFFICER BOBBY VARGAS

FRIDAY, 10:00 AM

Black, white, brown, or yellow, on Chicago's South Side, your neighborhood is your surname. Put on a gun belt, a suit, or a nun's habit, and all you did was accessorize.

For those of you exiting the 'L near Eighteenth and Laflin in the Four Corners, the etiquette is: grab a length of rebar, scratch a cross in the concrete, set both feet solid in the quadrant that best fits your skin tone, lean back, and start shooting. Welcome to Chicago, the "2016 Olympic City." We're glad you're here.

How *Olympic*? We have the best hot dogs, best pizza, worst baseball team, six months of weather that would give pause to a statue, and a river we dye green on St. Patrick's Day because we can. If the IOC could possibly require more, page two is fourteen miles of sandy beaches, blues bars that actually play the blues, icebergs in the winter, four racetracks, and street gangs with twenty thousand members. Think of Chicago as Club Med, but with issues. Wear clean underwear and socks in case there's an accident, and you're good to go.

On a good day.

Which, unfortunately, today isn't. Chicago isn't California-broke/bankrupt, but we're guaranteed citywide layoffs, school closings, and half-staff hospitals if we don't win the 2016 Olympic rebid now that Rio folded. Because our civic karma is a bit spotty, we're submitting our rebid during a Latino gang war on the West Side that won't stop making headlines, telling the IOC they'd be lots happier in Tokyo.

A Chicago defeat is worse than bad, but I/we have larger problems. Outsiders have come to the Four Corners. Outsiders who don't understand that some history will kill you dead if you don't leave it alone. These people weren't here twenty-nine years ago. I was.

Right over there, winter of 1982.

Above the unpatched asphalt and broken glass, in those four-story brick tenements.

It was cold and dead silent then; it's a hundred and six now. Frayed curtains flutter through windows propped open with No. 10 cans. Sharp voices bark from inside, blending with radios singing songs and making promises in three languages. Beneath the windows, lowriders and highriders idle their Chevys and pickups at their respective curbs, eyeing each other for insults they work overtime trying to see. Their neighborhood runs on friction, blame, violence, and reprisal.

America, the great melting pot? That's where Mayor Daley said we were headed when I grew up here, before the '68 and '72 riots changed everything. The truth is, that version of America is dead. We're the Balkans now, waving foreign flags from an idyllic old country that wasn't there when we left.

I lived two blocks from here when the riots went off, around the corner behind St. Dominick's. Grew up singing in the kitchen with my mom; wore what no longer fit my brother, Ruben; snuck Pall Malls from my father's pack before lung cancer and his two years in Korea finally killed him; and combed my hair as *American* as I knew how. We had a flag on our stoop every day it wasn't raining and I put it out there. My dad and I would stand at the flag, shoulder to waist, and salute it. I miss him and the country he died for, every morning when his picture watches me buckle on the body armor and 9-millimeter.

When I was a toddler, the Four Corners was home to "Ricans"—any shade of brown was considered Puerto Rican, like we'd all gotten off the same boat in Humboldt Park. Back then three other groups made up the neighborhood: shanty Irish, the I-talians who never made it to Taylor Street, and a sprinkling of Lithuanians from what they called Jewtown. The blacks were expanding toward us from the north and west but weren't here yet. Residents of the Four Corners didn't live on an island, more of a refugee camp with bad history and worse on the way. Not to say that blacks caused what happened. Everybody caused it.

To the south, the Chicago River kept us away from the bungalows of Mayor Daley's working-class, but way better-off, Bridgeport. If you were Irish and beholden to the Daley Machine but hadn't achieved *working class* yet, then you lived farther south, beyond the parking lots and souvenir sellers of Comiskey Park, in violent, insular Canaryville. If you were Irish and *aspired* to be beholden to the Daley Machine but were too poor or not tough enough for Canaryville, you lived *across the river* with us "Ricans" in the Four Corners; you listened to the White Sox on a neighbor's radio, drank Hamm's Beer on your stoop, and nights someone in your family mopped blood in the stockyards until it closed for good in '71.

To our east, fourteen elevated lanes of Dan Ryan Expressway and a hundred years of urban legend separated us from the First Ward. Within its boundaries the patronage jobs were doled out, as were the graft and violence necessary to run a major American city. The river ran through the First Ward's heart, ferrying goods to and from what was once the third-largest port in the world. Planes from the world's busiest airport flew over the First Ward. All the money coming into or out of Chicago made a stop in the First Ward. Big-boss aldermen brokered the city's future, beginning with Kenna and Bathhouse John, and ending with Toddy Pete Steffen who's still a kingmaker. One block farther east of Toddy Pete's dominion was Chinatown, but when I was a kid that trek meant braving the First Ward so Chinatown might as well have been fifty miles by camel.

To the north we could breathe a little; the Burlington Northern Railroad merely separated us from Jewtown—"Maxwell Street" we called it—a crosshatch of sweaty jangling street market where drinking-age restrictions hadn't caught on and goods-and-services warranties weren't given or implied. Jewtown we "Puerto Ricans" could go to if we were careful, which being young we weren't, until the riots changed the rules.

On Sundays, Muddy and Junior and Howlin' Wolf and anybody you could name played Maxwell and Halsted. Black men sportin' canary-yellow fedoras and girls on each arm mixed with nervous teenagers shopping for Mexican switchblades and factory-reject cowboy boots. Men with the musicians had walking sticks with voodoo heads and their women had nickel-plated revolvers. On the corner, Jim's Original grilled onions and Polish sausages all day. Nighttime white girls arched their backs under high-piled wigs, wore boots and tiny shorts and looked at you too long. The blues singers sang with half-a-man in each pocket, sipped those bottles between two fingers and each song till they were empty—song, bottle, and man.

Maxwell looked sort of like Eighteenth and Laflin does now, but acted way different. Fred Hampton of the Panthers was dead; so was Martin Luther King and the tension was high, but Sunday was a black/white truce day and Maxwell Street was the DMZ. Just before my big brother Ruben became a cop, he found me my first music-industry job sweeping the sidewalk out front of 831 West Maxwell at Maxwell Radio and Records—a real nice Jewish guy owned it, Bern Abrams and his wife, Idell-Idy. Ruben was their friend, made it a point that all the bad guys knew.

A week into my music career sweeping the sidewalk, Ruben walked out with three-hundred-pound Chicago legend Chester Arthur Burnett, the Howlin' Wolf himself, harmonica in one world-class hand, guitar in the other. Howlin' Wolf called me by name, took my broom, and slung his guitar over my shoulder. Un-freakin'-believable. Told me playin' was better than sweepin'; that he'd done a truckload of both and knew whereof he spoke.

Howlin' Wolf's why I bought my first guitar. Okay, it was the girls, but Howlin' Wolf was second. Big brother Ruben rode with me to a pawnshop in his friend's squad car the very next day and put up half the money; told the steel-eyed man behind the counter I was good for the other half. And ever since a guitar's been my answer to the day's questions.

My guitar didn't save Maxwell Street, long gone to "urban renewal," and it hasn't saved the blues from rap, although I'm trying. The Four Corners has hasn't fared well, either. Out here I have to be *Officer* Vargas, but you can call me Bobby. Actually, if you're a girl and like weekend guitar players, you can call me whatever you'd like. Toss in one of those pouty smiles or a three-star hair move, or just clap real loud while everyone else is talking, and I'm yours till you're tired.

I'm not quite your rock-star moment? Well, this guitarist has done a demo/session-player audition at Wolfe City Recording Studio, ground zero for the blues after Chess Records closed. Granted Wolfe City hasn't called back yet, possibly because I stood in the outer office drooling on the framed, autographed eight-by-tens and album covers for an hour, trembling like it was first confession day at St. Dom's. But Wolfe City will call, you'll see. And then it's "Stairway to Heaven" time. Get me the full pompadour, Ray-Ban 2140s, thin black tie—*baby.* Makes me shiver just thinking about it.

Unfortunately my district's taxpayers, all the bangers, and most of my coworkers don't see my future as clearly as I do; they think I'm just another pretty face. What I am is almost forty-two, the divorced father of two German shepherds—one of whom I miss—a failed Catholic, and speaker of street Spanish with some difficulty. My parents were both born in Mexico and my mom spoke lyrical Spanish every day of her life, so some in the Hispanic section of the Four Corners call my language issue a mental block. Others aren't as kind.

Some in the neighborhood also say I have a problem with professionalism in certain situations. This might be true; I have received CR numbers (complaint registers) a hundred and sixteen times in nineteen years. Sounds like a lot, but it's less than one a month and not bad if you beat them. If you don't beat them, a hundred and sixteen would be a hundred and ten too many. Do I give a shit? Well, yeah, I enjoy beating the crap out of ghetto people.

Just kidding; we talk sort of tough down here. However, I do find some pleasure in trading punches with assholes, Hispanic gangsters in particular. Any gangster would do, but other than the Four Corners, the 12th District is almost exclusively Hispanic gangs, my homeys, many of whom I've known since they were shorties. They consider me a traitor; I have suggested they tighten up the hairnets and drive their '62 Chevys south a thousand miles, learn to eat sand and iguanas, then come back and see which country they like better. I also insult black, white, and Asian gangsters, but not as well. A cultural bias? Only if you consider street gangs with twenty thousand members a culture.

SIREN. Then another. A blue-and-white wails past the alley's mouth, a Crown Vic right behind him. A four-foot-tall tough guy backs away from the cars and into the alley's mouth—flannel shirt, baggies, white sneakers. I pull my SIG Sauer, slide it under my leg, and pop my siren. The kid spins fast, almost falls, IDs the car, and digs in to run.

"*Little Paul.* Get your ass over here."

Little Paul freezes, eyes cutting, trying to choose between whatever scared him into the alley or me, his seven-year-old brain not quite up to the task.

"Now."

Little Paul unfreezes, pimp rolls to my front bumper, eyes me through the windshield, then cups his balls. He walks dented fender to my window where he stops and stands one shoulder lower than the other. The smooth brown face says, *"Me llamo Pachito."*

"Your name's Paul. You're an American, in America. You speak English."

His head, even with the do-rag and flat-bill ball cap, barely makes the bottom of my window. But he be bad, baby. Squint-eyed, teeth bit together, don't-fuck-with-me bad. *Me llamo Pachito . . . Ramera."* *Ramera* means *bitch*. As in, that's what I am.

"All ganged up, huh? Your brother still dead? Your father? How's that working out for them?"

Little Paul steps back and taps his chest with three fingers extended on both hands. KK—King Killers, street mythology that says his set kills Latin Kings on sight; doctrine that's almost as stupid as the WTC-9/11-let's-bomb-some-firemen ayatollahs.

"Your ma still working four jobs so you can wear those rags? Hang with these losers?"

"Mi madre—"

"Speak English, you little fuck, or I'll throw your ass in those trash cans."

He looks away—*fuck you* in street Spanish.

I pop the door, knock him off-balance, and exit, SIG 9 in hand. "Hands on the tire."

He does. Seven years old, a second grader, and he knows how to be arrested. And social workers wonder why this gang shit pisses cops off.

"Gimme the rock or I make you strip."

"TAC cops can't do that. Gotta call Juvy."

"I'll call the Sisters of Providence, too. But that'll be right after I fuck you in the ass. The rock or strip. One or the other. Now."

He does neither. I rip the dope out of his pockets and the pocket liners with it. Fourteen bags that should've been in his mouth but his mouth is too small. Ten dollars apiece. My left hand twists his shirt to his neck and spins him around to face me. My right hand holsters the SIG, then rubs black from my front tire. With my index finger I make a black dot on his forehead. Ash Wednesday for bangers.

"You tell Danny Vacco I catch you walking his dope again, I put a bullet in his head." My index finger taps the dot. "Right. Fucking. There."

"Don' think so."

"You don't, huh? Why don't we go find him now? I shoot the spic right in front of you. Make you boss."

Little Paul looks away.

I shove him backward. "Why do I keep trying to be your friend? Maybe you're just too stupid to save."

He throws me the KK again.

"Get the fuck outta here. Tell big bad Danny I got his dope." I draw my SIG and show Little Paul the barrel. "Right inside there is where I got it. And tell him Bobby Vargas don't have to hide in his own neighborhood."

Little Paul marshals his peewee-gangster dignity and slowly walks away to explain how he lost fourteen bags of rock. Later today I'll make a pass on Jourdan Court so Danny Vacco knows it wasn't bullshit. Even seven-year-olds don't live long if they steal from the gang.

Back in the car I consider today's *Herald* on the seat. The headline above the fold is Furukawa Industries and their billion-dollar support of Chicago's Olympic rebid. We get the Olympics, money flows in from everywhere; Chicago's budget is in the black for the next five years; developers make a ton of money; and a whole bunch of ghetto along the lakefront and ghetto gangsters are pushed out of the city.

Beneath the fold the news isn't so good. Part one of an "exposé" written by Tracy Moens, Chicago's star crime reporter. My name is prominent, as is Coleen Brennan's, and so is the Four Corners' troubled history—*special* problems like rape, cop killings, cop reprisals, and dead little girls. History that's better for everyone if it stays buried with the victims and families . . . but won't as long as there's money to be made and old scores to be settled. And a big-city newspaper on life support.

I knew Coleen Brennan and her twin sister, Arleen—not to play with; when I was a kid you didn't play with the white girls, especially the Irish—but by the time we were six Coleen and I had become real friends just the same. The last time I saw Coleen she was in an alley between here and Greektown before Greektown was six-digit condos and coffee cost five dollars. They found her lying faceup, crumpled in the trash, a mitten on one hand, a torn school-uniform blouse, and nothing else. February had frozen her fast, the screams still in her eyes. At the time, and maybe still, it was the scariest, saddest thing I'd ever seen. She and I were thirteen. February 3rd, year of our Lord 1982.

Year of our Lord—no way the God most people worship is real, not with the shit He allows. That said, I'll grant the preachers and faith healers that something powerful is out here festering in the dark, whatever it is. If you're a cop you can't help but believe in evil—not after a career of gag-reflex basements, eighty-year-old rape victims, full-auto drive-bys . . . every now and then a Mulwray (from the movie *Chinatown,* our name for a father-daughter; some stuff you have to rename).

The 12th District cops caught Coleen's killers and the state tried them—death sentence for the older one; triple life for the other because he only confessed to raping her. The killers were from Stateway Gardens, the projects by Thirty-fifth on the other side of the Dan Ryan, black teenagers who said they were in our neighborhood to see relatives who'd just moved in. It was the fearful era of white flight and the integration strategy of blockbusting and solid footholds. A week after the *Herald* printed the relatives' part in the boys' confession, the relatives' apartment burned to the foundation. Took the Irish firemen an hour to get their hoses right. But the blacks kept coming and their gangs came with them.

Coleen's twin sister, Arleen, stayed at St. Dom's but no one outside the school ever saw her other than a uniform cop who'd walk her both ways and a Child Services worker (shrink) who visited twice a week. Coleen's mom waitressed across the river in Bridgeport, tried to hold it together because she had Arleen to raise, but as it turned out Mrs. Brennan had only a year to live herself. After Coleen's murder, the father became a neighborhood fixture even the non-Irish cops left alone, a mean hair-trigger longshoreman who drank on the Brennans' stoop till the wife died and the surviving twin ran off a day later—fourteen years old and she didn't even stay for her mother's funeral—says something about that household. The father eventually disappeared into Canaryville or some other private hell. I never set foot on Coleen's block again. And prior to Coleen's father leaving, no black people did, either.

Life went on in the Four Corners. Harold Washington outcampaigned Mayor Daley's son and became the new mayor. Race and poverty and *new urbanism* dominated the city's agenda, but back then the state of Illinois could still kill somebody for raping a little girl to death. Anton Dupree, the black teenager they executed, was thirty-seven when he finally died at Stateville; the other perp died in his cell—thirty-seven stab wounds to the neck, face, and chest. Anton talked a lot in the six months before the state killed him, pointed his finger everywhere except the mirror. By then I was on the job five years, got the chance to attend the execution in place of my commander, sat second row and smiled at Anton when they walked him in, but I don't think he saw me—the state offers the condemned inmate tranquilizers ahead of time and Anton had accepted. Anton had a minister with him as well, a denomination-of-one preacher from Seventy-ninth Street who was sure this was a white conspiracy. The assistant state's attorney sitting next to me said they should execute the preacher, too, call it efficient governance.

I was twenty-six on that very day and surprised that I didn't feel any better when Anton died. It wasn't that I didn't believe in capital punishment—sure, doing it quicker would make it more of a deterrent; and making state-paid DNA mandatory would level the field for the guys who can't afford O.J.'s lawyers—but in the end, humans convicted of first-degree murder need to vacate the gene pool. And street cops can't shoot them anymore.

So, why the *Chicago Herald*'s sudden interest in digging up the distant past? For one thing, it turns out Anton Dupree probably didn't kill Coleen Brennan. I'm not saying Anton Dupree was an angel but it turns out he was retarded, "not operating with a clear understanding of his situation" when he gave and signed his confession. His public defenders say they didn't know; the ASA who prosecuted him three times says she didn't know; and I didn't know . . . or don't think I did.

But two of my fellow officers knew, one of whom was my older brother, Ruben. At least that's what the lawyers for Anton's family are saying. Wrongful death—$8.9 million from the city of Chicago; same from all four of the cops who worked the case, like cops have that kind of money. Hell, my brother didn't come on the job until the first trial was almost over.

Should the cops who worked the case have known Anton was retarded, possibly innocent? That's kind of the problem. On TV the hero cop bucks the system—takes on the role of the ASA, the judge, the jury, overrides the Constitution, does the *right thing,* and saves the accused as well as the American justice system from a tragic mistake. America can tuck the kids in, pet the dog, and go to bed knowing our system works—and when it doesn't, heroes (insert movie-star name here) will fill in the gaps.

Try that shit in Chicago and you'd be fired, your pension toast, followed by a short or long prison term depending on the public mood, and named in a civil suit to take whatever money or valuables your defense lawyers didn't. Why? Because *someone* would be positive you got it wrong. And some race, creed, or gender constituency would agree. There would be tabloid media and mainstream media, radio shock jocks, preachers, aspiring politicians, and law firms atop proud white horses. Time it just right and there'd be parades.

So cops stay within the system. Or you cheat *carefully.* And when you cheat for what you think are the right reasons, they say you're the devil. And when you don't cheat, they say you're a coward. And you're both, all the time, for a starting salary of $45K and the chance to die in a dark hallway for people you don't know.

My pager goes off, and I throw the newspaper aside. Time to go to work, meet friends for a gunfight that has nothing to do with Coleen Brennan's murder but everything to do with this neighborhood. I spend a last few seconds with her building, her window. So why won't I shut up about her? Let it go?

Two reasons: First, Coleen was nice to me—it was our secret. Started when we were six. We went to different schools, but our windows faced each other across the alley. She was white and back then I wasn't, and both mattered a great deal to me. Coleen was also my first real true and honest friend. Dangerous for us both because the Four Corners had race rules written in blood. Coleen and I weren't allowed to look at each other, let alone talk, or God forbid, touch, so we conjured a plan.

We'd sit in our windows every afternoon reading each other's books. She'd leave me one behind her trash can and I'd exchange it with one I'd get from our library on Loomis Street. By sixth grade, we decided we were officially boyfriend-girlfriend. I wrote songs about her. Coleen was the only Irish girl whose hand I ever held. By eighth grade, I was so in love with her and who we would become, that I didn't stop carrying a picture of us until I was twenty-five. Had it with me, soft in my hand, the day Anton Dupree quit breathing.

Reason number two is the *Chicago Herald*'s exposé: "MONSTER: The Murder of Coleen Brennan." Part one implies that in the days to come they will prove that my brother Ruben and I were the two boys who actually killed her.

2

She was alone because all little girls are alone on that day. Alone with a man—it's almost always a man, middle-aged, white—alone with the man who entices her into a car, a doorway, a vacant lot; a man who uses her in ways a civilized person can't quite fathom, can't quite add to their visual vocabulary.

—"MONSTER," by Tracy Moens; © 2011 *Chicago Herald*

ARLEEN CRISTA BRENNAN, ACTRESS

FRIDAY, 10:30 AM

Big grin for my bus stop: population six, a rainbow nation of very diverse hopes and dreams, all waiting for the Division Street Super-Shadow. Thirty seats scented with urine, vomit, summer sweat, and industrial disinfectant—the daily life cycle that cauterizes public transportation and keeps our fares down. Artie, our bus driver, calls us the United Colors of Benetton (I'd go with the Funkadelics) and says we're his favorite stop. Well, duh.

Six days a week we arrive here packaged from small closets and kitchens, semi-ready to meet another workday in our city, the Second City, the City of Big Shoulders. And just maybe the Olympic City, if the festival banners rehung along Division Street are right this time.

Horn toot, the 7-0 looms big and silver and pushes a slow-moving Pontiac forward. The bus door pops open and six Funkadelics bound up the steps. Artie smiles. I smile back. Today's my first day being me again.

It's not like I haven't been here before, but first days are always difficult. They're the final exit from intricate, intensely constructed fantasy back into an all too often blighted reality. Sound strange? It is, like coming down from a ferociously colorful LSD landscape to grayscale, soundless dust bowl; or a massive weekend romance with champagne and room service that leaves you flushed and tingly, but somehow emptier, some part of you lost in the exchange. And here's the kicker—you make this journey on *purpose,* with every ounce of your being, as often as they'll let you. And as often as your sanity can take it.

That's what it's like to audition, if being an actress is why you're alive. And 99 percent of the time the payoff is "Thank you for coming."

To do this well, it helps to be desperate or crazy, or both.

For the two weeks leading up to last Wednesday's audition, I slowly became Southern belle Blanche DuBois, meticulously purging any sense of "me" with yoga, intense meditation, and finally the deep-core exercises of Lee Strasberg that bring the tears and vomit. I've not had children, nor do I live in the third world where those children die young, but the process has similarities—death first, as the original you fades away; then new life, only to see your new identity, your creation, wither and die.

Our driver palms his cap, nodding as he accepts the paper bag I offer. He grins at the baked-apple-and-nutmeg aroma, follows my eyes to the Pontiac I'm watching drive away, then back. "Mighty nice of ya, Arleen. Mighty nice." His salt-and-pepper stubble hasn't changed in the two years I've been riding the Super-Shadow.

"Show business loves ya, Artie." No doubt, I'm the only passenger who brings him Belfast crumble muffins. Better his waistline than mine; each one of those nutty little monsters is thirty-seven minutes on the StairMaster. I bake them for luck. Not that they work all that often, but my ma said when you gave crumble muffins away it was buildin' a foundation in Heaven. She was a waitress, too, but over in Bridgeport.

Actually, I should say I'm "an actress who waits tables." At "thirty-nine" waitressing is one of the elemental ways you know you're an actress. The other is to learn every bit of craft and art anyone will teach you, prepare for every opportunity like it's your last, and, finally, pour your heart and soul into the auditions that all seem to end with "Thank you for coming," then do more auditions, then do some more if you can get them. Pay the price; take every part they offer and play it to the walls. And when you're finally in the running for Blanche DuBois, for a real part that might be the break you've earned, and you have a feeling that you might honestly have a chance—the casting director said something or his eyes did, something—then, and only then, do you bake Belfast crumble muffins.

My stop is State Parkway and Division. At the newsstand in front of P. J. Clarke's, I sneak a *Chicago Tribune* off the stacks surrounding the *Herald* and its tabloid headlines. In a month or two, the *Herald* will likely join America's newsprint graveyard. Where it belongs. Barney, the blind kid with the change bag says, "Hey, Cincinnati."

He means *The Cincinnati Kid,* the movie with Steve McQueen and Tuesday Weld. My middle name is Crista but "Cincinnati" has been my nickname since my twenties; a fellow hopeful at the Actors Studio in L.A. thought I resembled Tuesday Weld . . . if you squinted and it was dark. He's dead now, an OD after a final "Thank you for coming."

"We pitchin', Cincinnati?" Barney flashes a quarter between two black fingertips.

"I never win. Why don't I just pay double?"

"Could do that. Get me some actin' classes, too."

I put a dollar in his palm. "That's my lunch money, Barn. Trust me, only one of us has to wait tables; you're Broadway ready."

FRIDAY, 11:00 AM

Showtime in ten minutes. Apron on, ponytail just right. Chest out, lipstick . . . *man,* I can wear some lipstick. Tuesday Weld at "thirty-nine."

Sniffle. Sniffle.

Suzie. Poor thing; twentysomething, life ruined, and all she has is me. And I don't know one lullaby for girls already wearing long pants and makeup. In the Four Corners an Irish lass had to harden up a bit by then, hide what troubled her. And I'm not much of a singer anyway—dancer, forget about it, tiptoe you right off the floor—but singer, not so much.

Suzie shrinks deeper into her very attractive shoulders.

I lift. "C'mon, sweetie, let's get you some eyeliner."

Suzie continues to sniffle rather than participate in her reconstruction and a lunch rush that starts in eight minutes. She and I are two of nine waitresses at Hugo's on Rush Street, the North Side's one block of leafy boulevard de Montmartre. I hug Suzie's shoulder and lift—

Nope, she'd prefer to sniffle rather than prep her tables. Our manager notices and rolls his eyes—most of us are actors or actresses, so drama is occasionally on sale here, especially when we were sure we had the part. Today I have a right to a bit of drama, given the teaser exposé headline below the fold in today's *Herald,* but I'm not going there. No one in Hugo's knows I'm Coleen Brennan's twin sister. In the two years I've been back I haven't been near the Four Corners; that life happened to someone else.

I *have* spoken to two people who know me. One cop, and now one reporter from the *Herald.* Each time the *Herald* has asked for my cooperation, I've refused. And I won't read the article today, written by strangers about a beautiful girl they didn't know. Twenty-nine years ago I watched strangers bury Coleen, a part of me lost in the ether but not gone. A year later my ma died, and I ran . . . from my father and the Four Corners . . . all the way to Hollywood; was all of fourteen when I arrived. Axl Rose sang about it in "Welcome to the Jungle"—all the drama a scared Irish girl could stand.

I smile "sorry" at my manager, then tell Suzie, "Honey, Kylie Minogue couldn't wear the back of those pants any better; from the front you're Miss Teen USA; you'll work again, even if it's porn loops."

Suzie doesn't laugh, although it's true. She has talent and looks and youth, and she will work again—here, New York, or L.A. if she doesn't quit or self-destruct, self-destruction being a prime career hazard that claims as many of us as service revolvers do Chicago policemen. Window check—I know two Chicago policemen, and not in a good way, but like that Pontiac that spooked me this morning, both are part of another story.

"C'mon, we'll buy you some blow after work, you can saddle up a cowboy or five."

Suzie smiles perfect pouty lips and forces herself to her feet. She straightens an apron that will make four or five men risk their families before lunch is over . . . and sniffles. Suzie will work again. And like one, maybe even two of us in here with stacks of dog-eared scripts in our bedrooms, the kitchen Peg-board of wrap-party photos from the shows we got, and address books full of "contacts" from those shows we didn't get, lightning will strike—I've seen it, been so close I thought it was finally my turn—the stage lights will hit and we'll be whole.

Whole because beyond the stage lights and adulation, we'll be welcomed backstage into a new family, a joyous and dysfunctional troupe of drama queens and crew, for birthdays and doctor days, for new boyfriends and teary breakups, marriages and graduations, all the sinew and gristle that binds hearts to souls forever and ever. But only if we don't quit. In the actress business, persistence and will are all we have; they take the rest, all of it, and don't apologize.

The lunch rush starts like it's supposed to. Our customers act like the well-heeled are supposed to. Brass from Furukawa Industries are in booth 1, accepting heartfelt thanks, basking in their save-the-city limelight. One billion dollars buys a lot of PC/PR in protectionist times. Should allow Americans across the land to wave Old Glory whenever we buy Furukawa's made-in-America cars, or happily bank in Furukawa-controlled banks, or watch Furukawa flat-screen TVs. I don't blame Furukawa. It works for McDonald's. Selling obesity to schoolkids is okay as long as you also fund a clown and his rape crisis center.

Everything's rocking along like Friday should and: my cell phone rings with my agent's ringtone. *Shock. Panic.* Sarah calls rarely, almost never—and never, ever, ever when prayed for. And this week I've prayed every hour I wasn't waiting tables. I lit candles at St. Mary's and watched the sun come up over her steeples.

I flash on my ma's Belfast crumble muffins and flip the phone open, pushing it between shoulder and ear and the strawberry blond hair the real me reinvigorates twice a month. I dread hearing the "Thank you for coming" or just "Sorry," but I'm weak and blindly full of hope and acting is a soul addiction that kills you a lot of different ways. I'm already reaching under the hot lights for my order, telling the cheeseburgers and my agent: "Hi, Sarah!"

Pause . . . endless seconds . . . the "Sorry" from my agent's assistant about to begin my long dark descent into the well where Blanche

DuBois and I will say goodbye to her life and my dreams. Both eyes close to hide the death from my friends and fellow aspirants, the reality that yet again, after all the investment and risk, the Shubert Theater Company doesn't want Arleen Brennan as part of their family.

Sarah says: "Grab something, Arleen . . . The river parted, you got the callback."

I drop both cheeseburgers—$12.00 each, medium rare, no tomatoes. "For *Streetcar*?" The stainless-steel counter saves the burgers and most of the hand-cut fries. My other hand rescues the phone. "*Me*? The Shubert wants me?"

"Just spoke with the director. They're down to two for Blanche, you and—"

"Oh my God . . ."

It's almost too much . . . after two decades as Arleen the Also Appearing. Oh my God, the big time; lightning has struck. A hip bumps me sideways. Suzie has gently hip-checked me out of the way and grabs her order. "Sarah, this isn't a joke, right? Don't do that, not after . . . For real, I'm *half* the callback?"

"Yes and yes. Sunday, eleven AM at the theater. The director, producer, casting director, and Jude Law's agent. You'll read with Jude. I'll have the pages sent by the restaurant."

Oh my God. Finally.

Vivien Leigh was my age—way past her prime, they said—when she played Blanche DuBois. She showed 'em, won the Academy Award for best actress. Vivien was English, playing a Mississippi Southern belle. I'm Belfast–Four Corners–Irish; it's perfect.

"Sarah, don't worry; I know all the parts by heart." Oh my God . . . *finally.* "You're sure it's me?"

She laughs. "I'm sure."

Happy feet! Float on air. Waitressing at Hugo's is . . . *brilliant.* "Wait. Who's the other actress?"

"I'm sending the pages anyway. Worry about Tennessee Williams, not her."

"Is she big?"

"Honestly, I don't know. Just that she's flying in from L.A. tomorrow night."

"Sarah, I *am* Blanche DuBois. This is it. My turn. Has to be."

"I never promise clients, you know that, but no actress deserves this part more."

I deliver the cheeseburgers without touching the floor and kiss both recipients. Tinker Bell has touched me; I can fly. The most glorious lunch rush in history begins to slow. My cheeks have more lipstick than my lips. Tommy, the manager, is showing me where my picture will go—

A man steps into the bar window: Homicide Detective Ruben Vargas.

No. No. Not now; not here. I crane into the window, wide-eye for the Pontiac that was in front of my bus this morning. *Please, God, no Koreans*; they can't ever know my real name, where I work— The window fills. Two stunning models from Elite take turns kissing Ruben's cheek. He gently pats their bare shoulders, shakes their agent's hand, and sans partner, Ruben Vargas steps in off Rush Street. No square-faced Korean mafia gangsters follow.

My heart starts beating again. Ruben winks at Charlene, our fresh-faced maître d' assistant. She beams, hugs him with both arms, cranes for me on the floor, then the bar, and jubilantly waves me over like Ruben brought us the fall line from Prada.

Charlene's lost what limited poise she's acquired at Northwestern because whether you're a college girl, café society, or made gangster, Ruben Vargas is a street legend in Chicago. *The man,* don'cha know. Five foot seven, same as me, forty pounds heavier, all of it sinewy muscle, but tailored into a mint-green linen blazer and expensive jeans. His jet-black hair is cut perfect and combed straight back. A hint of cologne on smooth cocoa skin. The only mar is a razor-thin scar from mouth to ear. A fine doorway full of man, the Dublin girls would say.

I knew who Ruben was when I was little. He was grown and we never spoke. Ten months ago we were reintroduced at a theater party. An actress there described him as "coarse brown sugar." I didn't take the sample I was offered, but she had, and licked her lips when she said it.

My mistake, one of many, was dealing with Ruben with his clothes on. When I get to Ruben he smiles and turns us away from Charlene. "Lose your phone?"

"No, I—"

"We gotta get set up, baby." Ruben scans Hugo's patrons. "Finish that thing for me like you promised."

"Ruben, I can't, I have to prep. I made the callback for *Streetcar.* Sunday; can you believe it! The lead opposite Jude Law."

Ruben lingers on the Furukawa table and their corporate glow, then cuts back to me, grinning like a proud papa. "No need to thank me for openin' their eyes. Congratulations."

"Finally. I'm so—"

"So we gotta get this done tonight or you're missing Sunday."

Blink. Half the brilliant sunlight fades. "What?"

"You heard me. And no more losing your phone."

My back straightens. "In some other life, I'm missing my callback."

Ruben squares up. "*Princesa,* you forgettin' your responsibilities? What the fuck we're into?"

"Not *we,* Ruben. *You.* I'm an actress."

"I delivered your audition. Remember? And now you got the callback. And these are bad men who we gotta stop, whether you still believe it or not."

Ruben hooked me up with an impossible-to-get final-round audition for *Streetcar.* In exchange, I'd participate in a police sting operation. CPD needed a serious actress who'd accept serious risk for a good cause, a cause he knew would hook me, one I have very personal reasons to champion anyway. I got the audition. And the "bad men" are every ounce of that. But everything else Ruben fed me was a lie.

"Actress or waitress, what you are, *princesa,* is in too deep to be doing anything but what I say until we straighten this problem out."

The fading sunlight dies to dark; Tinker Bell flies away, replaced by years of aprons and promises and dreams that always seem to slip out of reach. I lean in at a dangerous cop who knows too much about me, about mistakes I've made—*his* mistakes in *his* sting, not CPD's—mistakes he and his crooked cop partner, Robbie Steffen, have set up to be mine if things go bad. And they have. The smart response, the survival response is shut up, say nothing.

But not today. Today I got the callback; today my sister and I are the winners. Coleen and I stare straight at Ruben's eyes. "Whatever you and Steffen are *really* into with the Koreans came this close to getting Robbie killed." My finger and thumb pinch together. "I don't know why you picked me for this disaster, but I signed up on a lie and I'm not dying for it. So fuck you, Ruben. And fuck Robbie Steffen. And fuck your psycho problems in Koreatown. How's that?"

Detective Ruben Vargas eases a toothpick into a smile that can mean anything from good wishes to cemetery. "Hope it plays in Koreatown, 'cause we both know they'll kill you if it don't. And we both know you're goin' back."

3

Some urban nightmares begin as graffiti on a dirty brick wall. Was 13-year-old Coleen Brennan's murder a reprisal for racist policing? Or was she raped to death as part of a gang initiation, an act so calculatedly savage that we refuse to believe it possible in our city? Maybe. Or was Coleen's murder the early work of a growing young sociopath, another Gacy or Speck, watching and waiting in the tenements where life and death are cheap and plentiful?

—"MONSTER," by Tracy Moens; © 2011 *Chicago Herald*

OFFICER BOBBY VARGAS

FRIDAY, 3:00 PM

Foghorns boom across the Laflin Maritime work yard.

Three nervous gang cops stare at me in the diesel-fouled air. Behind us and the four-story stacks of dented containers, Chicago's Sanitary and Ship Canal feeds the city her raw materials, the berthing docks loud with the shriek of barge cranes and stevedore shouts. Noise is good. Noise is cover from *on the record.*

Put cops under, or near, the spotlight of a big-city newspaper fighting to stay in circulation, and to a man, we'll all be nervous. Every cop has sins, some greater than others. And every cop has bosses, some you can trust, some you can't. Our boss was promoted to district commander three weeks ago while still up on the far North Side, arrived down here at midnight on the same night, and brought two non-sworn personnel with her. All we know about her is she has a law degree from

Northwestern, rumored judicial aspirations, and very little street experience. Not the choice downtown would make to stop a gang war.

Everyone in the 12th District who's awake believes our new commander's arrival is directly related to the $44.5 million federal lawsuit filed by Anton Dupree's family for his "wrongful execution by the state of Illinois." Those depositions begin in three days. Should one cop or several in this district need to burn to save the city money or embarrassment in the Olympic era, our new commander has no allegiances here, past or present. Shitty, but that's how the job works. And we've been waiting to see how the city and the department play it.

Then today's *Herald* lands with the opening installment of "MONSTER," naming police officers Ruben and Bobby Vargas as complicit in the murder that killed Coleen Brennan, executed the aforementioned Anton Dupree, and could cost the city $44.5 million.

Me and half of Gang Team 1269 are standing on this oily gravel because we don't believe the timing of the exposé and depositions is coincidental, and that means the plaintiff's lawyers and the tabloid are working together. Worse, we believe the department and our new commander *knew* the *Herald*'s exposé was coming. So as of today, we *know* how the department's gonna play it.

Should the other installments of the *Herald*'s exposé "deliver" on part one's promise, the city will settle with the Duprees out of court and the Vargas brothers are gone. Period, end of story. Then every cop Ruben and I have worked with will be thrown under the lights, then the bus if the investigation shows they've scuffed their shoes once or twice during their careers.

And that includes three-hundred-pound Walter "Jewboy" Mesrow, the gentlest giant ever to come out of Eastern European fairy tales. Walter removes a Texas Jewboys cap, wiping sweat with a leg-of-lamb forearm. His thick black hair remains in the shape of the cap and the wide-set eyes search mine for reassurance I wish I had.

"Yeah, Walter." I pat his size 56 vest and the neon cowboy shirt underneath. "Hasn't been a good day."

Officer Mesrow is one of my "sins," a work in progress, and always will be, not that we'd tell him that. He was nineteen when I met him, a big overripe Serbian immigrant kid surrounded by a gang of teenagers who'd spilled his four bags of groceries and punched him around a little. Walter was on his knees, blood on his lips, chasing oranges as my fellow Americans taunted him for his clothes and accent. Their girls laughed. I took offense, earned one of my hundred and sixteen CR numbers, and Walter Mesrow, like Little Paul is now, became one of "Bobby's projects."

Walter decided he wanted to become a cop. Had to take the test four times. Some have said that maybe I *helped* with his grade, then after he graduated had him ride with me as his training officer until he could survive on his own. And because of his repeated street mistakes, I took a gangster bullet, as did a bystander, then lied under oath to protect Walter's job. Our sergeant, Buff Anderson, now watches over Walter. Like I said, all cops have sins.

Walter's sin is his weekly Kinky Friedman/Texas Jewboys karaoke habit (hence the nickname), a practice that I've sadly participated in more than once. All in all, as every guy on this team would tell you, Jewboy's loopy grin is one of the day's little victories. And in this job, little victories are all you get.

His giant hand hikes a handful of brown Sansabelt pants, the other extends a rolled copy of today's *Herald* at our sergeant's chest. "*Out of the sky,* the paper decides Bobby's a *child molester*? *Three* days before the Dupree depositions? Nope, not for this copper."

My name and *child molester* . . . of a beautiful girl who meant more to me than breathing. In a few days the *Herald* will likely print that I take off Coleen's death day every year, that I'm the mystery man who leaves the flowers at Holy Sepulchre Cemetery.

Buff brushes the paper aside. He and my team won't fold on me, but Buff is not a happy sergeant. "What the fuck, Vargas? Library books?"

"I'm thirteen, for chrissake. I'm supposed to know library books make me a murder suspect? I'm still too young to buy cigarettes."

Buff looks away—thirty-two years on the job, balls like cantaloupes—then back, a move that says we're good. "But still, you should've—"

"*Should've what?* The Homicide dicks don't ask me, why would I say something? I'm *thirteen*; they're Irish, lynch-mob mad, hunting someone who murdered one of their teenage girls."

Jewboy's giant arm loops my shoulder. Buff smoothes arctic white hair, piercing blue eyes leveled on mine. Buff has three children of his own, one with muscular dystrophy, and works a second job six days a week to pay her medical bills. "Shoulda said about the books."

"*Books.*" Jewboy stabs his rolled-up *Herald* into his heart and the body armor covering it. "Always got me, too. What's your brother say?"

"Ruben told Tracy Moens to fuck off six months back when the Duprees filed the lawsuit. I heard she braced him an hour ago at Area 4, wanted his reaction to 'MONSTER'; had a cameraman and that ex-cop/investigator from Texas with her acting like he's some kind of avenging angel."

My partner, Jason Cowin, rests one meaty forearm on his automatic, turning to movement in the containers while he speaks. "Ruben Vargas ain't someone I'd accuse *in person* of anything this ugly. Even IAD would've called first."

Buff frowns. Then spits to his side. "IAD called you yet?"

"Woke up this morning to: 'Hello, Officer Vargas, you have an appointment with the Internal Affairs Division Monday morning at 0800.' "

Jewboy's hand mauls the *Herald.* "Nope. Still don't see it. Three days before depositions and the newspaper has to call Bobby a child molester?"

"Stop saying that, okay?"

"Makes no sense, you're not that Kennedy guy."

Buff squints, not following Jewboy's logic. Nor am I.

Jewboy shakes his head at stupid. "Kennedy's cousin? Michael Skakel? The neighbor; he's fifteen jacking off in the tree." Jewboy uses his free hand to show us how.

Jason turns back from the containers, laughing. "Can you imagine your *alibi* is you're in a tree with your dick out? Fuck the *Herald*'s ex-cop from Texas; we get us Mark Fuhrman; he busted Skakel thirty years after the murder when no one else could, *or would.*" Jason adds gangsta. " 'Cause Skakel a *playah,* he a *Kennedy.*"

Jewboy blinks twice, then grins big. "I got it. We'll chip in, hire Fuhrman to Rodney King the *Herald* . . . and their goons." He nods at Buff to agree, problem solved.

Buff slowly rubs his temples. "Fuhrman worked O.J., not Rodney King."

"Fuckin' Kennedys," says Jason. "Bunch of no-drivin' Chappaquiddick motherfuckers." Jason sticks his chest out, throws me and Jewboy a Latin Kings sign. *"Black and gold, never fold."*

I don't laugh. "Coleen Brennan was as nice as any person knows how to be and two shitheads took turns murdering her. Nothing, *not a goddamn thing* about that's funny."

Jason and Buff lean back from my tone. Jason says, "Don't go off on us, Bobby, gotta be the police . . . like in thirty minutes." Three Crown Vics arrive in tandem followed by a red, beat-to-death Toyota. The cars park facing the container stacks and the river beyond. The car engines die. This is the rest of our team.

For today's first adventure we have ten instead of eight; Jewboy is back from vacation plus two new kids whose first day with us is today, chicks from uniform we heard about three days ago. Rumor has it, the mayor and his Olympians are prepping a version of LAPD's Operation Hammer, when Chief Gates marshaled a thousand anti-gang cops into South Central and made 1,500 arrests in one weekend.

Two girls get out of the second Crown Vic; the larger one is Hispanic and butched up a bit beyond what I'd recommend for making friends today. I haven't met her, but her name is Officer Lopez. The other one is Officer Hahn, a five-foot-six blonde who I've heard hasn't said boo since she arrived at 12 the day she was reassigned. She closes her door, leans the back pockets of her jeans against the front fender, and thumbs at her nails. Officer Hahn has bruises on her face that have been there awhile and color on her knuckles that matches—gotta be deep South Side; probably a cop father or brother or both. The T-shirt under her vest covers half her bicep and none of a taut, veined forearm.

Jason stares, reading for the threat all cops feel with forced partnerships, then asks the butched-up Officer Lopez: "What's your name, dear?"

Officer Lopez drops her chin. "It ain't *dear.*"

"Oh." Jason smiles, but without his normal mirth. "Let's start over. Do you ah, fuck boys or girls? *Ma'am*?"

Lopez's brown skin reddens. From the fender, the five-foot-six

Officer Hahn says, "We fuck bun-boys. In weightlifter shirts and MTV pants."

Jason looks at his shirt and pants.

Pedigree or not, Officer Hahn doesn't want to start a fistfight with Jason Cowin. Throw on Jason first and your skirt won't matter till you get to the hospital. I chin at her bruises, hoping to ease her back a bit. "Fighting with the milkman?"

Her eyes cut to mine, steady, silent.

I can't help but smile; she has a bit of presence she probably earned; might even live through the whole day. "You don't say much; been on the job long?"

"Nineteen."

Nineteen means Officer Hahn would've gone through the academy the same year that ghetto legend Patti Black and I did. "Which class? A, B . . . ?"

"With Tom Duncan and Sister Rose."

"Julietta Rose? Father Dave's little sister?"

Officer Hahn nods.

My stomach sinks. "How Julietta doing? Haven't seen her. She went FBI right out of the academy."

FBI hangs like a bomb. Eight sets of eyes bore in on Hahn.

I watch Lopez's reaction, then back to Officer Hahn. "Where were you ladies before 12?"

Hahn makes a G with her left hand.

Six groans, one silence (our sergeant), and me: *"You're FBI?"*

"Was, went with Julietta. Then with the DEA in '97."

"Knew it." Jason glares at Hahn. "What the fuck are you doing here?"

"Working."

"Not with us, you ain't." Jason cuts to Lopez. "We get a new commander—a lawyer in the middle of a gang war. Then we get 'MONSTER' in the *Herald.* Then we get you and Hahn." Jason points at Lopez's face. "No chance you two walked away from cush DEA jobs to become gang cops. And you ain't here to save the Olympics. That leaves Dupree."

I look at Buff. He shrugs, but makes a point of looking at Jewboy's *Herald,* Buff's way of saying *watch your ass.* Jewboy steps up to Officer Hahn, literally twice her size. "Bobby Vargas is my best friend." She doesn't respond. Jewboy crowds her till there's no space between them. "Bobby didn't do anything this paper says."

Hahn raises her eyes to Jewboy's; the rest of her stays on the fender. "If you're considering putting those hands on me, fat ass, I recommend you don't."

Jason bumps Jewboy aside, taking his place. "Fuck with my friends, sistah, and the G won't save you from *this* fat ass, I kid you fucking not."

Buff forces his body between Jason and Officer Hahn. "Enough." With his back to Jason, Buff points all ten of us to his Crown Vic's faded hood. On it, he spreads a pencil diagram, then taps a seriously hot intersection with one finger. "We're doing the Latin Kings, Ashland and Twenty-first, the corner they took from La Raza last week."

Three dead, all La Raza. The second month of an escalating turf/dope war between twenty thousand Latin Kings and a thousand La Raza. The mayor and his Olympic financiers want the gang war shut down *now,* by any means necessary. Other than the selection of our new commander, our bosses are obliging. Buff points across a neighborhood where a shiny white, multimillion-dollar Olympic facility will obliterate a square block of ethnic rubble and the problems that go with it.

"None of these Latin Kings from north of Union Park know us, but be careful. They're wide-eye three-sixty all the time."

We all nod, the adrenaline coming.

"Two teams, five cars, Jewboy and I are the third car on each buy. We split the new officers—Lopez with Vargas, Hahn with Cowin."

"Fuck that." Jason spits on the gravel. "I ain't riding with no FBI plant. Not to a Cub game, and for damn sure, not into a Latin Kings' gunfight."

Buff stops. "You're the sergeant now? Maybe you're the commander?"

"Shit, Buff, even if Hahn ain't a plant, she's a goddamn rookie policing a ghetto gun—"

"I wanna be Crystal. Fucking. Clear." Buff's eyes are ice. "We are having no gunfight."

Jason spits again. "'Cause shooting back is bad pub for the Olympics?"

Buff stares Jason silent, then continues. "Vargas and Lopez go first, Lopez on the window. They pull up in the red beater, Lopez cops for ten or twenty." Buff hands her a wad of crumpled bills that he's probably xeroxed for the float. *Float* is when you intend to let the department's money go and don't immediately make the arrest/recovery. The G has high-tech budget to mark money. We use xerox copies.

Buff focuses on Lopez. "You're from the burbs; when the rock's in your hand—say 'Hell-o dreamland.' Everybody got that?" Buff waits for everyone to say so, then continues. "We do *not* bust the corner on this buy. An hour later when the Kings know the watch is changing, Hahn takes Vargas's place. She and Lopez will roll up in the beater, Hahn on the window. Hahn cops for twenty." Buff hands Hahn her money for the second buy. "When you have the dope in hand, you say, 'Wait, we ain't right.' Then we light 'em up from four sides; max arrest numbers."

Jason says, "*Excuse me?* We're doin' this twice? On the same corner, the same day? With two rookies?"

"Want to call the commander, tell her that her plan sucks?"

"*She* wrote this?"

Buff nods. Jason rolls his eyes. Buff finishes with: "We do this textbook, no deviations. Officers Lopez and Hahn are wired—"

"Oops." Jewboy steps back.

Hahn smiles an inch. Before Jason can go ballistic, Buff says, "Their wires aren't live."

I smile at Hahn—girl's got balls, gotta give her that. Or a death wish. I ask her, "You, ah, done this before? Walked in first?"

She nods.

"How'd you do?"

Hahn lifts her shirt, exposing a bullet scar an inch left of her lung. She has a second gun and the wire taped to her skin.

"Where?"

"Miami." Hahn pulls her Glock, half racks the slide, then holsters it.

Buff turns to me. "Can I continue?"

"Sure, sorry." I wink at Hahn, an "ex" federal agent who offered those sins to us when she didn't have to. She checks her second gun, then lowers her shirt. Normally I do better with the girls. Could be she's thinking about going in first, backed by a bunch of misogynist strangers who don't trust their new commander or see the Olympics as a good reason to die.

Buff points two fingers at Hahn and Lopez. "Your wires are to be live *before* the buy, dialed into our radios. The narcotics guys kinda forget this. And although they catch shit, they don't blow cases or spend the day with IAD for saying something on tape they wish they hadn't."

Buff's cell phone dances on the hood of his car.

"Anderson." He listens, then straightens—blinks at me and nods, turning away. "Ten-four, Anderson out." He flips the phone shut. "The buys are off for today. Gimme some numbers instead, but not on Ashland. *Tomorrow* we pop the Latin Kings."

Jason chins at Buff's phone for an explanation.

"Menstrual cramps, news cycle, who knows." Buff tells him: "Take Lopez in her car; she's your partner for the rest of today. Roll Ashland to Western, and shut the fuck up about her and Hahn being rookies. They aren't." Buff nods me toward the red beater. "Hahn takes the Toyota back to the lot. Put Hahn in your car, and don't get her killed."

Jason grabs Jewboy's shoulder. "Fuck this, Jewboy, we get us six frosties and some cheerleaders at the Cub game, let these idiots work with ghosts."

Buff shakes his head at a Cubs exit that won't happen, but not at "ghosts."

FRIDAY, 4:00 PM

My copy of the *Herald* slides into Officer Hahn's blue jeans as I turn left onto Ashland Avenue. She glances at the two-column header that has Coleen Brennan's name in it. Hahn and I are in my Crown Vic about to make a pass on the Latin Kings' corner we'll hit tomorrow.

Hahn picks up the paper. "Why do they call Tracy Moens the Pink Panther?"

"Red hair, major body, street PhD—Brenda Starr if you read the comics."

"That'd be a good-looking woman."

"If she catches up with me and you're there, be careful. Ms. Moens has teeth and isn't shy about using them."

Ashland Avenue begins to populate as we pass St. Pius V at Nineteenth. Hahn eyes the bangers but asks about the *Herald*. "Worried?"

I cut to her. Stare before answering. "Insulted."

Her eyes drop to the paper I'm sure she's already read. "Twenty-nine years, long time."

"Rape a child to death and help the state execute a retarded guy. Might not want to let two policemen walk around your city after they did that."

"You're guilty?"

"Define 'guilty.' "

Officer Hahn shifts ever so slightly into her door, adding distance and reaction time, then raises her shirt, showing me that the wire she was wearing is now in her locker, waiting for tomorrow's raid. Like I'm stupid enough to tell her anything under any circumstances.

"What I am is angry. And what it is, is none of your business. Okay?"

She looks out her window at tomorrow's corner. "Mak-ing con-ver-sa-tion. Mind if I drive tomorrow?"

"Not the commander's plan. She wants her girls making the buys."

Hahn braces one gym shoe into the dash. "Good to be queen." Her Converse All Stars have yellow laces. She nods at the *Herald*'s headline. "Know much about Furukawa?"

Headshake.

"Funny, a Japanese-controlled company backing a U.S. city against Tokyo . . ."

Hadn't thought of that. "Makes sense to somebody big or Furukawa wouldn't be doing it." I drive us a block east on Twenty-first Street toward Dvorak Park, slowing into the intersection to take the bump. "You never answered Jason: boys or girls?"

"That some of his business? Or yours?"

I glance. "Just making conversation."

Hahn studies the corner as we pass. "Girls, in the odd year a special one shows up; one of the reasons I'm no longer an FBI agent."

"So it's true; only J. Edgar could go both ways?"

Frown. "And we all have helicopters in our pockets."

Her verb is present tense. If I was undercover I'd be a ton more careful. Undercover cops die for much lesser mistakes. First, she offers that she was G, now she reinforces it. Makes no sense if working here matters.

"How long were you in?"

"Five years, nine months, sixteen days."

"Liked it, huh."

"All I ever wanted to do."

"Would you go back?"

"On the next plane."

"Any way they'd let you?"

Headshake. "Someone would have to admit a mistake, and that doesn't happen. I wanted to be a fed more than I wanted to win a sexual discrimination lawsuit, so I retired, went with the DEA."

"You stop bin Laden midair and the FBI wouldn't let you back?"

She thinks about it and tightens the knot on her shoe. "Yeah, they probably would. They'd say I was undercover the whole time, the whole girlfriend thing part of my story."

"Like now? Playing a part . . ."

"Real similar." She pulls out what appears to be breath freshener and spritzes. "Except there's no federal statute on murder. So if you and your brother did rape that little girl to death, it isn't *our* business."

"You're doing that on purpose, aren't you?"

She pockets the breath freshener. "Never hurts to make a good first impression. Even with assholes."

" 'Our' as opposed to 'their.' Present tense as opposed to past."

"What's the diff? You'll think whatever you want anyway."

Pause. "Yeah, but I might be nicer, until I can let one of these bangers cap you. Speaking of which—" Five La Raza soldiers are on the corner at Racine.

Behind us a voice yells: "Five-O! Five-O!"

The five gangsters don't move when they see us. I jerk the wheel to block the corner. Three drift to run; Hahn's out before me, pistol aimed, and yells: "POLICE."

Three shorties run between buildings.

I aim at the two adults on my left, "Get your ass back here," and fast-scan for their gunmen—shorties like Little Paul carrying the weight till it's needed.

Hahn yells behind her two-handed Glock. "Show me hands. *Now.*"

Ten dangling palms open up flat to us. I herd the three back to our car, glancing ground for the rock they either spit or dropped. I don't know Hahn, so I glance her, too. She's braced, like she means it.

A La Raza tests her with Spanish.

She insults him back, saying his dick better stay in his pants if he wants to use it tonight.

I scan again for gunmen I don't see. No visible gunmen doesn't mean they aren't aiming at us right now. Or this corner's gunmen could be these very guys, their guns hidden in loose building bricks, or trash, or the wheel wells of parked cars. Open-air drug markets have systems, all variants on the same theme: profit and survival.

I scan for the cameras. Whoever has a video camera or cell-phone camera has it on—neighbors and gangsters hoping for that Rodney King money.

I tell the gangsters, "On the car," then chin at Hahn. "Search these bitches."

She balks. "We calling in?"

She means for help since it's five against two not counting the windows. I show her my SIG. She frowns, holsters her weapon, and tugs Gangster One farther up the fender by his belt, then gently kicks his feet apart. I remind the other four, "Gentlemen, do not take your hands off the car. Clean or no, if you get lucky and I don't shoot you, you'll go to lockup, spend tonight fending off dirty brown dicks."

Hahn pats down Gangster One but doesn't shove her hand down the back of his jeans. Butt crack is a suitcase for rock. My pal Patti Black would've had the guy naked. Hahn gets to Gangster Two—a shirtless six footer with prison muscles and recent neck tats of the old Twenty-Treys; she pats him, pulls a roll of bills from his front pocket and tosses the money on the roof. Wind blows the wad apart. He's maybe twenty-five, twenty-seven, out-of-place older; I make him a serious felon, want to search his ride but don't see one that fits him. Hahn keeps patting, strips a gold watch and heavy neck chain, then moves up the car to stand behind Gangster Three. His head turns and he eyes her over the shoulder strap of his wifebeater. Instantly, Hahn's arm extends her torso away from his back. She says, "Wassup, homes?" Her other hand has gripped her pistol.

He stiffens, decides not to do whatever he had in mind, then focuses straight ahead at the car roof not her. She slaps his ass, half cotton jockeys, half jeans. "Too tight, my man. You get it or I get it."

No response.

Hahn makes sure I'm paying attention, then steps forward and strips Gangster Three's jeans to his ankles. "If it's rock, homes, you're jail-ready, you know that. If it's reefer, no biggie . . . unless you make me put my white-girl fingers up your ass. Make me do that, then you're on the bus."

His head and eyes go left to his homeys, then right; deciding.

"One hand, pull it out slow, and drop it."

He does.

One dime bag of ghetto-shit ditch-weed.

"That ass better be loose, homes. Not holding anything else up there, are we?"

Slight headshake. "*Nada.*"

Hahn squeezes his glute muscle; her other hand is again gripped on her pistol. She one-fingers the waistband of his jockeys, peers over the edge, then allows the waistband to snap back.

Other than their IDs and change spread on the car, Gangster Four and Gangster Five aren't holding, either. That means the rock is on the ground or they swallowed it or this was a community-service project we've wrongfully accosted.

We run all five sets of IDs and none have warrants, a surprise. Four have court dates pending, the charges range from possession to attempted murder. Attempted murder is Gangster Two, the convict with the heavy-gold accessories and the old-school Twenty-Trey neck tats someone inked recently. I nod Hahn back; she draws her weapon and I move around the car to stand behind him.

"Turn around."

He does.

"Where's your ride?"

He answers in Spanish.

"English, asshole. That's the last time I'm telling you."

"No ride."

"Where you from?"

"Here."

"Fuck you. *I'm* from here. You're from *elsewhere.*"

He gives me the stare.

"Street name?"

"Cop Killa."

I stare, maybe just shoot him now, general principles. "Attempted murder's pretty heavy. Where'd you catch the case?"

"Morseland. Say I did a bomb."

Morseland is a bar in Rogers Park, way north where I live, almost to Evanston. "You the Unabomber, huh? Danny Vacco bond you out? You somebody special? That shit on your neck?"

The eyes go empty, back to nowhere.

I lean in under his face and squirrel him up straight. "Hey, bitch, I'm talking to you."

His head flattens on the corded, Twenty-Trey neck. He eyes me sideways, silently saying the old-school mantra: *Wide 'n' tall, got it all.*

"Oh. So you the *bad motherfucker* riding these youngsters? Want nine cars here, we search every inch of Danny's corner? His whole fucking neighborhood?"

The flat nostrils widen, raising the tattoo under his eye, two tears for prison murders.

"That what you want?"

Cop Killa thinks about it; probably knows I can't get nine cars. "No. I don' see him."

"Fuck you, *no.* I got fourteen of Danny Vacco's rocks in my pocket. Rode his sister all afternoon."

The brown eyes flash at "sister," a display Cop Killa wouldn't have wanted; a small victory for me and polite society.

"What, you doing her, too? Right in her little cherry brown ass, I bet. Better than the joint, huh, all you Twenty-Trey wannabes bustin' each other's cherry."

"Mejor que la niña muerta." Better than the little dead girl.

"What? Was that Spanish?"

Cop Killa squints in the direction of Coleen Brennan's building.

I don't follow his eyes. "Do me favor, tell Danny Vacco you learned how to read, saw my name in the *Herald* this morning, and now you wanna be boss. In fact, I'm making you boss."

Cop Killa blinks, not sure where this is going.

"Danny Vacco gives Little Paul one more fucking rock—one more—the police shoot Danny dead." I finger-punch Cop Killa in his forehead, notice the *A* cut into his eyebrow for the first time. "We make you boss, then we shoot you." I lean in to his nose and prison-murder tattoos. "I promise."

Hahn says, "We taking any of these guys?" She's interrupting, like I might have a problem of some kind. The *A* is for *asesinos,* "assassins" in Spanish, a shadowy subset of the old Twenty-Treys—cold-eyed sociopaths who in their day were a new breed of street killer and as frightening as any ghost story a Four Corners kid could conjure.

I step back and tell the air between me and the five gangsters: "From this day forward, Little Paul ain't in your gang. He's in mine. I take him."

None of the five nod. I feel Hahn watching me, wondering what I'm talking about. I explain for her and them, in case they want to argue later.

"Me and these gentlemen just made a binding street deal. Little Paul becomes a taxpayer, these felons keep on keepin' on." Pause. "Anybody who wants to go to lockup instead, say so."

None of the five want to keep Little Paul that bad.

"Done. All of you'll be dead by twenty-six anyway."

Hahn smiles but keeps her pistol out. The gangsters don't move.

I tell them, "Get your shit off my car." Now they move.

Hahn and I get in. We make the block on all four sides without speaking or seeing the gangsters again. She says, "The Little Paul kid mean something to you?"

"When I lived here you had a chance."

"You lived here?"

"Right there." I point at the third floor, two windows facing the street, two facing the alley. Out front, plastic bags and papers are blown against the low chain-link fence, empty 40s lean near the gate. "Looked better—my mom didn't allow the trash, and no drinking on her stoop." The whole neighborhood looked better. "My dad and my brother could drink at their friends' or inside, but not on her stoop. She let me play guitar out there, though, and I did."

Hahn turns from her window. "Flamenco? Spanish?"

My tone drops. "Yeah, I'm a mariachi; my outfit's at home."

Hahn pulls her head back. "Something wrong? I say something?"

"No. I pick lettuce on the weekends, too."

While she's staring, I stop at 2116, slap the transmission into park, and tell her I'll be a minute. Halfway up the short walk I hear Hahn's door. Little Paul is on the stoop; his mother is, too, hand-washing clothes in a tub. She stops, wary. I hand him a guitar pick that he takes, not quite sure what it is.

"Guitar pick. Stay outta the life for one day, I'll show you how to use it."

Little Paul looks at me, then the street where his world begins and ends.

"We'll go by Wolfe City, see how the big dogs make their records."

I hand Little Paul's mother ten dollars. "Sorry about the pockets."

She hesitates, eyes me like we don't know each other all of a sudden.

"Little Paul had rock in his pockets. Danny Vacco's rocks. Take the money, okay? Make me feel better I did something."

She's no older than me but could pass for sixty. Part of that's *árbol de bruja*—the witch culture—and part of it's four jobs, a dead husband, dead sons, and no hope.

"Take the money or I take your son to Child Services."

She pulls Little Paul to her then takes the money, whispering to him in Spanish, "Don't be afraid. The police is afraid. The dark has him."

I know I'm the police but I'm not the devil . . . then I get it: the *Herald.* Me and Coleen, a girl not a lot older than her son stolen off these streets and . . . I start to explain, stop, and wonder why the fuck would I explain? What, *exactly,* would I say? I didn't kill Coleen? I didn't rape her? I'm not a midnight monster, the chupacabra?

"I'm the police, Mrs. Cedeneo. We ain't afraid of Danny Vacco and we ain't afraid of the dark."

She pushes Little Paul inside and shuts the door. In Spanish she tells me, "The light will not have you. An' you are afraid, no? When hell is the only place left to go."

I turn for the car and she keeps talking, telling me my future according to the *árbol de bruja.* Officer Hahn watches. I shrug; Hahn smiles at the ten dollars and Little Paul in the doorway giving me the finger.

"That's me, hero of the neighborhood."

We exit the curb and I turn us onto Cullerton facing a Crown Vic coming our way. The headlights flash and I stop. When we're window to window, my brother Ruben punches my hand. *"Eh, buey, como'sta?"*

"What's up, Homicide?"

Big-brother smile. "Nothing but you, baby. Who's your girlfriend?"

"Officer Tania Hahn. New, direct from the commander . . . via Miami, the DEA, and the F-B-I."

Ruben keeps his grin, doesn't show what we've all been thinking. "That a fact? Timing's interesting." Ruben cranes past me. "Hello, Officer Hahn, welcome to the West Side of Chicago."

She tips a hat she doesn't have on.

"Take care of my little brother. He can play guitar, make you weep, but this police thing we do . . ." Ruben winces. "Send 'em to school, they chew the covers off the books."

Hahn smiles.

Ruben says to me, "Where you having dinner?"

"Wherever you want."

"Pink Panther found you?"

Headshake.

Ruben's brown eyes remain cool and steady like when we were young. Ruben saved me once a week on the street. He wasn't the toughest guy in the Four Corners but Ruben Vargas would go—all day and as far as the other guy wanted. "Moens and her investigator get to you, behave yourself."

"Fuck 'em."

"I mean it, *buey,* these *pachingas* laying for the brothers Vargas."

I glance at Hahn. Then back at Ruben.

He says, "You and I are having dinner with a lawyer friend of mine," Ruben holds up a folded *Herald,* "get my retirement money lined up; buy you into that recording studio on Halsted you'd sell your soul for." He drops his chin and narrows his eyes. "*If* someone don't go *loco,* get all *Mexican* on everybody."

"And fuck you, too."

"*Carnalito.* All American in the land of plenty." Ruben winks. "Seven o'clock, Levee Grill."

I tap my vest and T-shirt. "Kinda underdressed." My real issue is geography. The Levee Grill is in the First Ward, the very same building as the old Counselors' Row Restaurant—ground zero for the FBI's Operation Greylord back in the early '80s, not exactly a brain-surgeon choice for the brothers Vargas, considering.

"We'll sit outside." Ruben cranes around me again. "Nice to meet you, Officer Hahn."

"Likewise."

Ruben drives off and so do I. Hahn says, "Handsome fellow. Seems nice enough."

I stare. " 'Cause you heard different?"

She makes that face black girls make when they think you're playing them stupid.

"Ruben's been the man a long time. Made major cases on connected people the bosses wouldn't touch."

Hahn points at the *Herald*'s front page.

"Fuck them. Police this city for real, a guy'll make an enemy or two along the way. The big dogs don't scare Ruben. They bite and so does he."

Hahn nods, reading me for . . . something.

Brake lights ahead. "Tell me about Miami."

She presses her Converse All Star into the dash again. "Palm trees, cocaine, and Cuban showgirls. Sun shines all the time and no one gets skin cancer."

"Like on TV, huh?"

"Sonny Crockett 24/7. You should transfer; hell, you play the guitar, handsome as you and your brother are, if you had any money at all they'd be in your pants with both hands."

Left turn onto Eighteenth Street. "And you'd introduce me around?"

"Wait till season, though; all the models are down from New York."

"Models are good; keep 'em under six foot. You work dope down there?"

Nod. "More cash than you can imagine. Boxes of it. Literally."

"All federal?"

"Worked with MPD and Dade County all the time. The cops who want to work, work. The ones who don't . . . no different than here, eighty-twenty like it is everywhere."

I turn us onto Ashland. "Be tough for you here, being from the G, assuming 'from' is the right word."

"Tough being a woman wherever you go. Most of your coworkers either want to bend you over or piss on your pumps. If a woman wants to wear a 9-millimeter instead of lip gloss, she better get used to it."

Yup, an unfortunate but healthy assessment. "You should be speaking at the academy."

Hahn finishes with her shoe. "Probably have too much history for that."

"Meaning?"

"I'm starting over as a street cop after nineteen years as a fed. What's that tell you?"

Smile. "That you're undercover."

She laughs. "Call me Frank."

Frank would be Frank Serpico—Hollywood's poster boy for a good cop busting bad cops—a distinct possibility. "You're saying you might've stumbled into trouble somewhere? In Miami?"

Nod; she taps the bullet scar under her shirt. "It's possible that a group of DEA agents overstepped their authority; two were killed, and a major case compromised."

Left turn.

"The case was against Santo Trujillo. Some said the DEA agents in question made the move on purpose to compromise the case. Rather than air that dirty laundry, those agents were given choices. All I ever wanted to be was a cop; my boss knew your mayor—"

"You know Mayor McQuinn?"

"Met him."

Headshake. "Buff was right. I better not get you killed."

4

A boy died. Hispanic—Puerto Rican this paper reported—but he was Mexican. Officer Terry Rourke shot and killed him in an alley just above the river at Halsted. Terry Rourke had a 30-year history of violent responses. The Mexican boy had none. He was thirteen, deaf and dumb. His parents protested; the neighborhood protested. No one listened. And that's how it started.

—"MONSTER," by Tracy Moens; © 2011 *Chicago Herald*

ARLEEN BRENNAN

FRIDAY, 7:00 PM

Don't do this. Fast breath, face wipe. If the VW I'm driving had velvet lining it'd be a coffin.

Wheel the car, Arleen. Turn around. Drive straight to the U.S. attorney's office and confess. Tell the whole truth on videotape—Detective Ruben Vargas and TAC cop Robbie Steffen are scamming the Korean mafia. I was/am the unwitting front woman. Vargas and Steffen will kill me if I don't continue and the Korean mafia will kill me if I do.

There. Police corruption. Send in the FBI. Okay?

My heart rate stays at one-sixty.

The U.S. attorneys will nod to each other, then ask, Okay, Ms. Brennan, we'd certainly be interested in malfeasance by Ruben Vargas and Robbie Steffen. What is your part in the scam?

My part? Oh, no, see I wasn't actually *in* the scam, I was tricked—

Oh? So you weren't participating in exchange for the first audition at the Shubert?

Well, yeah, but, not like, you know, a bad guy, partner in crime person would.

The U.S. attorneys will nod to each other again. Okay, Ms. Brennan, let's say you're an innocent pure-as-the-driven-snow good guy. Explain the scam, how everyone fits.

I'll wince, apologize, and say, Don't actually know. Vargas and Steffen have *something* scary valuable that belongs to the Koreans. Ruben denied he had it until the Koreans got ugly. Ruben brought me in—*tricked me*—to do the face-to-face. Through me, Ruben admitted he and Steffen had a third partner who actually had the stolen property. I told the Koreans that Ruben would get the stolen property from their partner and return it, but Ruben keeps stalling. See? Okay? Can I go to the Shubert now?

Why won't my goddamn heart slow down?

Onstage it would work out, if that's what the writers wanted. In street-world, the U.S. attorney will charge me as a coconspirator—either because they think I'm lying about being tricked or because they want max leverage on me when our partnership gets ugly. And it will get ugly. I'll be told to wear a wire, finish the scam—whatever the scam is—and if I don't die, I can testify against two cops and the Korean mafia for a reduced sentence or maybe, if I'm extremely lucky, catch a spot in the Witness Protection Program.

Sounds good, huh? Like a solution? My fist pounds the seat.

Bet it'll be hard to do *Streetcar* from prison or the Witness Protection Program. But, hell, why care about that? I touch the *Streetcar* pages on the passenger seat—*my* pages; *my* part. My shoe presses gas pedal; the VW stays pointed at Koreatown and the fantasy that I can make Ruben's patchwork of lies stand up. Sweat stings my eyes. I am an idiot, a certifiable loser on the pathetic dream-sick express.

Make no mistake, nothing in this universe is more powerful than a working actress's dreams, not drugs, not sex, not safety. Maybe not even love, although I can't speak for those girls. The only time I was in love, I was thirteen.

Not even death. Mirror check. Dry swallow. Three weeks ago I took the bait. Ruben and Robbie Steffen asked me to help CPD make a case against Korean child traffickers. In return, Robbie's father, Toddy Pete Steffen, would get me the impossible-to-get short-list audition for

Streetcar. I went to Koreatown for Ruben and played my part to the scariest men I've ever faced. An hour later I told Ruben to forget my audition—maybe for the part I'd die but not for an audition. Ruben and Robbie reminded me kids' lives were at stake, little kids like my sister. Two days later the audition at the Shubert came through. Even then I said no, but the casting director called, said he was seriously, seriously interested and would I please come in. My agent called and Sarah almost never does that; my whole goddamn life called me.

Ruben fed me more lies: "We'll protect you—we're cops for chrissake—you're in and you're out. No biggie, be an actress for us and a Shubert star is born."

They produced the *Streetcar* audition, that wasn't a lie. Toddy Pete Steffen is one of the founders of the Shubert Theater Company. And I nailed my minutes like I was born to play Blanche. Lap glance—Ruben's gun bulges my purse. Then today I get the *Streetcar* callback; fifty-fifty I get the lead—and here I am, six blocks from another face-to-face with Korean butchers who have special drains in their basement.

Both hands death-grip the wheel. Left turn onto Lawrence Avenue. July sunset glares my windshield opaque. Breathe, Arleen. Don't die in a car accident. Do Koreatown. Get Vargas and Steffen their seven more days. Don't die in a basement with special drains; don't go to prison. Dodge both and you're off the hook. Don't get fat, or pregnant, or stupid—*way* too late for stupid. Be soooo much better if the Valium would kick in, if my hands were as dry as my mouth. If Koreatown were an indie horror movie.

A pothole swallows my tire; big bump and half of Ruben's .38 Special pops out of my purse. I throw the purse onto the passenger seat. *Try not to get arrested, okay?* The gun's a goddamn felony even if you don't use it. Mirror check. And God can damn Ruben Vargas, too. Lying mockie wanker. *Hooooorn.* I jerk back to my side of the center line. *Pay attention* or Blanche DuBois will die before she gets to Mr. Psycho Choa's restaurant. Where you probably *will* die chained to an autopsy table in his basement.

Taillights. Lawrence Avenue bunches. Downshift, red light. Breathe. Prepare.

You're not Blanche, you're Arleen, and she'd better plant her Stair-

Master ass in the present. She's skin on skin with two crooked cops, one of whom the *Herald* will say raped and murdered your thirteen-year-old sister, then helped send an innocent man to the gas chamber . . . to close the case. And in my present situation, he's one of the good guys.

Except I don't have to read the *Herald*'s exposé to know it's muckraker crap; I won't read it. Black gangbangers from Stateway Gardens kidnapped, raped, and killed Coleen. Maybe Anton Dupree was retarded, maybe not. The state tried Dupree and his partner three times; 100 percent conviction rate. Tore my family apart. End of story. And there aren't any *good guys,* anywhere.

At Kedzie Avenue, banners announce Albany Park; Lawrence Avenue stops selling Michoacán tacos and begins selling kimchi. The Shubert wants to give me my lifetime chance and I haven't rehearsed one line, not a word or a gesture. Koreatown smells like . . . *Turn around.*

Yeah? Then what? Run?

At least you'd be alive tomorrow.

But run means no *Streetcar* . . . run means waiting tables in flower-shirt Mexico or the Dominican Republic under another name, listening to midnight promises that aren't good past breakfast or pulling palms off my thigh until even the married tourists aren't interested.

Gobshite. Both fists pound the steering wheel. *Stupid, Belfast jackeen knacker.* I should've slept with Vargas and Steffen. "Lay down, honey" is the standard trade for a serious audition. But no, I've been through that, I have to have *pride* now.

Mr. Choa's restaurant appears on my right; instinct reaches for the .38. The pistol's an Airweight but shakes in my hand. I make the sign of the cross. Five shots, all hollow points. If Choa's done talking, *gulp,* then even from close-up Ruben says I'll need all five.

Right turn onto Hamlin, ease a block north, and park.

Mirror check. Ruben says the Koreans don't know my real name—yet. They'd love to ID my neon-red '69 VW. Mirror check—last chance to be smart? I'm not, and slide the pistol into my jeans; my blouse drops over the grip. Deep breath—be an actress, play the role, not the reality; don't go to the restaurant's back room or the basement. *Shudder.* Tell the Koreans Ruben's story and make them believe it. Actress. Actress. Actress. Do what you do. Own the stage.

No part of me exits the car.

C'mon, baby, the Koreans are gangsters and have to believe you are, too; that's how you played it the first time. Played it perfect and they bought it. The Koreans want their property. If they'll wait seven more days and stop trying to kill people, they'll get their property back. Simple—wait seven and everyone's happy. Seven days for Ruben and Robbie to coax their partner into capitulating—that's the script; who knows what the truth is.

Ruben's .38 bites into my skin. I could use stronger deodorant. The Valium must have been a placebo. Two Korean women walk past; both peek at me.

Out of the car, Arleen, or out of the neighborhood. Brave the horror-house restaurant or give up *Streetcar.* My door opens before I can stop my hand. 'Cause I'm a goddamn actress and we can't help it.

Lawrence Avenue is hundred-degree hot. Standing mid-block, five tiny storefronts before Mr. Choa's restaurant, is a blockish man in an inexpensive black suit, the sleeves bunched at his elbows. The man squares up, obstructing my path. Late thirties, pockmarked cheeks, cruel hands, and a rose tattoo on his forearm.

"You have?"

"I'm here to see Mr. Choa."

"You have?"

Arleen is a gangster. "Want me to leave, Chopstix?"

He stares. I stare back.

"You have?"

"Yeah. But not for you."

On my right, a second black suit crosses Lawrence Avenue. He's older, better dressed, a lieutenant in Mr. Choa's family or whatever the mafia calls them in Korea. "Where is Ruben Vargas?"

"Couldn't make it. Double homicide uptown."

The three of us stare. Cars pass. The sun dips behind a cloud.

The lieutenant has a cell phone open in his hand. He grunts in Korean and nods the first man back toward the restaurant, then turns to me. "Mr. Choa is unhappy."

Shrug. "Not my problem, but tell him I'm sorry."

"Mr. Choa speaks with you inside. First, I must search your person."

"No."

"We go to the back, not to interrupt those who eat."

"No." I'm a gangster and *will* my hand away from the pistol.

"First, you must be searched, then we meet Mr. Choa."

Where they'll torture me for any information I have, then slaughter me to make their point to Ruben. The Korean nods small and smiles smaller. His open palm invites me to walk between shadowed buildings to the back.

"The front, Chopstix; not the back, not the basement, either."

Negligible Korean headshake. Veins in his neck.

"New deal; Mr. Choa comes out here." I step back as my hand drifts to my waist. "Find some other girl to kill."

His eyes go tight to my hand. "Furukawa will be *our* client, not belong to you. You must do as told."

Blink. *Furukawa?* I flash on the Olympic headlines, their table in Hugo's for lunch, Ruben lingering. What does Furukawa—

A Ford Taurus screeches to the curb. I jump back and reach for the pistol. The driver's door pops. It's Ruben's partner, bull-necked, six-foot-two, two-hundred-pound TAC cop Robbie Steffen. The silk Tommy Bahama camp shirt doesn't soften Robbie's appearance. Robbie reaches the sidewalk in two steps, squares up on the remaining Korean, slaps the man's chest with a butcher-paper package that bounces off and lands on the sidewalk. The butcher paper unravels, revealing the meat—a man's severed hand and forearm, a rose tattoo obvious on the gray-yellow skin. I gag and stumble backward. Steffen cocks his head sideways, then screws his face into the Korean's.

"Next time you wanna kill somebody, motherfucker, send Luca Brasi."

The Korean's eyes cut to the severed arm, hesitate, then refocus on Robbie. The Korean's cell phone rises slowly to his ear. My part in this play has ended. Robbie Steffen pivots to tell me something I know I don't want to hear. Mid-turn, Robbie stops, draws a blue-black .45 automatic from the back of his jeans, slams it into the Korean's hip. And pulls the trigger. The Korean screams, spins in the explosion and blood spray, and lands in a pile.

Robbie steps over him, aims the smoking .45 at the Korean's head, and . . . I'm already running when I hear the second shot.

FRIDAY, 7:45 PM

Drive. Steer. Talktofuckingme— My skin won't quit vibrating. Dan Ryan, southbound, never setting foot on Lawrence Avenue again. Are the car doors locked? My knees are butter, pistol on my lap. *Streetcar* pages on the passenger seat. I'm breathing in fits, sweating. *Sweet Jesus—*

The DJ voice says Chicago is sweltering. I'm shivering in some kind of fog. The DJ segues my car radio into "Highway to Hell." I can't quit seeing the severed arm, hearing the explosions, then—cold-blooded first-degree murder. Mirror check, window check. *Robbie Steffen sawed off somebody's arm— Then he executed . . . a made man in the Korean mafia.* I have to get help, apologize. The Koreans are old-school butchers, Ruben said. Guys who massacre entire families to prove a point.

I can't know people like this, not for real. I'm an actress.

And Robbie Steffen's not afraid of them. And Robbie Steffen knows where I live. Make a plan. Go home, get my Blanche clothes and— *You can't go home—* But Robbie shouldn't want to hurt me, should he? The sun drops the last inch behind the West Side. Shadows cover the rearview mirror and my mom's crucifix but not the blood splatter on my arms and blouse. OFF-RAMP. I veer, miss the concrete abutment, back off the gas, and drop my window. The scent of storm replaces blood and fear-sweat. I can ID Robbie for murder, *of course* he'll want to hurt me. Kill me—

My brain's not working, won't keep thoughts together, just jumbled flashes . . .

Go to the cops.

Robbie *is a cop.* His father's one of the most powerful players in the city.

Thunder crashes to the east. A siren wails, then another. Rain sheets across the windshield. I hurry the window up and hit the wipers. The light ahead blinks to green as a CPD cruiser shoots across the intersection. I duck and steer toward the inside lane. Sweat drips onto my lips; my hand squeezes the wheel. Mirror check—blurry cars crowd behind me—oh, God, Robbie Steffen. *No, stop it. You're not Coleen.* Lightning drills into the city. *Not a victim. Not alone in that alley . . . their hands, their . . . tearing you apart.* I suck air to scream but fight it down. More lightning—the city goes staccato black-and-white—the gun on my lap, the crucifix hanging on the mirror. Thunder crashes again. The night Coleen was attacked I started screaming and couldn't stop, woke up and knew Coleen was dying. Spent the next six nights in a child psychiatric hospital.

Go to the FBI, the U.S. attorney.

Right, *innocent good guy* was a tough sell *before* I was an accomplice to first-degree murder.

You can *try* to convince them.

And then, win or lose, you can *give up everything.*

The steering wheel sweats in my hand. My radio says the police are at a gangland murder scene on Lawrence Avenue . . . *Wake up, goddamnit.* Out of the fog. Shift gears. Eyes in the mirror. Don't end up alone in that alley. *Don't be Coleen.*

Sorry, sorry, I love you, honey. This is for us. Matching hopes and dreams. I'm the actress for us both. We are one, then and now, identical twins forever. I tell the windshield: "*Streetcar.* Twenty years for one chance. The Brennan sister who didn't die. Who didn't quit."

Actress. Both of us brave and bold. Venice Beach. L.A. Hollywood. Santa Monica. We bought this ticket. *Paid* for it. Paid *big.* It's *ours,* goddamnit.

Since we were three feet tall, actresses were what we wanted to be. Coleen died; I ran. By the '90s I'd made it to *actress.* Two waitress jobs in L.A.—not just one—in Hollywood, that's how I knew I was a *serious* actress. Add regulation 34C's from the best guy I could afford in West L.A., the strawberry blond hair from a salon on Sunset. And the teeth—a $16,000 smile I agreed could be billed one weekend a month in Palm Springs. Aspiring actors and actresses call those weekends paying the dentist, or the plastic surgeon . . . or the rent if things get bad enough.

Oh, and they can. Be a runaway in the City of Angels for a year or two. Rely on the kindness of strangers. *Swallow.* Gun on my lap—my new solution? No. No. Not a . . . or a victim, an actress, *the lead* in *Streetcar.*

Actress. Actress. Actress. When I stepped off that bus into Venice Beach I was fourteen, scared and alone, but would've laughed out loud had anyone told me how far I'd go to become an actress. But promise something every night, crave it down to your heart and soul, more than food, sex, and safety, and a teenager starts to see things differently. Flirting with the devil seems doable . . . or as things begin to unravel, *survivable.* But by then you're often alone in a dark room with something the old you couldn't quite have imagined, and he has his hand out.

So you pay him—and you never, ever talk about it—and just for that one time, never again. And like the thousands of ingenues who preceded me, each time I confronted the *next* time, I closed my eyes tighter. And buried deeper those parts of me I wanted to keep real and mine. And paid him again. I said yes.

Yes to the City of Angels—her casting calls and lineups, and readings when you could get one, each office or waiting room electric with preparation and hope . . . and then invisibility. I said *Yes* to the big theaters with bright marquee promises and darkened empty seats, heartbreaking voices saying "Thank you for coming"—because that's all an aspiring actress does every day until she *aspires* so hard and so often she can't remember which parts of her are the real ones, not with any certainty, not like back home in wherever you came from, population 6,042.

So you stay in L.A. or Los Feliz or West Hollywood, hanging on as part of the glittery nightlife that passes for real life, enjoying the dead desert wind and smog-filtered afternoons that pass for golden California; you stay through your new family's overdoses, doomed Vegas weddings, bankruptcies, and spikes of hope; all of you living for the next call, the next brush with career *something.* And when there's just a few of you left, after *years* of holding on to each other's dreams and promises and the next audition, 80 percent of those valiant, tenacious, bet-everything souls hit the wall . . . career finito. Your dreams and family are over. Then you die or you run.

I ran. Got so scared one night on the Santa Monica pier that I didn't bother to pack; ran ocean to ocean, to New York. But when I got there I couldn't quit, couldn't *transition out* as they say at the SAG office on Wilshire. A fellow actor once said that *the life* wasn't a lot different than a heroin addiction, Hollywood just takes longer and the methadone clinics are waitress jobs.

Rain continues to sheet. The street's a blur. I wipe at my fogged windshield and drop my window, downshift, and— POP, POP, POP echoes somewhere in the grainy streetlights. Gunshots? Mirror check. Robbie Steffen doesn't care that I'm an actress; he'll be coming for me. Can't go home; Robbie will figure me for home.

My radio crackles. Billy Idol and band pound into "L.A. Woman" circa 1992, tonight's gunshots, Billy and me doing Hollywood déjà vu: *"Another lost angel . . . City of Light . . . City of Night."* POP, POP, POP.

Back then the Hollywood dream was my fix-everything plan. Erase it all—my da, the Four Corners, the sunny California runaway years that followed . . . backseats of rental cars, teen modeling offices, the afternoon dinner-vigils at supermarket Dumpsters. All gone. Coleen would see the marquee lights, she and I would build a brand-new girl, a bright-and-shiny actress with no history, only future.

"Hollywood" officially began after a juvenile court judge pulled me off the street and placed me in an L.A. County youth home run by a couple from South Africa. They were ex-military, tough and blunt Afrikaners, but protective. I stayed there until I could work my way into a crowded six-flat near Western and Wilshire. Every boy and girl in the building had both hands gripped on the show-business express. The Rodney King riots had just ended, and just like tonight, "L.A. Woman" was on the radio, Billy Idol singing to me over the sporadic pops and early days of the truce between the Koreans and the looters.

Billy'd come in the Troubadour the night before, lit the place up, tipped me my first hundred, and left with every girl who could fit in his limo, a death-trip rock star who told me it was safe to walk with angels. I believed him, too starstruck to wonder how he'd know the angels' intentions were good, that my trip wouldn't be through the Old Testament.

Rain splatters through my open window.

Both hands begin to steady. The windshield's clear.

I could hide from Robbie at the L7 Bar with Julie. Julie McCoy's my best friend . . . or the Playhouse Theater; talk to Ruben from safety. Threaten, talk, *something*. I could make a plan that includes my hopes and dreams. And safety—my back stiffens—feel good? Arleen Brennan, victim? Lap glance . . . the .38.

I'm not a victim.

My mom's crucifix glints as I pass underneath a tight series of streetlights. The lights flash my *Streetcar* pages on the passenger seat then the .38 in my lap. Light to dark; dark to light. Is that the message? God gives me an asterisk on the Fifth Commandment? He'll consider Robbie self-defense even if I shoot first? God doesn't answer; the voice that does, doesn't care about self-defense. He's a recurring nightmare, always with the same solution: *Just pull the trigger.*

And that's what'll happen if I go home to my apartment—*my goddamn house.* No threats, no discussion; just Robbie Steffen, the dark, and me.

HORN. I jolt into the steering wheel and turn into a motel parking lot. Just get a grip, ease up long enough to *think.* Be *present*—you're on the South Side, the L7 is way north, lots of cops between here and there—maybe they're after me, maybe not. Robbie's a cop, Ruben's a cop—who knows what that means? My phone rings. RUBEN VARGAS on the screen. I don't answer. It rings again. RUBEN VARGAS.

"Stop calling me, goddamnit."

I look left. A squad car is alongside my window, the cop staring at me. I jolt back, then struggle the window all the way down.

He says, "Nice car."

Actress smile. Heart hammering.

"Are you all right, miss?"

"Ah, yeah." I point at the motel. "Checking in, got a call and— Sorry."

He nods. "You're stopped in the middle of the road."

"Shit. Sorry." I drive into the parking lot I thought I was in, stop, kill the lights and engine, pop the door, and— *BLOOD on your blouse.* Cop still watching me.

Can't sit here.

Can't drive away. Mirror check. The cops know something's wrong.

Deep breath; do something; *move.*

Purse to chest, I slide out into the rain with my shoulder to the police car, shut the door, and walk fast toward the motel office. Please, please, please, give me this one.

5

Officer Terry Rourke died in his front yard, shot to death from a slow-passing 1962 Chevrolet Bel Air. His daughter, Siobhán, died with him. Two thousand Chicago police officers attended their funeral. Before the sun had set on that snowy day in February, 29 Hispanic members of the Twenty-Trey Gangsters had been arrested. Four were killed and 16 critically injured.

—"MONSTER," by Tracy Moens; © 2011 *Chicago Herald*

OFFICER BOBBY VARGAS

FRIDAY, 8:00 PM

Meeting here at the Levee Grill, *now*, my brother is taunting the lion, telling the FBI: Suck my dick.

Out front, sixteen summer tables are topped with red-checked tablecloths and Chianti-bottle candles. A box planter spilling bougainvillea separates customer from passing pedestrian, ward heeler and political fixer from civilian.

Ruben rises from the table nearest the front door and introduces me to his attorney, James W. Barlow, mid-fifties, no necktie, 2016 Olympics pin, starched cuffs; a man known for his appetites, not his philanthropy. Mr. Barlow and I shake hands; he eyes my gun, jeans, and vest, then motions me to sit. The long patio is mostly men in expensive suits with happy hour or regular tee times glowing in their faces. Twenty-five years ago Chicago's power structure imploded right here. The feds tape-recorded and convicted a slew of judges, policemen, deputy sheriffs, Outfit bosses, union bosses, and forty-eight members of the Illinois State Bar. Operation Greylord remains the FBI's single biggest case against the Chicago Machine. Half these men probably don't know that; the half that do are the ones who worry me.

I scoot my chair toward the wall, but still have to sit with half my back to LaSalle Street. Mr. Barlow's nails are manicured; the TAG Heuer watch is the only non-knockoff I've ever seen and probably cost as much as my car. But then, any watch that runs probably costs more than my Civic. This morning's *Herald* is open on our red-checked tablecloth.

Mr. Barlow swishes a highball above "MONSTER." "Whatever you have to hide, Bobby, I should know."

Ruben sips Scotch.

"Have we met, Mr. Barlow?"

Barlow levels his eyes, accustomed to making demands that border on insult. A courtroom lawyer unconcerned with real-world reprisals.

"And we're not engaged?"

"No."

"So, ah, why would I answer a question like that . . . at a time like this?"

Ruben winks at me, then rolls his eyes at Barlow. "Told you."

"Two reasons, Officer Vargas—money and jail."

Cute. I ask Ruben how well he knows Mr. Barlow.

"Well enough I take him to the cockfights."

I nod small, but don't answer.

Ruben quits smiling and adds diction. "When Mr. Barlow isn't assisting slandered and libeled police officers from the Hispanic community, he walks and golfs with the city's movers and shakers. His firm is *the* firm for a fight with the *Herald* and he'll take our case as a personal favor."

"Favor to who?"

Ruben looks down his nose at his little brother, reminding me who was the man of the house after Dad died. Who kept the wolf from the door and who made sure Mom and I always had what we needed while Ruben often went without. "A favor to *me*."

"My brother's a mover and shaker? Not a homicide detective making ninety a year?"

On Ruben's left, a man exits a limo with a bodyguard-assistant and strides toward us in a $3,000 suit. This is the man who just delivered a billion-dollar Olympic sponsorship from Chicago's newest skyscraper, Furukawa Industries. He has a perfect haircut, wire-rim glasses, a light tan, and a 2016 Olympics pin in his lapel. Toddy Pete Steffen could be the mayor of Dublin or the CEO of General Motors. He is, for sure, a cop's worst nightmare before facing IAD on Monday morning.

Mr. Steffen stops, his hand light on my shoulder, and smiles at lawyer Barlow. "Jimmy, Jimmy, Jimmy. Why do I pay, if you never work?"

Mr. Barlow raises his glass and adds an Irish accent. "And here's to ya, Peter."

When Mr. Steffen ran the First Ward he was referred to as the Prince of Darkness, and still is. Cops can go to prison because they shook hands with him once or stood next to him at a parade. Mr. Steffen grins. "My office tomorrow? We've an Olympic rebid to win."

"Ten AM, bells on and biscuits in the bag."

"Enjoy your dinner, gentlemen." Mr. Steffen nods to Ruben and me. "And any extra effort to quell our gang problem in the 12th District would be greatly appreciated." He squeezes my shoulder, then turns toward two well-dressed Japanese men as the maître d' says, "Dr. Ota is inside, Mr. Steffen."

Ruben seems surprised at the reference to Dr. Ota, the Furukawa CEO headlining today's paper, and turns to look. "T.P.'s looking fresh as ever."

Mr. Barlow adds, "Toddy Pete joins the immortals if the Olympics rethink Chicago." Mr. Barlow cuts to me and taps the newspaper. "If we beat the *Herald* and the paper doesn't go Chapter 7, we will be well paid. If we don't beat them, Officer Vargas, the *Herald* will put you and your brother in prison. Ten years minimum, maybe life."

"No offense, but tell me something I don't know."

"Late this afternoon, counsel for the Duprees filed to exhume Coleen Brennan's body."

My eyes close. Barlow waits, then surrounds the images with: "The federal lawsuit filed by Anton Dupree's family names the city, your brother, and three fellow officers for wrongful death. It's possible the *Herald* will join the Dupree motion for exhumation, or already has, as a silent partner. What that means to you is that although you are not yet named with your brother in the Duprees' wrongful-death suit, you will be added if the *Herald*'s evidence against you is only *moderately* compelling."

I open my eyes, disgusted. "The Dupree lawsuit is civil. What's their plan, take my shirt?"

"The Dupree lawsuit is civil, but the accusations the *Herald* says they will make are *criminal.* First-degree murder, rape, suppression of evidence. I assume you've been contacted by IAD?"

Nod.

"I'd be willing to bet the *Herald* is already sharing whatever criminal evidence they have with the Duprees, who already have civil depositions scheduled for Monday. And a civil trial date shortly after that."

"And?"

Barlow cants his head an inch. "Do you want to face the U.S. attorney under oath? Because federal *criminal* court is where the civil suit leads if the *Herald* gets the public behind the case. U.S. Attorney Jo Ann Merica already hates the Chicago Police Department and wants to be governor—she'll file a criminal case against you and Ruben, crucify the *corrupt* Chicago Police Department, force a deserved restitution to the family of a retarded black man wrongfully executed, then convict the *real* monsters who 'raped a thirteen-year-old Irish girl to death.' " Pause. "Forget governor, Jo Ann rights so many wrongs she could run for president."

Ruben sips his Scotch, nodding, no smile. I ask if Mr. Barlow is representing him.

Ruben says, "Not yet. City's paying for my civil fling with the Duprees."

I nod down LaSalle Street at city hall. "Will the city stay with you after the *Herald* says you and I are John Gacy?"

Ruben sets his glass by the Chianti-bottle candle and removes his toothpick. "Now you have it, *buey.* Before today's paper, Ruben Vargas was either hero cop/*patrón del barrio*; or a cop who knew too many of the bad people; or a racist cop—all depended on whose story they were selling that day. No six o'clock news there. But in here"—Ruben taps the *Herald*—"they make the brothers Vargas into *monstruos* who have to die . . . then, *esé,* you and I *día del muerto.*"

Mr. Barlow adds, “One way or another.”

A cute waitress stops next to my shoulder, hesitates because it’s obvious I’m some kind of cop and on duty, then asks if I want a drink anyway. I tell her no thanks. Mr. Barlow spins his finger for another round. She leaves and I tell him: “I knew Coleen when we were kids. I liked her, a lot. I don’t hurt people I like.” I cut to my older brother in his expensive sport coat and concerned expression, then back. “But I have no problem hurting people I don’t like. So I’ll do my job until the department or the city decides to submarine me. If and when that happens, maybe we’ll talk.”

Barlow stares. “Suit yourself. I can’t make you want to survive.”

“Take care of my older brother. He thinks being a Mexican legend makes him immune.”

“No. Ruben knows better, that’s why we’re here. He knows this will get ugly. They won’t play fair and neither can you.”

Instead of standing like I should, I sit back. “What do you have in mind, counselor?”

“The investigator from Texas working with Moens is an ex-cop with nasty Mexico history that he doesn’t know I can prove. The Pink Panther, storied crime reporter for the *Herald,* continues an on-again, off-again lesbian affair with her ex–business partner in the L7, Julie McCoy.”

“That the kind of lawyer you are?”

“The ownership of the *Herald* is negotiating a bankruptcy plea that will invalidate its pension requirements and generate a sale to a U.K. conglomerate. Headlines help the sale. You and your brother will be dragged through the sewer. ‘Tabloid’ won’t quite describe it.”

“I don’t hide behind character assassination.”

“Noble, but child murder and rape accusations require rebuttal.” Mr. Barlow adopts his jury voice: “Either we fight their salacious innuendo and hyperbole masquerading as ‘fact’ with similar tools or—”

“Why not use the truth?”

Barlow blinks, confused. “Because the truth doesn’t matter. Winning matters.”

I look down the patio at customers busy with their own conversations. Being somewhere else would be good, and by Monday night—

after IAD, federal depositions, and the *Herald*'s next installment of "MONSTER"—probably *someone* else.

Barlow continues. "Bobby, I can't help you or your brother without your cooperation. That's a decision the two of you have to make. But be assured this fight will only be won dirty, and not without you and Ruben taking some hits."

Ruben crosses himself. "Or we can sit back and take it up the ass. Enjoy being *mártires*."

"I'm not a martyr . . . nor am I an asshole, most of the time." I nod at Barlow. "Thanks for your time and advice." Then to Ruben: "Talk to you tomorrow."

Ruben chews his toothpick, stands, and walks me to my car. "What kinda questions your new girls askin'?"

"Officer Hahn asked about Moens and the *Herald*—if it bothered me. Today's paper was on my seat; she was just making conversation. Did say something interesting, though. Furukawa's run by Japanese guys. How come they're backing Chicago against Tokyo for the Olympics?"

"Above my pay grade. Anything about me?"

"Nope." My phone vibrates. I answer.

Buff says, "Are we sober?"

"Twelve-pack ain't nothing for a musician."

"We're a go for the Latin Kings corner in thirty minutes. Train tracks and Damen—you and Hahn—now."

"Ten-four." I flip the phone shut.

Ruben grips my neck like when we were kids. "Where you at tonight?"

"Ashland and Twenty-first. Got me a red Toyota, buy money, and two girls the commander wants to make famous. Buff thinks it's the beginning of an Operation Hammer."

Ruben shakes his head. "No more ghetto. Won't need us, we'll all be one big happy Olympic village." He squeezes my neck. "Think about what Mr. Barlow said."

"Don't need to. I'm not joining the rape-and-pillage club."

Ruben slaps my head, then hugs me tighter than usual. "By this time tomorrow, little brother, you won't know a soul who doesn't think the rape-and-pillage club is *exactly* where you and I belong." He pushes me to arm's length. "And watch out for those girls. They ain't in your team to *make conversation*."

FRIDAY, 9:00 PM

Officer Hahn buckles her seat belt. "How'd dinner work out with your brother?"

"All good. New plan. Latin Kings are a go. We're meeting by the train tracks."

She nods, less than excited. Her right hand removes a plastic sack from a rugby kit bag she threw in our Crown Vic—the sack contains the wire and harness she'll be wearing. "Had a hot dog with Lopez. She told me we're a go." Little blond smile. "Guess some of the boys decided to talk to her."

I make a G with my right hand. "I'm smarter."

Hahn pops me her version of the FBI gang sign. " 'Always and forever, homes; blood in, blood out.' "

I turn left at the next corner, make my new team member forty-sixty undercover like Ruben says, but stay with the I Love This Gang moment: " 'We da G; we die under those colors.' "

She laughs. "Been shot once, that was plenty."

"Me, too. BB gun. Hurt like a son of a bitch."

Hahn smiles big and turns away, hiding the grin in her window.

"What? All of a sudden you'll hate putting me in Marion?"

She stays with the window, laughing now, and nods.

"Don't worry about it. I'm not guilty of anything the feds could care about."

She turns back, still smiling. "What? Ruben and you go to confession?"

FRIDAY, 10:00 PM

Sergeant Buff Anderson, T-shirt, jeans, and body armor, stands between four Crown Vics and the Burlington Northern tracks. His posture is street-boss confident, but there's concern in his face that his tone matches. "The girls make the first buy." He thumbs over his shoulder at the red Toyota Vice probably lent us. "Lopez drives the beater. Hahn buys. We four-way the corner—Vargas and Cowin from the west; me and Jewboy coming east; Candy and Romero on Ashland from the bridge; Gonzalez and Fez down from the Jewel."

Good plan; makes sense and should; Buff knows how to organize a gunfight, be it in the jungle or the city. The girls doing the buy is stupid and dangerous, and I'm sure he hates it, but our new commander wants her girls in the gang crimes and TAC units with street victories as their pedigree, not affirmative action.

"This is the commander's mission." Buff looks at the girls. "Her choice to put you in the buy car." Five-second pause. "Assuming you ain't feds, *Do. Not. Die.* Am I clear?"

Hahn smiles, Lopez doesn't, the adrenaline apparent in their faces.

Buff checks both his pistols, then looks directly at the girls again. "The Kings are stone killers; this corner's hot. Iraq hot. Am I clear?" Buff waits for the girls to nod; he doesn't have to wonder about us. "All of you who checked shotguns, I want 'em chambered and in the front seat. These assholes go live on the girls, come at 'em all the way. We'll worry about our Olympic image tomorrow."

Lopez finds no solace in her über-Olympic value. "If it's that bad we should have marines."

Buff continues. "Nothing on you two that says La Raza. No Spanish, you're white chicks from the burbs."

Lopez straightens, looking at her hands, then Buff.

"I'm not the commander. If you're calling in sick, do it now."

Lopez glances at Hahn, who shakes her head. Lopez strips her vest and belt to become a dope-buying civilian, pulls her Glock, checks it, and slides it into her waistband. She frowns at me . . . like her situation is somehow my fault, then glances at Hahn again.

Hahn says, *"Girls Gone Wild."*

Jewboy grins big, "'Ats the spirit." He points at Lopez's chest. "Now that we're working together you could flash me, you know, team spirit and stuff . . . sort of."

Lopez keeps her shirt on. Hahn strips her vest and belt, hands both to me, and asks for help taping up her wire. Lopez watches. Again, I get the odd flash I'm in some kind of spiderweb three-way with these two strangers.

Over Hahn's head I tell Lopez, "Tonight's the King's first weekend on your corner; big money changing hands Friday and Saturday. Whoever's out there will be shooters."

Lopez nods. Hahn inhales deep, winks, and walks toward the red Toyota. Buff hands her the money and says, "Same as before. When

Hahn or Lopez says 'Wait, we ain't right,' I repeat, 'Wait, we ain't right,' all cars roll. Clear?"

All of us nod.

"Check your radios." Buff watches till we're done, then taps the muscular dystrophy pin he wears for luck his daughter didn't get. "Do. Not. Hesitate. Chicago may need the Olympics, but none of Gang Team 1269 dies today."

FRIDAY, 10:30 PM

Jason makes the turn onto Twenty-first Street, lip curled under his teeth. "Got a bad feeling."

"Imagine that."

"Yeah, *imagine that.* All of a sudden we can't work the ghetto without chicks? And they do a double buy on day one? In the middle of a gang war? It's like they gotta get in with us so fast that suicide's worth it."

"Ate dinner with Jewboy, huh?"

"Yeah, but—"

"He still think Jimmy Hoffa shot JFK?"

Jason looks at me instead of the windshield. I reach for the 12-gauge, half rack the pump, then check the rest of the tube—six rounds total, lots of damage if the Latin Kings make me use it. Our car quiets into silent preparation, the personal inventory when you're driving toward a gunfight instead of away. Five cars, ten cops, all well armed. And yet we're the underdog. What's that say about America? The big gangs in the ghetto districts outnumber us twelve to one and have better guns. They don't have rules of engagement, we do. Their shooters hit the pipe to stay crazy, and fire till they run out of bullets.

Twenty-first Street darkens.

To break the silence I say, "If IAD has anything other than the *Herald*'s bullshit on Coleen Brennan and the Duprees, I gotta believe I'll see those cards Monday morning when I'm under IAD's lights. Whatever I hear should help us piece together where this train with the commander, Hahn, and Lopez is headed."

Jason's eyes cut to me and Monday, then back to the threats directly ahead of us. "Feels wrong. Buff feels it, too; I can tell."

"Call in sick."

"Fuck you." Jason focuses on something in the middle distance. "And fuck the commander. Her two FBI agents. And Operation Hammer."

"Go to the Cub game. Call in a beef; nobody has to work with strangers who fall out of the sky."

"But you will?" Jason frowns for real and pushes his radio at me. "Only if everybody agrees. This is stupid, but I ain't leaving you guys short."

"Guess we're going to work, then."

We stop in the dark two blocks west, one car alone on the war's Friday-night front line, Jason and I sifting shadows and shapes for Latin King lookouts or La Raza gunships neither of us see. Used to be bangers didn't murder policemen in their cars; crack changed that. The radio's back in Jason's lap, the girls' voices talking to his jeans.

Lopez: "Approaching southeast corner of Ashland and Twenty-first."

Hahn: "Four males, Hispanic, eighteen to twenty-five; T-shirts, caps, baggies. Black and gold. Pulling up."

Black and gold are the colors of the Latin Kings. Jason draws his 9-millimeter and slides it under his leg. We're too far away, but as close as we can creep and not get made. "This is fucked up, Bobby. I say call it off."

Hahn: "Got twenty dollars, wanna holler."

Hispanic male: "That right?"

Hahn: "Yeah."

Male: "Don' see it."

Shuffle noise.

Lopez: "Hey, man, why three guys to do—"

ROAR OF AN AUTOMATIC.

Jason slams the gas and me into the seat. I grab the radio, flipping the frequency: "Ten-one! Ten-one! Officer down, Ashland and Twenty-first. Gang Team 1269 on the scene." Both feet press hard into floorboard. The radio drops, I two-hand the shotgun, and we're airborne over the first intersection; Jason rockets the next block, makes the intersection at Ashland, and slams the brakes. Four males fire flame and roar into the Toyota's windows and windshield.

Jason skid-stops sideways and we're out of the car. Two shooters have their backs to us both slamming new magazines. A third shooter catapults backward from the Toyota. The fourth turns to run, leaps into the street, and Buff's front bumper smashes him into the pavement. I level the 12-gauge and fire twice. The nearest shooter goes down; the other turns mid-intersection, spraying us full-auto with a converted Tec-9. Bullets bang the fender. Our windshield explodes; I duck; Jason's hit, stumbles up aiming his pistol. Our southbound car screams into the intersection. The last shooter standing spins too late and is crushed at forty miles per hour.

I spin toward the Toyota. Hahn is standing, but crumpled over her fender. She aims her pistol down at Shooter Three pancaked on her sidewalk. Both fire. Hahn twists away, fires again, and goes down. Sirens careen in from three directions. I fan for targets in the flashing lights. Shadows. Adrenaline. Instinct. Doors pop on the arriving cars; body armor floods the intersection; ten more cops rush into our perimeter.

I twist one-eighty for my partner, then three-sixty. "Jason!"

No answer.

Nine minutes since the shooting stopped; the air's still adrenaline and death.

Radios crackle. Lights strobe the pavement blue-red-and-white. Armed men and EMTs move in and out of staccato 8 mm reality. Four TAC cars are stopped at odd angles, doors open. Shell casings and glass shards litter the intersection.

Mouth dry; pulse at one-twenty and coming down.

More beat cars roll in to block the side streets. Gas and oil and blood puddles glare in the crisscross of headlights. Officer Lopez is dead behind the wheel of the Toyota. Two Latin King shooters are dead from Crown Vic bumpers, both bodies splattered into the intersection. The gangster I shot is being placed in the nearest ambulance with two EMTs feverishly attempting to keep him from bleeding to death. Hahn hit the shooter on her sidewalk at least twice but he's conscious and breathing as his EMTs stretcher him past me. Same with Hahn, thankfully.

How she is a survivor is one of those mysteries that can happen; the bullets go everywhere you're not. All but one—a .38 ricocheted, then hit her second gun. The .38 didn't break her hip, but bruised her so badly she couldn't stand. Hahn is loaded into her ambulance, windshield pieces buried in her face and arms; her eyes remain locked on Lopez's lifeless body.

Jason is bleeding but not bad. Buff is about to tell him a second time to get his ass to the hospital but has to turn to more uniforms piling out of their cars. "No, back it up to Paulina, nothing eastbound past Paulina." Buff walks the uniforms west, pointing at where he wants them.

Radios bark that Homicide is on the way in, as are the crime-scene techs. Jason spits a glass fragment. "Shit, that hurts."

I'm still trying to figure what happened, what I just saw. The radio squawks inside our car. The call tape won't sound like a dope buy that went bad; this was an execution; the Kings were waiting for that red Toyota. And until a few minutes ago I was supposed to be driving it.

"Officer Vargas?"

I turn to a white male in a sport coat. He introduces himself as an investigator from OPS and asks what happened. OPS is the Office of Professional Standards—any officer-involved shooting is investigated by OPS. Our commander is for sure on her way, same for the street deputy—he's a deputy superintendent and the highest-ranking policeman on duty when Superintendent Jesse Smith isn't. I start to answer the OPS investigator and four Homicide dicks screech to a stop in two cars; my brother Ruben is one of them. He runs to me instead of walking to Officer Lopez dead in the Toyota. "We cool, *buey*?" Ruben prods my vest and squeezes one shoulder.

"Yeah."

Ruben nods a professional acknowledgment to the OPS investigator, then back to me. "Sure you're okay?"

"Fine."

"Remember what I told you at dinner." Ruben scans the scene. "Three dead, two dying gonna make the Olympic village major-unhappy."

I nod again; he does the same, turns, and walks toward Lopez. I will see Ruben again tonight when the officer-involved interviews start at ADD, the Area 4 Detective Division. If my shooter dies, I'll be under the lights all night and be offered days with pay, pending the investigation's outcome. If he lives, I'll only be at ADD half the night, till OPS and Homicide and the ASAs and the street deputy and finally our commander all are satisfied that what we did passes all the best second-guess tests modern man can devise. Then I can type reports till my fingers go numb.

The OPS investigator separates me from Jason and asks me what I heard, saw, and what I did. He writes it down, asks to hear it again and follows his notes while I repeat my answer, then confirms: "Shooters One and Two on your side of the Toyota were both firing?"

"Yeah. The Tec-9s. Both were firing at Lopez. I shot Shooter One; he went down. I shot Shooter Two as he sprayed us. Fez's car caught him."

Ten feet away, Jason picks at the glass in his cheek and tells the flashing lights, "Motherfuckers blew up my car."

The OPS investigator focuses on Jason, then the 9-millimeter magazines by the bodies, and asks me, "Both shooters had reloaded and had commenced firing?"

"Yeah."

"You're sure?"

Frown. "Compared to what?"

He stares, but for some reason doesn't press it. "And you have no explanation for the firepower present or any precondition for its use?"

"Like I told you, no way they light up the Toyota if they know we're cops. But they knew something, expected some kind of car-bomb, big move, and they knew it was that exact car. Maybe not the people in it, but the Toyota for sure."

"Who else knew about the Toyota?"

"Don't know." I glance at Jason who can't hear us. "Probably on loan from Vice."

"Who else knew the details of the mission? Day, time, location?"

"Don't know. Came straight from the commander and at the last minute."

"Last minute?"

"We heard it was a go thirty minutes before we rallied. Like it could've been part of an Operation Hammer or something."

Buff steps between me and the investigator. Using one arm and both eyes, Buff hugs me hard. "Good job, Bobby. Did everything you could."

Buff doesn't bitch about the gunfight. He turns to Jason still picking at the glass in his face. "Good job, Jason, damn good. Now go to the hospital."

Jason eyes Buff and his tone. It's obvious Buff wants time to talk with Jason before OPS does; Buff will know what I said, and this way, Jason will too before he goes on the record. Heads will roll for this gunfight and Buff's trying to keep them from being ours.

The OPS investigator does not appear comfortable or confident. He says to Buff, "We better talk, before you and your team head uptown."

Buff nods, gives me the same cover-your-ass look Ruben just did, then walks off with the OPS investigator.

Jason watches them avoid the headlights of more unmarked cars arriving. Halfway to the perimeter, Buff and the OPS investigator stop in the oscillating shadows, the investigator talking, Buff listening. Jason steps to me. "Cap rabid dogs and we gotta worry?"

I scan the death scene: haphazard cars, bodies, and weapons, now surrounded by methodical meticulous police reaction. It's a surreal moment—the sharp roar of the street, followed by the blanket silence of the system—surreal, but in most big American cities it happens once a day. A clearly shaken Jewboy steps around the broken glass, blood, and brass casings, but stays inside yellow crime-scene tape being strung.

"That was bad." Jewboy exhales long and slow, then chins toward Buff and the OPS investigator. As those two talk, they stare at a parked black Ford SUV that usually means FBI. Two men in dark suits stand either side of the SUV's headlights, both talking on cell phones.

"I fucking knew it." Jason turns his back to the SUV. "Lopez was undercover. She and Hahn are after us . . . and we got one of 'em killed."

Jewboy nods, unusually somber, head bouncing from Jason to me. "But why be after us? We didn't do anything. Did we?"

Everybody's waiting for me to say something . . . like I have the answer.

FRIDAY, 11:30 PM

The Area 4 Detective Division is a big building at Harrison and Kedzie. Buff has us all here, sans Jason who's at Mercy Hospital till they remove the glass from his face and arms. In these situations, Buff operates in full father mode. We're his charges, like his grunts were in Vietnam. If bullets are in the air, be they foreign or friendly, Buff leads from the front.

And that's a good thing, 'cause if Officer Lopez was a fed—and it appears she was—then an assistant U.S. attorney and other FBI specialists will be added to the normal rounds of post-shooting interrogations. Not debriefings: *interrogations.* Unfortunately, it has to be that way; when a public servant kills a citizen *or three*—even murderers armed with machine guns—the system has to satisfy itself that you acted properly. Properly is defined by hard-and-fast rules of engagement that are then interpreted subjectively. And you don't get to whine, because you knew all that when you took the job.

Two gangsters were killed with cars; I shot another who, as of ten minutes ago, is still alive; and Officer Hahn shot a fourth one who isn't. Officer Lopez is dead and anyone who's been the police more than an hour knows this incident was a setup, an execution. The fact that Sheila Lopez probably was a *federal* undercover officer points the finger at the police who organized the buy. As of this moment, we—make that Gang Team 1269—haven't been told what case Officer Lopez was working for the FBI but it stands to reason that it was against our TAC and gang crimes unit. There is the possibility she was working a case on the Latin Kings and hadn't involved us because a) we can't be trusted, and b) how would we know "b" if we can't be trusted?

Our new commander—who organized the buy and should be under the lights with the rest of us—is seated next to an ASA (assistant state's attorney—"the DA" in TV shows) and the OPS investigator who conducted the crime-scene interview with me. The fact that our commander isn't under the lights means either she did her interview previously or she put the mission together with the full knowledge of the ASA. And that is not required policy for a street-level, stand-alone dope buy.

Our commander asks me to explain what happened.

I do.

When I'm done reliving the gunfight a fourth time, she mentions, a fourth time, and on the record, that my brother Ruben is one of the

Homicide detectives investigating the murder of Officer Lopez. The first two times she mentioned Ruben, I agreed. For the last two I have remained silent.

She asks, "Did you speak with your brother tonight, prior to the shooting on Ashland?"

"Yes."

"When and where."

"Levee Grill for dinner. Eight o'clock."

"Two and a half hours before the shooting?"

Nod.

"If your nod indicates an answer in the affirmative, please say so."

"Yes."

The ASA takes over. "Did you and Detective Ruben Vargas discuss the Latin Kings mission?"

"No."

"Did you discuss officers Hahn and Lopez as possible federal agents?"

"No."

My new commander leans in, extends a finger toward my face, and—

Commotion behind her produces three more professionals led by a six-foot woman wearing a perfectly pressed suit in the middle of the night. The hair tightens on my arms. Jo Ann Merica introduces herself as the U.S. attorney for the Northern District of Illinois and sits down uninvited. Seeing her here and *in person* at pushing midnight is so out of line I have to rub my eyes and remember to breathe.

On TV you cowboy-up and tell the G to stick it; in real life you don't. They have all the money and all the time required to ruin you, guilty or not. And they will, if they think ruining you serves some higher federal goal. Or if it helps run for governor. Jo Ann Merica studies me like the motionless, ghetto pit bulls do when you're about to step into their yard. She's famous for putting cops and politicians in prison, and for "thirty-two-degree eyes that don't blink when children die."

The ASA shows me a copy of this morning's *Herald*. "Is this what you and your brother discussed? And if so, what was the substance of that discussion?"

"The Olympics is a bit off my beat."

The ASA frowns, flips the *Herald* over, and points to the exposé teaser.

I silently count to five before answering. "Help me here. I'm not named in the Dupree lawsuit. And why does libel in the *Herald* on an unrelated case that happened when I was *thirteen years old* matter tonight?"

"Answer the question please."

"I will, after you explain why it matters."

"You shot a man tonight; we want to know why."

"Because he had a machine gun and he'd just murdered one of my fellow officers."

"Please answer the question."

"I forgot, what is it?"

"What information do you have on the Coleen Brennan murder?"

"Coleen Brennan was my friend when other people wouldn't be. Whatever we were is none of your fucking business."

"That's your answer?"

"If that's your question."

Uninvited, the U.S. attorney for the Northern District of Illinois, one of the most powerful federal officials outside Washington, D.C., takes over. "Did you ask Officer Lopez if she was a federal agent?"

Neither the ASA nor my new commander challenge Ms. Merica's right to take over, so I turn to her and answer, "No."

"Did any member of your gang team ask Officer Lopez if she was a federal agent?"

"Don't know."

"That's your answer? On the record?"

"Yeah." Bit of adrenaline.

"Have you discussed Officer Lopez with Chicago Police Department officers Anderson, Cowin, and Mesrow?"

"Yeah."

"Did you discuss the possibility that she was a federal agent?"

"Don't remember."

"You're certain you don't remember?"

"I don't remember if I remember."

A meticulously dressed subordinate supplies Jo Ann Merica with papers and points mid-page. "Officer Mesrow remembers. Does that help?"

"No. Sorry."

The subordinate's finger points Ms. Merica to another section. She reads it, then says, "You told the OPS: 'No way they light up the Toyota if they know we're cops. But they knew something, expected some kind of car-bomb, big move, and they knew it was that exact car.' Is that what you said?"

"Something like that."

"How would the Latin Kings know?"

"Somebody tipped them. And no, I don't know who. I was told by my sergeant who was told by our commander"—I nod across the table at my commander, intent on saving her career—"to perform the buy at a specific time and in a specific manner. That's what I did; that's what we all did, including Officer Lopez." I cut to the ASA. "And I was not notified of this mission until *after* I left my brother and Mr. Barlow. And no, I did not speak to either man again until I saw Ruben at the crime scene."

The U.S. attorney taps her pen. No one speaks, not the ASA, my commander, or the OPS investigator. The U.S. attorney continues. "Did you and your brother discuss the red Toyota at the Levee Grill?"

"I already said, no."

"Not to me." Pause. "I understand former First Ward alderman Toddy Pete Steffen was at your table."

Uh-oh. Either the Levee Grill is under federal surveillance or Ruben and I are being tailed. "Mr. Steffen said hello. To Ruben's lawyer."

The U.S. attorney nods. "And the two Japanese men from Furukawa Industries?"

Staring at Jo Anne Merica, it hits me that she hasn't asked about the Duprees' *federal* lawsuit that might make her governor. Her only focus, *at midnight,* is me, Ruben, and federal undercover agents. And now Toddy Pete and Furukawa—

"The gentlemen from Furukawa—did you or your brother speak with them?"

Blink. "Why would we?" My commander and the ASA stare bullets at me. I cut back to the U.S. attorney. "One of you three wanna tell me what's going on?"

Small smile; unlimited budget, thirty-two-degree eyes. "I wonder how the Vargas brothers—street cops from the Four Corners—can afford James W. Barlow as their attorney. And why they're in the same restaurant with Toddy Pete Steffen and Dr. Hitoshi Ota, CEO of Furukawa Industries, Chicago's Olympic benefactor. It looks like a meeting, smells like a meeting, maybe it *is* a meeting."

Barlow I understand; the rest I'm clueless. "Wanna repeat that in English? 'Cause this *street cop* doesn't know *what the fuck you're talking about.*"

The U.S. attorney leans forward. " I think you do."

My new commander waits until she's certain the U.S. attorney isn't continuing, then says, "You're given two days with pay, pending the review of tonight's shooting. And, per previous notification, you are to report to the Internal Affairs Division Monday morning at 0800 regarding the Coleen Brennan accusations. You may appear with or without an attorney."

My hands unfold damp. There should be FBI specialists in here if Hahn and Lopez are FBI, and there aren't any. That black SUV and its two guys belonged to somebody.

Jo Ann Merica says, "Do not leave Chicago without prior notification to my office. You're excused."

6 SATURDAY

ARLEEN BRENNAN
SATURDAY, 1:00 PM

The alley behind my apartment radiates fight-or-flee. One hand squeezes a cocked murder weapon, the other squeezes the steering wheel. Heat prickles my neck. Through bit teeth I repeat, "I am not a victim." I am Arleen the Bold, clutch down, in gear, engine running. And have been for twenty-eight minutes. July sun glares my VW's windshield. *Fight-or-flee.* Robbie Steffen is here, has to be. Robbie has to kill me. I was on Lawrence Avenue, and a player—the state's attorney can charge me with murder. The U.S. attorney can charge me under RICO. Robbie knows I'll get some kind of immunity on the murder charge to bury a crooked cop. I release the steering wheel, keep the cocked .38 in my other hand, and call my landline again.

No answer. The window curtains don't move. But Robbie *has* to be here.

Robbie couldn't find me last night because I slept in my car and moved every two hours. Now if I can just survive a fast trip up my back stairs . . . Run up, pack the Blanche clothes for my audition—the ones I wore that got me this far—grab my hair and makeup case, I'll hide out at Julie's till audition time. By then, something will have worked out. It's my turn.

I squeeze the .38 and glance at the *Streetcar* pages. Fight-or-flee?

Arleen the Victim or Arleen the Bold? My hand reaches for the *Streetcar* pages, *my* pages. Pick. Choose. I cut the ignition, pop the door, and bolt. At the stairs, I leap two at a time, key the door, jump inside, close it, and listen . . . to the city outside, me breathing, nothing else.

Don't be here, Robbie . . .

I slow-walk out of the kitchen into the hall, three steps, then four. My apartment wasn't electric dangerous before— Noise. Was that a creak? The front door? Forget the clothes—no have to have the clothes— Don't be here, Robbie. Don't make me shoot you.

"Arleen?" Front door, ten feet away.

I freeze. Someone knocks—knuckles or a gun barrel. "Arleen? We gotta talk. Your neighbor called me, said you were home."

The front door arcs open. I stiff-arm the .38 and brace into the wall—

"Whoa . . . *Niña* . . ."

Ruben Vargas sitting on my living-room couch is world-class scary, but not as scary as Robbie Steffen. Ruben adds *smooth* to his pimp smile and voice. "Baby, I know Robbie's nuts. What can I tell you? Grew up with too much money."

I show Ruben composure I don't feel. "*Nuts?* Robbie's a murderer, slight difference—"

"Hey, now. How could you know? You weren't up there on Lawrence Avenue. Maybe you *heard* something somewhere, but . . . 'Cause if you *were* up there, then you're an accessory and just as guilty as the shooter. Whoever that was."

"I'm out, Ruben. If that means you try to take *Streetcar* away, use my phone, take your best shot. Koreatown, you, and Steffen are a train wreck I'm done riding."

"Why would I take your dream? Robbie's a problem we can fix."

"*We* can fix?" I bluff a small femme-fatale smile. "The next time you say 'we,' I'm using your .38 or calling the U.S. attorney. Either way you're dead."

Ruben glances at my hands, then the *Streetcar* pages on my table. He sits back and removes his toothpick. "And tell Jo Ann Merica what? That your whole life is my fault, or Robbie's? We made all your decisions for you?"

"Threaten somebody else. I'm out."

Ruben's eyes narrow. "I have friends in California, detectives."

California? Heat burns my skin red. *California?*

Ruben smiles, tracing the long scar at his mouth. "But why would I want to take your dream?"

Take my dream? Like Ruben owns it, like *he* paid twenty years of soul poison for it. I grab the *Streetcar* pages and shake them at his chin. "I'll be at the Shubert tomorrow, you monumental asshole—on time, ready for my chance—go ahead, do your threats. Steffen and you want a goddamn fight, I'll give you one."

Ruben shakes his head and replaces the toothpick. "Arleen, baby. Work with us—sort it out so everybody's happy. Tomorrow morning you probably get the part at the Shubert, become a big star, and put all your worries behind you." The toothpick changes sides. "Or . . . you'll have to deal with the Koreans on your own, same with Robbie and everyone else you harm. All for the good of who? The U.S. attorney? So the bitch can be governor?"

"Your partner shot that Korean. Dead."

Shrug. "*Our* partner. One less gangster who was probably illegal anyway."

"He's not my goddamn partner and neither are you."

Shrug. "Maybe I'm not, but Robbie is for sure . . . *if* you were there . . . and *if* he pulled the trigger. Accessory before and after, twenty to life. Even with immunity, Robbie's father can't let you bury his son—"

"Leave me alone!" I jump halfway into Ruben's face, grabbing for anything that might scare him. "What about the *Herald*? Want me to—"

"What? Feed Moens a story you know isn't true? C'mon. Read what Moens says. If she exhumes your sister's body and they find new DNA, we both know it ain't gonna be mine. Then where are you?"

I will read Moens's *exposé,* if for no other reason than to use the lies against Ruben. My head starts to pound. "I'm out, Ruben, done. I worked my whole life for a chance—"

"And *I* gave it to you. Didn't I?"

Balk. "You said it was Toddy Pete Steffen. He asked the director to call me in."

Headshake, teacher to child. "*I* told that director to give you a fair shake. Not a ride, just an honest shot. She was undecided on her Blanche—owes me big for keeping her cocaine headliners out of jail—and you aced your chance. I'm happy for you." Pause. "So we calm Robbie down, convince Choa to be cool, and the rest doesn't matter."

"Doesn't *matter*? The Korean's dead—two of 'em—counting the one Robbie cut up."

"Did Sinatra have a fifty-year career?"

"*What*? You're saying . . . What are you saying?"

"I'm saying calm the fuck down. This isn't the first time somebody from my world helped somebody in yours. The Koreans don't know your real name, yet. We have a situation, that's all, one that's manageable in my world."

"*Manage* two dead members of the Korean mafia?"

"We don't deal in face paint and scenery. This is what we do, then there's tomorrow and we do it again."

I stand there, lost in the insanity. Ruben points me back to my chair, and like an angry child, that's where I go.

He points at a copy of *Rolling Stone* with soldiers on the cover. "Collateral damage. We killed seventeen people in Afghanistan today, you gonna be all crazy about that, too?" Ruben waits for a response. "Choa wants his property returned, a package, and I want to give it to him, but we deserve *something* for finding it. Choa decided he could pay less than agreed. Robbie and I ain't doing that. So there was an argument. Choa tried to clip Robbie." Headshake. "*Toddy Pete Steffen's* son. And Choa's real lucky he missed." Ruben smiles, but it's cold, reptilian, like the smile that went with "California." "The ramifications have been mentioned to Mr. Choa, who now sees the error of his ways."

Not that I believe a word of Ruben's story, but killing Toddy Pete Steffen's only son could never have been a good idea; all the proof anyone would require to be scared of the Koreans. "A package of what?"

"Not important to us, but a big deal to the Japs and Koreans." Ruben sits back. "So before becoming a star tomorrow, you gotta behave today. Meet with Robbie—"

"The hell I am."

Ruben leans forward. "Explain to Robbie—"

"You explain. I'm not getting within fifty miles of him."

"Arleen, I'm trying to help. If you wanna die or rot in prison on dyke patrol, be my guest."

"Do I need to say it in Spanish? The answer's no. Your lies got me into—"

"And I'll get you out." He taps at my *Streetcar* pages. "But you're *in* and you better get a grip on that . . . too."

We stare. I send him as much hate and as little fear as I can.

"Things are a little warm out there for Robbie and me, U.S. attorney–wise. I got something you have to give Robbie and something you have to tell him."

"No. Chance. Never. Happen."

"Till we get this done, Arleen, you'll be carrying the mail. Robbie's not gonna hurt you; you gotta get past that. He'd have been here waiting and he wasn't. We need you; you need us. Feds can't help you. Simple as that."

SATURDAY, 3:00 PM

"Calm and cool." Me mumbling to me. "Just another audition." Gun in my purse, walking toward suicide or prison. Jackhammers and diesel engines shake the ground. Steel skeletons of unfinished mid-rises checkerboard the sky above the "new" Greektown. Deep breath, right turn into the alley, and . . .

Thirty feet down the alley at the T junction, six-foot-two TAC cop Robbie Steffen waits in the shadows. Half his body armor and gun belt are hidden by the brick corner. Behind his right leg he has a handful of metal that glints. A crane boom crosses the narrow sky above the alley. The air tastes like concrete dust and throat bile. Robbie flinches at the crane moving above him, then glares at me and the street beyond my back. He was expecting his crime-partner Ruben Vargas. Robbie wants the package he and Ruben owe the Koreans, not additions or explanations to a story that can only get him killed. He hugs his brick corner and fast-eyes the alley to his left, then right, waiting to see if I'm alone.

A rat runs between trash cans. Overheated July breeze skitters homeless debris past my feet and excrement stench past my nose. Robbie stays protected by the brick corner and waves me closer. I don't want to be any closer; the Valium I took has had thirty minutes to work but my heart's pounding louder than the jackhammers.

Robbie waves again, more of his gun visible. When I'm ten feet from him, his gun comes all the way out. Robbie focuses on my hands, then my purse with the pistol in it. He locks on my eyes, but comes no closer. "Who's with you?"

Swallow. "No one."

Robbie does not look or sound good.

"Drop the purse. Pull up your shirt. Do a circle."

"What?"

"Pull up your fucking shirt. If you got a bra on take it off."

I show him my bare chest, then my back.

"Where's Vargas?"

"Too much heat. He gave me— Wants me to—"

Robbie leaps out halfway to me and stiff-arms his pistol at my forehead.

"Don't!" My hands jump up between us. "I'm just a messenger. I saw nothing in Koreatown; honest, if anyone ever asks, I wasn't there. All I want is *away* from you two maniacs."

Robbie's head jerks three directions, comes back to me, and he squeezes tighter on the trigger.

"Do you have to point that at me? I'm an actress, not a—"

"What'd Ruben tell you?"

"Nothing. Honest. He wants me to give you something. In my purse. Said things were too hot—the U.S. attorney—for him to come."

"And you *believe* that?" Robbie jabs with the pistol. I duck left and away but bump into a trash can. Robbie hard-eyes the alley, then comes right at me. "Put your hand in that purse; come out with anything but my share of the White Flower money, and you're dead."

"Jesus, Robbie, take is easy. I know zero about flowers or money. Ruben said—"

Robbie's pistol cracks me in the ear. Lights go black and bright and I tumble over the trash can. Blink; stars, blink, a voice talking— "Goddamn set up. Ruben made a deal with the Koreans, didn't he? Serve me up as an apology."

"No, Robbie, I . . ." I palm and heel the alley, scooting back on my butt, try to stand.

"*No?* Then Ruben made a side deal with Furukawa's boss, motherfuckers cut me out. Ruben and his Vietcong bitch cut me out, *didn't they.* Send you to kill me and they cut you loose. *Right?*" Robbie swings. I cringe under the punch.

"No!"

Robbie jams his gun in my face, looking everywhere at once, then back at me. "Fuckin' cunt. I ain't the one dying here."

"Not a setup—" I crab backward through trash cans, palm and heel more alley until a brick wall bangs my head. Robbie's gun barrel is a giant O in my face. "*Stop it, Robbie*—"

"Got a gun in that purse, don't you? Uh-huh, got Ruben thinking with his dick. The goddamn Brennan sisters. You think if I die, Ruben's strong enough to fade Furukawa? Jap motherfuckers will eat you three alive."

"Robbie, c'mon, I know nothing about that. Honest to God—"

Robbie ducks, spins, and two-hands his pistol at the alley's other end. Concussion and roar bangs off the walls. I jolt into the trash cans and Robbie fires again. The alley flashes red-white from both directions. Robbie blows backward in cordite smoke. I curl in the trash cans. A blinding explosion splatters me with heat. Can't see, can't hear—

Eyes open, eyes open. Trash cans and smoke; no gun pointed in my face. Has to be Koreans. Please, God, no gun in my face, no rose tattoos. Please. Not like Coleen. Koreans will kidnap me, torture me to talk, cut me up— My hand fumbles. *Purse, get the gun.* Vibration? They're coming. A trash can kicks away. My hand fumbles for the purse; I grab the .38. Heavy black shoes appear in the refuse, then pant legs to the knee—oh, God—then the square head bending down. His eyes are predator intense, set deep in a wide pocked face. A pistol smokes in his bloody fingers. *Please don't.* The pistol rises into my face. NOT COLEEN. Flame-thunder explodes between us. He leaps straight back into the other wall, then slides down, mouth torn apart, eyes and forehead gone. I squeeze the gun with both hands until it shoots him again. His face and head are inside out, blood spraying everywhere. I'm frozen in a horror movie, aiming a gun at a . . . headless gushing monster. I try to scream and can't. My feet won't move; both arms are locked—

SIREN.

My head bangs brick wall, I suck a breath, then another, see the gun in my hands and jump to my feet; both shoes slip in the blood and trash. Robbie Steffen moans on his back. A second Korean is sprawled in the puddles. I jump Robbie's torso, run blind, bounce off the alley's T junction, veer left, and sprint, gun in hand, aiming for the next . . . Korean. No one charges. Car, where's my car? BREATHE. The alley ends at a street. Construction workers. Hide the gun. Cars pass in both directions. MOVE. RUN . . . siren, coming this way? My feet tangle; I stumble, palm the building for balance, don't fall, and run for my car.

Drive; c'mon, *drive*! Two CTA buses block the intersection. I jam second gear, veer into a side street. Rearview mirror, nothing, look left— Robbie had a vest on; he could be alive. Steer, both hands on the wheel, think later. And the Koreans don't know me, do they? Brake lights. Somehow they followed Robbie to that alley. Or me? If they followed *me,* then they know me and that I shot their man. Arleen Brennan just a shot a man. *To death.* Blew his head off. Vomit rises in my throat. *Hooorn.* Brake lights—

"Sorry, sorry." Bile, swallow, grimace. Right turn. Shift. Breathe. Residential; trees. North Side. The gun bounces on my seat—not a gun, a murder weapon. Mine. Yesterday I was an actress . . . now I'm a . . . oh, no. No, I'm not. I shot that monster in self-defense. He had a gun; he shot Robbie Steffen and would have killed or grabbed me.

Slow down; this is a side street.

Slow down? Ruben Vargas just tried to kill me—

Oh. My. God. The alley *was* a setup. Ruben put Robbie and me together, tied a bow on us, and called Mr. Choa.

But why? Why have the Koreans kill us? I fumble out Ruben's envelope and tear it open.

Blank paper. Machiavellian. A setup from go. Robbie and I die so Ruben can settle an eye-for-an-eye debt in mafia world. Ruben also has one less share to pay in the scam he and Robbie are running. And most important, the psycho Koreans and Mr. Choa are now real busy surviving Toddy Pete Steffen's wrath.

Plain as day. And Ruben wins the bonus round, too: both potential witnesses—me and a cop partner who's facing a retrial by the U.S. attorney—aren't available to roll after the scam is complete. Headshake. I've been expendable since this started, one of the reasons I'm sure I got the job. Gotta hide. Maybe upstairs above the L7? My best friend's bar. Julie's hideout room, the Butch and Sundance suite.

Traffic bunches ten deep at the light on Ashland Avenue; all four directions? *I'm trapped*— Calm down, calm down. Wrigley Field is eight blocks up; must be a Cubs home game; shit, the L7 will be packed with visiting-team fans wondering *why are all these women in here*? No, it won't—Wrigley traffic this late means a national TV game—watch check—they're ready to start. I'll hide my car—that's the plan—then walk to Clark Street mixed in with the fans, call Julie on the way in—my anchor, a smart, fearless, tough man in a pretty-girl suit—Julie will know what to do. She left me a voice mail on Friday when the *Herald* came out with their exposé and their support for exhuming Coleen, said she'd go with me to beat the shit out of Tracy Moens for writing it.

The *Streetcar* pages stare from the passenger seat. That's what I'll do—me and *Streetcar.* We'll rehearse in Julie's hideout suite. Then, then in nineteen hours I'll take the stage at the Shubert Theater . . . and save the Brennan sisters.

Right. Be Blanche DuBois; that's who you are; she wasn't in that alley. Ruben's not trying to kill her. Make that work. Find a parking place; be invisible. Coleen and I win this one.

I brake for two girls in the street. They're wearing bright yellow 2016 Chicago Olympics 10K T-shirts, walking down the street's center line. Passing out bumper stickers. One girl turns her back. Across her shoulders the font is big, bold, and Japanese: Furukawa.

My breath catches. Robbie said, "Jap motherfuckers will eat you three alive." Then everyone started shooting.

SATURDAY, 4:15 PM

Walking. Took another hit of Valium and changed my bloody shirt in the car. Been over an hour since I shot a man, think I'm in shock—floaty like after a car wreck that demolished your car but not you. The two hits of Valium are working better than one. Red VW is parked, blue tablets swallowed—I think I covered that—journey to friendship and safety begun. Just stay away from Koreans and *Jap motherfuckers* who will eat me alive.

Block three of a five-block walk to the L7 begins to feel good—me floating through leafy normal world—anonymous—with happy people in Cubs blue-and-white preparing to drink beer and eat peanuts. People who haven't murdered anyone. The not-so-good part is everything else. At block five, Bushmills or Jameson will level what the Valium hasn't. I flip my phone open with some difficulty and dial a large, athletic, saloonkeeper who loves me.

Bagpipes and singing answer. Julie McCoy yells, "*Blanche! Did we get it?*"

"The audition's tomorrow. I'm three blocks from you. Is there room at the inn?"

Over the din she yells: "For a star? Any bed she wants." Riot noise. "We won the Chicago 7s! Beat South Africa—the natural-blond bitches—Chicago RULES. *Boo-yah!*"

She means women's rugby. "Any men in there . . . asking for me?"

"Men? What are they for?"

My foot skips a sidewalk crack, don't want to break your mother's back. We loved our ma, most of the time; our da not so much. "Never mind. Be there in a sec."

I fold the phone, walk two more blocks, and hit Clark Street at Addison, the Valium OD beginning to numb-shuffle my feet and knees, weird feeling for a dancer. I loop fifty pregame revelers out front of the Cubby Bear Lounge and sidestep into Clark Street's game-day Mardi Gras—car horns, cops with Cubs hats directing traffic, fans in the street, flags, banners. They don't care if they win, the North Side's past that; this is ritual. Must be wonderful to belong to this kind of world.

Mid-block at the L7, the two smiling female doormen don't ask for my ID or the gun in my purse. The chunky one with the "Kesey Does It" T-shirt says, "Busy in there."

Kesey must mean Ken Kesey of *The Electric Kool-Aid Acid Test* . . . makes sense . . . I think. The L7 is a "woman's bar" but it's also the Beat capital of Chicago. Been here since the '30s, a beer hall/tavern with a Jack Kerouac pedigree. Julie added John Waters and Tallulah Bankhead, and our friend Beth Murphey painted the a/c ducts like snakes that only get that big in Imax anaconda movies.

The brunette opens the door and LOUD rocks me back a step. If Annie Oakley lived in Chicago, this is where she'd drink. Visiting-rugby-team banners hang haphazard from the high tin ceiling. Bagpipes wail across thirty tables pushed aside by muddy women in colorful jerseys and questionable haircuts. Have to be a hundred girls in multiple uniforms, all of them singing and sloshing a beer in each hand. To my right the long historic bar has *five girls marching on it*? Parasols on their shoulders, throwing beads at the crowd? Right, right—the Mardi Gras March, the New Orleans team Julie played for. The stage at the back is the only spot that's empty except for the band equipment.

Julie McCoy will be in the mosh somewhere—probably guest-starring with the pipers. Jesus, it's loud in there. Julie was a world-class athlete and well on her way to becoming a concert cellist before "the accident." The accident is depicted by a huge twenty-foot back-bar photo mural of Julie crashing her Ducati into a Nice café, showing off for a girl whose name she couldn't remember.

Brilliant red hair. I duck the flash—not sure why—just know I should. Two or three dead in an alley may be the reason . . . or twenty milligrams of Valium, or giant snakes squirming overhead of an all-girl riot. I veer toward the bar, shuffling for traction, staying close to the front window and the lesser violence. The doorway to Julie's office and the stairs up to the Butch and Sundance suite are all the way at the back, stage left, or to the right if you're a civilian.

Bump, shuffle. Young faces with bulletproof grins. The crush of shoulders and feet and hips and hair and singing—singing is way too kind—all this might be more than the Valium OD will allow. Keep moving. Four minutes of snaking through the crowd keeps me upright. This is a post-tournament party that will be off the hook in another hour. I've been to a few of these; wild like a badger, as me ma would say.

Hey! There's my picture, an eight-by-ten framed with others, each with a lipstick kiss and autographed to the L7. Mine is from *The Argonautika* four years ago. If I get *Streetcar* Julie will do a life-size poster and put me next to the Lisa Law photo of her hero, Allen Ginsberg at 9 rue Gît-le-Coeur. If I get *Streetcar* . . . loopy grin, three dead in an alley, homicide cop trying to kill me, Japanese motherfuckers wanting to eat me alive—no problem, take twenty milligrams every day and everything's everything.

The door to Julie's office is unlocked. I slip through, shut it behind me, and lean for a second. The noise cuts by half. Her oak desk has a folded copy of the *Herald* that won't quit following me and a framed photo of her adopted daughter, Hannah, playing the guitar. I pick up today's *Herald.* Please have something in here that can be used against Ruben Vargas for real, and soon, like today. Big picture of Dr. Hitoshi Ota, the Furukawa CEO, with the mayor. I fold the *Herald* and reach to lock Julie's door. Nope, double deadbolt that requires a key. The other door leads to the tiny hall and stairs to Butch and Sundance, and safety for now, and I'm through the door, pulling it closed behind me and—oh, shit.

Shit. Shit. Shit.

Sitting on the stairs— *No possible way*—Ruben Vargas couldn't have known I was coming here. The door is shut tight behind me. Blink. He's blinking, too, both hands on a red guitar, not a pistol. And he's younger than he looked earlier today, my age now, and his eyes are kind, not cold and reptilian. The devil's last cruel trick before he grabs me, his newest killer.

My ma says, "No, you baked the crumble muffins."

Blink. Half swallow. *Do something.* Gun . . . I have a gun.

I reach for the gun. And all the saints of heaven.

7

OFFICER BOBBY VARGAS

SATURDAY, 4:30 PM

Eighteen hours ago, Officer Sheila Lopez was murdered during her third shift with the Chicago Police Department. The dead shooters ranged in age from sixteen to twenty-two. My part of the officer-involved interrogations ended at 4:30 AM when U.S. Attorney Jo Ann Merica cut me loose. I drank two hours, semi-slept six, then ate breakfast at one o'clock watching the national news cycle marry gang wars and dead policewomen to Olympic rebids. The comments in Tokyo were of great shock and sympathy for the victims.

Officer Lopez's parents came in from Ohio; limp, washed out, holding on to each other and the cloudy, fuzzy hell-walk you see when somebody's child dies. And the cameras were right there. The Lopezes' parish priest was with them. Mayor McQuinn made a statement, called Sheila Lopez a hero in the war on drugs. The parish priest called Sheila a daughter, a casualty of this society losing its moral compass. The reporter said, "Back to you, Jim."

Twenty minutes till showtime.

I'm here at the L7 but my bandmates aren't. My cell vibrates. I put phone to ear, knees balancing my guitar.

Ruben says, "Lopez was a fed. Dead-bang." Pause. "But neither the ATF, FBI, or DEA had people at Area 4. No one on Hahn's hospital room, either. I've been seeing feds a long time, *esé*—and G is what these girls are—but this ain't how their organizations act."

"You're sure about Hahn?"

"They rolled in together, no?"

Exhale. My eyes squeeze shut. One hand presses my cell phone tighter, the other covers my ear to block out the party noise beyond the greenroom wall.

Ruben continues. "Homicide's investigating the Lopez murder—we got jurisdiction, but can't get the U.S. attorney to tell us what Lopez was working on. And I know Merica knows, which means it's all about CPD, maybe another Greylord . . ."

My back slumps into the stairway wall. Floor polish and mop disinfectant mix with Ruben's words.

"*Or* . . . we got us some kind of wild-card situation. Hahn give you any idea who she is? Who they work for?"

"Nope. Said her history was FBI, then DEA; got sworn here through Mayor McQuinn. We figured if they were feds, it had to be for Dupree."

"That don't wash. The mayor's not gonna help anyone with the Dupree lawsuit. And even if he wanted to give city money away, why would feds be undercover in your team for that? None of you was even on the job then. No, has to be the G's after someone in your team for something else." Pause. "And whoever that *vato* is got their girl killed."

My Stratocaster slides half off my lap but my elbow catches the neck. A cop killer in my gang team—my family; guys I bet my life on every day.

Ruben says, "Our lawyer wants a conversation tonight, eight at the Mambo; get you thinking right for IAD on Monday—"

"Damn, Ruben, I don't want—"

"*Carnal.* Trust me, this you have to do. Don't know how Barlow did it—probably Toddy Pete—but Barlow got a judge to sign an injunction against the *Herald.* No part three on Sunday. Barlow and them go to court Monday, we won't have to read about us again till Tuesday, maybe Wednesday at the earliest. Even if we lose, Barlow will have seen whatever Spanish news the *Herald* is selling; gives us a chance to buddy up with the *Tribune* or WGN with a rebuttal."

"The U.S. attorney asked me about you ninety-five times."

"I saw the transcript. Watch your ass. I'm your brother. I know you think I'm nine-foot armor-plated, but I can't keep a U.S. attorney off you."

"I didn't do so good in the interviews, huh?"

Pause. "People running for cover, *carnal,* they gonna run over whoever they have to. You hear *anything* about what Hahn's up to, let me know. See you at eight."

I flip the phone shut and reset my guitar. If you have to fight giants or bet it all, no one better to stand with than Ruben Vargas. The door to the stairwell opens. A svelte, curvy woman slips through with her back to me. She closes the door, leans into it, and exhales deep. Professional dancer; it's the posture and her jeans couldn't fit any better. She turns, shaking strawberry blond hair out of her face—

My heart literally stops.

The ghost at the door sees me and goes rigid, welding her back to the door to stay standing. Her eyes widen to their limits and so green they take your breath away—

Never ever forget those eyes, not as long as I live. Not in summertime across our alley, bold and timid sitting in her window, peeking up from her book after every page. Or a year later making a Neverland promise from three inches away, both my hands in hers. Not in the rose-red blush of a first kiss, and not in the harsh white of winter, pleading terror frozen in the prettiest eyes God ever made. Someone uses my voice to say: "But you're dead."

The ghost fumbles for her purse but is having trouble keeping her feet. "So are you."

My Stratocaster and I lean against the stairwell wall, hoping for stability. "No, really, you're dead."

The ghost doesn't move or agree. We're too close for me to be wrong . . . even after twenty-nine years. My first girlfriend, my first heart-to-heart partner in hopes and dreams, a girl I would've fought every Irish boy in the Four Corners just to walk home. Coleen Brennan is grown up, not dead, and standing five feet from me. And she's shaking.

I start to stand— Behind her jeans, Coleen's hands fumble fast for the doorknob.

"Wait." I sit back down. "Wait. It's okay."

Coleen's hand stays on the knob. She swallows or tries to, then lowers her chin. "Bobby?"

"Uh-huh. Twenty-nine years later, but it's me." I'm talking to a ghost, losing my mind from no sleep and tabloid fantasies.

"They said . . . I asked . . . they said you died in a car accident, in Milwaukee."

"Never been to Milwaukee." Blink. I've been confused before, but not like this. "You died in an alley. I . . . I saw your body . . . Your dad wouldn't let me come to your funeral. I stood outside at St. Dom's. It . . . was snowing."

Coleen stares, trying to decide if I'm real. She squints at my guitar, then back to me. "The flowers every February?"

I nod again. Flowers on her grave—me and Joe DiMaggio; bluebonnets and pixie dust and a promise I couldn't keep. *Her grave,* Bobby. As in dead person. Who they want to exhume. My hands are shaking, too.

Her mouth trembles into a smile that doesn't happen. She stammers "Tinker Bell," and waits, eyes on mine, her hand trying to turn the knob. The first book we traded was *Peter Pan,* a book that became her Bible. We promised each other we'd fly away from the Four Corners *together*; take her sister along, too. Flying away was so important to Coleen she said we had to hold hands every day we could, close our eyes, and promise that Neverland was only one tomorrow away. But the Four Corners killed her before we could make it happen.

Talking to apparitions leads to pilgrimages and straitjackets but I can't help myself. "But you're dead, Coleen."

She stares—the eyes so green, the soft freckles—and doesn't have to answer. It *is* her, impossible but true, not a no-sleep, tabloid fantasy, and I am, literally, without words or breath.

Coleen exhales, scared, confused. "It . . . wasn't you, the accident in Milwaukee?"

"No. But . . . you're a ghost, right?"

Headshake. Finally she says: "I'm Arleen."

"No, you're not. Your eyes, the freckles, the alley, our books. You're Coleen."

She shows me her hand without bringing it closer, the little warm, electric one that held mine, the long scar on the palm. "My da . . . we weren't allowed . . . Coleen was braver, wanted you and I to be together. She'd be me at school or after when I was with you . . . in case our da . . . we were kids, foolish, somehow we thought it would work . . . if—"

"*You* were my girlfriend?"

She nods. "And you were my boyfriend. Coleen and I would've told you before we all flew away."

Well, holy shit.

As I lean back, my shoulders land soft on the banister and it's the only reason the rest of me isn't on the floor. A really long time passes, or not. My heart keeps beating; my mouth says, "But after your sister died . . . Why didn't you tell me? We could've . . . Something."

Her hand regrips the knob behind her.

"Wait. Did, ah, you come here to see me?"

Arleen has trouble with that, too.

I point at the *Herald* in her hand. "Are you back in town for . . . because of the article?"

Her head shakes slow and only an inch. "Been back two years." She stares, forming words that tremble her lips. "Why are you here?"

I point at my guitar, then the wall separating us from the rugby party. "I'm in the band, weekends around town." Still nothing. "The L7 every six weeks or so—Julie's rugby parties?" I point at the wall again. " 'YMCA'? 'Margaritaville'? Once the girls get cranked up?" Still nothing; obviously not a regular or a rugby player.

"Julie and I usually meet downtown . . . not in this neighborhood so much."

My hands pat the electric air separating us. "Are you okay?"

Arleen licks her lips then bites the lower one between her teeth. "Surprised. It's just—I don't know, you're a shock after . . . twenty-nine years. Peter Pan returns from the grave and on a day I'm . . . trying to fly away. Wasn't ready."

She sounds like she means it. It hasn't fully hit me that she may be here on purpose and for bad reasons. She is, quite simply, happy ever after, strawberry blond hair, and freckles in blue jeans that fit really well. If my fingers worked I'd play her a song; self-protection has left the building. "So you live here, in Chicago?"

She nods. "West Side." A hint of little girl creeps into the posture that she quickly erases. "And you? Your, ah, family still around?"

"I live north. Up by Evanston. Ruben's downtown living large. You remember Ruben."

She hesitates at Ruben's name, or maybe it's "downtown," or maybe

I can't see through the fog in my head. Yesterday I shot a guy who had a machine gun and the U.S. attorney wants to put me in prison. Today I'm a thirteen-year-old playing with ghosts. "What do you do? Are you . . . with Julie?"

"Am I gay?"

"No. Yes, I mean, ah, I don't know what I mean."

A grin materializes. "Julie's my friend." Pause. "I'm an actress. And waitress at Hugo's."

"Really? An actress?" My hands need someplace to be. "I saw *Forrest Gump* ten, fifteen years ago at the Pickwick, and big as life, there you were, Jenny on that dirt road with Forrest. For real. Dropped my popcorn and the Pepsi; hit me all of a sudden that you might come back somehow, grown up, running across Grant Park instead of the Lincoln Memorial." My hands are flippers; I cannot believe I just told her that.

The green eyes soften but not all the way. "I auditioned for Jenny. They were casting right after the riots. I made the callback, thought I had a shot, almost."

"Bet you'd have been good."

"I knew her life, but I guess so did Robin Wright."

"That where you went when you left?"

Nod. "Golden California. Kinda rough at first."

"You were just gone—we were freshmen, first day at Benito Juarez—no one other than the kids at St. Dom's had really seen you since . . . Coleen. High school was starting. Nobody knew where you went. Your mom had just died; lots of rumors . . ."

Arleen shifts her purse. "She died on Saturday night. Sunday was bad. Monday morning I put on the school clothes I'd worked all summer to buy and snuck out of the apartment before my da and his friends came to." Her eyes cut away. "Anything was better than staying home. I walked toward B.J., had my enrollment money, all the worries any kid would have . . ." Arleen shifts her purse again. "Made it to the bus stop at Twenty-fifth Street and a carload of older black kids yelled at me. They knew who I was; Coleen was gone but the murder and rape trials were about to start again. Beat my ma down until all the racial stuff killed her, and Da was . . . what he was, a long way from being safe harbor." She exhales and pulls herself straighter. "Caught that bus and decided not to get off until no one knew me. Caught several others and stayed on them until one stopped in Venice Beach, California. Coleen and I talked the whole way. We agreed, she and I would be movie stars in the sunshine."

"You had family out there?"

Headshake.

"You were a *kid.* We were fourteen, fifteen—"

"Fourteen."

I search the green eyes for things I've seen in other kids' eyes, things cops know and see that changes them forever. Maybe she got lucky; it can happen—

The door bumps Arleen out of the way. She jerks backward, hands up like she's being attacked. Julie McCoy, proprietor, pops in with bar noise following her, yells "Blanche!" and bear hugs Arleen, then sees me, and grins. Then stops. "Damn—the crap in the *Herald*—are you two . . . okay?"

Arleen and I are deer in the headlights, anything but okay.

Julie unhugs Arleen and back-steps toward her door. "Should I—"

"No, we're fine." Arleen drops her hands. "Just catching up. Kind of a shock."

Julie says, "No kidding. I called you yesterday after one of the girls read me the *Herald*—meant to call you back, but got tied up with the crazies." Julie nods at the post-tournament party, then shakes her head. "Damn, Bobby. Tracy's good, but she's lost her mind on this one."

I fidget my guitar, no idea what to say.

Julie notices. "Bobby's nice, *especially* for a guitar player. Can sing the blues, too, if you don't listen too close." Julie hugs Arleen again. "Blanche can't sing, but *man* can she dance."

My eyes cut to her jeans before I can stop. "Blanche?"

"Ms. Movie Star didn't tell you? Tomorrow morning she's up for the lead in *A Streetcar Named Desire. The lead.*" Julie hugs Arleen again, this time with one arm. "Hard to be as famous as we're about to be. I'll be a size four, *bo*-dacious tatas, living that big blond Hollywood life."

Arleen's eyes roll. There's a distinct possibility that if I speak I will say something stupid, again. Arleen pushes Julie away. Julie frowns at her, then chins at me. "Ask for a man, I brought you a good one."

I blush and haven't done that in twenty years. Arleen just seems jumpy, edgy with me and not enough space. Or maybe all actresses are like that. Or maybe it's the obvious, the *Herald* in her hand.

Julie shows me her watch. "Your pal Rita isn't answering her phone. You're going on without them."

"No, thank you."

Frown. "Are we scared?"

"Yes."

"Without Rita to protect you, big bad Bobby Vargas is scared of a roomful of girls."

"Yes."

Arleen is not smiling as much as I'd hoped. Julie says, "I'll be back in fifteen minutes. No Steve and Rita, then you're on your own, but you're *on*."

I turn to Arleen. "How bad a singer are you?"

Arleen's watching me more than she's thinking about it. "How loud can you play?"

I grin, but hers is posed, more protection than playful, someone marking time until they can run, like a bank robber at the glass door . . . or a tough girl but with a very bad vibe on a very dark street. But she's forty-two years old, piña-coladas-under-the-palm-tree breathtaking no matter how you clock it.

My cell vibrates again. Jason Cowin's name on the screen.

"Make it fast, Jason, our set starts in a couple minutes."

"At the L7?"

"Yeah. What's up?"

"Just finished my OPS. Fuckin' commander acts like we staged a gunfight just to tank her shot at Olympic poetry judge."

"She'll get over it."

"I don't know. News Affairs is barely done making our statement for the reporters and somebody shoots Robbie Steffen and two Korean gangsters three blocks from the office."

"Dead?" I cringe *sorry* at Arleen and Julie.

"Koreans are. Robbie's in ICU at Mercy."

"1269 okay?"

"Everybody but you."

"What?"

"We gotta talk, man, and it ain't about Steffen or last night. Don't go onstage. I'll be there in thirty."

Steve and Rita choose that moment to barge through Julie's office. I climb two stairs to get out of the way, still talking to Jason. "What do you mean?" But Jason's already disconnected.

Julie says, "Rucks and kisses," and grabs Arleen to make room for Steve and Rita.

"Wait. Coleen, I mean *Arleen*—"

Julie hurries Arleen past Rita, who does not appear happy, and *happy* is Ms. Longhofer's trademark. At a svelte five foot five, Rita has that flower-child '60s vibe, so pure and joyful you think you're at Woodstock. But today she's wearing denim lederhosen over a T-shirt, sort of Debbie Harry does Dallas. Today there's something seriously wrong in Rita's land of sunshine.

Band meeting lasts three minutes, all business, no chance to say the love of my life just walked in and made me a teenager—and it's *show-time.*

SATURDAY, 6:30 PM

The L7 crowd is way past civilized behavior—the *new* Rita's fault—and has been since we took the stage. Rita can belt or ballad Bette Midler so pitch-perfect Barry Manilow couldn't tell the difference, but so far she won't sing any Divine Miss M songs. After way too many beaming requests and room keys, from way too many beer-and-sweat-drenched Bette Midler fans, one hundred rugby girls threaten to kill Rita. We do "Delta Dawn" three times.

Julie and Arleen are barricaded behind the far end of the bar. Every time I peek at Arleen I miss my strings with both hands. Man, is she something or not? A voice from the mosh screams, " 'Freebird'!"

We have one guitar, but need three.

" 'YMCA'!"

We *can* do the Village People. "YMCA" goes over dance-on-the-tables big. Steve goes topless behind his drum kit and twenty of the rugby girls match him. The stage shakes my feet sideways. A bruised and busty topless fan shimmies her shoulders and shoves a bottle of

Jack Daniel's at Rita, demanding: "Anastacia! Anastacia!" The Rita I know and love does fine with *other diva* requests. The *new* Rita growls and grabs the bottle, swigs more than I've seen her drink in an entire evening, then exits our set list for a trip to "Jumpin' Jack Flash."

The L7 levitates with my first seven notes. I check Arleen; she's still behind the bar, safe from the riot, but arguing with a flaming redhead—exposé writer, Tracy Moens.

We finish "Jumpin' Jack Flash." Rita steps in front of me, drops the Jack Daniel's on my foot to put my attention where it's supposed to be, then fires Steve the look no cornered animal wants to see. I refocus on the new Rita and whatever she wants. Rita pivots to face her audience who loves other girl singers better and yells, *"SO, YOU BITCHES WANNA PARTY?"*

All of the drunk, muddy, violent women in Chicago scream incomprehensible rock-concert affirmation. Over her shoulder at Steve and me, Rita yells, "Kenny Herbert, 'Mornin' Ain't Comin' '!"

Steve stares, mouth open, and doesn't move; he knows these jobs are hard to get. We're supposed to close with "Margaritaville," not start an indoor riot. I sneak a quick look at Julie McCoy. She doesn't know what's coming and would stop us if she did. Arleen and Tracy Moens are—

Rita spins, glaring at Steve through her bangs, "Count it out, Crossett, or leave," turns back to the audience and yells: *"ANY GIRLS GONNA GET LAID TONIGHT?"*

A hundred-plus rugby divas scream more incomprehensible rock-concert sex-for-money give-us-a-reason-to-riot, "Yeaaaaaahhhhhh!"

Steve "Sonny-boy" Crossett cocks his sticks overhead, tells the ceiling, "We're going to hell," and on *four* we light it up. Half the crowd recognizes Rab Howett's guitar line and their hands leap skyward throwing beer everywhere. Rita marches left pounding both feet into the stage, then right with one arm jammed at the ceiling. She hits the middle of the stage on cue, plants her feet get-some-of-this wide, and belts:

"YOU GIRLS GET READY,
FOR LOSIN' YOUR MIND,
MORNIN' AIN'T COMIN'
AT THE END OF THIS LINE—"

The L7 goes insane. Rita grabs both sides of her shirt to rip it open as if she's lost her mind, waits for Steve and me to catch up, strips the mic off the pole with both hands, and:

"ZIPPERS ARE DOWN
NO GETTIN' OUT SOON
HAVE TO BE NAKED
TO HOWL AT THE MOON"

A bar full of wild animals pound each other, yelling louder than my amp. Rita crushes the last verse, does the chorus twice promising to fuck every woman in the room, then spins and throws the mic at me and the floor like she hates us both. Stage left she jumps off into the crowd, elbows her way to the office door, and disappears.

Steve and I finish because we're afraid to stop. The girls scream for a Rita encore that won't happen and we run through brothel/locker-room steam for the door that swallowed Rita minutes ago. Steve slides through first, I glance for Arleen at the bar, don't see her, then slide through as well. The office wall saves us from a riot our employer didn't purchase. Rita has her back to me, packing her gear. I want to hug her but don't; gently I put my hand on her shoulder.

Rita turns fast and squares up. "We had lawyers and their investigators at the apartment this morning. They told me they could protect me from you and Ruben, but only if I cooperate."

"Protect you? From me?"

"Everyone close to you and Ruben is being investigated by the FBI, IRS—any police record anywhere." She looks at Steve, then back. "Bobby, I lied about the pot conviction back in college. I'll lose my job, so will Steve—"

"I'm not even *named* in the civil suit—"

"They said you would be. No more band, Bobby; no more drinking sangria on my living-room rug, no more *us* till this is all over. Write your songs at your own house." Rita tells Steve "Meet you at the car" and is gone to the fire-door alley exit.

Steve chugs half a beer, then sets it on the stair. "Sorry, man, she's scared; why we were late." Shrug. "Let us know what happens." He stands, pats my shoulder so lightly I can't feel it, says nothing else as he passes, and he's gone to the alley exit as well.

My guitar and I are alone in the stairwell with today's *Herald* that I haven't read and don't intend to. I contemplate the fire door, try to imagine "lawyers and their investigators" dead in the alley. My phone vibrates again, but weaker. I switch to the ringtone and answer. Over riot noise Jason Cowin says, "Where you at?"

"L7."

"No you're not. I'm at the bar. Fuckin' nuts in here."

"I'm in back. Be out in a sec—"

"No. Tracy Moens is out here bracing the owner and another chick—"

"Strawberry blond, five foot seven, jeans that won't quit?"

"That's her."

"Fuck it. I'm coming out."

"Don't. They call you about Little Paul yet?"

"Did who call me?"

"Child Services."

I slump into the wall . . . Danny Vacco killed him. A seven-year-old. "What happened?"

"Little Paul's down at Child Services saying you molested him in your old alley; did a dope search and fondled him up, then went to his house to get some more little-boy love or pay off his mom."

"*What?*"

"Child Services has witnesses, Bobby. La Raza debs, two of 'em who say they saw you go into the house, come out zipping your pants. They say Little Paul's been crying about you for months."

The *Herald* stares at me. "Where's his mom? She knows that's bullshit."

"Not around, and her being MIA don't smell good, either. Child Services and the *Herald* gonna make you Michael Jackson even if Dupree's lawyers don't."

My throat goes dry. I replay yesterday—Coleen's alley, Little Paul, the gang stop with Tania Hahn. "Danny Vacco's doing this, the street-king piece of shit. Had my chance to shoot that motherfucker ten years ago. Had him cold but I let Ruben stop me."

"Don't even think that now, man; not out loud. Way too many

wolves at your door already. Media's gonna say you got kids under the floor."

Street-king piece of shit. My hand pounds the wall. I see the entire frame come together around my portrait: Ruben and I start the day in a *Herald* exposé, then a four-dead shootout later that night—bingo, Danny Vacco smells opportunity like the street-fucking animal he is, and adds present-day child molester to my résumé. A *serial* molester, a cop monster in the shadows for twenty-nine years . . . the media will go nuts with that; won't have to prove anything for Bobby Vargas to be headlines, just "investigate" and print. The Duprees' lawyers will leak innuendo like they did to Steve and Rita. I'm guilty until proven innocent, and then probably never, no matter what the facts are.

"Tania Hahn was with me at Little Paul's house. She's out of the hospital—"

"That's true? You were at the *house*?"

"Yeah. And I did the dope stop, too. Little shit had fourteen rocks on him. Danny Vacco's rocks."

"Tell me you wrote it up. Took the rocks to property. Where the fuck was I?"

"No, I didn't write it up. If I do, the kid ends up in Child Services."

Bar-riot noise. "Where was I?"

"How do I know? It was fifteen minutes before we came to work in the yard at Laflin Maritime."

Bar-riot noise.

"Jason?"

"I'm here. Watching Tracy Moens figure out who I am." The riot noise begins to lessen. "Man, she's pretty in person. That whole Pink Panther/Brenda Starr thing isn't a lie."

"If you had children she'd eat them."

"I'll get her to leave with me, see if she does front-seat blow jobs. You slip out, then call me as soon as you're somewhere clean up the block. We'll figure how to play Danny Vacco."

Woman's voice, semi-Southern, and loud over the others. "Hi. Aren't you Jason Cowin? Bobby Vargas's partner?"

The phone goes dead. My hand wants to crush it; I dial Ruben instead. He answers, "*Carnal* . . . No good, *buey*."

"Danny fucking Vacco."

"*Sí, pocho.* And very strange. Danny V don't throw down with the brothers Vargas. Somebody big and bad pushing his buttons."

"He just did. Stars lined up and he took a shot."

"No, Danny V ain't that stupid. Could be the feds pushing him, maybe the U.S. attorney. For sure the *Herald* ain't enough. And Dupree's lawyers ain't, either."

"Heard Robbie Steffen's in ICU."

"Took two .45s in the vest, but he's alive, so far. Had two dead Koreans with him—mafia from Lawrence Avenue, badass hoodlums, those *vatos.* We have bullets from a third shooter who walked away."

"Jason told me. But no mafia guy's that crazy, shoot Toddy Pete's only son? Has to be a cracked-out banger. No way it's a mob guy, even Korean."

"Whatever Robbie's into will play itself out." Ruben's voice slides into older brother. "Don't you and any of your cowboys go by Danny Vacco, promise me."

"Sorry."

"Bobby, so you bust him up. How's that help?"

"Danny's 'witnesses' quit lying; his crew lets Little Paul's mom go; if I'm lucky, Danny gets shot in the head during the argument."

Silence. "Can't cover you for that." Ruben's tone drops. "Every step you take the wrong way makes whoever's behind Danny V stronger."

"Fuck 'em. I'm dragging that piece of shit out into the street for the cameras. Tonight's Danny's last night as street king of the Four Corners."

"No, *buey,* don't help the U.S. attorney put you and me in prison. Think about it—hell I'm your brother, *I know you,* but it adds up too good: Coleen Brennan twenty-nine years ago, then Little Paul. Throw in the fed Lopez last night—"

"All bullshit."

"Yeah, but what if other Little Pauls walk into Child Services, *vatos* grown now, like the archdioceses altar boys back in '06, *vatos* who say you molested them when they were *niños*?" Ruben's voice ramps. "Gives Officer Bobby Vargas *history.* 'Chicago cop as serial child molester'? Shit, *buey,* the department cuts you loose *instantáneo,* all your friends say bye, and the tabs make you Carlos Cruz."

Carlos Cruz was a child-molester cop in Mexico City; a street mob broke him out of jail and hung him from a bridge in Chapultepec Park. Cruz's name is a nasty reality check—Danny Vacco could go down the line in his crew, pick any five guys he wanted, and tell them to testify that they were my altar boys. The bangers would hate it, but they'd be on the stand the next day describing every unnatural act. My eyes squeeze shut—how the hell is this happening?

"Listen, *buey.* When you get the call from Child Services for Little Paul—and that's gonna be any minute now—don't go without Barlow or one of his people. Same for IAD; hundred percent they're adding Little Paul to your interrogations on Coleen Brennan and me."

I try to interrupt but Ruben stops me. "*Esé,* we can't afford bold. Lay low, let the lawyers talk for us. Being out front is asking for Stateville."

Arleen. Jesus, what will she think? Believe? Shit, at least wonder? "I just saw Coleen's sister, Arleen. Damn near had a heart attack."

Silence. Ruben says, "How she doing, the sister?"

"She's an actress, works at Hugo's. You'll never believe this, but she's who I traded the books with, not Coleen. She was my girl—"

"Yeah. I know her."

"You do? Didn't she ask about me?"

"Who?"

"Arleen. Somebody told her I was dead."

"Was me; eight or ten months ago at a party. But, shit, I was *joking,* meant the little *niño* you used to be was dead." Pause. "Where'd you see her?"

"Here. The L7. She's out front right now with Tracy Moens. I swear, Ruben, she was . . . looked like happy ever after in blue jeans."

"Little brother, wake up. Stay away from Arleen Brennan and Moens. And now that I think about it, your commander gave you days. Don't answer the call from Child Services, either. Let Barlow handle it."

"We're that sure about Barlow?"

"Even more now that T.P.'s son is down. And we all want to be on the right side of Toddy Pete Steffen when T.P. answers." Pause. "Can you fire-exit the L7 without being cornered by the Brennan sister or Moens?"

"Don't want to. Arleen's—"

"*Buey.* We got wild-card feds in your gang team, your childhood's in the *Herald,* Danny Vacco makes you Carlos Cruz for Child Services to crucify. Then, all of a sudden, Arleen Brennan and Moens are where you are?"

The cramped hallway shrinks, the way our world did the year the Four Corners came all the way apart—the deaf-and-dumb Mexican kid from my block, Anjel Pion, shot dead for who knows why; then Officer Terry Rourke and his daughter die in their front yard; then four Twenty-Trey Gangsters; then Coleen Brennan. Took less than two weeks.

Ruben says, "Get your ass uptown to the Mambo, little brother. No cowboys, no Danny Vacco, no Brennan or Moens. I'll call Barlow. We'll meet him early, as in *now.*"

I stare at the wall that separates me from Arleen. Barlow feels wrong, like a bad decision you'll want back but won't get back because you'll be in a corner, alone, with a train coming.

"*Pocho?*"

Twenty-nine years of dead or missing children in the Four Corners; Bobby Vargas as John Wayne Gacy; Bobby's basement full of their trophies. Even Steve and Rita see the possibilities.

"*Pocho,* you there? We seeing Barlow, right?"

Goose bumps, a bad, bad sign. "Okay."

8

ARLEEN BRENNAN

SATURDAY, 7:00 PM

"RITA! RITA!"

My hand steadies against the back bar and my Valium OD. If Bobby and his band don't do an encore these rugby girls may tear the L7 apart.

"RITA! RITA!"

Bobby Vargas—be still my beating heart—and just over there behind Julie's office door. Love it he didn't lose those kind, mischievous eyes or the crooked smile that stays there when he sings. The wide shoulders and tight jeans are new—

"RITA! RITA!"

We were all of nine when it started in earnest, but I'd already loved him since the first grade; I think all the girls did. Coleen, too. Bobby was gentle but sort of fearless; inquisitive, thoughtful. When we were eleven we'd plan sick days and stay home from school; Bobby and I would sit on the stoop. Mrs. Logan or Mrs. O'Hearn would walk by and growl, then threaten him with their sons and husbands, but Bobby wouldn't shoo; he'd be scared, but he'd stay. I liked that. On the stoop, Bobby taught me to draw using chalk and rocks—portraits, caricatures of our neighbors, but nice even when the neighbors weren't. I liked that, too. When the Irish boys skipped school, too, I made Bobby run; told him he couldn't cause me more trouble with my da, but Bobby would stay by me till the very last second.

How different would today be if I'd told Bobby that it was me who was his girlfriend . . . if I'd snuck back to the window after Coleen . . .

told him about my father, what I knew about the police and the troubles in the Four Corners. *Blink. Swallow.* Only wondered that a thousand times. But I didn't because my da and the Four Corners would've killed Bobby. Like it did Coleen.

My hands keep hold of the bar. The Valium OD makes it tough to focus.

Bobby Vargas . . . Not exactly the way I sketched him when I first arrived in sunny California, whenever I was hungry and scared—in the flesh he's less invincible but kind of better. And the hands . . . those were some hands, there, playing that red guitar, and for the first time in the longest time, a man's hands like that didn't put me off, actually wondered what they'd feel like . . . Bobby could play that guitar, couldn't he?

Julie's stereo booms on with "Margaritaville." Commotion at L7's front door. Men barge in, colliding with riot-tested rugby girls. I duck and the bartender on my left reaches to keep me upright. If the men are Koreans or cops I'm so dead—no, it's baseball fans. *Crash*—six stacked chairs clatter into the back wall of the L7. *Jesus Christ* rugby girls can party. Julie steps up and yells in my ear: "Naked chair bowling."

"What?"

"Make a lane. Stack six chairs, three on the bottom, then two, then one, then bowl."

A naked girl untangles from the chairs and stands into backslaps and beers. Thirty of the players have created a bowling lane on Julie's floor and sloshed the floor between them with beer. Julie yells in my ear, "Convince the rookies to get naked. One after another they bowl themselves down the lane into the chairs."

The chair bowling is a good diversion to no encore, but if Julie had a fire hose I'm sure she'd use it. The front bar is my protection; I'm safe behind it, wobbly, but safe; no telling where I stand in the rest of the world. Other than the Shubert Theater Company. In sixteen hours I'm their next Blanche DuBois. Blurry squint at the door, then the windows. Tighter grip on the bar. At least Tracy Moens is gone.

Chicago's star crime reporter said we have to talk, tried to tell me why she supports exhuming Coleen. I told Moens to crawl back under her rock. Almost mentioned Ruben, thinking I could somehow walk a tightrope between a scorched-earth reporter and a Homicide cop who already wants to kill me . . . testimony to what twenty milligrams and one whiskey can bridge. There has to be leverage in Tracy Moens somewhere, but I don't know how to use it.

My phone rings twice, but it's dead when I answer. The door to Julie's office opens; out pops Bobby Vargas with his guitar case. My phone rings again—my agent's ringtone—and I fumble it to my face. "Sarah! Is . . . everything okay?"

"Could you come by the theater? Informal, but it's important if you could. Now."

"Who? Why? Sure I'll be there."

"Two of the investors for *Streetcar.*"

Well, that's a first—*investors.* I spin to use Julie's back-bar mirror. "Sarah, I've been at the Cub game . . . take me a few minutes to fluff."

"No time. Don't worry, investors understand makeup and lights."

"They say they do, but—"

Tone drop. "Arleen—"

"On my way." I grab one of Julie's Cubs caps off the back bar. "Traffic won't be easy; I'm still at Wrigley."

"Fast as possible."

"Leaving now, but—" Sarah clicks off before I finish. Bobby and I lock eyes as he slices through the crowd toward the door. I step out from safety and fight through cheering, sweaty, half-naked bowlers toward the door. He gets there first. I yell "Bobby!" but he's out and I'm still stuck at the door. The "Kesey Does It" girl grabs me and yells something in my ear. I jerk loose and jump out onto the sidewalk crammed with Cub fans. "Bobby!"

He turns and three men stumble into him. Bobby goes down and they tumble him over his guitar case. One bitches, one apologizes, and they keep schooling south. Bobby stands, grabs his case and steps back to the wall. The case has a long scuff down the front.

He's smoothing at the scuff when I get there. "Sorry. My fault."

Bobby frowns, red-faced, holding back temper and embarrassment.

"Loved you and the big finish." I'm grinning like the teenagers we were, amazed that I can and can't help it. "Sorry." More grin. "And you fall like a stuntman."

Bobby exhales and loses the anger. "Only I would do that. With you watching."

"Should've said goodbye."

He stares, starts to say something, and I step in, kiss him lightly on his scarred cheek, and step back. He smells, I don't know, good.

"Wow, ah, thanks. Didn't know . . . you know . . . what you thought. The *Herald* and all."

"The *Herald*?"

"Me and Ruben, and you know, Coleen."

"You're mentioned with Ruben?" It feels filthy, awful just to think it.

"But I, we . . . didn't do that. We—"

"The *Herald*'s a bankrupt tabloid. You'd never hurt someone that way. I knew you, Bobby, heart to heart. Better than any boy I've known before or since."

He actually blushes. "It's . . . God, I don't know what to say . . . really great to see you." His hands fumble and he hugs his guitar case.

Cub fans pass, loud, raucous. Bobby and I stare across three feet and twenty-nine years; his brown eyes have the light; they have dark, too, but the hopeful little boy is still there. I want to touch his hands, his arms above the elbow, but don't. He smiles at me like he used to, twenty-nine years and I remember that smile, how weird is that? My boyfriend and I on a stoop, the world rushing past . . . Peter Pan's Neverland in our future, the whole world waiting to help us be happy.

"Arleen, I, ah, well, I don't know what to say. That simple."

I step in again and put my hands lightly on his. We're eighteen inches apart, eye to eye, only the guitar case between us. "Ask me out."

"You'll go?"

"If you ask."

He smiles, boy mushrooming into man, sort of. "That'd be . . . swell. I mean, great, good, I mean—" He laughs, adding composure. "We could get a drink, tonight?"

"Can't. I'm at the Shubert, leaving now, then—"

"We could eat lunch tomorrow."

"How about dinner? More drama at dinner. I audition for *Streetcar* at eleven." My hands make two sets of crossed fingers on top of his guitar case. "Should be a star by midafternoon; you could be my date to the party; we could stay out all night, midnight picnic at the lake. Tell each other twenty-nine years of . . . of whatever we want to tell."

Siren pop. Bobby and I jerk to the street. An unmarked Ford pulls to the curb. I have a murder weapon in my purse.

Bobby says, "I'm in. But can I call you?" He nods at the Ford. "I have to figure something out first."

I'm backing up to run from the police. His hand stops me, brushing my purse, his eyes confused at my movements. No one exits the car. I suck a breath I'd forgotten to take and tell Bobby my number. He punches it into his cell phone, breaking into a comfortable grin. "This is like the coolest day of my life. Never ever would've believed it really *would* feel like this."

He blushes at the admission. I blush back and half laugh. "You thought about me . . . all these years?"

Now he blushes solar. "I'll be the handsome prince calling you." Bobby slides the phone into his front pocket. "Bearing gifts and food and—"

Red hair and athletic shoulders slip in between us like a referee. Tracy Moens beams. "My goodness. The two of you know each other . . . in the *present*?"

Bobby steps back, something I'd bet Moens doesn't see a man do often. The siren pops behind us again. Moens smiles at Bobby, then me, trying to read my expression.

Bobby steps around Moens and touches my shoulder. "Call you tonight, okay?"

I nod, fast like the high-school girl I never was. Suddenly I'm buying a prom dress.

"Good luck at the Shubert. You'll get it." He taps his heart and grins. "I feel it; Peter Pan."

Moens moves to block his exit. "Officer Vargas—"

Bobby says, "Excuse me," loops us and streaming Cub fans to open the back door of the unmarked Ford. He carefully slides in his scuffed guitar case as a trapped Chevy behind the Ford lays on his horn. Bobby jumps in the Ford's front seat. The driver pops the siren of what has to be a plainclothes police car, veers into oncoming traffic, and drives off.

Tracy Moens shark-eyes me. "Care to explain?"

"*Officer* Vargas?"

"He's a gang-crimes cop in District 12—the Four Corners, Greektown. The driver's his partner, Jason Cowin. They were in a shootout that killed four people last night."

Bobby Vargas is a cop? Like his goddamn murderous brother? My heart ramps through Valium, prom night, and a murder weapon with my fingerprints. I stumble and Moens reaches for my shoulder like I might fall. Her hand is man-strong.

"Arleen?"

"I'm late." I shake off her hand and slide south into the crowd. Moens stays with me.

"I'll give you a ride. We can talk."

"No thanks."

Moens hangs at my shoulder but is sheared off by a large man. She jumps around him and back to me. "I can help."

"Help? Leave Coleen alone, that'll help."

"I know who killed her."

The crowd splits us again. Moens is pushed three-deep but fights her way back to my shoulder.

"Don't you want to know who murdered your sister?"

"Already know"—glare, shoulder bump—"and so do you."

"No, you don't. Trust me, you don't know." She steps a half step ahead to stare at my reaction. "Or if you do—"

No cabs, tons of traffic; I'll never get to the Shubert. I jump into the street and start running. My purse bangs my hip. Gun. I still have the gun, a murder weapon. Moens jogs next to me like she runs crowded sidewalks every day.

"My car's right here." She grabs me off stride and pulls us to a stop. A uniform cop smiles from near a red Jaguar's fender. She hair-flips him. "Thanks, Tommy."

The cop leers politely and says, "My pleasure, Ms. Moens," and moves on.

"Hop in. No questions, just a ride. If I'm lying, get out."

SATURDAY, 7:30 PM

The Jaguar smells like money and power. For the last nine blocks Tracy Moens has placed a red/blue flashing light on the dash that complements the siren she blares when looping into oncoming traffic. "What time at the Shubert?"

"Now." I make a ponytail and slip it through the Cubs cap.

"Business or pleasure?"

I glance at her question.

" 'No questions' doesn't mean we can't talk about anything." Moens smiles at the windshield. "C'mon, I got a $500 ticket for this last month and I was looking *good* that day."

Exhale. "I'm up for the lead in *Streetcar.* The investors want to meet me."

Moens eyes my jeans, shirt, hair. "Don't take this wrong—you look good, you do—but we could stop; you could primp a little? I can—"

"—drive the car? That'd be great. I'll worry about my career."

Moens overtakes a bus, brakes hard, weaves through three cars, and runs the last of a yellow light. "I know your director, Anne Johns."

"Congratulations."

"Anne's a good friend. We go way back, still share a trainer when I'm in Santa Fe."

"And you'll help me any way you can, right?"

"Don't know about that, but . . ."

"Stay out of my life. Stay out of my sister's life, what little the Four Corners let her have."

Moens drives us another five blocks of serpentine roller coaster. "I'm sorry about Coleen. She's why I became interested in the story. That's all."

My eyes roll at the passenger window.

"Then the other evidence surfaced—the Twenty-Treys, the Vargas brothers—and in good conscience I couldn't leave it alone."

"Pull over."

"We're almost there."

"Shut up or pull over, one or the other."

Left turn onto Monroe. She drives the block and slows approaching the Shubert marquee. "Arleen, I can be the confidant you and Coleen never had . . . I know the truth about what happened, We can talk about it."

I jump out, skirt behind the trunk, and run across traffic toward the Shubert's front doors. Wish I looked presentable, smelled better. My purse bangs against my hip. Wish I hadn't shot anyone, either. Sarah's outside with two women, neither of whom I recognize. Sarah smiles, glances past me to the red Jaguar, and asks, "Is that Tracy Moens?"

"Yeah." I beam at the two women, me, the full actress-in-waiting loaded on Valium and gunfire. "Hi, I'm Arleen Brennan."

They introduce themselves, say Sarah was just telling them about me. One offers good luck; they excuse themselves and Sarah does an air kiss with both. Sarah watches them walk toward Tracy Moens, phone to her ear in her shiny red Jaguar. Sarah blinks, recalling what she knows about me, where I'm from in the city, and what she's read in the *Herald*. "Coleen Brennan was *your* twin sister?"

"Yes, she was."

"I'm so sorry." Sarah hugs me. "I didn't know."

"Not many do. But that's about to change."

Sarah glances at Moens again. "The *Herald*'s exposé, while painful . . . could be a help. One never knows, and investors want publicity if it's positive."

Frown. Now I'm thankful for the Valium. "Sarah, I want to be Blanche DuBois with my whole heart and soul. Would die for my chance. But Coleen being murdered is not part—not now, not ever."

Sarah hesitates again. "I understand completely, I do. But this tragedy will be revisited in the *Herald* no matter what we want. And likely on every channel if there's actually a new story there."

A Ford Crown Victoria turns onto Monroe.

My eyes lock on the windshield. No, *please*. Fight-or-flee ramps up my back. I force myself still. Doesn't have to be Ruben Vargas; Ford made millions of— Threat radiates off the car. I step back, flex to run— Ruben eyes me over his sunglasses, slows, then notices Tracy Moens and accelerates. Sarah feels the adrenaline in my posture, thinks it's stage fright, and turns us to the Shubert's doors. "Not lions, *investors*. Let's show them their next franchise."

Ruben passes between Moens and me. Poise. Be the lead, not the victim. I take three steps away from murder world—*bury it; be Blanche. Be Blanche*—and into the Shubert. My eyes acclimate, framing . . . Renée Zellweger? She's at the lobby bar chatting with a ring of admirers. If they can afford Renée Zellweger as Blanche DuBois, why am I or anyone else here?

Sarah guesses and presses her hand into my back. "Not Renée. She flew in for tomorrow's Olympic benefit."

I feel Ruben in the shadows, somehow, and turn to look. "Who, then?"

"Right after we meet the investors." Sarah turns me back, focusing our attention forward. "Ladies of the South don't worry, or perspire."

Two men disconnect from the bar group and walk toward us, one late forties, the other early sixties, urbane summer suits, one with tie, one without, both with 2016 Olympics pins. The one without the tie used to be the theater critic for the *Sun-Times*. He eyes my Cubs hat and extends his hand. "Ah, a Cub fan; you know betrayal."

I megawatt smile and shake his hand. "Arleen Brennan."

"Kevin Nance, we've met before." He points. "This is Peter Steffen."

In person Toddy Pete Steffen is a shock. He could be Robbie, if Robbie had class and education. Six foot two, sturdy shoulders, lean hips, kind eyes, perfect haircut in white. "*The* Peter Steffen?"

Mr. Steffen smiles and offers his hand. "Let's hope you mean that in a good way. You're Ms. Brennan, Arleen, as I remember?"

"Yes." I take his hand. "Sorry. Yes, in the best way. For . . . thanks for supporting *Streetcar* and all the other productions." He hasn't let go of my hand. "Without you and Mr. Nance we wouldn't have theater companies in Chicago."

Toddy Pete Steffen, father of a son I left bleeding in an alley six hours ago with two dead Koreans, extends his arm lightly around my shoulder and says to the others, "I saw Arleen in *Jersey Boys* and *Chorus Line* but didn't know you'd cast . . . were considering her for Blanche." He hugs my shoulder. "Wonderful in both. Absolutely magnetic for such tiny roles."

His arm feels fatherly. I smile past him toward Anne Johns. "Please tell your director." His son has to be alive or Mr. Steffen wouldn't be here, smiling. I want to glance for Ruben but don't.

Kevin Nance says, "Sarah tells me you're up for *Chicago* and *Toyland*."

First I've heard—and highly unlikely. Big grin, fingers crossed, like the possibility isn't complete agent-sales-job fantasy. "We're hoping this is my year."

"Would you prefer *Toyland* over *Streetcar*?"

My shoulders and ponytail ease into Blanche DuBois. I wilt her accent, a Southern patrician on a hot day. "I know Blanche, Mr. Nance, in the way I know my mirra' on a woman's sad day. And would be pleased, proud to portray her for this comp'ny more than anything on God's earth."

Mr. Nance grins as his eyes widen. "I always felt you were quite good."

I half curtsey in my Cubs cap and ponytail.

Mr. Steffen's arm stays around my shoulder. He says, "Let's all go to N'awlins, gumbo and sherry at the Napoleon House."

Sarah brightens. "I'm free."

Mr. Steffen says, "Wish that I could, but I'm due back at the hospital." He grimaces, explaining to me, "My son was shot—he's a policeman."

I don't have to make my eyes go wide. *Poise, Arleen, own the ground.*

"He'll survive, thank God, but it will be touch and go for a while. I did want to meet you, though. This production of *Streetcar* is crucial to the Shubert Theater Company and our plans for its future, the entire theater district for that matter." He touches his Olympics pin. "A great asset we have that Tokyo doesn't."

"I'm *so* sorry about your son."

His arm tightens slightly and lets go before my trembling is obvious. "Thank you, and thank you for coming by."

Kevin Nance adds, "It was a pleasure, Arleen. Go Cubs," and shakes my hand. "Let's hope it's their year, too." He and Mr. Steffen return to the alcove bar and Renée Zellweger. She beams a stunning movie-star smile. Sarah pats my shoulder. "That's us one day very soon."

"I'm 'thirty-nine'—better be *Sun*-day."

Sarah turns us away and toward the front doors. "Glenn Close couldn't have played those five minutes any better." Sarah doesn't mention how unfortunate it was that a megawatt movie star dressed for the evening was here, too, not the comparison any girl would want—taffeta prom queen versus sandlot baseball fan.

"Who's the other actress? She here yet?"

Sarah stops us at the front doors, puts both hands on my shoulders, and stares. "She doesn't matter. You matter. All your energy—fear, hope, love, anger, death, life—all of it goes into Blanche tomorrow morning. You will win this role if you do that. I feel it here." One hand pats between her breasts. "Arleen Brennan will go on to Broadway and then . . . anywhere she wants."

I glance through the doors for Ruben Vargas and complications Sarah couldn't quite fathom.

Sarah kisses my cheek. "I'll step back to the bar to chat, keep us on everyone's mind." She winks. "Go on home, chil', and think those New Orleans thoughts."

I smile, turn and wave to Mr. Nance waving from the bar group, then use both hands to push open the doors. The marquee lights are on and illuminate the sidewalk. I stand underneath, bathed in the fire and let it incinerate Ruben's horror world. One actress to beat and, *finally*, this fire will be mine. I'll walk out here after a show—maybe opening night—into a crowd, and cameras, and flashbulbs like the '50s . . . and people love me, love my work. And inside I have a family that bet their present on me and won. Me.

My phone rings. Bobby Vargas says, "Been thirty minutes, just wanted to say hi."

I pirouette into my answer, the glorious future that— Ruben Vargas, ten feet away, staring at me. Shit! No, chill, he can't, won't shoot me out here under the lights. If I don't get in his car he can't try to kill me again. I tell my phone, "Can't talk."

Bobby's voice goes to static and the call drops.

Ruben scans my face, posture. I don't show him fear or rage, nothing but control. Two brown fingers remove his toothpick. "How'd our meeting go?"

"Couldn't get within a block because every squad car and news van in Chicago was there."

"You weren't there?" Ruben eyes my purse and his gun in it.

"I just said I wasn't. That means I. Wasn't. There."

"First good news I've had today. Our Korean friends are smokin' opium." Ruben Vargas, Homicide cop, homicidal criminal grins his pimp smile. "But I think I can put a lid on 'em. Let's go somewhere and I'll explain—"

I jump at him, halfway across the wide sidewalk. "I talked to Tracy Moens, she already *explained.* I didn't tell her about your little party, but I could've. So, yeah, you *explain* how that alley's full of dead people and why I wouldn't have been one of them."

"You think I—" Ruben shakes his head. "No, no, that's crazy talk, *niña.* We're in this together." He gestures toward his passenger door. "Hop in."

"Can't. Toddy Pete Steffen's inside, one of the show's investors, don'cha know. He wants to talk to me. *Again.*" I want to spit "Furukawa" at Ruben—Toddy Pete's gigantic sponsorship victory that Ruben and Robbie are willing to risk destroying—but don't because I wasn't in the alley, so Robbie couldn't have screamed "Furukawa" at me; that "the Jap motherfuckers would eat us alive" if Ruben and his Vietcong partner cut Robbie out.

Ruben stops smiling and replaces the toothpick. "Careful, Arleen. Careful with my little brother, too. Bobby's in a fair amount of trouble. Don't get him thinkin' you two got some kinda reunion comin'."

"Your brother's a cop. He can probably take care of himself."

"Read tomorrow's paper. It won't be about Coleen"—Ruben shakes his head—"it'll be about Bobby and another kid from the Four Corners, Paulito Cedeneo."

I don't know what that means, want to ask, want to know how Ruben knows I talked to Bobby, but don't want Toddy Pete Steffen or anyone else to see me here with Ruben. And I don't want Ruben Vargas to corner me anywhere and "explain" the alley or his blank papers in the envelope. And I don't want him to grab my purse—find a gun with my fingerprints that killed a man five hours ago. If I hail a cab he can stop it wherever he wants. "Okay, meet me at Hugo's in thirty minutes."

Cop fish-eye. "Gonna be there?"

"As soon as *Mr. Steffen* and I are done."

"Better you get in the car, give me back the envelope and that protection I lent you. We talk, I bring you right back."

"Sorry." I step back. "Mr. Steffen's waiting."

Ruben stares, not believing, then points one finger at the marquee above me. "Looks like you might belong here, shame to blow it now. Age 'thirty-nine,' doors startin' to close . . ."

"Keep that in mind, asshole, next time you hire an errand boy to front your lies. If I'm lucky enough to have something to lose, you and your partner have nothing to worry about."

He accepts the threat like he didn't hear it. "Always good not to worry." Both Ruben's hands push him off his car.

I jump back, showing fear I wish I hadn't.

"Girl, we can work things out, but what we *can't* do is walk away, just pretend we ain't where we are. Choa—and others—ain't having that. And we got business to do."

"Not *we*, Ruben. I already covered that with you."

"Saying it don't make it true." Movement at the corner. Ruben's hand slides fast to his gun. He hard-eyes three Asian men a hundred feet away; crouches like he might draw but doesn't. Still fixed on them, Ruben says, "We get the business done, this thing cleans itself up," then nods at the marquee. "Bright lights, kid. Your turn maybe. Hope so, but the wrong people can see these lights, too, know right where you are."

"You heard me, right? Who's inside this theater? Who has money in this show? That was his *son* in the alley. And it's *your* fault."

Horn. A red Jaguar turns the corner at Dearborn. We both guess who it is. Ruben taps his watch, angry, off-balance. "I'm trying to help you not be stupid. Thirty minutes. Tell your good friend Toddy Pete I said, '*Qué onda, vato?*' " The Jaguar tries to change lanes but can't. Ruben's tone drops to ice as he turns to open his door. "*Be there,* Arleen. We get our business done, now, or it swallows you."

I focus on the Jaguar, then the three Asian men on the sidewalk . . . Ruben lunges and rips my purse off my arm. I scramble for it with both hands, miss, and he throws it through the driver's window into his car. We're three feet apart, close enough he could grab me or me him. He can't have the purse; I swing; he ducks, pivots, but doesn't grab me.

Horn. Horn.

Ruben doesn't look. "Be at Hugo's." He jumps in his car and accelerates east before Tracy Moens can cut through the traffic.

I watch his taillights. A Homicide cop has a murder weapon with my prints. But I wiped the gun, didn't I? When I was behind the bar at the L7. Used a bar towel stuffed down in my purse. How much wipe is enough? I wanted to dump the gun in the trash but the bins were overflowing with cans and bottles.

Ruben turns at State Street. Meet him in thirty minutes means I have thirty-five to disappear and not die. But Ruben Vargas has the gun, and he's a Homicide detective. He can get the real ballistic evidence and manufacture more, make up whatever matching story he wants. I check the sidewalk; the three men weren't Koreans. The Jaguar pulls to the curb; not Tracy Moens. Voices gush behind me; I spin and five strangers exit the Shubert. Don't stand here. Do something.

I fast-walk east toward State Street, want to run, want to cry— *Cry?* My feet stop and I look east into the coming night, see all the way to Venice Beach, to the Four Corners, to my sister's alley in Greektown. *Cry?* I turn back to the Shubert's brilliant marquee. The thirty-foot illuminated wedge reaches to the street. On opening night it will cover patrons in suits and gowns, alive with laughter and anticipation. Photographers will pop and celebrities will arrive in shiny black cars. Backstage, the crew and my fellow actors will hold hands in a big ring. I know exactly how it will be; I've seen it almost every night since Coleen and I were kids.

And this time, the dream is not a five hundred to one cattle call or a Palm Springs promise or a cocaine dream. I'm one director's decision, one unnamed actress away from winning a *starring* role, a chance, a *career,* family forever. I can make all that happen. All I have to do is win. Stay alive, play my one chance to the walls, and win.

Siren. A squad car wails east.

And don't be Coleen.

We were so sure we would be famous, then Anton Dupree dragged you into his car. Do you see where I'm standing, *Éire Aingeal*?

My feet plant the Shubert's sidewalk like it's mine.

I'll dedicate *Streetcar* to you from stage center every night. Chicago will know Coleen Brennan like they should have, the joyful, brilliant Irish girl from the Four Corners. I'll get this part; you'll live again, as a *Brennan.* Not a *Dupree* victim. I promise. My eyes cut to another siren; an unmarked car like Ruben's racing toward criminals and their crimes. Both hands ball to fists; tears run down my cheeks. *I fucking promise.*

9

OFFICER BOBBY VARGAS

SATURDAY, 7:30 PM

Wrigley Field gushes fans into a traffic jam/street party that will last another hour before it gets sloppy and people get arrested. Jason and I are in his Crown Vic, trapped front and back.

Coleen Brennan! I mean, Arleen Brennan. Oh my God. On the sidewalk grinning at me and our *future.* I may be too dizzy to ride in a car. From the sidewalk, Tracy Moens yells for me to wait, to talk to her *now.* Jason pops the siren twice, jerks the wheel, and jumps us into oncoming. My guitar bangs to the floor in the backseat. I stare through the back window and say, "Easy, that's my future," meaning my guitar and the prettiest green-eyed, swimsuit-issue, strawberry blond ever to breathe.

Jason stays on the siren, creating a middle lane. "Man, Moens wants you all the way."

Moens has Arleen cornered. They're not together like Ruben said. Arleen's eyes were so green I would've stood there all day, awestruck as my man Forrest Gump. Jason slams the gas. Cars and Cub fans blot Arleen out.

She's really back! Different name, which is weird, but she's here. I twist back in the seat, grin like a schoolboy, and exhale deep.

Jason waves "Thanks" at an oncoming car granting us room. "Moens honestly believes you did Coleen Brennan; that you and Ruben are the *monster* she's gonna expose. And if Little Paul checks out she intends to—"

"I was *thirteen.* How do you *motherfuckers* keep missing that?" Paradise to hell in two seconds. “Sorry.” I rub my face with both hands. Arleen can’t believe it, I won’t let her.

“You’re definitely popular.” Horns. Bumpers. Siren. “Buff and I and Jewboy went by to see Sheila Lopez’s parents.” Jason shakes his head once. “Only daughter. Jo Ann Merica was there . . . bunch of other suits.” Jason floats one eyebrow at me. “But no Chicago FBI or DEA.”

“None?”

Jason makes a zero with his thumb and index finger.

“Lopez and Hahn are feds, Ruben’s positive, but can’t figure what branch, and Merica won’t say.”

“That ain’t kosher, Bobby, even for the G.” Jason brakes and pops the siren. “Now you got Little Paul—”

“No way Little Paul checks out, not if Merica or Moens are interested in the facts.”

“That’ll be brand new.”

I think about dead cops and girls of your dreams coming back to life while Jason center-lines us through cars and buses, and . . . accusations that I molest and murder children. *Me,* focus on me ’cause there aren’t any real assholes out here; I don’t see those motherfuckers every single fucking day feeding on the weak.

“Take me to my car.” My car’s five blocks the other way buried in Cubs-victory traffic and will be for another hour. I pull the Airweight I carry off duty, check the cylinder full, then slide it back clipped to my jeans. “Danny Vacco will back all this down or he’s dead defending it.”

Jason nods. “No problem. Who’d suspect Bobby Vargas?”

“I’m not gonna be guilty of being a child molester.”

“Ease up, Bobby.” Jason backhands my shoulder. “We’ll get a beer, figure it out. The boys want to talk.”

“The boys” is our gang team. “We can talk. *After* I find Danny Vacco. Drag that motherfucker to 12 where he can admit what he’s doing or die in our lockup.”

“Let’s do the boys first; go by Jewboy’s basement, everybody’s there. Maybe they can slow you down, keep you out of Stateville.”

Blink. “Everybody’s there? We figured the red Toyota? Who?”

Jason shakes his head. “Buff said we ain’t spending another day wondering.”

The headache that’s been chasing me since last night begins to pound. "Ruben thinks Lopez and Hahn were put in 1269 to hunt one of us, but not for the Duprees' lawsuit—we weren't on the job then." I stare at Jason until he glances me. "Ruben can't figure what Hahn and Lopez are after, but he thinks one of us gave up the Toyota to stop 'em."

Jason turns right, eyes three shapes peeing in the shadows. "Could've been the commander said something; she's got the street sense of a watermelon. Could've been Hahn. They knew everything we knew. Hell, Lopez could've told someone. That adds everyone in the federal government."

"So, what, we'll all take polygraphs?"

Jason pulls us up in front of Jewboy's bungalow on the far West Side, throws the car in park, and says, "Yup." He exits the car and rounds the fender.

I show him my phone through the windshield, then dial Arleen. Her voice makes me a schoolboy instead of cop in a sea of shit. I say, "Been thirty minutes; just wanted to say hi."

Silence, then a frigid "Can't talk" and she clicks off.

I blink at my phone. Thirty minutes ago we were going on a midnight picnic, gonna talk all night, probably hold hands. I'd get to kiss her again. I fold my phone. But not anymore. My stomach knots. Had to be Moens. Moens must've fed Arleen the exposé back at the L7. Bobby the monster.

SATURDAY, 8:00 PM

Jewboy has named his basement Walter's Love Hotel, but as far as I know, no girl's ever been here who wasn't with Jason or me. The Love Hotel is state-of-the-art, unmarried-cop, wood-paneled hip—pretty much a copy of the old *Saturday Night Live* skit with the Czech brothers. Orange-felt Brunswick pool table, slot machine, Hamm's OTB beer sign, beer-tap refrigerator Candy Cook painted as the paddock at Arlington Park, autographed life-size Girls Next Door poster he stood in line all day to get, bobbleheads of Earlie Fires, Mike Ditka, Ernie Banks, and Walter Payton; gun-range trophies because Walter Jewboy Mesrow may be more mascot than cop, but he *can* shoot; flat-screen TV and three outdoor, triple-strength chaise longues. My spare amp lives in the corner for our weekly repeat of the same three-chord lesson. I've never been down here when I wasn't laughing. Till today.

The polygraph guy is set up with a laptop and printer on the pool table. Jewboy's three vinyl kitchen chairs crowd the five-foot bar. I'm on a stool next to Buff, having just told my cell phone and Ruben I'll be an hour late for the Mambo.

"*Buey,* Barlow ain't a lightweight. Not the kind of man the brothers Vargas keep waiting."

"So buy him a drink. I'll be there."

Harder tone. "Stateville's a cold lifetime, *esé.* I want us to stay out."

"*I said I'm coming.* Barlow waits or he doesn't."

Silence. Ruben lightens his tone. "Be cool, little brother. Don't be getting all Mexican, not now. We got—"

"Have two stops to make. After I've made them, I'll be there. Bye." I fold the phone and it snaps like teeth. Buff stares, his hand wrapped around a rolled-up *Herald.* The basement is tense with eight guys, each of us wondering who gave up the Toyota. Nobody asks about Little Paul. It's an odd tension, a basement room filled with personalities, guys you thought you knew so well you could *be* them. All of us are armed.

Buff says, "Give me your weapons. Everybody."

We stare.

"On the bar. Those of you with two, put 'em all up here."

We do; ten weapons total. Buff puts them in a box, then strips his nickel-plated pimp rig and drops it in the box. The box goes on the floor between his barstool and the wall. He nods at the polygraph and says, "Alphabetical. Three baseline-control questions about nothing, then the Toyota. Nothing else."

No cop likes polygraphs; our eyes bounce from face to face. Before yesterday I knew everything there was to know about these guys. Buff taps the rolled-up *Herald* against his jeans. They may or may not have thought the same about me.

Alphabetically, Buff goes first (Anderson). He sits the chair and straps himself into the clips and pads. The operator asks him if he's ready.

"Yeah, c'mon."

"State your name."

"Bob Anderson."

Seven sets of cop eyes watch our sergeant. We can't read the screen that shows his reactions, the infinitesimal changes in pulse, respiration, and skin conductivity that some say are bullshit anyway.

When Buff finishes, Humberto Candelario goes next—Candy's got private-security jobs all over, for all kinds of weird people, worked dope for the DEA. Jason is strapped in next—he drives a new car, rides a $15,000 Harley, buys $80 Cubs tickets like he has a trust fund.

Then Rick Gonzalez—Pretty Ricky buys borderline-ghetto three-flats and rehabs them to sell as yuppie condos when the yuppies are ready to take another block. Ricky's money is always working right up against the gangsters, one midnight fire away from losing it all.

John "Fez" Kelyana is next. Fez is from Syria and has family desperate to get out of harm's way. What isn't spent on food and rent, Fez spends on immigration lawyers. One by one we take the chair. The basement becomes a bullpen, not enough room for our shoulders and nervous feet. No one is told if they pass or fail. The air worsens as each cop is put on trial, all of us wondering who sold us out to die.

I'm last to be strapped in. Other than Buff, my team has backed away, flexing their hands, their necks, working the tension out, wondering.

"State your name."

"Bobby Vargas."

"What is your legal name?"

"Roberto Vargas Ruiz."

"Are you a woman?"

"No."

"Are you a member of the Chicago Police Department."

"Yes."

"Last night Officer Sheila Lopez was shot to death in a red Toyota on the corner of Ashland Avenue and Twenty-first Street. Were you present?"

"Yes."

"Prior to the murder of Officer Lopez, whom did you tell about the red Toyota?"

"No one."

The polygraph operator looks up. "Did you discuss the red Toyota with members of your team?"

The headache kicks in. "Well, yeah. Yes." Behind the operator and Buff, all seven are looking at me.

"Did you discuss the red Toyota with anyone else?"

"No."

I am not asked about Coleen Brennan. Or Little Paul. The polygraph operator nods at his machine, then me, and says, "Done."

I unclip and remove the waist strap. The polygraph operator gathers papers from his printer, then begins to pack his equipment.

Buff says, "Well?"

"Oh, sorry." The operator hands Buff the results. "Everybody passed."

"BOOYAH!" Big grins, backslaps. Gang Team 1269 just won the World Series. Half are on duty but all grab beers with both hands. Somebody fucked us—the commander, the feds—but it wasn't us, and for the next twenty-four ounces that's what matters.

Buff rolls up the polygraph results, backs me away from the others, loses his grin, and says, "Leave Danny Vacco alone."

I toast with beer. "Can't."

"Listen, shithead, I'm telling you to leave Vacco alone, not that he's being *left* alone, it's just not you who's doing anything . . . if something were to happen."

"Thanks, but Vacco's not your fight."

"He's not? I don't work the Four Corners? Some day Danny Vacco don't pull Little Paul on me when I'm in the box?"

"You're retiring next year. And you're smarter than that."

"I'm smarter than *you,* that's for fucking sure." Buff fixes me with his steel-blue stare. "Somebody close gave up that Toyota."

I toast again. "Wasn't us."

Buff bangs his beer against the Hamm's I'm holding, eyes staying on mine an extra second too long, then pulls out the box with all our weapons. "Wasn't us, but it's somebody who knows us."

I grab my Airweight. Buff grabs his pimp rig.

"Something's out there." Buff chins at the wall as he slides his pistol and holster into his belt. "A wild card, and it ain't working well for those involved. How do I know this? We have a dead undercover fed in our team that no federal agency wants to claim. Our commander isn't talking to me, and my one friend in OPS—the investigator who took your statement at the scene—poor guy's married to my cousin, the loud one who likes to eat. My friend in OPS and I go way back, knew him in 'Nam, and last night all he says to me is 'Shadowland' and walks away."

"Shadowland?"

"A box-canyon plateau up above the A Shau Valley, between Hue and Khe Sanh. For the whole of the war—ours, and the French before us—neither side could hold it more than a year. The CIA/SOG guys operated in there with the LRRPs." Buff's fingers snake-paint his face. "The long-range recon, special operations people."

I don't speak Sergeant, Chicago OPS, or Vietnam, and ask Buff to explain.

"My friend's telling me to stop being stupid. Hahn and Lopez aren't who or what they say; their mission *and ours* isn't what we think it is; and we better figure Shadowland before we take another half step into the jungle."

"Kinda what Ruben said. The feds have to be after us for something else, 'cause when Coleen was killed none of us were on the job."

"I was." Buff sips the beer. "And two hours ago Dupree's lawyers noticed me for Monday's depositions."

"You? Why?"

"Back in the day I worked with Ruben and the other three coppers who put Dupree in the gas chamber. Lawyers must think I can tell 'em something. Your brother say anything else?"

"Nah. Ruben's focused on the depositions and the *Herald*. He's hooking me up with a downtown lawyer, big hitter, who I guess already got an injunction against the *Herald*. They go to court Monday when I'm at IAD and you guys are being deposed."

"This guy your lawyer or Ruben's lawyer?"

"What's the difference?"

"You know the fucking difference."

I lean back. "He's my brother, Buff."

"Yeah, I know. Answer the question."

Heat rises on my neck. Deep breath. I am real tired of being prodded, questioned, doubted, threatened, and pushed around, friend or foe. Tired enough that I— Deep breath . . . another. Buff's my friend, I know that, and my boss. "Why"—I swallow beer—"do you think I need a different lawyer than my brother?"

Buff says, "Why aren't you looking at me?"

My eyes cut to his. I want to leave.

Buff says, "That's why you need a different lawyer."

I stand; so does Buff. From behind, Jason throws his arm around me. Buff tells him to give us a minute. Jason slaps my back, grabs his gun and yells, "Pole party at Jewboy's. Then we find the rat who fucked us."

Buff waits for Jason to turn, then says, "Ruben's a legend, but he's a player. Doesn't make him guilty of shit, but it for sure doesn't make him innocent, either. He has history, your brother. People talk about him—who he knows, how he operates. I'm a blue-collar guy; people say shit about me, too, but it's different. And you know it's different."

We stare at the polygraph results Buff holds between us. Buff's telling me something he won't say.

"Everybody passed, right? That's what the guy said."

Buff nods, but his eyes don't. "Your brother *could* be a federal target for something other than Coleen Brennan. I underline 'could,' Bobby. I'm not saying he is. I'm saying *maybe* he is."

Target doesn't mean *guilty.*

"He's my brother, Buff, my only brother."

Buff starts to say something but stops, then: "Robbie Steffen and your brother are friends. Ruben was in his wedding. The dead gangsters in our alley *with Robbie* were Korean mafia from up on Lawrence Avenue—rose tats on the arms, evil sons a bitches, I promise you. I knew some in Saigon."

"I still don't see—"

"Robbie was off duty and wearing a vest."

Buff lets me think about that, then adds:

"IAD don't convict Robbie on a vest, but I do. Then there's you. Interesting how fast Danny Vacco put you together. After the ten years you been jerking with him, all of a sudden Danny V picks a fight to the death?" Buff shrugs. "Could be all your shit lined up so perfect Danny took a flyer." Pause. "But I doubt it. I see shadows, Bobby. Don't know that they belong to your brother or Robbie, but I see shadows."

"Ruben's my brother. He'd take a bullet for me."

Buff nods, but not with conviction. "Your lawyer won't. Bobby Vargas don't mean shit to him."

I turn to leave. Buff stops me.

"No Danny Vacco. The rest is up to you. But as your friend"—he points the rolled-up polygraph results in my face—"I advise you to at least get a different attorney for the Child Services charge."

"Charge?"

Nod. "Child Services will try to set the Little Paul interview for tomorrow, Sunday, like they're investigating the Little Paul complaint on the straight-up, not connected to IAD interviewing you on Monday for Coleen Brennan. When their interview's over, Child Services will have the ASA charge you for Little Paul in time to make the next prime-time newscasts. When IAD interviews you on Monday for Coleen Brennan, you'll already be in handcuffs and a jumpsuit. Whoever used Danny Vacco to put you together knew what they were doing."

"You honestly think Robbie and Lopez being shot has something to do with all the shit falling on me and Ruben?"

"I don't believe in coincidence, and I sure as fuck don't believe in explanations that require three ifs in them." Buff glances our team. "The G's got their bankroll; the bad guys got theirs. We got each other." Buff extends his fist to knock mine. "Even if some of us ain't going directly to Heaven."

SATURDAY, 9:00 PM

Whatever Moens said to her, Arleen hasn't called back and it's been an hour. I only resist calling again because the phone isn't in my hand. River North revelers herd across Clark Street wearing T-shirts for tomorrow afternoon's 2016 Olympics 10K through downtown. I brake, then pull up at the Mambo on North Clark.

My plan is: meet Barlow, get Arleen to call back and say we're okay, then hunt down Danny Vacco. I don't know what I'll say to Barlow or Ruben; Danny Vacco's different—he'll have an epiphany or a funeral.

Tania Hahn steps out from the alley by the valet stand. She limps to my passenger window, leans on the sill, and smiles with three lines of stitches on her face and round Band-Aids on her arms. "Wanted to say thanks."

I fish-eye her, then the street for how she knew I was coming here. "You lost?"

"Nope."

I check the street again. "Sorry about Lopez."

Hahn nods. "Good girl, worked with her in Miami; liked her a lot."

"Undercover there, too?"

Sad smile. "That's what we do."

"Who gave us up?"

"Thought maybe we should talk about that."

I wait for her to do that but she doesn't.

Hahn looks south down Clark Street. "We—*you and I*—should talk first."

"*I'm* the guy you're after?"

Instead of answering, Hahn reaches for her back pocket, pulls out an ID wallet. It unfolds on the sill. CIA in capital letters, emblem, her picture. "This ID's true. Mind if I get in?"

"You're a spy? Working the West Side of Chicago?"

"Sort of."

"Why Chicago? Why me?"

"Mind if I get in?" She opens the door, slides in with a wince, and sits back, the door still open, the interior light on us.

"Close that."

She laughs and pats at the stitches. "Painkillers make a girl brave and forgetful."

Frown. "Sure thing."

Her eyes brighten. "You're smarter than you look. Lots smarter than you act."

"Why am I talking to the CIA?"

"I have a problem; you have multiple problems. Possibly we can help each other."

The Mambo's front door is where I should be. "I'm gonna kill Danny Vacco in a few minutes. Wanna help with that?"

"Maybe." Smile, both eyes blink. "We occasionally step over the line." The smile remains. "Allegedly."

I make it fifty-fifty she actually means it, or it could be that Danny's already on her payroll. "You were with me on Little Paul's porch. You know I didn't do shit."

"I was there." She doesn't agree that I did nothing wrong.

"What do you want, Tania?"

"Help."

"With what?"

She studies me. "How well do you know Robbie Steffen?"

"Never spoken to him."

"Robbie Steffen has something I want."

"Guess the Korean mafia wants it, too."

Her eyes widen again. "Can't wait to hear how you know that."

"The two dead guys with him in the alley, rose tattoos on the forearms, that's the Lawrence Avenue pedigree."

"*Right, right,* you're a policeman." Wider smile. "Definitely should try some of these painkillers, stuff works. *Now* I understand why dope's all over everywhere."

"You were saying . . . Robbie Steffen?"

"Robbie's father is kind of important, too."

I stare, confused. *I'm* worthy of the CIA infiltrating a CPD gang team? Makes no sense, not if she wants Robbie Steffen and his father, Toddy Pete. "You live?"

She shows me her wrist, then tugs a mic and wire through her sleeve, and hands it to me. "I won't tape you; you have my word."

I accept the equipment because I'm curious, not because I believe her.

She says, "If we're working together, you'll have to trust me."

"Now we're partners?"

"Barlow and your brother can't help you. I can."

"I'm a child molester, maybe the rapist murderer of a thirteen-year-old."

She shrugs. "Some of the people I work with have faults."

Silence. Cars pass on Clark Street. We stare for a moment. I don't ask her how she knows who I'm here to meet. "What the fuck do you want?"

"First, you wear a wire. On Robbie Steffen; then your sergeant, Buff Anderson; and maybe Toddy Pete Steffen *if* I can get you close enough—"

"Buff's got nothing to do with those guys."

Hahn holds up her hand. "Along the way, maybe we have to shoot a corporate CEO and a couple of girls who work for him—collateral damage, we call it. If we're successful and don't die, I'll make Child Services go away; I'll make Tracy Moens and the *Herald* print a retraction; and I'll kill Danny Vacco while you watch." Her face goes cherubic even with the stitch blotches. "Then we'll pop down to the D.R., dance with some topless Latinas, smoke a Cohiba or two. Lopez and I used to do it every Christmas, lotta fun."

I focus tighter on her eyes, a bit of sadness masked in the happy ever after. "How much of that shit did you take?"

The cherubic mask remains, but the sales pitch hardens to the original. "They don't give these jobs to the Spice Girls. Lopez and I were the Wicked Witches of the East, we just didn't look like sisters."

10

ARLEEN BRENNAN

SATURDAY, 9:00 PM

The Shubert marquee is twenty blocks behind me.

Rush Street vibrates with its Saturday-night expectations. Limos and taxis crowd the curbs; revelers parade the European-style sidewalks under festive pole banners for the 2016 Olympics. Cole Porter drifts out from inside the Whiskey; Sinatra from Jilly's. The tables out front are full and will be till closing. Soft neon and high-limit credit cards blush everybody beautiful.

Everyone but Ruben Vargas.

Ruben eyes the valets at Hugo's eighty feet north, then tells me what we're about to do—what *I'm* about to do. He says it matter-of-fact, but his posture is caged-animal calm, now both predator and prey. Ruben explains how he and I and his unnamed partner are going to "clean this up with Robbie and the Koreans." Ruben says I'll deliver a small package to two Japanese women who have, in the past, attempted to kill Ruben's unnamed Vietcong partner. Not to worry; should these women misbehave again, Ruben and his partner will kill them.

More *murders,* like we're discussing spoiled fruit. Robbie's warning: *Jap motherfuckers will eat you three alive.* I'm considering those futures four feet from a cop who set me up to die six hours ago. My feet want to sprint but I force them not to move. Coleen and I win this time. The Olympics banners flutter above Ruben and me. I look and a slow, knowing smile breaks across Ruben's face.

Ruben tosses me my purse. "Technically, if we drop the two Japs we'd be committing murder, but that'd be for a jury to decide." He shrugs a summer-weight jacket that doesn't hide his gun or his hand near it. "Get a good lawyer who can sell you as a non-player? Then it's self-defense." Pause. "But Robbie's alley in Greektown . . ."

My purse is light; Ruben kept the gun.

I step away from the bank's shadows and into the only streetlight so Ruben can't grab me and can't misunderstand. "I'm calling Choa—your psycho Korean mob boss—how's that? Telling him you're selling his package to some Japanese women. Then I'll call the *Herald* and tell them you're threatening me with all kinds of frame-ups so I won't talk to Tracy Moens about her exposé. Then you and I can go to the U.S. attorney, spill our guts about the Ruben-Robbie show. I'll give her your envelope and we'll see who wins."

Ruben's eyes widen. "I'm trying to help you and you wanna fuck me? *Chica,* you gotta get right. Hurting you doesn't help me, and hurting me doesn't help you."

"Leave me alone or it's Choa, *Herald,* U.S. attorney."

Ruben's reptile tongue shifts his toothpick. "Must not want to be in your play."

"I'll take my chances."

"Uh-huh. Do anything other than what I say we gotta do, and I wouldn't call your chances *chances.*"

"I don't need your advice, but thanks."

"The Japanese meet is set for tomorrow afternoon, Sunday—"

"You're outta your goddamn mind. For real. Make an appointment; see somebody."

Low-shoulder, street-gangster headshake. "*Chica,* we can wrap this up in a couple of days. I haven't told the Koreans who you are. If I do, the Shubert's over, finito, *se acabó.*" Ruben shrugs with upturned palms. "But if I don't tell 'em your name, how they gonna know? And after they're paid, why would they care? Gives us plenty of time to work these misunderstandings out for everyone. Robbie, too."

I wave hello at a valet and scan Rush Street for kidnap cars. Ruben was always capable of anything—trying to kill me earlier today was new—but he's completely lost his mind now, thinking I'll trust him, walk deeper into his nightmare in order to get out.

"*You'll* work it out with Robbie? After you got him shot. Ten to one both the Steffens are gunning for you right now."

"Then T.P. and son are hunting Arleen Brennan, too."

"No sale, Ruben. This is all you."

"Arleen, baby, I called the ballistics lab since you and I chatted at the Shubert. Three guns were used in the alley—Robbie's 9-millimeter, the Korean's .45, and a .38. Like the one you had in your purse. Haven't matched the bullets yet—and maybe I don't—but it's funny, you know? The gun that killed one of the Koreans was like yours. So maybe somebody like you was in that alley. And if she was, Robbie's gonna think bad things about her, *setup* kind of bad things. Might even tell his father." Ruben shrugs, and glances the banners again. "And if Robbie does tell T.P., goodbye Shubert Theater, you know?"

"I wasn't in that alley. No matter how bad you want it that way."

Ruben studies me—the actress—and removes his toothpick. We're both running bluffs and we're both professional liars. Ruben shrugs again. "Let's say you weren't in Greektown, the truth is you were right about Robbie and Lawrence Avenue. The man's a cop; unless he gets paid big to be cool, Robbie can't have a witness there. Not if he shot a Korean. To death."

More threats, alibis, and handguns. More leverage/life insurance—Ruben's never ending circle of shit. My father's temper adds venom to my tone. "This girl isn't fronting for you with Japanese women. Already did that with your psycho Koreans." My hand balls to hit Ruben in the mouth, knock his shiny teeth out. "I. Don't. Kill. People. Get it?"

"Your dead Korean in Robbie's alley doesn't count? *Somebody* blew his head off. Won't be anywhere to hide from that, *niña*. Career's over before it starts." Ruben shakes his head, mumbling something that sounds like "Santa Monica."

My breath shortens at *Santa Monica,* my face so red it hurts. "Fuck you."

"Women's prison . . . and you were so close. For you and your sister, God rest her."

The temper begins to boil. I flash on Coleen's funeral, Route 66, try to blink out the bus trip but can't. My purse slides off my arm. Both hands are fists. *Don't do it, Arleen. Don't.* Rush Street becomes America the Strange, passing too slow in a grimy bus window. I'm fourteen, talking to Coleen in our private language, picturing a future she won't have and I don't yet understand. The bus seat smells of previous riders. I finally fall asleep and wake to breath on my neck, a man's hip touching mine. I kick and scream him away. *The Four Corners will not find me. Da will not find me.* Finally the ocean—weeks, months. Waves crash on cold nights spent outside; colder still in the backseats of Venice Beach, mouthfuls of businessmen who pat my head—but my father did find me. Goddamn him, he did.

Blink. And goddamn Ruben Vargas. Eighteen inches from his pimp smile and reptile eyes, my vision begins to blur. This will not be Coleen again. *God rest her . . .* Not this time. Will. Not. Happen. I lunge ten bloodred nails at Ruben's eyes. He bats my hands, sidesteps to punch me but I pivot with him and stomp his instep, stomp again, and slam an elbow across his eye. Ruben stumbles into the wall. I kick him in the pelvis but miss. Ruben straightens in a blur, cocks his right hand, and the lights go out.

11

OFFICER BOBBY VARGAS

SATURDAY, 9:30 PM

The valet at the Mambo Grill takes my car keys as Tania Hahn disappears back into her alley. Her deal hangs in the hot summer air—wear a wire on Buff, my sergeant and friend. Be a rat and Hahn kills Child Services, kills the Moens exposé, and kills Danny Vacco—I clean up pretty for my girlfriend. Don't even know Hahn's script yet and have thirty minutes to decide.

Gonna be tough to explain the undercover CIA agent in our gang team as my savior. Why? What's so tough? Just tell your team you sold her your soul. Then sold her your friends. Simple.

Then, five years from now, after Arleen has found out what a swell friend you are, you can take a last inventory of your dingy-motel-room life and commit suicide.

I button my phone, hoping for a call from Arleen. Nope, no call back to keep our connection, to play teenager with me, something I really, really want her to do. Maybe call Tracy Moens, line her up on a wall, and ask what bullshit she said.

Before I can do something that stupid I step inside the Mambo. Tito Puente's timbales and Celia Cruz's voice fill the doorway. A five-ten Latina maître d' smiles red lipstick and brown eyes at the two customers in front of me. I search for James Barlow beneath the bamboo ceiling fans swirling saffron and cachucha peppers.

Odd spot he picks to meet. The Mambo on Saturday night is Calle Ocho in Miami—Little Havana—dark-eyed players in guayaberas and torcido panamas talking with their hands; their women in slip dresses, chins high, gold crucifixes tight on cocoa skin, eyes and shoulders slow-dancing a dangerous salsa behind their cocktails.

The maître d' says, *"Un momento, señor,"* and escorts the two customers past the bar into the dining room. The Mambo has straight-back wooden booths along both walls with hand-painted Havana scenes above them. Two rows of tables run down the center. The music's Cuban and so are the waiters. If you saw *The Godfather,* where Michael murders the corrupt police captain, this is that place with paella and plantains.

In the back corner, my brother isn't sitting with lawyer Barlow, a curvy blonde is, not wearing much more than imagination above the waist. In the back-bar mirror, Ruben walks in behind me. He has a cut over his left eye, a napkin to it, and dried blood on his collar.

I turn into his approach. "What happened?"

"A drunk. Woman, no less. Was trying not to be late, thinking about you and the new paper coming"—Ruben's eyes harden—"and she clocked me."

New paper means complaints or arrest warrants. The cut's not deep but his eye is bloodshot and the skin already coloring. "The lady can hit."

Ruben's tone drops. "Be awhile before she does it again." Ruben wads the napkin into an ashtray. "Let's talk to Barlow, get the new paper straightened out. I got other things to chase tonight."

"What new paper?"

Ruben pushes me forward down the Mambo's bar, past the low necklines and mojitos. We approach Barlow's table; he sees us. "Gentlemen. About decided you weren't coming."

Ruben smiles politely at the blonde, then tells Barlow, "Homicide. Argument after. Unfortunate timing, my apologies."

Barlow studies Ruben's cut, avoids looking at me, then touches the blonde's shoulder. "My niece, Mary-Charlotte Masterson."

"Ruben Vargas. My pleasure." Ruben introduces me. "My brother, Bobby."

She smiles twenty-five-year-old happy, a big contrast to Ruben's and Barlow's expressions. I've seen her before but can't place it; good vibe whatever it is. I'm about to say pleased to meet you and she says: "Wolfe City."

Wolfe City is the recording studio where I did my studio-work demo, the cathedral of blues history. "Right. Right." I push my hand at her to shake. "You dress different at night."

"You don't." She leans back from my hand, grinning at one more starstruck, join-the-club blues hopeful. "If you're here, the cell number we have must be wrong. Doc's chasing you, or was. Ed Cherney heard your demo this morning and wanted you on behind Kenny Herbert and the Memphis Horns."

"Me?" Ed Cherney? Jesus, he works with the giants. I grin at Ruben, the man who paid for half my first guitar.

Ruben says, "I was just about to tell you."

Mary-Charlotte continues. "Ed's in town for the Chess Records/ Blues Heaven Benefit. The tie-in CD for the mayor's 'Stir the Soul' Olympic hook. Cameron Smith had your demo and gave it to Ed."

If you play jazz or blues, Cameron "Superfly" Smith is Chicago radio. Chess Records is . . . well, Chess Records. A man steps up behind Mary-Charlotte and rests both hands on her bare shoulders. Mid-forties, Armani black T-shirt and linen pants, Cameron Smith in the flesh and reaching for my hand. Cameron smiles, surprised. "Bobby, Bobby, how you doin'? Loved the demo. Son, you best be up the street. Wolfe City'll be firin' up about now." Cameron shifts to Barlow, saying he and Mary-Charlotte have to go. "We're emceeing part of Furukawa's star-power fund-raiser. You should come." Cameron squeezes Barlow's shoulder, then tells me, "Personal-swag auction; Chicago-connected star power doin' it for the cause."

Mary-Charlotte stands. "Call Doc *right now.* Tell him you're on the way."

My phone's out before she finishes. Ruben pushes my arm down and I pull it away. "What's the number?"

Mary-Charlotte gives me the number. "Doc's private line."

I dial. A voice answers, "This is the Doctor."

I step away from Ruben and tell Doc who I am.

"All good. Cameron and I liked your demo when you did it, you know? Ed Cherney's from here, wants some of your Four Corners behind Kenny Herbert and Rab Howat doin' 'Calumet City Blues,' so . . . come on by. We're just getting started."

Silence. I can't speak.

"Yo? Bobby Vargas?"

Finally my lips work. "Yeah. Sorry. Thirty minutes be okay?"

"C'mon."

I flip the phone shut and sit down before my knees give out. Me recorded by Ed Cherney playing with Kenny and Rab and the Memphis Horns? I blink for focus. Barlow's talking to Ruben, saying, "No. She actually *is* my niece." Barlow turns to me, feigning interest, but his tone is cold. "Good news?"

Skin pinch—yeah, I'm awake. "*Me,* I'm recording with Ed Cherney."

Lawyer Barlow doesn't get it or doesn't care.

"Grammys with Bonnie Raitt? Jackson Browne? Emmy nomination with the Rolling Stones? With Eric Clapton for *Crossroads*?" Still nothing. "Ed's the man. I mean, like, *the* man."

Barlow nods, "Congratulations." Then loses the happy-for-you face he was faking. His finger taps the cell phone next to his plate. "Not good news."

I glance at Ruben, his lips flat, eyes hard—this must be the new paper—then back to Barlow. "What?"

"Child Services has another complaint."

I lean away like it will help, sense the revulsion around me.

Barlow says, "Not Little Paul. This time it's a young girl—"

"Danny Vacco. That Mexican motherfucker keeps making—"

"No. This little girl is white Irish." Barlow's eyes narrow at Ruben, then back to me. "From your apartment building."

12

ARLEEN BRENNAN

SATURDAY, 9:30 PM

Someone . . . speaking . . . Spanish? Blink. Brick wall ten feet away . . . bank ATM . . . traffic noise behind me. Blood taste in my mouth. I pat my face, check the fingers for blood. Blink. Café tables to my right. I'm against a fender, neon, summer, Sinatra. "What . . ."

Fast Spanish. Green valet vest and shirt; cigarette breath. Hugo's. I jerk left and off the car's fender. Ruben Vargas.

Two valets step back, hands patting air. "*Calma, señorita.* Calm."

Ruben's not here, left or right. My purse is on the ground. The gun didn't spill. No, I don't have the gun; Ruben has the gun. *Kidnap car.* I jerk to the street. No kidnap car. "What happened?"

"You fight, yell. We help."

Blink. Ruben knocked me out.

"*El halcón,* your policeman, he leave."

Ruben knocked me out then left before more police came. Rush Street isn't his area; he doesn't want "us" on the record. Maybe that's good.

"*Señorita* . . ." Both valets examine my eyes. A car stops too fast. I jerk and the doors pop. TAC cops—body armor and blue jeans. The driver is pointing at me but looking at the valets; his hand has a pistol exiting his holster.

"Wait. No, don't. They helped. I work here."

"*Alto!*" The passenger-side cop circles his fender, gun in both hands. "*Vengan aquí!*"

"No!" My hands wave. "We all work here."

The valets freeze.

"No, wait." I jump between both cops and the valets. "They helped me."

One cop sidesteps me; the other grabs my shirt and jerks me out of the way. "Easy, ma'am." His hand pulls me toward the wall. "It's okay. We got it."

My hands go to his vest. His head jerks to mine. "Hands down." He presses me away.

"No. No. We work here."

"So do I. Calm down. Everything's okay."

He glares, but not angry, then cuts to his partner putting both valets on the wall. We're in District 18, Robbie Steffen's old district. He's a TAC cop just like these two. "Wait. C'mon. These valets are my friends."

"Then they got nothing to worry about."

The other cop tells the valets, "*La migra.* Hands on the wall. Don't fuck with me."

I slide left toward the second cop. "Don't do that. They're just working, for God's sake; they pulled the mugger off me."

A hand grabs me back. "You speak fucking English? Stay. Right. Here."

I struggle and he bangs me into the wall. What if Ruben called these guys. What if—

"Calm down, lady. Don't make this something it isn't."

Tommy the valet boss walks toward us. The second cop yells, "No," and Tommy stops cold. The cop tells all of us: "If you folks will just be cool, let us be the police, everything will be fine. We aren't here to hurt anybody. For anything. No *migra,* okay?"

Me—the valets pressed into the wall—Tommy frozen on the sidewalk—we all take a breath.

"If you two gentlemen have IDs let me see 'em. Pass 'em behind you."

Faces on the wall, the valets pass something back. The cop studies one ID, then the valets, then the other ID. "Okay, turn around." The valets do, nervous. The cop says, "Sorry for the inconvenience." The valets accept their IDs and turn to leave. "Wait." The cop stops them. His partner asks me, "Wanna file a report?"

I want to get away from District 18 TAC cops. "No."

He picks up my purse and holds it out. "Yours?"

"Yeah. Thanks."

He nods to let the valets go. His partner does. "What happened?"

"I don't know; a man grabbed me; I hit him; he hit me," I wipe my cheek and lick at the blood, "the valets pulled him off . . . I guess, ah, think the guy knocked me out."

The cop puts his finger under my chin until my eyes rise to meet his. "Sure you're okay? Looks like a pretty good shot you took."

I brush at my hair; sniff, and wipe at my lip.

"Need a ride? We can take you."

"No. Thanks. My car's over there." I point at my still neon-red 1969 Volkswagen.

The second cop comes up the sidewalk and stops. Same as the first, blue jeans, gun belt, and fitted black body-armor vest. Batman for the city. He says, "That your car?" and points at the VW I just pointed to.

Nod.

"Nice." He's focused on me not my car. "Not many of those around."

Nod.

"Live by Greektown?"

Jolt. "West of there. By Union Park."

"But you go to Greektown." Not a question.

His partner is inspecting my VW.

"Mind if I see your driver's license?" The new cop nods to my purse. "And registration."

"Why?"

"Because I'm the police and I asked you."

I dig out my license; if the gun had been in my purse I be in handcuffs already. All three of us walk to my car for the registration and insurance. The second cop writes down my name and address. I ask his partner, "What's the problem with my car?"

"Guy we work with was shot in a double murder. Earlier today in Greektown. A witness remembered a car like yours."

"Is your friend . . ."

"He's alive. So where'd you have lunch?"

"Huh? Oh, at home."

"Anyone with you?"

"No. I was . . . am rehearsing for an audition tomorrow morning." I cross both index fingers. "*Streetcar* at the Shubert."

The cop cocks his head; his partner quits writing.

"What?"

He says, "Our friend, the cop who was shot, is Robbie Steffen."

Stare. Stutter. Fidget.

"Robbie Steffen. The guy who got you the audition."

Both hands go to my temples. "I'm sorry, what?"

"Robbie's big with the Shubert." The cops stare, both add posture and interest. "Were you in Greektown today?"

"No."

"Not once?"

"I said, no."

"Did Robbie get you the audition?"

"What? No. I don't know any Robbie Steffen."

"Bet he knows you."

I look at the cop, then his partner. Don't show them my heart beginning to pound.

"Mind if we search your car?"

"For what?"

"A witness to the Greektown shooting remembered a car like yours. Do you mind if we search your car?"

"I'm attacked on a street corner and now you want to search my car?"

The cop nods and holds out his hand. "Keys?"

Hands to hips, circa Maureen O'Hara. "And you'd want to strip-search me, I suppose?"

"No, ma'am, just your car—"

"My boyfriend's a policeman. Should I call him? Tell him your hands were all over me?"

"What's his name?"

"So that matters? Now you'll treat me like a human being? His name's Bobby Vargas. He's a TAC cop just like you, except he's a gentleman. When it's called for."

The cops glance each other. "We'd still like to search your car."

"Get a warrant. Or arrest me." I snatch my papers back. "Tell my lawyer and the *Tribune* your 'probable cause.' "

Left turn onto Division. My heart's still doing one-sixty. Why did I say "arrest me"? What if they did a paraffin test like on TV? *So, Ms. Brennan, you fired a gun today. Your car was in Greektown. And you have no alibi* . . . Why did I say Bobby Vargas? That's a half step from Ruben Vargas.

Bobby called me *just to say hi.* I fumble for my phone to call him back. Why does the devil have to be his brother? Anyone but his brother and I could tell Bobby—

Tell him what? That you shot a Korean to death? But it's okay because Bobby and Arleen have a date to the prom? You're not going to the prom; go home, clean up— Can't go home; no telling what Ruben intends to do after I threatened to go to Choa. *Cringe.* Ruben might get past the Choa threat, but the U.S. attorney was way too strong.

Will Ruben hunt for me at the L7? He might.

Left turn onto Clark Street, southbound, not north to the L7. Headlights behind me blink to brights; I swerve and they pass. Cameron Smith's on my radio doing some Olympic hipster pitch. Can I make tonight any worse? And Ruben has the gun. If my prints are on it I'm *so* in prison— No, no, no I'm not. Tonight *can* be worse. Ruben will make sure I die in a shootout with the police. He can't risk me talking, trying to save myself with the U.S. attorney. After I'm dead, the gun and prints will be proof I was guilty. Ruben or his cop accomplices will be the good guys. That's what will happen. Right after Ruben and I finish with the Japanese women.

Jesus, God, the Japanese women. What are Ruben and I doing to/with Furukawa? This whole city will lynch Ruben if he burns Furukawa. But no mob's hanging me, I'll already be dead. The light at Kinzie turns red. Or . . . or . . . I could shoot Ruben first before he kills me. My foot hits the brake. The Koreans don't know me . . . Murder? That's Arleen's solution?

Car next to me.

Maybe.

What about Robbie? Kill him, too? Robbie *knows* you were in the Greektown alley and he knows you were on Lawrence Avenue. Robbie knows you're a civilian; you'll blurt everything two seconds after you're arrested. Deep breath. Robbie will kill you as soon as he can. And he'll kill Ruben Vargas, too.

Jesus, this is awful. But Bobby Vargas is a cop. What if he helps me? Somehow?

The car next to me accelerates to the Clark Street Bridge. I follow across the river, change lanes and pass the Thompson Center lit up for a Saturday-night event. Then past city hall lit up because the mayor wants it lit up. Monroe Street. I make a left, then one block and park. Across from the beautifully lit Shubert Theater. The marquee tells me and the whole world:

STREETCAR starring ARLEEN BRENNAN
SOLD OUT

Horns honk and loop my VW. Just scam Furukawa, Chicago's new patron saint, and murder two crooked cops. I conjure the marquee lights and two-foot letters that will solve everything.

Except I'm not killing anybody.

And crooked cops aren't taking my dreams away.

Goose bumps in the July heat. My name up there. An entire family inside who loves me. I want to call Bobby Vargas, promise we're having our picnic, it'll just be awhile, but dial Ruben's number instead, then stare at the marquee while I wait. The marquee begins to play Coleen's stark winter funeral; then the boardwalk in Venice Beach—Fellini's grotesques in and out of the neon—the dark cars and sticky upholstery; then the men, the promises.

Ruben answers his phone, "About fuckin' time, *chica*."

The marquee goes black.

Lightning hits beyond the pier in Santa Monica. The solution to evil has a high price, but it's clear and it's simple: *Just pull the trigger.*

13

OFFICER BOBBY VARGAS

SATURDAY, 10:00 PM

I run lights toward Wolfe City. For the date with destiny I've worked for since I was sweeping sidewalks at Maxwell Radio and Records. Me, Bobby Vargas, on the Chess benefit record—holy shit. Wish my parents and Arleen could see this . . . stand behind the mixing board and watch *me* play next to the greats. Gonna be so good, if I don't faint or drool.

I brake for three young girls in white T-shirts, start to yell at them to get home but don't. Barlow's *little girl from your building* is my new tag. The discussion isn't if I molest children; it's what brand I prefer. I watch the girls across the intersection. How does Danny Vacco put an *Irish* girl together ninety blocks north?

He didn't, not without help. Mexican motherfucker. But he could've; odds are against it, but he could've cornered the mother, scared the hell out of her—he's an animal—then . . . then *what*? Child molestation is a monster charge to make, and ten times worse to defend. The mother and daughter know I'll fight . . . and they filed the charge anyway.

So if it isn't just Vacco, who? The *Herald*—maybe. Hahn—she's capable all the way; I'm already half an hour late telling her I'm ready to be her rat. Could be the U.S. attorney—if the mother was jammed on something federal, the U.S. attorney or an FBI agent could drop a hint for the mother to follow, then the G rolls me, I roll on Ruben for their Coleen Brennan case *and* whoever got Lopez killed, Jo Ann Merica becomes governor. Mother and daughter walk away.

Or, maybe the kid really *was* molested and . . .

Be here, Bobby, not there. *Be the blues, baby; be the blues.* Deal with what you can deal with. Wolfe City won't know about a little white Irish girl from your apartment building. Or Little Paul. Or that my own brother—my hero for half my life—gave me *the look.*

Once Ruben, Barlow, and I were alone at Barlow's table, the new paper was explained. Ruben said the little girl at my apartment building had come forward after her mother read the *Herald.* The little girl said I made her read about Coleen and threatened to do the same thing to her if she told. Barlow's advice was brutal but true: if I'm innocent, we break both children—the girl and Little Paul; if I'm guilty, we break both children. Officer Bobby Vargas becomes seriously Hispanic, a Mexican American civil servant of immigrant parents, a victim of stereotyped race hatred because I had the nerve to police white people, not just brown and black.

Barlow didn't ask if I was guilty, but he didn't want to touch me and then return to his food. Ruben gave me the blank face he uses in his interrogations. *My own brother.* And stayed in his chair at the Mambo. Made me want to hit him; broke my fucking heart is what it really did.

Don't be there, be here. Be the blues, baby.

I pull to the curb on Halsted. Half a block south of Wolfe City, four bangers eye me from the corner, their white wifebeaters sharp contrast against the abandoned storefronts and shot-out streetlights. Four teenage ghosts with gang promises blue on their skin, two-way radios, do-rags, and futures so short they don't add up to yesterday.

A car door pops. Banger number five exits a parked Chevy, straightens, and— Cop Killa, the North Side import with the Twenty-Trey tats who Hahn and I braced, muscled-up from prison and out on bond for attempted murder. My hand lands on my Airweight, not my guitar. In all of the Four Corners, Cop Killa *happens* to be standing here? Staring at me, hands hidden? The street knows I'm up against it, that I'm weaker than yesterday. Is Cop Killa here to make a move? Danny Vacco gets me before I get him? A block beyond Cop Killa and his lineup, the main body of Danny Vacco's La Raza set are out representing the colors, ruling their real estate in the war with the Latin Kings. If I'm tonight's target, I'm already surrounded.

Across Halsted, the dim blue neon WOLFE CITY R. S. arches above a warehouse doorway. One hand stays on my pistol, the other pulls my guitar out of the trunk. Lose *today,* Bobby. Be *tonight.* Play the blues for as long as Ed Cherney will let you. My eyes close tight and I squeeze the guitar case. *Be the blues.* You're a musician; this is the Crossroads, baby; highways 61 and 49 in Clarksdale, Mississippi.

Eyes open—Cop Killa's still watching me. Still can't see his hands.

The WOLFE CITY R. S. neon dims then brightens. The Chess Records benefit session is on; the studio's in use, sucking power into the hands of my heroes. I'll be a part, no matter what the papers say tomorrow, no matter what my own brother believes. My playing will be on this record forever. My fingers tingle to my wrists.

Out front, three limos are double-parked, the drivers all leaning against the center limo's fender, their backs to Halsted and me, and Cop Killa a hundred and fifty feet south. Tonight's no biggie to the drivers, but this might be what you'd call my Big Chance, that single moment when your entire world changes, where bad things shift just enough to crumble under their own weight, where the miracles happen. I close my trunk and pull the Airweight. Maybe when tonight's over, after I've played for Ed Cherney, Kenny, Rab, and the Memphis Horns, maybe I won't have to kill Danny Vacco, or his pit bull Cop Killa, or wear a wire on Buff Anderson and sell out my gang-team family. Maybe Ruben changes his mind and says he's sorry.

Arleen's image materializes . . . Neverland, that's the answer. Arleen and I get out of the Four Corners after all—just like the bluesmen in the Delta. I start to grin; the door to Wolfe City opens; two men exit: one white, one black. The tallest of the limo drivers jumps to attention and grins at the Memphis Horns, Wayne Jackson and Andrew Love. Holy shit, star time for forty years. Wayne, the white one, possibly the best trumpet player alive, waves off the driver; he and Andrew walk north. Bad night for that.

I go instant hall-of-fame, blues-royalty fan and yell from my car, "Wayne?"

Both men turn. I put the Airweight on my leg so Cop Killa can see it but the Memphis Horns can't, and jog across Halsted with my guitar case in the other hand. Slipping through the parked limos, I say: "Hi, ah, not that good a neighborhood; kind of a Latin gang war under way. Don't think you guys should be walking out here."

Both men search Halsted for threat they missed. I holster the pistol and point behind me over my shoulder. "Those T-shirts are La Raza lookouts." Neither man twitches like crack cocaine is part of his lifestyle. "Honest." I tip the guitar case and show him my gun and the badge clipped next to it. "I'm a gang cop." Smile. "When I'm not playing in the studio."

Andrew Love smiles his famous wide smile. "You're on the Chess record?"

"Supposed to play behind you." I push my hand out. "Bobby Vargas."

Both shake it; Andrew's has a tremor. Wayne says, "We'd like to walk off a bit. Any idea where—"

"Sure." I pull my cell and speed-dial Jason.

Jason answers, "Man . . . Bobby?"

"Do me a favor, okay? Get a car by Wolfe City. Two guys I'm playing with need an escort. They want to walk a few blocks, thirty minutes or so."

Jason says, "Just heard that's where you were."

I smile at two all-stars, telling Jason, "Wayne Jackson and Andrew Love, the Memphis Horns. Can you can believe that?"

Bad tone. "I'd believe anything."

"Huh?"

"I'll get your friends a car, but you already got some coming."

I see the lights before I realize the sirens have been amping. Uniform cars come in from two directions; four uniforms exit and circle us on the sidewalk, same way you'd do a street stop. I recognize all four cops. One says, "Bobby, you have to go in." One of the other three cops pulls my guitar out of my hands, another steps into my face while the third snatches my gun and badge while I'm wrestling for my guitar.

"Hey." I grab for my gun and miss. "No. I'm going in Wolfe City, got a gig with these guys." I nod at Wayne and Andrew moving away. "I'm playing on the Chess Records benefit."

"Sorry, man, but you gotta come in." He has handcuffs out. "Have to, sorry."

"Fuck you. What are you talking about?"

Two of the uniforms re-crowd me. One pulls my arms behind my back. I twist, step left and shove him away. "No. *Understand?* I'm playing on a record. *Me.* A big record. And I get one chance. Whatever you think you have to do, we can do four hours from now."

They clamp me hard and twist me into the wall. My cheekbone scrapes on the bricks. I hear one of the uniforms say, "Sorry, man. Guess fucking the second little girl was one too many."

SATURDAY, 10:30 PM

Handcuffed to a bench. Rocking back and forth. Be stone, Bobby, block of stone.

My guitar and case are twenty feet across the room, along with my badge and gun. *Evidence.* Officer Bobby Vargas is in lockup, and not just any lockup but the twenty-five-by-twenty-five basement I see every day. This is District 12's TAC/Gang Team lockup; it's in our office, *my* office. I'm handcuffed to an anchored pipe that runs along the bench's back. *The rack,* we call it, for the felons and gangsters. In the room's center, five communal desks are topped with wire baskets for our paperwork and computers too old to sell for salvage. For seventeen of my nineteen years I've sat at one of those desks. Was the good guy, the guy you called when you needed help. And I came; every single time.

Third watch is still on the street, doing what I used to do. The only people in the basement are our secretary Shannon, one of the four arresting uniforms, and me—felony arrest, rape, sodomy of a child. At the end of my bench, Shannon peeks out of her tiny office next to Buff's, stares till I look, and says, "What the *fuck,* Bobby?"

I can't answer; I'm busy rocking back and forth. How do you tell people you know that you're *not* a child molester? That they could leave their kids around you and not worry?

You don't; you sit on this bench in silence. Like the criminals do. When we're done processing your paperwork, you'll sit here, waiting for the bus to county jail. At county, you'll wait for an arraignment and try not to be raped, beaten, or stabbed. If you're a child molester or a cop, county will take special precautions, both in your transport and your housing. If you're a known gang member they will sort you by affiliation. What they *won't* do is guarantee your safety. Jail world has many levels, all bad, all the time.

Shannon retreats behind her open door but her voice doesn't. "Better not be true."

Buff Anderson walks in and nods the uniform out. The uniform shakes his head. Buff stares and the uniform leaves. Buff cuts to Shannon and says, "Smoke break."

Shannon doesn't smoke. She leaves without looking at me.

Buff stares, hard and angry. "True or not? Any fuckin' part of it."

If I could stand, I'd hit him.

"Answer me."

"You believe it, huh? After five days a week for seventeen years?"

Buff sets his jaw. "You tell me."

"Yeah, me and your kids, too."

His fist lands before I can jerk out of the way. I blink through stars and flashes; shake out the blur. His eyes and teeth are most of his face. "Say my kids again." Buff un-holsters his pistol. "Go ahead."

I blink until I can glare, and shut up.

Buff shakes his head, no. "Answer. True or not?"

"*What the fuck do you think?* It's *me,* asshole. *Me!*"

Buff hits me again. And again. "Gotta have an answer, Bobby. We all do."

Blood drips into my eye and mouth. I focus on the concrete floor, not pride, not friendship, not trust. "No. I did not rape Coleen Brennan."

"Little Paul? The girl in your building?"

"No." Dry swallow. "I'm not a child molester. The first time I had sex with anyone but my hand I was twenty."

"Look at me."

"Fuck you."

Buff slaps me upright, slams a boot into my chest, and pins me to the wall. "I want you to swear on your mother and father, on your guitar-hero future, on all of us who've stood with you since you put on the uniform. *Our uniform,* motherfucker. Swear to God you did none."

I stare.

"Swear it, Bobby, or I shoot you where you sit." Buff stands back and aims his pistol at my head.

Blink. "You honestly think—"

"Swear it!" echoes off the walls of what used to be my home away from home, off the yellowed cartoons and fight gouges, the gallows humor and shared lifetimes. Buff has three little girls and tears in his eyes. He thinks I'm capable of child rape.

"I did none of it. None."

Buff breathes in the words but doesn't lower the gun. His skin is red against the white hair, eyebrows, and mustache. He doesn't get this angry at work. I think I might kill him if I could.

"Somebody's framing me—Danny V for sure, maybe others—you said so yourself. I don't know why, or what they want, but I'm innocent. They can bring in five more little kids and I'm still innocent."

"I said it *smelled* bigger than Danny Vacco."

"Too much weight on me. From too many directions, and all at the same time."

"That's how you *know*?"

"Tania Hahn."

Buff's pistol slowly lowers. "What about her?"

"She braced me an hour ago. Wants me to wear a wire, maybe shoot a few people. If I do, and her and I live through it, she solves all my problems."

"Nah." Buff shakes his head.

I yell, "What the fuck do you care?" My hand jerks at the cuffs. "You think I'm guilty."

"We got three kids saying the same thing. *Three,* asshole. *Children.*"

"I didn't do it! If I had, there's no way Hahn could beat that. She says Robbie Steffen and maybe his father have something she wants, that her and Lopez wanted." Buff starts to interrupt and I out yell him. "Hahn's CIA. So was Lopez. Lopez was Hahn's girlfriend."

The south door opens; Jason comes in talking to his phone but stops dead when he sees me, then Buff with his pistol out. "*Shit,* Jesus. We . . . okay in here? Somebody . . . know something I don't?"

Buff points Jason out of the room.

Jason balks, blinks, adds horror possibilities, implications . . . "Bobby, don't tell me—don't."

"Out." Buff jams his empty hand at the door. "Now."

Jason stumbles on his heels, then pinches his face like he might puke, doesn't want to leave, but does.

Buff continues. "The *CIA* wants Robbie Steffen?"

I nod.

"What's Robbie got that the CIA wants?"

"Don't know."

Frown. "Who else?"

"You don't want to know."

"Yeah, I do. We all do. Robbie ain't part of Gang Team 1269. Wear a wire on who?"

We watch each other until I say, "You."

Buff blinks once. The door opens again, this time it's a uniform escorting a good-looking white woman in fitted black pants, coral blouse, and expensive jacket. She hands Buff papers, then makes a tight smile for me. "Cindy Olson Bourland. I'm your lawyer."

Buff hasn't looked at the papers. "And who the fuck is Cindy Olson Bourland?"

She taps the papers. "That's a release order signed by a federal judge. Judges appointed by the president of the United States rarely work late on a Saturday."

Buff reads the papers, looks at her, then reads again.

"I'm Mr. Vargas's attorney. The document in your hands instructs you to release him to me forthwith. I'd be pleased if you'd do that now."

"You would, huh?" Buff stares at my new lawyer. "Where's Mr. Vargas going?"

"None of your concern, Sergeant."

Buff stares at me, then wags the pages. "The paper has to check out. Have a seat."

Ms. Bourland smiles without warmth. "We won't be here that long."

14

ARLEEN BRENNAN

SATURDAY, 11:30 PM

Just pull the trigger. That's the answer, the only answer.

Sweat beads on my forehead. Dry grass crunches underfoot. Do it, Arleen, *here,* now. Dark presses inward from every direction; soundless, starless, cemetery dark. In twelve hours I'll be on the Shubert stage. Arleen the Innocent should be wrapped in beauty sleep, not creeping through a walled, tomb city at midnight, planning what I'm planning.

I'm not running a scam against Furukawa or murdering more Koreans. I'm not risking being shot by Japanese women and I'm not dying here.

Ruben Vargas is.

Ahead in the dark is Holy Sepulchre Cemetery's only light. Atop the shadowy knoll, a cluster of twisted oak trees rises out of an ethereal haze. Dim footlights serpentine down a pathway toward me. Long segments of the path die into the darkness. I squint for threat that prickles my skin. It was me who chose this spot, but Ruben could have beaten me to the pathway. *Slow, silent exhale.* I'm afraid of the dark—not nighttime—the *real* dark. Very bad things like Ruben Vargas live and hunt in the real dark, but that's where our confrontation has to happen. Ruben will feel at home where the grotesques can look and act like what they are. He will believe he has the upper hand.

Swallow. Sweat wipe.

A gust rustles unseen oak leaves, adding sound and the sweet-sour of dying flowers. I hear the echo of bagpipes, decades of grand funerals for Chicago's Catholic policemen and firemen. The mothers and wives are crying; the children frozen in little suits that fit. The echo won't reach the periphery along the far wall; the far wall is reserved for the less grand: the waitresses, stockyard workers, longshoremen—the citizens of Canaryville and the Four Corners who had a mass and a *time* to help collect the funeral costs. The far wall is home to the Brennan family of Belfast. Coleen's grave is half size, four rows away from our parents' plots and their American dream.

My heart begins to ramp. I hide a key-chain penlight with my leg; the tiny patch of light helps my feet avoid most of the gravestones and tree roots but none of the mounting fear. At the far wall I shiver in the heat and cut the light. Coleen's gravestone is no bigger than a greeting card and glints in a dull sliver of brief moonlight. Under an etched Celtic cross her whole beautiful life is three lines I can't read but know by heart.

Coleen Crista Brennan
Daughter—Twin Sister—Éire Aingeal
Born: December 19, 1969 — Died: February 3, 1982

"Aye, *a stór,* 'tis your season, it is."

I don't glance toward my parents. The dry grass I smell covers the dirt that covers Coleen's casket, earth that has hardened into a protective shell in the twenty-nine years since her murder, a shell the Dupree family and their lawyers and the *Chicago Herald* want to rip away like the rapists did Coleen's school uniform. On Monday I will be served with papers, legal demands that I will have to answer if I am to defend Coleen's right to be left alone, if our diary—which I buried with her—is to be left alone. The lawyers will argue about the greater good. They and the court will keep score on the service of this greater good—for the state, for the Dupree family—a score that will be kept with money.

My phone vibrates, the ringtone muted. I answer, hiding the screen light, and tell Ruben Vargas I'm at the knoll, not Coleen's grave. He's nervous and should be. Holy Sepulchre is an odd place to discuss his plan to rob Furukawa, maybe kill Japanese women, and make me a star. But if Ruben wants to kill me, a deserted cemetery is a good place . . . and he has to wonder why I chose it.

Ruben has promised to bring me the gun he took back at the Shubert so I can defend myself if the Japanese women try to hurt me. I hope he does, and if he does—if there's no proof I shot the Korean in the alley—then I will kill Ruben Vargas with his gun or the gun I brought from home, a 9-millimeter Beretta bought on the street in Los Angeles during the Rodney King riots and never registered.

The dim pathway lights will illuminate Ruben's torso as he climbs the knoll . . . he won't take that route. Ruben will approach from the back, from the deep shadows where he's always comfortable. He will have a gun in his hand; he will be worried. After I shoot him I will go to St. Mary's, light a candle for a saint with a soft spot for girls who pull the trigger, ask her to forgive me. She'll say, "Sorry, three strikes and you're out." And I'll have to live with that.

But Bobby won't. I won't tell him I had no choice but to murder his brother.

My phone vibrates again. I answer, again hiding the light. Ruben says he's almost to the knoll, wants to know if I'm on top in the oak trees. I say yes and don't move. Our phones remain connected, and as he climbs through the dark I can hear his breathing. I ask where he is, why he isn't on the path.

He says he's almost to the trees. "*Niña,* where are you?"

I press the phone to my chest, cock the Beretta, and feel-crouch my way through dark.

Ruben talks, but I don't answer and continue to climb. Higher on the knoll, Ruben silhouettes in the branch-sifted moonlight. He turns slowly, peering the dark in all directions, either a phone or a pistol in his hand.

"Ruben?"

His hand presses to his head. "What are we doing, *niña*?"

"Being careful. Making sure you mean me no harm."

"*Niña . . .*" He keeps turning, unaware he's silhouetted. "We're here to work this out . . . I gotta help you; you gotta help me."

I reach the bottom of the knoll, the last spot I can answer him safely. Ruben continues to turn as I climb toward him. I wait until he stops, his shoulder and empty hand nearest me. I step out, level the Beretta at his chest, and tell him: "Behind you."

He pivots, sees my shape in the shadows and the pistol pointed at him. When I don't shoot he relaxes and holds out both hands, one empty, one with his phone. "Guess the other gun isn't required."

"Guess not."

"We okay, Arleen?"

"No. We're gonna die and it's your fault."

"*Niña* . . . Things happen. But like I keep telling you, they can be worked out."

"Save it. Say I agree to face your Japanese, how's it work for me the day after? Why won't you or Robbie kill me if they don't?"

Ruben flexes to step forward, but stops fast when I don't flinch. "Easy, Arleen. Easy, I'm staying right here." Pause. "I don't know why you think I *want* to hurt you, that it's somehow my plan."

My finger can't be any tighter on the trigger. I start to tell him I know Robbie's envelope was empty, but don't. "Running out of patience, Ruben."

Ruben tries soothing. "The Japanese know I have a woman partner; hell, they tried to kill her. You're not her; you're a civilian, not a threat. We'll make a deal with them, use part of the money to pay the Koreans. Clean slate for everyone. Arleen goes to the Shubert—"

"I go to the *cemetery.* That's what I *do.*"

"Will you take it easy? Arleen? Please?" Ruben's hands slowly drop to his sides so I can still see both, one palm with his phone, the other open. "The Japs want the package and zero publicity." Ruben pushes a hint of happy into his tone. "You'll give them a sample. No reason whatsoever to kill the messenger."

"A sample? Of what? We're doing blackmail?" I jam with the Beretta. "*That's* the plan that will save me from you and your disaster?"

Ruben steps back. "Easy, baby, shooting me isn't what you want to do."

"It isn't?"

"Doesn't fix anything."

"It'll fix one thing. You're dead. That leaves Robbie. I make a deal with him; tell him I have a file you built on him that I'll trade for exit money. He comes to get the file . . . and bang, he's dead, too. Koreans don't know me. I have no more problems."

Ruben winces and semi-shakes his head. "Arleen's gonna out-game Robbie? And not die? C'mon."

"Won't matter to you."

"*Niña,* what about the police ballistics on the alley?"

"*The alley?* That gun is in your waistband. And since my prints aren't on it and it didn't shoot anyone in the alley. Who gives a damn?"

Ruben winces yet again. "My little brother might. Could ruin your honeymoon reunion, no? Maybe the *Herald* wonders why I die in your sister's cemetery a day after I come by your work. Cops might think the same thing, being that I might've signed out to come see you here."

"The *Herald* and anyone else who matters will think you were here and Hugo's because of the *Herald*'s exposé. You screwed up, Ruben. About time you died for it like everyone else around you does."

"*Niña,* don't start killing innocent people. It ain't good for the soul." Ruben shifts his weight. "Yeah, you're mad. Hell, so am I, but trying to kill me and Robbie—if you could get it done—is a one-way ticket. We're *cops* for chrissake. CPD won't ever let that go. They can't—not good for the morale."

Shoot this man. Now.

My finger stops before I squeeze the last millimeter. "Give me your gun."

"Real cops don't do that."

"Not your CPD gun, the .38 you grabbed to frame me."

"*Niña, niña* . . . Don't confuse me with those backstabbin' assholes at the actors guild. I'm trying to *help* you so you can help me."

"Give me the .38."

Ruben blurs—I fire. Nothing. Squeeze harder. Ruben's hand goes cop-reflex and FLASHES loud. I lurch backward, fall over an oak root, smash my head, and tumble down the knoll. Can't see. Ruben doesn't fire again. My heart's hammering in my ears. The Beretta's in my hand. I flick off the safety and, and . . . Still blind from the flashes. A minute passes. Is the safety off or on?

Ruben's voice: "God*damn,* Arleen, we don't have to kill each other."

I make a knee, brace to run, then yell up, "Prove it," and run left until I crash into something and fall.

Pause. Ruben says, "Just did. If I wanted to kill you, you'd be dead."

My heels and palms crab left into more dark. "Throw me the gun."

"Can't do that." The voice turns with me. "Gotta keep it to make you behave."

I stand, run left, and a divot grabs my foot. I twist my ankle, spin and fall, roll, try to stand and can't.

Ruben's voice moves in the dark. "The Japs just want the package. You help us with Furukawa, then everything's okay—provided you don't point that gun at me again. Everybody gets paid, okay? Nobody else has to die if you just back the fuck down and play it smart."

My ankle throbs, might be sprained. If Ruben has a flashlight—*of course he has a flashlight*—and he's willing to risk using it—

"Arleen?" The voice turns, uncertain. "Arleen?" Flashlight beam. Twenty feet to my left, creeping down the knoll. "Arleen?"

I jump up, my ankle holds, and both hands aim the Beretta at the light. The beam clicks out. Can't hear him. Can't see him. The flashlight beam clicks on, brushes my feet. . . . I fire blind. My feet tangle; I stumble and fall.

Ruben screams, "Bitch! Crazy—"

Hands and knees. I crawl grass, stand unsteady, slip, then sprint into the pitch-black. Ten strides and—bang. Stars. Knocked down, hands and knees on the grass.

The flashlight fans grass. "Arleen?" The beam sweeps closer, then quits and the dark swallows everything. Soundless . . . only my heartbeats and tombstones. Both hands press me up to my knees. I two-hand the gun, aim where the light was, and— Nothing but black. Where is he? Twenty feet left, the light snaps on.

Twist, aim— The light snaps off.

Ten seconds, then: "Arleen, *niña,* you gotta quit shooting or I gotta shoot back."

If I run, I'll smash into something again; he'll hear me and I'm dead. The flashlight blinks on and fans the opposite way. I crawl into the dark, adding five feet, then a tombstone, then another, then get up. Three strides and—

"Arleen?" His voice lacks confidence, not sure it has a listener. Jesus, was I out cold? How long has he been hunting, saying my name to the dark? The flashlight pops on, farther away, then off. Then on again and farther away, then off. He's leaving. Ruben's leaving. My cell vibrates. I open it, cover the screen, and Ruben says, "Where are you?"

"Why?"

"*Niña,* we can be done by Monday. By then you're a star, all this behind us. *Promesa, es sencillo.* It's that simple."

"You'll kill me anyway or Furukawa will. Put me in prison. Something."

"No, *niña*—"

"Furukawa tried to kill your partner. That's what you said. They'll think I'm your partner, too, just like you made sure the Koreans do. Furukawa will think I know all about their stuff."

"Write up a paper; put it in a safety deposit box; give the key to your friend Julie. If anything happens, she gives it to the U.S. attorney; I go to prison; Furukawa's headlines."

What would I write? I could tell about Lawrence Avenue, but that's Robbie. I could tell about the alley . . . but that's nothing against Ruben. "Give me the gun with your prints on it."

"What gun?"

"The one you took from me. Give me that gun with your prints on it, then we can talk."

Silence. No flashlight. No sound.

Ruben says, "Okay. Meet me at—"

"Leave it on Coleen's grave. Then go to your car; flash your lights and honk your horn as you leave."

Pause. "So you're still here? We can talk now—"

"Give me the gun—*with* your prints or I'm on my way to the U.S. attorney."

Pause. His voice adds confidence. "You *were* in the alley with Robbie and the Koreans. *Chica, chica, chica,* two men died in that alley."

"Gun or goodbye. I don't need your empty envelope to negotiate with the U.S. attorney." I flip my phone shut.

The phone vibrates. I don't answer. It vibrates again.

Three minutes pass. A flashlight pops on by the parking lot, then walks toward Coleen's grave. If Ruben's "Vietcong bitch" partner is here, I'm dead—she'll be waiting at the grave when Ruben's car leaves. No, Ruben's partner isn't here, not yet. If Ruben stalls, she's on her way. If Ruben goes away quick, I have a chance.

The flashlight fans, then walks closer and closer to Coleen's grave. The flashlight halts. My phone vibrates. I open it and Ruben says, "Leaving the gun. Call me in an hour. And *don't* make me come looking. I'm done dancing, *chica*. We got business with the Japs."

I hang up before he can add more threats.

The flashlight walks back the way it came. I half stand and extend one hand at the dark, then duck-walk toward Coleen, my 9-millimeter tight to my hip. Ruben's headlights flash, the horn honks. I duck. The headlights sweep the north entry's limestone towers, then turn out onto 111th and become red-dot taillights. Stumble, trip, bump . . . so completely dark. Coleen leads me in her thirteen-year-old voice: this way, that way, sweat in my eyes, and I'm here. I pat grass until my fingers touch Ruben's gun. It may or may not be the same gun; it may or may not have Ruben's fingerprints. *The same gun* I could prove just by seeing it in the light; fingerprints will be much harder—

Coleen whispers not to linger. And don't listen to the hateful voice. The pier is not the answer, was never the answer; find another way.

15 SUNDAY

OFFICER BOBBY VARGAS

SUNDAY, 1:00 AM

My guitar stays behind, locked up in property. Angry eyes burn into the back of my head as Cindy Bourland walks me out of 12 into the night. Outside, two uniforms I work with don't hide the disgust in their faces and don't move their cigarettes out of our way. We sidestep the uniforms. Bourland stops when we're clear, locks her eyes on mine, and annunciates: "Be. Careful."

Before I can speak, she palms my elbow, walks me to a waiting Pontiac idling with the windows down. She places herself between me and the passenger door, mouths "Careful," and walks away.

I check the Pontiac's backseat, empty, then the front seat to ID the driver. My hand pops the door, I force calm into my demeanor, and slide in. Tania Hahn is behind the wheel. "Forget to call me after the Mambo?"

I nod back over my shoulder toward "my" lawyer.

Hahn sips from a can of Pepsi One. "Yep, Cindy Bourland works for me." Hahn sets the can on the Pontiac's dashboard. "And now so do you."

The uniforms watch. I watch them back, consider a short trip to their personal space and a brief, bloody fistfight. "No reason to call you. Not wearing a wire on Buff. Never happen."

"Sergeant Anderson thinks you're a child molester."

I turn to Hahn. "Fuck you."

"Enjoy prison, then." Hahn studies the cut above my eye, then waves to Cindy Bourland passing in a Porsche convertible. "Cop? Child molester? Maybe you last a week in Stateville."

"I didn't do it twenty-nine years ago and I didn't do it now."

"Two out of three ain't bad, if that's what you mean." Hahn turns slightly. "Where's your guitar? I can drop you back at your gig. Heard Ed Cherney was in town."

I bite my teeth and stare at Hahn. Taking the bait won't help me kill Danny Vacco or find who's behind him framing me, somebody big like the CIA. "The Chess session's over; I called from inside."

"Pity. Cindy said it was a big deal you were invited."

Maybe hit her first, then the two uniforms. "Suppose you can fix that, too?"

Headshake. "More into country, k. d. lang, Bekka Bramlett, cowboy-chick stuff."

"You wasted your money. Feds rat. Chicago cops don't."

Hahn purses thin lips. "Should we add up your problems one last time? Before your only hope tosses you out of her Pontiac and signs up another *Chicago cop*?" Pause. "Let's see, the *Herald*—child-sex murder; Little Paul in the 'hood has you wagging your dick at him or worse; add the white girl in your building, then the red Toyota that got my girlfriend killed . . . I miss anything?"

"What the fuck do you want?"

Hahn turns the Pepsi One can so I can see the logo. "I already told you."

"Not from me, asshole. From Robbie and his partners. You said they had what you wanted. I'll go with you. Give me a gun and we'll go get it."

She attempts ingenue. "I know I'm just a girl. But if it were that simple, wouldn't I already be doing it?"

I stare, squeeze my hands to keep them off her. She doesn't speak or blink. Just stares.

"I'm not wearing a wire on my friends, no matter what you threaten or promise."

"Somebody will. Might as well be you, survive all these awful accusations you say aren't true."

"They *aren't* true. I'll prove it."

"How? Your friends are already walking away. Hell, you can't blame 'em. Come Monday all the city, state, and department agencies will be all over you. The newspapers, tabloid TV; shit, Bobby, you're fucked. And if we were talking about somebody else you'd know it."

"Not wearing a wire on my friends. Price is too high."

She shrugs. "Depends. Only injures the guilty. That's your job, isn't it?"

My job . . . I take a long look at the uniforms, Bobby Vargas already convicted. If cops who know me think I'm guilty, what will the agencies, the social workers, the feds say? Every ghetto kid I meet will be scared to death of me. Hahn's right, I *am* fucked. I toss her some of my own bait. "You want me to roll? Tell your rat why."

Headshake, pursed lips, Pepsi sip. "Explanations aren't part of my job description, sugah."

"Then we're done." I pop her door, leave it open, and walk south on Racine, mumbling, spitting. Good job controlling your temper. *Fuck my temper,* how's that?

Guess it's James Barlow time. Assuming he'll still have me. Maybe he can't afford a multi-accusation pedophile client; Toddy Pete insures the Archdiocese of Chicago; Toddy Pete might not want to share a lawyer with a pedophile. *Horn.* A hundred feet past the District 12 parking lot Hahn pulls up with her passenger door still hanging open. "Compromise."

"Fuck you."

"Wear the wire on Robbie Steffen. You *know* he's a crook."

I stop, scout Racine for listeners, and stay on the sidewalk. "And how do I know that?"

"Because you're a cop, even if these other assholes aren't. And if I'm right, you don't like crooked cops. So it's not being a rat; it's payback for him shitting on your uniform."

Eve and her apple; little blond reptile ought to be a game-show host.

But she's right, I hate crooked cops, most of us do, but I'm not Frank Serpico, not that I think Serpico was on the level. "If I wear a wire on Robbie there isn't a cop in this department who'll talk to me when it's over. Even if the prick's guilty of treason."

"Probably won't come to that. No testimony; nobody has to know."

"Only way it *can* end—bright lights, U.S. attorney, federal court, reporters and cameras everywhere. Jo Ann Merica wants to be governor, remember?"

Hahn tosses her can of Pepsi One at a wire trash basket between us and misses. "If I can unpack Robbie, he'll roll to stay free, white, and alive." Eyes tight, focused. "I'm not interested in lawyers or law and order. Couldn't care less."

"You can override a U.S. attorney? Bullshit. God can't do that."

"Not override."

"Jo Ann Merica's on a mission for Robbie Steffen, he's one of her tickets to the governor's office in Springfield. If she finds the ammunition she'll crucify him . . . assuming Toddy Pete doesn't get stupid and put her in the river."

Hahn pops another Pepsi One. "Jo Ann's part of the federal government—a big place with lots of competing agendas—and you're right, Jo Ann Merica would put me in prison next to Robbie Steffen if it would make her governor of Illinois. But she'd also cut a deal with Toddy Pete—a kingmaker in Chicago, you'd have to admit—if it earned her the same thing."

"Nah. You don't know Chicago."

"I know the federal government, and I know Jo Ann's bosses. What I'm hunting trumps crooked cops and governor's races."

I stare at District 12 a block behind us, then at Hahn. "All my shit goes away? Clean? The *Herald* prints a retraction?"

Hahn nods. "Do Robbie the way I want, then Toddy Pete; and if you're still alive, you're free. I'll even shoot Danny Vacco for you, just like I said."

"What about Buff?"

"Maybe I explain some, let you decide whether to wear the wire or not." Shrug. "Or we put Buff on hold . . . for now."

Half of me is shadowed by the lights of the 12th District station. My home of seventeen years, old and worn and full of my dysfunctional family. My lungs exhale and I hear my voice use words I would have bet my life against hearing. "Ask Robbie what?"

"Hop in, time for your education."

SUNDAY, 1:30 AM

Wacker Drive still has Saturday-night traffic passing the window of Coogan's Riverside. Our large table in back is lit dim by a green porcelain shade overhead. From the chair next to her, Tania Hahn lifts a government-issue folder and slides it between our pints of Guinness. Her hand presses down on the folder.

"Open the folder and you're pregnant." Pause. "Bobby Vargas is in till I say he's out."

I focus on her, not the folder. "Everyone in the CIA a drama queen?"

She smiles—half the time it looks real. "Nah, just me." The smile quits, becomes a blank like it was never there. "I'm not kidding about being *in.* And I'm not kidding when I tell you I can act *way* different than I look."

I sip the Guinness and try not to hear the music that's playing. Bonnie Raitt and John Lee Hooker dueting "I'm in the Mood." A song John Lee wrote and I can play top to bottom; can hear it come out of my fingers. Mine.

Hahn says, "WMD . . . BW."

More Guinness; it's easier, several is a good idea. Me and Chess Records were right there. Now I'm a child molester pedophile. A rat. Hard to fucking believe—

"Biological warfare."

"Huh?"

"I'd listen if I were you." Hahn's face is a blank, a serious one.

"Yeah. Sorry."

"BW is biological warfare, my specialty, my calling if you will. Not chemical weapons; *pathogens, bacteria,* and *live virus,* the kind that finds a living host—mammals like you and me—reproduces inside millions of times till the host bursts."

"That's *warfare*?"

"Enough hosts and you have a strategic weapon—*not tactical,* strategic. There are only two types of strategic weapons on this planet—nuclear and weaponized live virus."

"Nuclear. We're talking *nukes*? Like the A-bomb?"

"Not nukes, but Robbie Steffen and his partners say they have weaponized live-virus matériel. Old stuff from the 1940s, but scary shit nonetheless. We don't believe they have it *yet,* but they very well might know where it is. They tried to blackmail a major corporation with direct historical ties to the creation of this matériel. The corporation tried unsuccessfully to recover the matériel . . . were a bit heavy-handed. Do we at the CIA care about blackmail or heavy-handed recovery? Somebody on the fourth floor might, but I don't. I want the BW matériel—or proof Robbie's running a scam; which he probably is." Hahn checks me for understanding, then lifts her pint and drinks a quarter. "Agent Tania Hahn, over and out."

"Nah. Doesn't add up. Why be in my gang team?"

"I need a cop with your history. The rest you don't need to know. Not yet."

I turn the pint once in my hands. "I wear a wire, trick Robbie into convicting himself, then do the same to his father. Risk my life twice and *then* you'll explain?"

Nod. "After we try T.P., you and I are probably dead, so knowing the rest won't matter."

"I take it back. You're too stupid to be a drama queen."

Hahn taps the folder. "In or out?"

"Last chance. Who the fuck are you?"

"Think of me like the Secret Service guys working counterfeit hundreds. Lots of attempts and passes that don't amount to much, but the Secret Service takes all of them seriously because when a well-done, well-distributed outbreak occurs, the ramifications are huge." Pause. "BW—when it's live and on the ground here in the USA, and it will be one of these days—has a lot more teeth and lot more dead people than bankers jumping out of windows. I'm someone who runs down the leads to see if they have teeth." Hahn taps the folder again. "In or out?"

I stare at her, not the folder and her bullshit story. "So, like the movies, I open this, then change my mind about being your bitch, and you shoot me?"

Small nod. No smile.

"Bullshit."

She makes a pistol finger at me. "Whenever and wherever I feel like it." No smile. Icy blue eyes that don't blink.

"We prosecute murder in this city, arrest people and put them in prison."

"They all say that, Bobby. Then they'll hold your funeral."

It's two in the morning and I've had a long day. I open the folder; if she really is CIA there's nothing new *she* can do to me. On top is a black-and-white eight-by-ten dated 1945 in white ink at the bottom. Approximately a hundred bodies, outdoors, the Kool-Aid die-where-you-fall of Reverend Jim Jones's Jonestown.

Hahn says, "Manchuria. Northeastern China, not far from the Songhua River."

I stare at the bodies but don't see the trauma that put them there.

"A research facility named Pingfan, Unit 731."

I lean back. She's looking at me for a reaction I don't have. She waits, studying like cops do when we think you're guilty. Her fingers pull out another black-and-white eight-by-ten. This one's bad, vivisection—a live man in agony, cut open on a table, surrounded on three sides by other men in lab coats.

"1944. Notice the doctors."

"Doctors?"

"The doctors are Japanese." Agent Hahn extracts another eight-by-ten. This one I don't pick up: more vivisection, a woman; she's in agony, the women and men in lab coats are unmoved, scientific, passive in the victim's terror. The woman's pregnant. I blow my air out slowly and focus on the wall. How do people do this and remain people?

Hahn taps the photo. "Before and during World War II, Imperial Japan had a bio-weapons research facility in Pingfan, Manchuria, called Unit 731, the one I just mentioned."

"*Our* Japanese? Sushi restaurants, Toyotas—"

"The same. For the last sixty years America's strongest ally in Asia; home to our fast-strike bases against Red China and southern Russia." Hahn adds emphasis: "And our most important economic trading partner off the American continent."

I look up from 1944, thinking what cops think—always follow the money. "And sixty years later our partner has a problem."

Hahn nods, then points out the window to the newest skyscraper on Wacker Drive. "The partner is Japan; the *problem* is one of Japan's premier *good guys,* Furukawa Industries."

"No." I cut back to the horror photographs. "Furukawa did . . . mass murder?"

Nod. "Pay attention. Asking Robbie questions isn't the whole show. You have to play a role, convince him he has to cut you in. To play that role you have to understand how Robbie and the rest of us all arrived at that alley in Greektown yesterday."

"*The rest of us?*" I glance at the three eight-by-tens and the file underneath.

Her eyes harden. "This mission killed my girlfriend. And people aren't done dying, that includes you, me, your sergeant, and some others who matter to you."

"Who?" Photo glance. Skyscraper glance. "What others?"

Hahn waves off our waitress and my question. "Ready? This is survival stuff."

Nod, teeth bit together. "For you, too, honey."

"It's 1937, Japan is 'provoked' to invade China. At that time China is in a multi-way civil war—Chinese Nationalists, Chinese Communists, opium warlords, and Vietminh guerrillas, the precursor to the VC your sergeant and his friends faced thirty years later in Vietnam—each battling the other for local control of China, all of them being hunted by the Japanese Army and their colonial pacification policy of *Sankō Sakusen*—'Kill all, burn all, loot all.'

"By 1944 *millions* of peasant bodies are rotting in the rivers, farms, and villages. Those who can't hide or don't die in the pacification are captured and sent to Pingfan 731 or a similar facility for experimentation." She taps the vivisection photos. "All told by mid-1945 it's believed the Japanese conducted some five hundred thousand such *lethal* experiments on the Chinese peasants and captured soldiers; British, American, and Australian soldiers as well. There's no official estimates for the numbers killed in the field trials of weaponized plague, anthrax, and cholera, but it would be in the millions. That August, President Truman dropped bombs on Nagasaki and Hiroshima. Japan surrendered, saving the emperor and the annihilation of his population."

I push the nearest photo up against her Guinness. "A shame, huh?"

Hahn doesn't blink or vote; she continues. "President Truman officially ended World War II on December 31, 1946. Japan was forgiven for what some experts would later estimate at thirty million civilian deaths, then 'reconstructed' on the Western democratic model.

Japan—a once-demonized enemy, a society capable of sanctioning repeated massacres on the scale of Singapore, Nanking, and the Bataan Death March—was to be rebuilt into the West's Pacific Rim bulwark against Communism. Rural China, the West's *ally* in World War II, would not be rebuilt nor remain an ally. While Japan rose out of the blood and ashes of her neighbors, rural China descended into hell.

"The descent wasn't only the continuing civil wars fueled by hate, revenge, greed, and opium. China's descent into hell was also biological—the germs of Japan's massive BW experiments don't die because a peace treaty is signed—and sixty years later no official will discuss any of it on the record. The mainland Chinese Communists won't because they were the victims and don't want to be seen as weak; the Japanese won't discuss it because they had successfully outpaced Adolf Hitler. And *that* wouldn't be good publicity."

"And we're gonna marry war criminals . . . so we can put on the Olympics?"

"Won't be the first time."

I rub my eyes. Hahn continues. "Five years ago I was in China chasing Robbie Steffen's package before he owned it or its location. It's been sixty years, but when the Chinese peasants want to scare the incorrigible children working the chicken barns"—she taps the vivisection photo again—"they whisper *'Hiou hiou'*—the emperor's plan to trump America's rumored *super bomb* and win World War II. Imperial Japan's *'Secret of Secrets.'* "

I've never heard a word of this; not in school, not at work, not in the papers. Tracy Moens and the *Herald* will print a twenty-nine-year-old murder/rape exposé fantasy but not this.

Hahn points out the window. "The 'major corporation' blackmail attempt I mentioned happened across the street nine days ago. Dr. Hitoshi Ota, worldwide CEO of Furukawa Industries and Chicago's Olympic savior, is the target. The CDC in Atlanta was tipped by an 'unnamed source' inside Furukawa—probably another exec's power play for Ota's job—but not until after two full days had been wasted. The CDC authenticated the paperwork and tested the threat sample. They believe the BW agents the blackmailer provided are a direct derivative of the plague agents developed at Unit 731. And while these agents are not nearly as virulent as the agents developed by the Russians in the 1980s and '90s, they are lethal and easily dispersed in any number of ways. In an amateur's hands—and Robbie's crew is for sure that—Chicago could have a serious event on the immediate horizon."

"Robbie Steffen has *plague agents*? More than the sample?"

"Maybe. And if Furukawa doesn't pay, he'll do a test dispersal downtown, then tell the world that Furukawa invented the BW agents sixty years ago, lied about it to protect their brand, and wouldn't pay the ransom to stop it."

I flash on British Petroleum's commercials after the Gulf oil spill, telling us they were the good guys. Hard to imagine what Furukawa could say. For sure, the mayor and his economic plans could say sayonara to the Olympics. "No way Robbie does that."

Frown. "'Cause Chicago arguments don't kill lots of people? St. Valentine's Day was fiction?"

"Capone didn't use the *plague*—"

"It's a *weapon*, Bobby, like a tommy gun. But with more bullets."

"Who're Robbie's partners?"

"In a minute. Dr. Ota has spent fifty years buying and destroying the hard proof that ties him to Unit 731, but he was there, and so were many of his prominent university and corporate colleagues." Pause. "Robbie's crew told Furukawa that if they don't pay after the 'test dispersal,' round two is disperse the rest."

I read Hahn for the better-than-airport-novel-constructed lie the FBI/CIA would put together to get whatever they *really* want. "Okay, what's Robbie's demand?"

"Forty million. Assume the blackmailers would settle for twenty."

"Furukawa can afford twenty; why not pay?"

"Don't think they believe Robbie's crew has the 731 matériel."

"But you do?"

"Don't know." She stares at me. "But I need to."

"Say your story *isn't* an FBI/CIA fantasy. How come Dr. Ota and his 'university/corporate colleagues' weren't tried after the war? When the proof was still around?"

"The Tokyo War Crimes trial was a whitewash. Why? The cold war. MacArthur and Truman felt the 'Secret of Secrets' research was crucial—if you can call these photographs *research*—to stay ahead of the Russians. We pardoned three thousand Japanese scientists and put them to work developing the next generation of WMD—*bio war.* Cheap, deadly, terrifying. Back then nobody wondered what would happen if the genie popped out of the bottle."

"We *pardoned* the people in these pictures?"

The cherubic smile again. "Life outside *Mister Rogers' Neighborhood.*"

"Nah. Sorry, Robbie Steffen's an American. If he's got it, he's not letting this shit loose."

"No such thing as Timothy McVeigh?"

"Nah. Nowhere in the world Robbie could spend the money."

"Maybe it's not up to Robbie anymore. His partners want to get paid. Either way, want to risk it? And they kill ten or twenty? Maybe they screw it up and kill five hundred, at least thirty or forty of them cops and early responders. With families. And you could've stopped it. Want to be part of that?"

"Why me, Tania? Why Bobby Vargas, child molester? Why not some guys in white spacesuits and helicopters?"

"Planeloads from Atlanta. The minute we know they actually have it."

"Still doesn't explain making Bobby Vargas your bitch."

She stares. "Big tough Chicago cop gonna listen?"

I wave come the fuck on.

She leans back instead of forward. "If you want to survive Robbie's hospital room, Robbie has to believe you're a player, a silent partner stepping in to smooth out whatever it was that tried to kill him. Knowing what I know will be the only way."

"So tell me. Make me a believer."

She points. "Pay attention, tough guy. It's 1945, we're on the island of Japan, five months before the atom bombs will obliterate Hiroshima and Nagasaki. The Allied invasion is imminent—the reprisal for thirty million deaths is about to visited upon the Pacific's master race. Knowing what's coming, the Japanese military speaks for the emperor and orders all records of the *Secret of Secrets* and its research facilities destroyed. But not the weapon.

"Prior to demolition, the Pingfan laboratory packages its weapons products under the careful direction of one Dr. Shiro Ishii, the bacteria's creator. Ishii is shipping to Tokyo. Imperial Japan's intent is to mass produce the plague for use against the first wave of invading Allied troops. Japan's military commanders also create a backup supply—a negotiating threat should a second or third wave of the Allied invasion survive and succeed. They order a separate repository of Unit 731's formulas and plague samples to be created and suspended in a balanced salt solution they pioneered. Gives the samples a probable half-life of a hundred years. This repository is thirty glass vials, boxed and sent under armed escort to the island of Hokkaido. Since that day sixty years ago, Western, Soviet, and Chinese operatives—government agents and private contractors—have been chasing that repository, nicknamed 'the Hokkaido package.' Sort of a deadly sunken treasure, BW instead of doubloons.

"Preinvasion, President Truman estimates the Allies will lose one million men so the atomic bombs land instead of the invasion. Japan surrenders. The *known* Unit 731 formulas and samples that had arrived in Tokyo are turned over to General MacArthur. Dr. Ishii and his scientists are pardoned, then enlisted in the cold war with Soviet Russia, the world's new merciless enemy.

"In early 1950, while Dr. Ishii is clandestinely in the USA at Fort Detrick, Maryland, his father is kidnapped in Japan by radical elements of the Korean Catholic Church, a sect who'd been enslaved inside Japan during the war. The Korean Catholics intend to use the Hokkaido package to prove the emperor's involvement in crimes against them and humanity, atrocities the Allies have denied and declined to prosecute.

"The Hokkaido package is demanded of Dr. Ishii. He reveals its location as his father's ransom. At some point during the three months the Korean Catholics negotiate with the Japanese government, an excommunicated church member steals the package and sells it to the Korean mafia. The mafia smuggles the package to Seoul. The Korean civil war breaks out a month later; the package remains hidden while the Korean War is fought well into 1953.

"Fast-forward seventeen years." Hahn searches the file and finds another photo—three men behind an ornate iron gate set in a plaster wall capped with tile, and guarded. Behind them, a colonial building's second floor rises to a balcony with shuttered windows. She taps: "Courtyard of the French embassy in Saigon; 1970, the same year Nixon renounced the U.S. use of biological weapons and promised we'd dispose of our existing stocks."

Buff was in Vietnam in 1970. I squint to see better, definitely not Buff.

Hahn says, "The tall man is the Japanese ambassador. The man in the middle is Dr. Hitoshi Ota, in Saigon to buy back the Hokkaido package from the squarish fellow on the end, a ranking member of the Korean mafia."

"Dead Koreans here, Koreans in Japan, Koreans in Saigon. Lotta Koreans."

"They're the bridge, that's all, not the problem. Can I continue?"

"Be my guest. Korean gangsters got zip to do with anybody I care about."

Hahn hesitates, staring at my comment. "The Korean mafia was the street power in Saigon, the final arbiters for the river of overspent money and contraband matériel that all wars generate. In this case, U.S. money. The Koreans ran the war under the war, brokers for everything and everyone—for the corrupt South and the Communist North, for the VC in the city and the up-country opium warlords bringing their poison to market.

"When that French embassy photo was taken, the American war effort was under severe stress from the NVA and their Chinese Communist benefactors. With the help of a Carmelite nun and a child prostitute, the CIA disrupts an auction for the Hokkaido package, the bidders being the Chinese Communists and Dr. Ota. Dr. Ota is representing his own interests as well as the Japanese government and its closely aligned corporations."

"How do you know all this stuff?"

"I told you, it's like a treasure hunt, same as the *Atocha* in Key West. I've been on this one on and off for eight years. Let me finish, then you can ask."

Shrug. "So finish."

"The package disappears into the chaos of the U.S. withdrawal and the eventual fall of South Vietnam. Ho Chi Minh takes over the country. Crime doesn't go away, just morphs into the Communist version. In 1982 the elements of the Korean mafia still running parts of Saigon open another sale discussion, this time with the governments of Israel and South Africa, a project called the Ethnic Bullet. Before a sale of the vials and papers can be completed to either, the Hokkaido package is stolen by the same prostitute, now twenty, Lý Thi Loan aka White Flower Lý. The Koreans have been whoring Lý to the rich and powerful since she was eight. Lý murders her way out of Saigon, then requests the help of an American GI and the Carmelite nun for old times' sake." Hahn pauses, reading me for . . . who knows?

"What? I wasn't in a convent. Or the army."

"White Flower Lý smuggles herself and the package to Bangkok, then hops a plane with the ticket the GI provided. No one from her past sees or hears from her again until the blackmail attempt nine days ago against Furukawa's CEO, Dr. Ota."

"And who do I know who knows White Flower Lý?"

Hahn stares. "Robbie Steffen." She keeps staring, waiting for me to see another face.

"No. No way . . ." I close my eyes.

"He knew her in Saigon and he knew the nun."

"No, not Buff. Not with the plague—"

"Sergeant Anderson's been interviewed several times over the years but says he never saw White Flower Lý get off the plane and never knew the nun's real name."

My eyes stay shut. "And you don't believe him."

"Be a cop. How many innocent lives should we bet?"

16

ARLEEN BRENNAN

SUNDAY, 1:30 AM

Prime DUI time. Any traffic stop and I go to jail for felony gun possession, one of them a murder weapon. Jail is Rubenland. Rubenland is not survivable and has no place in Arleen the Innocent's new plan.

Arleen the Innocent has a new beginning—she did not successfully "pull the trigger" at the cemetery. The twin sister to an angel has that bit of pixie dust, her sister's guidance, Ruben's gun, and a way to check the fingerprints. With just a little luck and one major bluff, I will tightrope my way through the nightmare voices of my past and Rubenland of the present. Less than ten hours till *Streetcar.* I win the role, somehow I stay on the good-guy express and everything works out.

My phone vibrates. I lay the L.A. 9-millimeter on my lap and palm the phone. Bobby's text message reads, "Call me, text me, something. Okay? I want to talk, see you. Something."

Both hands tingle. Bobby Vargas, my boyfriend. I'm "thirty-nine" and my hands tingle.

I pull onto Waveland Avenue east of Wrigley Field and parallel park into a street space. Bobby's your boyfriend? Bobby is Ruben's *brother,* Arleen; his *family.* Except . . . except it felt so strong at the L7, so right now, and I saw it in his eyes, too. It was there, for real.

Grown-ups now, Arleen, not thirteen-year-olds. *Twenty-nine years ago* Bobby was your boyfriend.

I grab my purse with the *Streetcar* script and Ruben's .38, dropping my phone in just as it vibrates again.

Ruben says, "Talked to the Japs."

I leap out of the car, the 9-millimeter stiff-armed over my roof, then behind me, then east and west on Waveland. *Don't make me* . . . I do another three-sixty, finger tight on the trigger. *Please don't make me* . . .

Muffled: "*Niña,* you there?"

Ruben. But inside my car, in my purse—must've hit the button. I lower the 9-millimeter, thank pixie dust, dig the phone out, and tell Ruben part of the new plan. "I'll meet the Furukawa women *after* my audition, do your goddamn felony. If I don't make it back my written sworn statement about you and Robbie scamming Furukawa and killing Koreans goes to the U.S. attorney. Same with your .38."

"Got all that done since Holy Sepulchre? Lotta work in sixty minutes."

"Think of me as a bomb in your pocket. Yes or no?"

Silence, then: "See you at the Shubert. Maybe I bring little brother for luck."

I fold the phone and tuck the 9-millimeter in my jeans. Intermittent drunk voices echo in the dark. Wrigleyville is a good neighborhood, but on a postgame night with all the drunks . . . men do bad things to girls when they're drunk or in bunches or . . . Men just do bad things.

Waveland Avenue is dark, even darker at the L tracks viaduct as I pass under. At Murphy's Bleachers, I press down on the 9-millimeter in my waistband and start running. I sprint Sheffield a block to Addison, veer west down Wrigley's first-base side through more aftermath of the postgame party that ended hours ago. Approaching Clark Street I'm starting to pant. Two squad cars share the corner.

My feet stop so fast I almost fall over. I make myself two AM innocent with two guns, turn south, breathing hard, and walk toward the L7. The L7 is mid-block and across the street. Eight drunk rugby girls are out front singing arm in arm. Past them is the alley. One of the girls whistles at me and waves. I diagonal across the street past her, waving "no thanks," and duck into the alley, hoping the girl doesn't follow. Light spills into the alley from the open fire-exit door. Julie leans big against the bricks, beer in one hand, cell phone to her ear. She knows I'm in trouble from my five-second phone call after Holy Sepulchre, knows I want to hide here (part of the new plan), but not why.

I duck in past her. Julie follows, closing the door behind us. Sweat stings my eyes. I lean into the hallway/greenroom wall where Bobby Vargas stood smiling at me—nine hours ago, right after I shot the Korean. A lifetime ago. Both knees ache and I slide to sitting. My watch snags at my knee. Nine hours till my audition.

Julie listens to her phone, but shrugs at me, asking if I'm okay.

I mouth "Fine," and point upstairs to the Butch and Sundance suite.

Julie points at her phone and mouths "Tracy."

"Tell her to come over."

Julie's eyes widen.

"Tell her, okay? But it has to be now."

Julie tells her phone, "Right here with me. Wants to talk to you but it has to be tonight." Julie listens, then flips her phone shut. "Pink Panther's en route. Think I'll sell tickets if that's okay."

Downstairs, the L7 has finished last call after an eight-hour rugby-girl party. Upstairs, Julie's resting on an elbow on the Butch and Sundance bed, waiting for my explanation, her part in the plan. Twelve inches from her, I quit rubbing awake into my face. "Do we have a wee screwdriver?"

Big blond grin. "Tracy's not that bad."

Frown. "I have to fix something."

"It's two in the morning, movie star."

Movie star sits up, opens her purse, inserts a pen into the barrel of Ruben's .38, and lifts out the gun. Julie stares; I lay the .38 on her bed. "Have to remove these grips."

Julie's seen a gun before but can't be happy there's one on her bedspread being handled by an actress like we're *CSI* Chicago. She says, "And why would we remove the grips?"

"The less you know, the better."

"As in 'like we've never met'?"

"Be best. But after I get *Streetcar* later this morning we'll be Broadway babies . . ."

Julie nods at Ruben's gun. "So . . . that's a prop."

"Can I have the screwdriver? I don't want your ex to see the gun."

Julie doesn't move.

"I want Tracy to match the fingerprints." Exhausted-actress smile. "And you don't want to know the rest."

Julie reinspects my throbbing forehead and cheek. "Arleen, you didn't . . ."

"No. I didn't." Frown. My eyes roll to cover the lie. "Had I shot somebody, *my* prints would be on the gun. Right? And I wouldn't require Tracy's help to ID them."

Because Julie's a saint, she blows past the sarcasm. "So somebody else shot somebody?"

I continue the lie. "No. Someone shot at me, lost the gun, and I want to know who it was. But I don't want to tell the police, don't want the Shubert to get scared of me and cast the big-shot actress from L.A."

Julie's eyebrows arch. "The other actress did it? Oh my God, a Tonya Harding moment." Julie grins all the way across her pretty face. "Hollywood's gonna be so much fun."

I lay back and close my eyes, wish I could pass out. "The screwdriver. Please?"

Julie rolls out of bed, heading to the door. "Somebody should have a drink."

"And a screwdriver. And a plastic baggie. And Blanche DuBois clothes for tomorrow."

SUNDAY, 2:30 AM

Tracy Moens ponytails her trademark flaming red hair out of a face that doesn't have, or require, makeup at two thirty in the morning. Easy to hate her just for that. I have better reasons. She stares at me from the chair in the Butch and Sundance suite, well-muscled legs yoga-ed underneath her. Julie sips at an Anchor Steam. Tracy forgot to button her blouse and does that while she glances at the pistol grips on the bed corner between us. "Could give them to a friend. She could take them in if the ghetto isn't busy. But I'd have to have a reason."

"A favor. To Julie and me." I nod at Julie.

"What do I tell my friend and CPD?"

"You're the Pink Panther. I'm sure the options are limitless."

Tracy purses lips that will never require collagen. "What's up with you and Bobby Vargas? Are you crazy kids an item?"

"Coincidence." I'm asking favors from someone I'd like to watch melt in a fire. "First time I've seen him in almost thirty years. Just saying hello."

Julie waves her Anchor Steam at me. "I'd say y'all were packing for the Love Boat. Too bad it had to be the day Ms. Moens accuses Bobby in the *Herald*."

Moens says, "I *mentioned* him, didn't accuse him. Yet."

I drill straight into Miss Bottom-feeder. "Meaning what?"

She blinks, or maybe bats, the green eyes. "We go to court with his lawyer tomorrow. James Barlow. Know him?"

James Barlow is dangerous money, old First Ward kind of money. He brings clients to Hugo's for lunch, tips well, and always sits in the back corner. Bobby Vargas is a cop/weekend guitar player; they don't have big dangerous money, or shouldn't.

Tracy hugs her knees. "Love to know who's paying. Barlow's not known for pro bono."

"I'd stay and referee," says Julie, "but I have to count money downstairs. Been a long day for this saloonkeeper."

I point at my watch. "Seven o'clock, okay? Not a minute later."

Julie kisses me on the cheek. "Just like a hotel." Then she kisses Tracy. "Be nice, both of you have reputations to protect, sort of."

Julie closes the door behind her. Tracy says, "Where's the gun?"

"Sorry. Grips are all I have."

"Whose prints are we matching?"

"Don't know."

"But you know *why* . . ."

I feed her the lie I practiced. "I need a favor. Do it and I won't block the exhumation of my sister—*you're* the neighborhood *monster* for soliciting exhumation, but I'll get out of the way."

"I'm a reporter." Pause. "Julie said someone shot at you."

"Julie's drunk after a big day and a bigger night."

"Someone *didn't* shoot at you?"

Hard frown. "Match the prints, give the grips back to me, *then* I'll talk to you."

Tracy fingers at the pistol grips encased in the baggie Julie provided. "Robbie Steffen?" She looks up. "He comes in Hugo's, doesn't he?"

Nod.

"Isn't his father, Toddy Pete, one of the backers for *Streetcar*? Where I dropped you this afternoon?"

She probably called the director, her friend Anne Johns. "You know he is."

"Small world. All of us, six degrees of separation. The Vargas brothers, the Steffens, you and I . . ."

"What'd you tell the director?"

"Anne Johns? Nothing. And I wouldn't say anything, not if it hurt your chances. I'd be happy to do the opposite, if you thought it would help."

I glance her toward the pistol grips on the bed. "I have to sleep, my audition's at eleven."

Tracy picks up my script, not the pistol grips, and muses. "A long journey to here, finally." The room goes silent and stays silent. Tracy fingers the script. "The Shubert might prefer a lead actress without serious . . . problems."

Belfast creeps into my voice. "That they might."

"So what do we do?"

"We cut the crap and you decide."

"Had I known about you and *Streetcar,* I would've waited a week to break the story." Shrug. "But I didn't know, I had the new information about the Twenty-Treys and . . ." She looks up from my script for a reaction.

I know all about the Twenty-Trey Gangsters, about the Irish cop Terry Rourke who killed a nine-year-old Mexican kid and the street war it started. I was there. And that's right where Moens goes.

"Terry Rourke was related to your mother, wasn't he?"

No one outside our family has ever said that before. People whispered—not because they knew—just because people whisper. "Terry Rourke was my ma's brother. They didn't speak."

"Because of the . . ."

"Because Officer Terry Rourke raped my ma the week she and the family came over from Belfast. My ma was eleven; he was twenty something, already a cop, had helped bring them over."

"And your father knew."

"No." Long exhale. "That one you have wrong. Had my da known he wouldn't have married my ma. Had he found out after they were married, Da would've killed Terry Rourke long before the Twenty-Treys did."

"But the police in the Four Corners knew. And didn't prosecute."

"You're Irish; our families bury things like that. Had Ma told after she was married, she'd have been raising two daughters without a husband. Da kills Terry, then Da's either shot dead by Terry's fellow policemen or put in Joliet and executed."

"Could your mother have . . . She knew the Twenty-Treys from the neighborhood. Knew they were gunning for Terry. She knew her brother's address. She could've . . ."

Through my teeth I tell the bedspread, "I asked you for a favor. I agreed to get out of your way if you do it. Period."

Moens waits, then gathers her things to leave. She picks up the baggie with the pistol grips. "Could take all night, *if* I can get it done at all. Next time we talk—if I have your answers—you'll have to have mine. Sorry, but that's how it works."

I don't respond and don't raise my eyes until the door shuts behind her. I go to the door, lock it tight, and throw the bolt. Something nags me, something Moens said that didn't fit. Or was it something she did? Like help me. Help me because . . . Julie and I are friends? Because Moens wants Coleen's body exhumed? Because Moens knows about the diary she couldn't know about? Because underneath all that feral beauty Tracy Moens has a heart of gold?

Face rub. I'm missing something that's right in front of me.

Recap: The *Dupree* family wants Coleen's body exhumed. Tracy Moens doesn't have a heart of gold. She has her exposé story ready to go if the court will let her print it.

Then why all the questions? Why does she need *answers*?

What if she *doesn't* have her story ready to go? What if the *Herald* is about to go under like the rumors say? Tracy said an injunction has temporarily stopped them from publishing her exposé—but injunctions are *very* hard to get against a major city newspaper. What if her exposé is a stunt, a desperate gamble—Moens starts a fire just before the Dupree depositions start, then watches how and where the suspects run. The courts "stop" her from publishing the ending . . . an ending she hasn't written yet.

Because she doesn't have an ending.

Jolt. Then what *does* Moens have?

Coleen whispers, "Go to sleep; figure Tracy Moens tomorrow; fight Ruben tomorrow."

I smile. Say, "Aye, *a stór,*" and slide the 9-millimeter from the back of my jeans, stuff it under Julie's pillow, and curl up with my script hugged to my chest, wrapping Tennessee Williams and Blanche DuBois in the best embrace I can give. Us against the world: me, Coleen, Tennessee, and Blanche. And a plan that *will* work. Ridiculous schoolgirl smile. And maybe Bobby.

I'd cook us all muffins if I could, but Coleen's right, we have to sleep. Somewhere between exhaustion, survival, and stage fright I have to sleep. Tomorrow is my day; Coleen's day. I survived the Four Corners and Venice Beach and L.A. and Santa Monica for a reason. Today is over—thirty-one hours of Byzantine, Machiavellian hell. We have a plan; control. Tomorrow is my day. Coleen and Arleen's day. Tears bubble, then run down my cheeks.

I hug *Streetcar* tighter. *Please,* God, if you're out there, forgive me for just twenty-four hours and give me my chance. I will stand up there fearless and pour out Blanche DuBois, I swear I will. I'll be the best actress they've ever seen. Let them pick me—*one time, God*—pick one of the Brennan sisters for something other than penance.

17

OFFICER BOBBY VARGAS

SUNDAY, 2:30 AM

Chicago at the witching hour. Agent Hahn behind the wheel, driving me toward the crossroads to sell my soul. Robert Johnson did it; shook hands with the devil and learned to play the guitar like no one had before. Robert died at twenty-seven, howling on his hands and knees.

Neon dreams flash the passenger window. In a matter of minutes Chicago's River North will feel very different. After the throbbing, vibrant nightlife has finished and the revelers sent home, the city goes into a kind of shock for an hour. Block by block these bars and diners close, the hum of their a/c quits, and the neons blink out, the colorful splashes replaced by gray and steamy July heat. During this hour the streets quickly lose their possibilities; silent shadows rise, the alley air sours, and the playground becomes nocturnal. Every night on the job we watch it happen, and wait with our handguns and handcuffs, cups of coffee and gallows humor. Humor helps because this next hour—not night, not morning—is when the really strange shit happens. Robert Cray's "Night Patrol."

Hahn's Pontiac feels dirty, like germs you can't see, like infections that start small and take you over. She'll have me do Robbie Steffen first, then take what he says and go after Buff. Then who knows, I'll have sold my soul to Agent Hahn, I should be capable of anything. Won't be a cop anymore, that's for sure.

Maybe that's what happened to Robbie. Maybe Buff saw stuff in

Vietnam that thirty-plus years of ghetto failure finally convinced him to take money. Shit happens, stars align—Furukawa's Dr. Ota hits the front page with the Olympic rebid, White Flower Lý digs out her vials of plague, enlists Buff from the good old days, and *bingo,* they're all there with the devil at the crossroads.

But why drag Bobby Vargas into it? I've been on the good-guy side of the witching hour all my life. I don't harm children; I don't cruise for kid prostitutes pimped from doorways or troll for the runaways finding each other like magnets, grouping up for safety in the alleys nobody will want till the sun comes up. I don't roll drunks or mug girls who parked brave.

I was a good guy. Arleen needs to know that; I deserve one last little victory before I tape on the wire. I'm me, not the Bobby Vargas who puts his hands down little kids' pants.

I dial instead of text. Arleen answers a sleepy "Hello?"

"Hi. It's Bobby . . . Vargas, I—"

Dreamy, sorta Southern "Hi," warm and soft.

"Sorry to call so late."

Sleepy, like she's hugging her pillow. "That's okay. I'm glad."

"I just wanted you to know, you know, ah, it was great seeing you today. Better than great. Been thinking about you all day."

"Me, too."

"Really?"

"Uh-huh. Feels good, Bobby, so good I don't know what to say."

I smile into my window. "Good luck, you know, at the theater." Pause. "And, ah, don't believe anything you hear about me, okay? I'm chasing bad people who are trying to put me together. It's a cop thing, but it isn't true."

Silence, then: "I know Bobby Vargas; I told you, heart to heart." Muffled sounds of sheets I wish I was under. "You're not the only one in trouble." Her voice strengthens. "After the Shubert, win or lose, maybe we could sit down . . . like before when it was just us."

"I'm in. Promise not to believe what you hear."

"After the Shubert, then."

"Remember, the stuff they'll say or print isn't true."

"I already know that." A breathy "Bye," and Arleen hangs up.

I sit back in the Pontiac's seat and feel the smile. Somebody important trusts me. Someone who sounds like Anita Baker on a happy day, smells like Sunday-morning cinnamon rolls, and vibes so good you think about her instead of the crossroads you're approaching.

Hahn says, "Ground control to Bobby."

My smile dies. "Your deal with Robert Johnson didn't work out too well for Robert."

She nods. "Always better someone else braves-up and does the work for you."

"Robert wasn't enough? Gotta get me, too?"

"Hero time, Bobby. Time to walk it like you big bad Chicago cops talk it."

Face rub, eyes shut, exhale into my hands. *Sure, I remember Bobby Vargas, the rat, that spic Mexican who gave up his team. Candy-ass motherfucker.*

"No wire. And I'm no hero. Tell me what you want from Steffen and I'll go get it."

SUNDAY, 4:15 AM

Mercy Hospital is drab faded cubes stacked in the elbow of two rumbling eight-lane highways. Not the best neighborhood, but now advertised as walkable from Chinatown since the State Street projects were torn down or converted to "apartments." Bad, dangerous motherfuckers don't live in "apartments."

Hahn eyes me, sensing I may fold. She removes a handful of change from her pocket that she drops on the console between us. The fingers of her right hand line up the coins while she talks. "In Europe, before they had mega-dense populations centers like we do here, a strain of the plague less potent than the Unit 731 strain killed seventy-five million people, every third person on the European continent. Fleas, same as Dr. Ota tested in rural China, brought the germs from Asia by accident on wooden ships. Since then, the plague has been weaponized—first by Dr. Ota in World War II, then by us, then by the Russians.

"The 'modern' plague includes a highly effective airborne dispersal system, as witnessed by Dr. Bill Patrick in 1968 upwind of the Johnston Atoll one thousand miles southwest of Hawaii. At the time, Dr. Patrick was a top biological combat scientist attached to the U.S. Army at Fort Detrick. While Patrick watched, a U.S. Marine Phantom jet overflew a series of barges loaded with hundreds of caged rhesus monkeys. Patrick says the laydown killed half."

Hahn organizes her coins into stacks. "He concluded that a similar jet doing a modest laydown over Los Angeles would produce the death rate of a ten-megaton hydrogen bomb. Dr. Patrick said that *forty years* ago. Lotta scientific water under the bridge since then."

Hahn's fingers move the coin stacks together. "Downtown Chicago, twice the size of what L.A. was then."

My eyes drift to our skyscraper skyline. Two days ago I was fine. I turn to her. "Are you making a Roger Corman movie?"

"And your sergeant, Buff Anderson, helped White Flower Lý bring it here. And at least one of your fellow cops is threatening to use it." Hahn extends an envelope with "731" handwritten in the upper left corner—my credentials "proving" I'm a player, an unknown silent partner—and drops the envelope in my lap. She says, "Robbie Steffen is our first answer. Anything we can get from him is worth the risk."

Stare. "Assuming you're not full of shit. Assuming I like trapping policemen."

Her voice hardens. "*Somebody*, probably one of his partners, tried to kill Robbie thirteen hours ago. He'll think you were part of it so you better be convincing . . . or he kills you. Or worse, his blackmail crew, or Furukawa, make a mistake and we have to get biblical to clean it up."

Robbie Steffen has a private room adjacent to ICU but not in it. The guards on his door are uniformed Chicago cops; one I know. The uniform I don't know jumps up, pointing me back down the hall. "Nah, nah; get the fuck outta here."

"Robbie wants to see me."

The cop shoves me backward. "Ain't no little kids in there."

"Fuck you." I shove back. "You don't know shit."

"I know you're a spic, fucking greaser we shouldn't have let in our country in the first place." He shoves again.

I knock his hand away, pivot, and half trip. "You're positive, huh?

'Cause I'm not an American? Or 'cause you've seen the evidence they don't have?" I spit in his face.

The cop I know jumps between us—Steve, Rita, and I played his wedding last year at Park West. We both stumble to the hallway wall, his face in mine. "Easy. Bobby, you must want to go to prison. We have to write down everyone who comes up here."

Behind him, his partner wipes at his face. "Spic mother*fucker.* Let him go, Dave. I'll kick his ass to Mexico."

"Yeah, Dave. Let me go."

"Stop talking, turn around, and somehow I didn't see you."

We dance, but no closer to Dave's partner. "Can't do it. Here to see your patient."

Dave keeps his hands up between me and his partner and barks back over his shoulder. "Pauly, calm the fuck down. Get on the door." Dave turns back to me. "Cool?"

I nod, glaring at Dave's partner glaring back. Dave pulls out his notebook. "What's your badge number?"

I tell him. Dave stays between me, his partner, and the door to Robbie Steffen.

"Can't just go in. Steffen's bodyguards have to agree. And it's four thirty in the morning, in case your watch is broken."

"Steffen wants to see me."

Dave stays with me, then tells his partner to find out. Dave's partner taps the door five times. A voice asks him something and he steps inside. Thirty seconds pass. The partner returns with a serious fellow in a black suit and a wire in his ear. Toddy Pete's bodyguard at the Levee Grill could've been this guy or his twin. The suit eyes me carefully; he probably heard the commotion. "May I see an ID?"

I show my wallet, sans badge, and tell him I'm on suspension. He nods, then backs up into Robbie's room. A minute passes. The suit returns. Politely, he says he'll have to frisk me. He's thorough, professional, and dead serious in his movements. My cell phone is in his hand when it rings. He pops it, decides it's okay, and hands it to me still ringing.

Tania Hahn says, "When you hear your brother's name, act like Ruben sent you."

"What?"

"Ruben sent you."

Hahn clicks off. The black suit says something. I stare at my phone. *Ruben sent me?*

The suit says, "Understand?"

"Huh?"

"In the room, don't step past me. Any move forward and I'll respond at full capacity." The suit doesn't seem to care that I'm a child molester. "Are we clear?"

"Right. No problem."

The suit backs through the door and motions me to follow. Behind him, Robbie is in his bed bent thirty degrees to sitting. A second guard steps out behind me after I pass the bathroom; I'm now sandwiched, speaking to Robbie over the first bodyguard's shoulder.

Bandages crisscross Robbie Steffen's chest; his right hand grips a Glock automatic. With difficulty he says, "If you intend leaving Mercy's parking lot alive, this better be the best story I ever heard."

Ruben sent me?

I ease out Hahn's Unit 731 envelope and let Robbie see it. He has the bodyguard facing me read the inscription, then tells me to drop the envelope on the foot of the bed. Robbie pushes himself up under the sheets, Glock tight in his hand, eyes the envelope and says: "I'm listening."

I nod at the black suits sandwiching me. "Don't think you'll want witnesses."

Robbie doesn't want witnesses, but he doesn't want to die, either. "We frisked him?" The suit nods. Robbie grips his Glock. "Wait outside."

They hesitate. One points me to the wall under the TV. "Shoulders on the paint." Then tells Robbie, "Up to you, but if he comes off the wall I'd shoot him. We'll put a cold piece in his hand and call it self-defense."

Robbie aims the Glock at me. I flatten against the wall and both bodyguards leave. Robbie eyes me and the envelope. "So?"

I offer the envelope. "Not going on tape."

"Ruben think that'll keep him alive?"

Gut punch. My brother's name. "Read it. We got business."

"Business? All of a sudden I know you?"

I offer the envelope again. "You wanna get paid, read it. You wanna die, shoot me."

Robbie lifts the Glock with both hands and aims at my heart, then tells me to step forward and open the envelope. I do both, extracting a page sealed into a tight, see-through plastic letter holder. The page appears old; it has a government seal at the top and bottom that may be Imperial Japan circa World War II. There are two paragraphs of what Hahn said are Japanese characters; the letter is signed and dated. I extend him the page.

He points the page to the bedsheet covering his legs, his eyes and the Glock on me. "That it?"

I drop the signed page on his sheet, then pull out four four-by-five photos. The first photo is of a metal-and-glass receptacle being attached to the fuselage of an unmarked vintage plane. At the bottom of the photograph it reads "infected fleas" in blue ink. I show it to Robbie, who does not want to touch it.

The next photo is an aerial shot, looking down past the same receptacle to the ground below flooded with soldiers aiming their rifles upward. A plume of smoke trails the receptacle. The same blue ink reads "October 27. Ningbo, Zhejiang Province, Chinese Army." The third photograph is the same plane on the ground, a tall thin Japanese man in uniform stepping out. At the bottom the blue ink reads "Lt. Gen. Shiro Ishii, Director, Epidemic and Water Supply Unit." The fourth photograph is the front page of a Chinese newspaper. A large headline roofs a photograph of bodies littering a village. The blue ink reads "Results."

I toss the last photo to the others piled just below Robbie's knees and retreat to the wall. He bends, winces at the pain, then falls back with a deep exhale. He breathes until he's steady, then uses a pencil to move one photo after another close enough to view. When he's done, he studies me. Thinks about where we are in the crime, what I'm doing here, what he knows that I don't.

"Talk."

"Furukawa."

Robbie blinks, breathing with his mouth open, then stares, reading me for the trap. "Assuming you know what the fuck you're talking about—" He stops, squints. "Pull up your shirt."

I pull up my shirt. "Furukawa won't pay."

"Bullshit. They have to pay."

I shrug and roll out the lie. "White Flower wants to use one vial . . . at the 10K this afternoon. Lý does that, we're facing feds, not corporate criminals."

"Fucking psycho Vietcong. Her and his Irish bitch put a bow on me for the Koreans. Set me up in that fuckin' alley. And your brother let 'em."

"Wasn't Ruben. I wouldn't be standing here hoping you don't shoot me."

Robbie glares. "Not Ruben and Lý? Some cocktail waitress put the whole thing together?" Robbie's face is gray-red and blotchy; he can't take much more anger. "Tell your brother"—breath—"I want my full share." Wince. "And if he thinks he can fuck me like he did the Koreans"—Robbie tries to push himself farther up in the bed but can't—"then he's dead." Wince. "And so are you. Two less child molesters for Chicago to worry about."

"I came here to tell you it wasn't Ruben. And that we have to rein in White Flower."

Robbie stares, hand tightening on the Glock. "Am I missing something? 'Cause I'm not a fucking Mexican? White Flower is your brother's squeeze. How do we figure I can run her?"

"We thought maybe Toddy Pete could help."

Silence. Robbie goes a hundred percent wary. "You did, huh?"

SUNDAY, 4:45 AM

The stairwell on Mercy's east side feels like the morgue. I steady into the concrete wall and cue up Ruben's number. Three times he doesn't answer. Sweat stings my eyes. I call a Yellow Cab, tell them to pick me up outside the emergency room.

Ruben. My brother.

My eyes squeeze shut and I vomit down the stairs.

The railing keeps me upright. I vomit again, stumble back sucking fouled air, and my shoulders bang the wall. The heels of both hands wipe my cheeks and eyes. I spit bile, breathing short. My jaw clamps. I twist and kick the shit out of the metal door. Kick it again. "NO. JUST FUCKING NO." The echoes beat back at me and I kick again. My stomach cramps me to half.

Ruben can't be part of Hahn's horror show, can't be Robbie and White Flower Lý's partner, can't be willing to kill people for *money.* Sweat wipe. Ruben's my brother. He can't, wouldn't, couldn't do that. Just fucking NO. Maybe, hopefully, they tricked him, or if they didn't, they don't have Hahn's Hokkaido package; they're scamming a mass murderer and his corporate protector. Ruben would be a crooked cop, but he wouldn't be a murderer. 'Cause he can't be.

And Robbie never said Buff's name. And he would've if Buff was part of the blackmail, wouldn't he? Bile burns in my throat. I start down the steps. Who knows? But Robbie damn near shot me after I said Toddy Pete's name, that's damn sure a fact. Robbie smelled me fishing; I could see that in his eyes, even clouded with painkillers. Had we been in an alley with no witnesses, I'd be dead.

Ground floor. Hallway, movement, nurses, orderlies, business as usual. I semi-sleepwalk through the halls, buy a Coke from a machine to rinse out the bile. Outside the emergency room, a Yellow Cab idles with his windows up. I get in and tell him, "Wolfe City on Halsted."

The cab drops me at my car across from Wolfe City. The limos are gone, the curbs clear other than my Honda and empty King Cobra forty-ouncers. Above the door, the WCRS neon is dark. The door lever rattles in my hand. The great, life-changing, good things have quit happening. I press the doorbell just in case, then the intercom button and lean into the speaker . . . to say what?

My phone rings, Hahn's number on the screen. By now she knows I ran; knew my car was here. I'm not ready for her plan to crucify Ruben. Don't want to hear it, believe it, know it. I point my car north toward Ruben's condo and call him again. "Call me, Ruben. Now. I just left Robbie Steffen. You gotta talk to me."

I turn onto South Michigan at Cermak. Have to find Ruben. Now. Before—

Hahn calls again. For twenty-five blocks, I call Ruben everywhere I can imagine him being at five AM on a Sunday. City workers are already out stacking street barricades on the sidewalk, prepping Grant Park, downtown, and Millennium Park for this afternoon's Furukawa 2016 Olympics 10K fund-raiser. Right turn on Randolph. Ruben's building is at the far east end overlooking the lake. He could watch the 10K from his fifteenth-floor windows. I park in Ruben's drop-off circle, tell the doorman and then the deskman/security I'm Ruben's brother. One recognizes me. They let me in. I elevator up, pound Ruben's door, get nothing, then elevator down to his parking place. No car.

If just half of this stuff is true, Ruben could be in serious jeopardy somewhere. His partner White Flower Lý, Hahn, the Koreans, Robbie Steffen. Ruben's dancing in the big time with forty million on the table. Find Ruben. He's gotta be somewhere.

I bail downtown for Lawrence Avenue, no idea what or where to search other than Koreatown. But it's five AM on a Sunday, and even if mob guys were wearing signs, they won't be out now. Hahn keeps calling. Three trips up and down Lawrence Avenue yield nothing. Maybe I could modify her plan, use what she knows to . . . to what? Warn Ruben? Save him? My stomach rolls. Stop him? I need a gun.

Really need a gun. Ruben has partners who won't want to be saved or stopped.

I have a gun at my apartment, ten minutes northeast. Sneak in, turn on the a/c, grab a gun, touch things that prove I'm me. Risky—I'm already out on bond—exhale—for child rape. Any hallway confrontation with the little Irish girl "victim" or a 911 call from her mother and I'm either shot or in handcuffs doing a TV perp-walk to the street. I punch Recall on Hahn's number and head toward my apartment to sneak in.

Hahn answers on the second ring. "Taking big chances, Bobby, hoping these folks don't do something stupid while you do."

"Tough night."

"Today will be worse. Tell me you didn't warn your brother."

"Can't find him."

Her voice hardens. "I can help Ruben *and you,* but it has to be now."

My head throbs. "If you knew about Ruben from the beginning—assuming it's true—why drag me in? Why not—"

"We're about to lose control of the *plague,* Bobby."

"*If* they have it; if you aren't full of shit."

Hahn takes a breath. "Had I told you about Ruben, you wouldn't have believed me."

"And I'm supposed to now? Because Robbie Steffen says so?"

"If it wasn't Ruben's name, you'd be kicking in their door already."

"You say you're gonna help Ruben. How?"

"Tell me—in person—every word Robbie said. While we're talking, we'll find your brother. You'll save him by helping me trick him and Buff Anderson and anyone else who has their hand in or out."

"Me. Trick my brother, for you?"

"*That's* why I involved you. Why the CIA and the mayor let me involve you. You're the one person right next to both suspects, and the one person we could trust to do the right thing. Fast." Pause. "And you *will* do the right thing for two reasons—save you and maybe your brother, and save innocent civilians if Ruben and White Flower Lý do have the Hokkaido package."

"I didn't hear you mention the U.S. attorney on your team."

"She's on her own team. Best we keep her and the FBI dark."

No lights on at my apartment building. I pull into my parking space and kill the engine. "How can you find Ruben?"

"Trust me."

"*Trust?* Somebody—probably you—makes me a child rapist so you can save me? Just give you my brother because *you* say he's guilty. He knows Robbie Steffen, big deal."

Pause. "What if they have it, Bobby? The Hokkaido package—"

"I'm not giving you my brother."

"Running out of time, Bobby. Maybe Ruben's crew uses some this afternoon. At the Furukawa 10K."

"Not doing it."

"I'll give you one last chance to save your brother. Meet me at the bottom of Chinatown in an hour. I have someone for you to chat with. Maybe you and Ruben can have it both ways."

I flip the phone shut. I can't be talking about . . . what I'm talking about. I climb the stairs, creep the hall—my hall—past the door of my Irish neighbor and her "sodomized" nine-year-old daughter. *Jesus,* that sounds awful.

I key my door and shut it behind me. Bobby Vargas lives here, the

Bobby Vargas who returns every night after policing the city the best he can.

A wave of safe harbor washes over me. *Me* is an accumulation of the things I've done, not charges and innuendo and TV cameras and disgusted, angry glares.

A cleansing wave, affirmation, proof that I could line up if the media and courts will let me. My very first guitar leaning against the wall, signed by Ruben on the back and Howlin' Wolf on the front. A Wolfe City poster framed in scrap wood from 2120 South Michigan, the Chess Records building that Willie Dixon has now. Dreams regular kids have, regular grown-ups have. My parents' pictures; Ruben and me as kids; Gang Team 1269—me, Jason, Buff, Jewboy playing softball, fishing for lake coho we never caught, sunburned stupid in Jamaica at Eggy's Bohemian, drinking parasol drinks with both hands. Ruben in uniform, receiving his first of nine meritorious service awards.

I reach for the smallest photograph. It's in a soft plastic wallet holder I carried till I was twenty-five—me and Arleen on her stoop, heads together, shoulders touching, both of us with sidewalk chalk in our hands. For years, and at the oddest times, I'd think of her, us. Boyfriend-girlfriend, but way beyond—we were promise partners, a big colorful life outside the gray violence of the Four Corners, happy ever after. *So absolutely real* . . . then winter came and she was gone. Everything we were and were going to be, was gone.

My guitar stares at me. The best but saddest songs I've ever written are about us and the death of that dream, sad enough I don't play them. Then suddenly today, as the threats and accusations mount, there she is, five foot seven and smiling. Joan of Arc walks through the fire and kisses my cheek, tells me *she* believes me. Me and her, one more time. Makes me dizzy. Proof I guess that God does, in fact, work in mysterious ways.

The sun's up. Neighbors getting ready for work will see my car. Horrified neighbors who *know* I'm guilty, know I'm John Wayne Gacy up there in his window staring as their little girls walk to school.

I take a fast shower to wash off Gacy and wake up. I don't look in the mirror, or at my pictures, or at my couch. I grab clothes and the gun I'll need more than happy ever after to meet Tania Hahn, and leave.

In the hallway, my neighbor's door stops me. I want to walk past, but don't. I stare, visualizing the door splintering as I kick it in. Mrs. McKenna and daughter Katherine terrified at a *real* threat. I rock from heel to toe, twelve inches from mother-and-daughter's door, the daughter I raped and sodomized and threatened to kill if she talked.

Policeman bubbles up in the rage. Who does this Irish mother and daughter know that I know? Hahn? Danny Vacco? The U.S. attorney? The Korean mafia? Dr. Ota at Furukawa? What are Mrs. McKenna's sins? What or whom does she fear so much that putting me in prison as a child molester is a better option?

She'd tell me if I put a gun in her face. Oh, yeah, she'd tell me, because if I had to, I'd look at her daughter like she says I did. We all have family to protect, no? Why is theirs better, more important than mine?

Kick the door down, let's find out.

I leave before the rage and filth overcome the last of my judgment.

The drive south toward Chinatown doesn't help. I keep calling Ruben and get no response. I want to cry, to pound the dashboard into powder. Call Arleen Brennan and just fly away. Jenny and Forrest, Arleen and Bobby—we will save each other just like we promised. The sun glitters the lake on Lake Shore Drive. I dial Arleen's number, but don't finish the call, don't know what to say, finally typing a text message wishing her luck with her *Streetcar* audition.

Except Arleen doesn't need to be saved, she's about to become a star, and a Vargas around her neck would be the end of that dream. The Vargas brothers are from the Four Corners in every possible way, and we're never leaving.

SUNDAY, 8:00 AM

Chinatown's still dirty from Saturday night. Hahn pulls up to my car just west of Wentworth and says, "Get in." She's wearing last night's clothes, drives a block on Twenty-sixth, and turns left on Wells before she gets to Ricobene's. "I said I'd help you and your brother and I will, but you gotta get with the program." She nods at me. "Before Ruben buries our chances. The fight between him and Buff Anderson—"

"What fight?"

"The two of them went at it early this morning in the lot at Area 4. Twenty cops broke it up. Your pal Jewboy Mesrow hit Ruben from behind, knocked him over his car." She jerks a sudden hard left veering through a chain-link fence that's been recently knocked down. Instantly, we're under the elevated Dan Ryan access lanes, avoiding the tall columns and concrete bridging that blocks the eastern sunlight into checkerboard shadows. Her tires ricochet gravel and something rustles behind my seat. Hahn hits the brakes. Her Pontiac slides to a stop as dust clouds engulf us. A blanket sits up in the backseat, then half falls away. I cough, have to blink twice to see what I'm seeing.

Danny Vacco, La Raza street king, handcuffed in the backseat, naked to the waist. Duct tape over his mouth—

Commotion in the dust cloud. I twist to the windshield. Hahn has stopped us just short of two homeless men, one of whom staggers away; the other falls back over into the trash. She puts the Pontiac in Park, reaches across her hip, digs out a 9-millimeter Beretta, and tosses it in my lap.

"As promised."

Danny Vacco eyes me, then Hahn, then me again.

"All yours, Bobby, shoot him, gun's cold. Don't worry about the upholstery, car isn't mine."

I dig the Beretta out of my lap, drop the clip, check it full, then rack the slide—loaded—replace the clip, but don't lower the hammer.

Hahn says, "My word's good; for this *and* your brother."

I stare at Danny Vacco, the brown pockmarked cheeks and forehead. The faded blue Twenty-Trey tats circling his neck. Danny's pushing thirty-five, has poisoned my neighborhood for years. Ruben and I had a chance to kill him in a confrontation years ago and didn't. My decision that day has come back to haunt or destroy a lot of people in the Four Corners.

I stare at him. "Little Paul?"

No answer; wary eyes.

My hand squeezes the Beretta he can't see but knows I have. The headache hardens my tone. "Little Paul's mom? The girl in my building?"

No answer. Danny Vacco's street-king piece-of-shit face is twenty-four inches away.

Harsher. "I rape children, right?" Louder. "Sodomize them? You know what that means?"

No answer, no expression, but full attention. His eyes dip to the seat back between us, a silencer of sorts. I stare, hate clouding my eyes. My finger tightens on the trigger.

Danny Vacco shows nothing but street armor.

I keep staring, hoping he'll do something that will help me commit my first murder. "This spic right here is a gutless cocksucker coward, that's a hundred percent positive, but I'm not murdering him. Not today."

He and Hahn and I wait to see if I mean it, then, seemingly surprised, Hahn waves for the Beretta. I hesitate at a second opportunity lost, then drop the hammer and give the Beretta to her, afraid that if I keep the gun I'll use it. Hahn points the Beretta over the seat. With her other hand she rips the duct tape off Danny Vacco's mouth and slaps it on his shoulder.

"Here's the deal, Danny. I have some bigger business to do." She taps her watch. "So you tell me where Little Paul's mother is, and she better not be dead. Then we go see her and you tell her to get her kid back from Child Services. Two, you tell Little Paul to say he lied. Three, you get the two debs who think they're witnesses to recant. Four, you tell me who gave up my girlfriend and me in the red Toyota." Pause. "We do this right now and real fast. Any questions?"

Danny eyes me, then our location, then the little blonde pointing the 9-millimeter at him. *"Esta puta loca."*

Hahn blinks, then thin-lines her lips. "I work in Miami. Cuba, too, sometimes." She pulls her ID and shows it to Danny. "We have different rules than cops."

Danny smirks.

FLASH; EXPLOSION. The Beretta kicks in her hand. Danny bounces into the door, a hole smoking above where his left shoulder was.

"Jesus." I reach for my door handle and miss. "There's a gas tank back there."

The car's air is cordite. Hahn drops the hammer and holds up one finger to me, asking me to sit tight. I do, sort of frozen.

She speaks street Spanish to Danny. "Bro, not fuckin' 'round. My dog here has to focus on my business, you know? Big business." She waits, then slides back into English. "Give me what I want or I will paint my backseat with your little Mexican heart. Then I'll give your two debs five grand each to recant. Then I'll give your two street captains ten grand each to say it's okay, tell 'em to get Little Paul to do the same." Pause. " 'Cause that how it work, homes, in CIA land."

Hahn glances me, waits, then shakes her head at Danny acting unafraid. "Bro, you're dead, right now, right here at breakfast time, instead of walking tall, selling rock, killing Latin Kings. I'm out thirty grand, but to my bosses that's lunch money. Then—and here's the good part—after you're dead and your two captains roll for me, get my dog here cleaned up, I'll grab both your captains, put 'em in the very same backseat you're in, and ask, 'Who gave up the Toyota?' They won't want to tell me, so I'll shoot one. The other one talks, but I'll shoot him, too." Smile. "My dog's clean. I know who to kill for the Toyota, and your hated rivals, the Latin Kings, now own the Four Corners and chicken-fuck all your girlfriends."

Danny's listening, adding up if it could happen. For sure he's only seen the CIA in movies, but Danny's a Twenty-Trey, stone-killer street king, and he didn't get there by birth. If he's in any way responsible for Sheila Lopez dying, Danny Vacco isn't showing it. He cocks a one-inch smile. "*Soldado* ain't doin' none of that."

"See, the Latin Kings can't fuck my girlfriend 'cause she dead." Hahn un-cocks, then re-cocks the Beretta, looks at it, then Danny. "We both know this 9-millimeter is double action, but cocking it is what they do in the movies to say 'last chance.' And since you're a cold-rolled, twelve-inch dick who gets his life lessons from rap videos, I thought I'd give you one last chance. *Comprende, amigo?*"

Danny smooches at her.

Hahn fires twice. Danny's heart explodes through his shirt. His handcuffed hands flap once in the cordite smoke. Hahn already has her door open.

I yell: "What the *fuck*!" and jump halfway out the other side.

Hahn drops the Beretta in an evidence bag held by the now-standing homeless man. She peels almost-invisible gloves, gives them to him, and turns to me. "I know Danny deserved it, but you shouldn't have shot him. And all that stuff I told Danny I was planning for your witnesses? It's already done. That's the good news: Bobby Vargas just bought two slices of public redemption—you're no longer Little Paul's child molester and Danny Vacco's too dead to throw any altar boys at you. Bad news is, you're Danny Vacco's killer."

Dan Ryan traffic rumbles overhead. I'm backing away from the car, into bridging and deep shadows on three sides. The homeless man disappears with the murder weapon. Hahn loops the Pontiac and stops ten feet from me. "Now you help me corner Ruben and your sergeant—"

"Are you crazy! You just murdered a guy!"

She squints like she doesn't understand. "Not me. I didn't shoot him."

I scan one-eighty for her phantom partners, at the very least the other homeless man who has to be watching. A Mrs Baird's bread truck slow-rolls outside the fence on Wells. My prints are on the gun. I told at least two people I was going to kill Danny Vacco. Hahn's face has no expression. I step forward. "How'd you get Danny in your car? Danny Vacco's a gangster, street smart times a hundred. You didn't grab him, he *got* in your car . . . because you and him were already doing business."

Hahn shrugs, but doesn't step back. "That's a stretch, but possible."

"You put him up to Little Paul. Conned Vacco into your car today and—"

"And I had him shoot my girlfriend and me in the Toyota?" Hahn's eyes harden. "Your brother's in way over his head, Bobby, screwing with people who aren't street, who aren't stupid, and who have all the money in the world." She points toward downtown. "Furukawa's 10K starts in eight hours. I'm not privy to your brother's blackmail negotiations, but I know I'd threaten it."

I glance at Danny dead in the backseat of her Pontiac. "That how Ruben finishes?"

"Not if he gives me a choice. Dead cops cause a lot more heat than dead gangsters."

"Tell me where he is. I'll talk to him first, then you can—"

Hahn shakes her head. "We go together. You wear a wire, if he doesn't cooperate, we grab him."

"Fuck you."

SIREN.

Red, blue, and white lights careen onto Wells a block north at Twenty-sixth Street. I spin into the deep shadows and concrete bridging. Hahn yells, "Bobby!" Tires squeal and crunch the gravel as I sprint down a chain-link fence line crowded with wrecked cars. The siren quits. The fence turns ninety degrees. I slam into it, bounce big, land on one foot and fall. I crawl between cars to a far concrete column, climb twelve feet of chain link, teeter, bear-hugging the column, twist over, rip my pants from knee to hip, and jump.

I land hard, roll, jump up, hear squad cars, then sprint west, running three blocks of Twenty-seventh—all-out, past kids, cars, trucks—to the Norfolk Southern tracks, jump the fence, and flatten in the trash and overgrown grass.

More sirens. Gasping. Dogs bark, flies buzz. Hundred-degree air.

Maybe Tania Hahn *is* the devil. My heart slows to gunfight, then twenty over normal. Sirens, but no squad-car lights over here. Window curtains pull back in a third-floor six-flat and a head sticks out. The dogs won't shut up.

My car's a mile away in Chinatown. Can't stay here. I crouch, then tramp weeds north, hugging the tracks' embankment. At the first cross street viaduct I have no choice but to climb to the tracks and walk silhouetted against the sky. In this neighborhood I'm a transient the barking dogs know shouldn't be here. At the viaduct's other side I drop and skitter down the embankment.

My phone beeps that I have a message. I duck to my haunches. The phone is bloody and slips in my hand, a long cut on my leg. The message—*finally*—is from Ruben: "*Buey,* where you been? Took some magic, but Barlow's straightened out; he'll take care of that little girl in your building. But, *vato,* hey, we gotta talk about who you seein'. These people fillin' your head; sendin' you places you gotta stop arriving. Call me. We can make what's chasing you stop, but you have to help."

I punch Ruben's number; it rings through to voice mail. My phone beeps call-waiting. I answer, "Ruben?"

Jason Cowin says, "What *in the fuck* are you and Ruben into?"

A squad car turns northbound onto Stewart Avenue, nothing between me and their handcuffs but a low fence and high grass. The cop eyes the grass that hides me, then the embankment as he rolls north.

Jason barks, "Bobby?"

"Yeah. I have to find Buff and Ruben."

"What the fuck is goin' on? Buff and Jewboy fighting Ruben? Little girls pointing at your dick? Federal judges bailing you out? You ain't talking to us. The truth, for chrissake."

I watch the squad car turn. "Is Buff at work? There's something chasing him and me."

"No shit. He was looking for you. Went to meet somebody and some psycho Asian bitch shot him four times."

"What?"

"Still alive, but barely." Breath. "Jewboy was in the car with him." Jason chokes, breathing short in the phone. "DOA when they got Walter to Mercy."

18 A STREETCAR NAMED DESIRE

ARLEEN BRENNAN

SUNDAY, 9:00 AM

"Nine o'clock!"

Julie jumps back. I throw the sheet and leap out of bed. "I had to be up *two hours* ago." Blink, scramble. "You promised—"

"You were out cold. I made an executive decision." She grabs my shoulders. "Plenty of time. Everything's in the bathroom. Blanche's clothes are hanging right here." She points at the door. "Clean up, catch a cab ninety minutes from now. Even you can't take that long to get ready."

"Sorry." I kiss her, then push her to the door. "Me. Get ready. Bye." Julie backs through and I throw the deadbolt her key opened. My script's on the floor. I'll clean up, make up, dress up . . . then speed-read what I already know by heart. Then I'll . . . big exhale . . . then I'll do the absolute best I can.

I take the 9-millimeter to the bathroom and lock the door. The shower works wonders; clean is almost an orgasm. The clothes, not so much. I "Blanche" them up, belt the slip dress that's too big, and wish for bodice frills I don't have. Ruben's knuckles left bumps I can't cover but color that I can. The strawberry blond hair goes into the semi-bun that I can release mid-scene. Blanche drank; Blanche flirted; Blanche wielded a biting snobbery to lie about her lost social standing. Underneath it all, Blanche was desperate, only a gentleman of means could save her.

The 9-millimeter is on the bed. I do a turn for Julie's antique mirror.

The veined, aging silver reflects a tragic calculated lie in a cheap evening dress; a desperate woman unraveling toward suicide or a mental-institution future. My hand gently strokes my hair; I will not *unravel,* I'm a Mississippi Southern belle aging much too fast due to unreasonable circumstances, standing in my sister's squalid French Quarter apartment. I can smell Stanley, her apish husband, his friends; their lack of culture, their coarseness and vulgarity—

Door knock.

I jolt out of the French Quarter, grab the 9-millimeter, and two-hand it at the door.

Julie wouldn't tell anyone I'm hiding here. Would she? Unless . . . they made her. I step to the door. In the peephole is Tracy Moens—jeans, Nirvana T-shirt, ponytail, ball cap—she appears to be alone in the tiny section of hallway I can see. Can't tell if she's nervous. I grab Ruben's .38 from my purse, slide the gun under the mattress, unlock the door, then jerk it open using the door's blind side as cover.

Moens walks in, peeking around the door as she does. I slam the door behind her, expecting a shoulder crash that doesn't come. Moens squares up, sees my 9-millimeter aimed at her face, and stumbles back. "That, ah . . . for me?"

One hand lowers the 9-millimeter, the other locks the door. "I was in Blanche DuBois; you scared me." I lay the 9-millimeter on the leatherette table by the chair.

Moens sits on the bed; spreads her fingers on my script, rubbing the pages. Then nods like we're on the actress journey together. "I asked Patti Black to run the prints on your pistol grips."

"And?"

"Are you trying to kill Ruben Vargas? For Coleen?"

"What?"

"Ruben Vargas is a dangerous fellow, Arleen; not someone I'd threaten . . . if that's what you're doing. And Robbie Steffen is almost as bad."

"Your exposé isn't a threat? Exhuming my sister isn't a threat?"

"The *Herald* and I are different. I have protection you don't."

I snatch my script from under her hand. "*You don't have act three, do you?* Your story's a sham without an ending, a grandstand to save the *Herald.*"

"We're way deeper into the story than that." She pauses, but her green eyes stay on me. "Lots of secrets, Arleen."

"One of 'em is you're a fraud who's run out of brilliance and innuendo. Show me the grips or get out."

"Something's up, Arleen, something new that involves you, Robbie Steffen, and Ruben. Ruben was in a fistfight with a sergeant early this morning, a sergeant who was on the job when Coleen was killed, a sergeant who's being deposed by the Duprees tomorrow. We could talk about that instead."

I point her to the door.

Moens stands but not to leave. "Seven hours ago you gave me pistol grips from a .38 Detective Special. The gun they came from was fired within the last twenty-four hours. The same caliber gun was used in Greektown in the Robbie Steffen shootings. Robbie Steffen and Ruben Vargas helped you with the *Streetcar* audition, according to Anne Johns, your director."

My phone vibrates.

"Yesterday you were downstairs in Julie's office thirty minutes after the shooting in Greektown, and so was *Bobby* Vargas. Five minutes after you and I left for the Shubert Theater, Ruben came by the L7. Maybe he was looking for his brother, maybe he was looking for you."

"Get out."

"An hour later you were assaulted on Rush Street just south of Hugo's by an 'unnamed assailant.' The valets described a man who could easily have been Ruben. They said the two of you were talking, then bang, you hit him and he hit you. He was dragging you toward a car when they yelled him off."

I jerk open the door. "Are you leaving, or do I throw you out?"

Moens stares. "Bad news, Arleen. The only prints on the grips . . . are yours. Your parents filed them when Coleen was murdered."

"Out, goddamnit!"

"I can help you. The cops aren't reaching under the right rocks yet, but they will be. The secrets in the Four Corners won't stay buried, Arleen. It's too late. And whatever you're into with Ruben and Robbie—"

"If you have proof someone other than Anton Dupree murdered my sister, show me." My phone vibrates again.

"I will. First we finish last night's conversation. About your mother and *father*; your mother's brother. How the secrets in the Four Corners—"

"My sister's dead. I'm not." I grab my purse, stuff the 9-millimeter in it, then the script. "Coleen's at Holy Sepulchre where she's *staying.* I'll be at the Shubert. When you and your tabloid have *proof,* call me."

Moens follows me out, talking to my back. "Detective Richard A. Hirshbeck worked Anton Dupree's third and final trial. Hirshbeck kept an informal file, sometimes called a 'street file,' on all the cases he worked. I have his file. After Anton Dupree was executed, Detective Hirshbeck wrote a letter to the state's attorney's office asking that they reopen the case. Two days before he was to meet with the state's attorney, Detective Hirshbeck died in a gang-related drive-by." Moens jumps the last three steps to the bottom. "A gang-related drive-by, Arleen, seven years *after* Hirshbeck had retired."

Downstairs the L7 isn't busy yet. I recognize Anton Dupree's father from his photograph in the paper; he's the spokesman for their lawsuit and the only surviving relative. Mr. Dupree gets up when Tracy Moens and I exit Julie's office two feet apart. No question Moens brought him here to confront me and that's what he does.

"We must have your help."

I try to sidestep him but he slides left and won't let me. Tracy blocks me from the other side. Mr. Dupree and I stare from three feet. He's about sixty, looks older, frail the way some black men do when their hair is graying and their suits are too big.

"It's the right thing to do, Ms. Brennan. For my boy; for your twin sister."

"You mean for the lawyers"—I nod at Tracy—"and this bitch's newspaper."

"No—"

"Then don't sue for the money—don't demand any; none for you, none for the lawyers. We'll all sue just because it's good for *your boy* and my sister."

"No. My boy was—"

"Your *boy,* Mr. Dupree"—I lean into his nose—"was a *rapist murderer.* My sister was *thirteen,* wearing a school uniform when your boy *fucked her to death.*" I turn to hit Tracy Moens in her perfect pretty face but she's already stepped back. A Cubs fan opens the door to enter. I shoulder into him, bounce his hat off his head, and storm up Clark Street.

SUNDAY, 11:00 AM

The gypsy cab changes lanes, trying to beat southbound traffic that shouldn't be on the street. Moens emphasized *father.* Wanted to drag my ma in as well; wants to exhume Coleen. Under my script, my purse vibrates. Shubert. Shubert. Shubert. I'm about to be late to the single biggest chance I'll ever get. I dig out the phone careful not to spill the 9-millimeter. Ruben Vargas's number is on the screen. Fifteen minutes from my moment on planet Earth and he won't leave me alone.

Be Blanche. New Orleans.

My phone vibrates again. If the window would open, I'd throw the phone out. Ruben Vargas again. That monster better not be at the theater. I touch the 9-millimeter; he better not. Robbie, either.

The phone blips in my hand before I can shut it off—911 messages. The first is a text message: "BREAK A LEG . . . BUT IN A GOOD WAY—BV." BV is Bobby Vargas. We *did* talk last night, wasn't a dream. He was so sweet; hard to imagine he and Ruben are related. I dial Bobby, get his voice mail, and tell him: "Fingers crossed, Bobby. On my way in. Love you for calling, means a lot. Bye."

The other message is from Sarah, my agent: "WHERE ARE YOU?"

Twenty years. Breathing too short. Push back in the seat. Be calm; be professional; be *ready.*

The driver turns onto Monroe. Ruben's car isn't parked out front; he's not under the marquee or at the doors. My phone vibrates again. Ruben's number on the screen. I pay the driver and jump out. Sarah has her phone in her hand and greets me chest to chest at the curb.

"Blanche!" Her hands go to my shoulders and press us apart for inspection. "Absolutely awesome. Feel good? Everyone's ready. Waiting."

Sarah's nerves make mine worse. Today I'm her new project, the flavor of the day. I matter, and have a hundred percent of her attention. Blanche DuBois stutters. I squeeze my eyes shut—be *ready.* Blanche answers that she will be, has to be.

Sarah eases back. Worried? Or she understands, knows where I am. Where Blanche is. I push down the jitters, keep the energy, hold the energy; be bold, brazen, bet it all. But professional. For us, for Blanche. Hold back, all of it inside, ready. Stanley's an animal; Ruben's an animal. Stanley, Stanley, Stanley.

Through the Monroe Street doors into the Shubert's lobby. The lobby's empty, vast, and cold. Only one black-lacquer door is open. A gaffer gives me a thumbs-up. The aisle down is side-lit dim; the theater's dark, five heads are in the tenth row, center. As I approach, Anne Johns, friend of Ruben Vargas and Robbie Steffen, rises from the seats in a black Armani jacket, jeans, cadet cap, and wire-rimmed glasses. She sidesteps seats into the aisle, every inch of her the award-winning director she is, and says, "Hi." Her tone is delicate, almost somber, as is her hand when she touches my shoulder. "We're ready when you are."

Bring it. New Orleans, postwar.

I smile patrician, 1940s Southern holding on to the last of it, and don't speak. On the elevated stage Jude Law is seated on a brass bed across from a bureau and mirror. A trunk is open on the floor with flowery dresses—Blanche's dresses, my dresses—thrown across it. A flimsy curtain hangs between him and what would be the bathroom, another curtain separates what would be the kitchen. An end table by the bed—*my bed*—a partially consumed bottle of liqueur and a glass. Under an open bowling shirt, he's wearing a strap T-shirt. A jolt straightens my back: We're doing the *rape* scene, not the pages Sarah sent.

My eyes cut to Anne Johns. She hands me the scarf I used in the first audition and squeezes it gently into my hand. "Blanche might want it for the yacht."

Mr. Shep Huntleigh's yacht. The desperate creation—the last hope—of a woman spiraling into madness. The scarf is Blanche's talisman, "proof" that her imaginary Caribbean cruise and millionaire admirer are real, that her new life is about to unfold. The scarf is my talisman as well.

Sarah walks me down the last thirty feet of descending aisle, takes my purse at the stage, and whispers, "Everything that's ever happened to you. Your sister, Coleen. All of it."

Onstage my palms are wet when I shake Jude Law's hand. I haven't looked at the audience, the five heads who own Blanche's and my future. Jude has blue-collar eyes—sexual, violent, knowing. His hand is too strong gripping mine. Feet apart, shoulder dipped, he is motionless swagger; male, control. No good wishes are offered. He is Stanley and points me to my mark in the bedroom of the cramped, steamy, New Orleans apartment he shares with my pregnant younger sister. In ten steps he is offstage to where Stanley Kowalski will enter.

Arleen Brennan ceases.

Blanche DuBois steps into the bedroom and grins, twirling on the dark edges of delirium—drunk, rejected, retreating into the last of a shattered fantasy world that will save her from past indiscretions, elevate her to a position of dignity and safety befitting a Southern woman of charm and breeding.

"Toast to the future! *My telegram has arrived at the telegraph office! Mr. Shep Huntleigh, Dallas millionaire!* Oh my, yes, he and I. Our own Belle Reve and a return to the genteel days of finery and distinction."

I pirouette for the bureau's mirror and an audience of future admirers, glorious me in my white satin evening gown—and stumble. It's the heat, or possibly I've had a bit too many of my drinks for the day, and the exhilaration that comes when a lady prepares for . . . for her millionaire to whisk her away.

I smile out into the dark apartment and the night beyond. "Oh, what a wonderful life we will have in Dallas, Mr. Shep Huntleigh and I! Never again will I encounter those who think me pretentious, my overly fragile chin too high. *Me,* of all people, gossiped about as a shopworn Southern belle who may have known too many men, searched too diligently through the loneliness for the safety a respectable marriage can provide."

I pirouette, thanking a gentleman for a compliment.

"Have I lied? *Why?* Because I tell what *ought* to be the truth? That is no sin; a woman must protect herself in this world. The brutes and lowborn may savage me for a harmless prevarication, but not my faraway millionaire. No, no; Mr. Shep Huntleigh of Dallas knows me to be a beauty, a beauty of mind and a richness of spirit. This gown, all my dresses, will be spotless again—every one of my detractors will see—my rhinestone tiara will shine, no more casting my pearls before swine. Ha-ha!"

A door bangs open in the kitchen, then shut. The light pops on. Stanley Kowalski, my younger sister's apelike husband, a Polack of the worst sort, cradles a bag of quart beer bottles under the arm of his bowling shirt. He's been to the maternity hospital, but liquor is in his posture as well. He eyes my white satin gown and whistles low.

I want none of his sweaty attentions. "How is my sister?"

"Tomorrow's Stella's baby day; you and I are on our own tonight." His tone adds mock politeness men such as he foster. "You're all dressed up fine and well."

"Why, I have an urgent telegram, from a former admirer—"

Stanley grins his apish mouth, nodding. "Why, sure you do." He sets down his bottles and removes his shirt, leering his disbelief, knowing how his undressing will affect me.

"Please. Close the curtains before you undress any further."

Stanley shakes a bottle of beer instead, then opens it allowing the beer to foam and geyser. "Rain from heaven," he says, then offers the foamy bottle and continues his leer. "Shall we bury the hatchet and make it a loving cup?"

"No. Thank you."

"Well, it's a red-letter night for us both. You having an oil millionaire and I'm having a baby." Stanley walks into my room uninvited.

I shrink back, sensing . . .

He stops at the bureau, sets down his beer, and opens a drawer. His rough hands remove green silk pajamas that he shows me. "I wear them on special occasions, wore them on my wedding night. When they call and say you've got a son, I'll tear this coat off and wave it like a flag."

Stanley walks into the bathroom, undoing his pants. I tell his back and my bedroom, "It will be divine to have privacy once more."

From behind the bathroom door, Stanley says, "From your oil millionaire."

"Why, yes. I have been foolish, casting my pearls before swine, but no more."

"Swine, huh?"

"Yes, men like you and your friend Mr. Mitchell."

Stanley opens the bathroom door dressed in his pajamas. His tone is low, harsh, and ugly. "Swine, huh?" He ties the sash, hands lingering below his waist. "Take a look at yourself here in a worn-out Mardi Gras outfit, rented for 50 cents from some ragpicker. And with a crazy crown on. Now what kind of a queen do you think you are?"

No, all will be fine. I begin to hum "It's Only a Paper Moon."

"Do you know that I've been on to you from the start? And not once did you pull the wool over this boy's eyes."

I'll not listen. *"Only a paper moon. Sailing over a cardboard sea . . ."*

"You come in here and you sprinkle the place with powder and you spray perfume and you stick a paper lantern over the lightbulb—and, lo and behold, the place has turned to Egypt."

He's not here, threatening me with his uninvited presence in my bedroom, with more gossip about my . . . past. *"Only a paper moon. Sailing over a cardboard sea . . ."*

"And you are the queen of the Nile, sitting on your throne, swilling down my liquor. And do you know what I say? Ha ha! Do you hear me? Ha ha ha!"

"But it wouldn't be make-believe. If you believed in me . . ." I am busy with movements unrelated to his threat, movements of a fine lady who a brute would not dare sully. Stanley steps closer with his dirty thoughts; he wants me to see them.

I step back and bump my bed. "Don't come any closer."

"You think I'm gonna interfere with you?" He has the wanton look lowborn men reveal when they drink, or believe they have rights. "Maybe you wouldn't be bad to interfere with."

Stanley smiles with his filthy mouth open. His hands rise . . . to reach for my clothes, then my skin. I grab his beer bottle, shatter it against the bureau, and jab the jagged edges at him. "I will twist this broken end in your face!"

Stanley grabs my wrist, holding the bottle at bay. He pulls me to him, almost mouth to mouth and snarls, "Tiger, tiger. Drop that bottle top. Drop it."

His chest touches mine; his breath is hot. I fight him for the bottle and he rips it from my hand. I claw at his eyes and he whips me sideways to the bed. "No! *You won't have me.* You, you, *Pollack. Animal.*" My hand rips out of his grip and I jump toward the door.

He grabs for my shoulder, ripping away my gown. His other hand sinks into my hair tearing it loose from the semi-bun, and twists me back to him.

"So you want some roughhouse. All right, let's have some roughhouse."

"No! You leave me alone." His blue eyes blaze two inches from mine, awful horrible words bounce off my lips. I'm a lady. He can't take advantage, can't take the last of me. He can't . . .

He crushes me to him. "Tiger. Tiger. We've had this date with each other from the beginning."

I'm heaved to the bed; he lands between my legs, pounding into me, ripping at my clothes. I won't let him! I won't—

"SCENE." Loud, from out there in the black.

Fight him off. Motion, blur, my hands . . . Stanley's weight lifts—

Applause. Blink. Applause.

Jude Law. Movie-star smile. He's standing, offering me his hand I don't, won't, can't take; he's pulling me up from the bed, waits till I'm standing, lets go, and begins to clap. For me, us. Tears pour down my cheeks. I'm shaking all over. Jude Law ducks an inch and looks up at me, hands open, palms up. He approaches gently and hugs me okay. "Wonderful, Arleen. Powerful, powerful. Blanche DuBois."

I think he means it. I'm at the Shubert Theater, not in the French Quarter, not Blanche, not Coleen being raped. Anne Johns the director is coming to the stage. She hugs me, too, then turns me to the audience, still holding my hand. Sarah, my agent is applauding, both hands over her head. For me. I think, I think . . . I did it.

Anne Johns says, "Arleen. It was . . . awesome. Sex, fear, terror, disgust . . . just oh-my-God awesome."

"I . . . I get the part?"

"Don't know, one more to go. But you—"

I don't hear what Anne says. It's hot, way too hot, and I have to hug her shoulder to stay standing. She adds a bit of support until I regroup, then holds me at arm's length, still beaming. The last forty-eight hours is as much of the performance as I am.

Anne Johns says, "So totally *Southern.* And you were right there—I was terrified. Wish we'd filmed it."

I feel the eyes of Jude Law, an actor's actor, and smile through my tears. A combination of Blanche and I half breathe, half say, "The kindness of strangers." He winks. I peek at the audience. Chicago-girl Amy Madigan has her hands clasped together squeezing them in affirmation for what her friend and I just did. Forty rows beyond her, two figures walk partway down the side aisle. One is a theater security officer.

The other is Bobby Vargas. I'm so glad he's here. It's perfect, it's—

Not Bobby.

It's Ruben. He stops when he's sure I've seen him and can't blink him into nothingness, then gives me two thumbs-up and his creepy café-society grin. He's here to own part of my moment, to remind me that this is his ground, too, that I can be Cinderella or he can drag me from the sunlight into the sewer anytime he wants. Stanley and Ruben, deep breath, Ruben and Stanley. I never have a gun in my hand when it's time.

"BRAVO." Applause. "BRAVO." In the other aisle, Toddy Pete Steffen walks toward the stage. He's wearing a tailored summer-weight suit, and applauding. For me, a beaming boyish grin on his face. The First Ward's Prince of Darkness applauds all the way to the orchestra pit.

"*Fabulous.*" He's still clapping. "Wow."

Jude Law bows twenty degrees and points at me. *Me.* Mr. Steffen continues to applaud. I scan shadows for Ruben Vargas and don't see him. Not midnight for Cinderella after all. I can't help it and hug Jude Law who hugs me back. And when my feet leap off the stage and hit the carpet in Toddy Pete's aisle I hug him, too.

He wipes my tears off his cheek and kisses my forehead. "Young lady, you deserve it. If for some reason it doesn't happen, come see me." Toddy Pete turns us to his director. "Blanche DuBois isn't the only lead role with your name on it."

My hands flatten on his jacket. "Please, Mr. Steffen, just let me have Blanche. I've had so many tomorrows that never came." My voice is half Blanche; my hands are pleading and I pull them back. "I'm sorry." Wince. "Honest, I'm more professional than that." Both hands press at his jacket. "I'm just—"

He smiles again, boyish at sixty, handsome not dangerous, not the First Ward's Prince of Darkness. Then hugs me and turns us again to the decision makers. "My girl's not bad, huh?"

Amy Madigan, yells, "Spectacular."

The gaffer yells, too: my new family. Sarah applauds over her head, then grins at the man next to her to include him in our celebration. Ruben Vargas nods, says something to Sarah, and begins to clap.

19

OFFICER BOBBY VARGAS

SUNDAY, 12:30 PM

Nobody kills Jewboy, ever.

I run all the lights on Canal, brake hard at Harrison, miss the CTA bus, and slide westbound through the intersection. Jewboy's not dead. Walter E. Mesrow goes on to become president after Obama. Buff's not fighting to stay alive in Mercy's ICU; Buff doesn't die; he retires; his daughter gets better and goes to college. My foot stomps the gas. Wet fingers wipe at my eyes. Robbie Steffen's a liar; so is Hahn. My brother's not into a blackmail business that killed Jewboy. Ruben didn't, couldn't. I call him; voice mail for the hundredth time. "Answer your phone!"

Call-waiting beeps in my hand. Hahn's wrong. Robbie Steffen's wrong. It's a scam, a frame. And Jason's wrong, Jewboy's not dead, not shot by *some psycho Asian bitch.* Wet fingers wipe my nose. I jam the brakes, jerk into the parking lot at the Cook County Morgue, bounce hard and park. Jason's been wrong before. Jewboy is not here.

The room is large and cold. It smells of disinfectant, and it's silent. Officer Mesrow is almost too large for his stainless-steel table. A dull green sheet covers all but his neck and face. No grin, no red Hawaiian shirt. Tucked under his head is Jason's favorite Cubs hat. Wet dots appear on Jewboy's sheet. I apologize and pat at the dots. An assistant medical examiner walks past, heading toward an autopsy table; his face says he's sorry, too.

Except this place doesn't need any more of my friends. Me and Walter E. Mesrow aren't saying goodbye, not here, not like this, not after seventeen years. Jewboy's basement is where he belongs, where we should all be, with the beer signs and Hawaiian shirts, planning for Jamaica and WaveRunners that sink, girls and rum punches, planning our next Cubs game, softball game, somebody's wedding. We have too much to do. The guitar lessons were going great. And we agreed, none of us would die this year; in November we're all flying back to Jamaica, Frenchman's Bay, to Eggy's Bohemian.

I squeeze Jewboy's hand so he knows I'm not screwing around. "If anybody can beat this room, Walter Mesrow can." I stare thousands of conversations, regrets and losses, hopes and dreams, and *family* into his face. I will him back to life. Jewboy's sunburned skin is yellow, his hand stiff and icy. He doesn't move. "C'mon, man, gimme this. Everybody's outside, we got beer, the entire Dallas Cowboys cheerleaders. Hef's plane is waiting; we're flying to the mansion." Jewboy may be on a cold stainless-steel table covered by a sheet, but he's Serbian Polish, he can do this. I ate pierogi and pelmeni suppers with his parents, saw him do stand-up comedy sober and carry dogs out of apartment fires with his shirt burning. I will him to sit up. But Jewboy doesn't.

"C'mon, Jewboy. You ain't leaving me and the guys here." Choke, eye wipe, trying to hide it from him. "It isn't right, we'll have nowhere to party."

Nothing.

"Okay, okay . . . I can give you a minute. We'll be fine till you get back." My voice breaks and my eyes squeeze shut to stop the tears. "I'll make sure your mom gets through till then. That's a promise, me to you." I squeeze Jewboy's hand harder with both of mine, rubbing heat into his. "But it'd be way better if you came back now. Before you take this too—"

A door opens behind me but I don't react, don't need to know. "Officer?"

Didn't hear that. Way too early to give up.

"Officer? Sorry, we're scheduled to do the autopsy . . ."

Two men in surgical gear stop six feet away. I look down to Jewboy. No one comes back from autopsies. They cut the big Y in your chest, saw half your head off, and you're gone. You go from the last time anybody saw you to a carved stone in Holy Sepulchre or Waldheim, dead brown leaves and twenty-four-hour silence bunching under your name.

"Please, Walter, c'mon. These guys aren't kidding."

The Red Sea doesn't part. The stone doesn't roll away. Because all that's bullshit.

My eyes fill all the way and I squeeze his giant hand one last time. "I'll take care of your folks, Walter. Got my word, whatever it takes." My best friend doesn't squeeze back because Walter E. Mesrow is gone.

Outside the morgue the air is thin, loud, and thirty-five degrees hotter. The parking lot is full. It's always full. I walk between cars to mine and key the door. The interior is an oven. My key reaches the ignition, fumbles, and falls to the mat. Both palms squeeze the steering wheel. I grimace my eyes shut to absolute black. *Walter, I am so sorry.* A sob wracks my shoulders. My hands hide my face but can't stop the tears. I slump down across the seat, curl fetal, and weep like a child.

Empty and weak, I push up into the seat and wipe my face presentable. The morgue fills my windshield gray. From Hawaiian shirts and ten-mile loopy grins to . . . nothing, and for what? Now it's on to Mercy to see Buff, then cry in their parking lot, too. I start the car but don't put it in gear. Maybe nineteen years is enough.

At Roosevelt and Michigan I loop a '62 gunship and change lanes toward the curb. Two black bangers sit the front and back. The gunship turns south behind me, away from downtown. No bangers crossing Roosevelt today. Today is Furukawa's 10K, a law-and-order day in downtown. Today we have the right to police that part of the city.

I pull my phone to call Ruben but listen to a message from Arleen, her voice nervous, but strong: "Fingers crossed, Bobby. On my way in. Love you for calling, means a lot. Bye." Watch check; two hours ago, hope she got it; hope she gets out of Chicago and never looks back. Exhale. No I don't; I wish, I wish . . . I don't know what I wish.

I try Ruben again and get voice mail. Again. My hand cocks . . . hesitates, then drops limp to the seat. Hahn was right when she said the Hokkaido package wasn't done killing people. She lost Lopez; I lost Jewboy. And maybe Buff. A CTA passes through the intersection; Furukawa's Olympics flag covers the entire bus. Furukawa gets police protection because they're the good guys. That mass-murder shit back in China? We'll just sorta overlook that because they build a park every now and then. But Jewboy gets to die; that's okay.

I try Ruben again, then make the right turn into Mercy Hospital's crowded parking lot. Buff may or may not still be alive. Not sure if I can face him *and* Jewboy being dead. A doctor's space is empty nearest the entrance and that's where I park. My phone rings again—I answer getting out of the car.

Tania Hahn says, "Don't know where you are, Vargas, but in the next five seconds I better. If not, that body and your Beretta's public domain."

"Where's Ruben?"

"Clock's ticking, Bobby. If you're not wired to do your sergeant and Ruben in fifteen minutes, I'm dropping this bundle at Area 4 and finding a new horse to back."

"Jewboy's dead. Buff Anderson's fifty-fifty. I'm walking into ICU now." My car door slams and I turn toward Mercy's emergency entrance. "Give me thirty minutes, then you and I go find Ruben."

"No. Don't go in till I wire you. We need your sergeant on tape to convince Ruben he's gotta give this up."

"Buff isn't part of your Hokkaido package. I don't know what he and Ruben were fighting about, but it wasn't that—"

"Ground control to Bobby—their fight was about the package or Coleen Brennan. Or both."

My feet stop on Mercy's sidewalk. "Leave Coleen Brennan out of this. Last time I'm warning you." I hate what it might mean, but repeat what Jason told me anyway. "The shooter who got Buff and Jewboy was ID'd as Asian, a female."

"Asian, female—gotta be White Flower Lý."

"Why?"

"She's their *partner*, Bobby. Your *brother's* partner. For whatever reason, Ruben's crew is disintegrating. Get your sergeant on tape, if he's not dead. Anderson can tell us why the crew's coming apart. Tell us if *today's* 10K is a target."

"Fuck you and the federal government. Robbie didn't say shit about Buff."

Hahn's voice ramps. "Recovering the package *from your brother* isn't about the federal government, asshole. It's about your city and three million innocent people."

"Yeah? Well fuck them, too."

The ER door opens. It smells like the morgue and I start crying all over again.

20

ARLEEN BRENNAN

SUNDAY, 12:45 PM

Traffic zips past the Shubert and a marquee that later today may be mine, should be mine. *Will* be mine. Sarah my attentive agent hands me my extra-heavy purse and beams at me like I'm her only client. Her smile is dazzling and I can still taste her lipstick. She claps again and says, "There is a God and she is a woman. You were . . . *monumental.*"

I can almost walk. Ruben Vargas has stepped away, into the netherworld where the Stanley Kowalskis congregate. My feet have finished floating, I think. Maybe I'll do spins, a leap or two, throw flowers at the buses, even the Greyhounds to L.A. Could the sun be any shinier? The Brennan sisters are about to win; call Bobby Vargas, the three of us and Tinker Bell are finally out on tour.

My phone vibrates its hooray. I dig it out and flip to tell whoever it is that I am the new queen of England. It's Ruben Vargas. My eyes and attention jump to the shadows, the street. *No*—I delete his presence and his memory and scroll past. Bobby's earlier text message appears, bright and shiny. I punch Call and his voice mail answers. After twenty-nine years Bobby comes back to us on our day. That cannot be coincidence.

"Bobby, it's me. I did it. They loved me." I grin at Sarah. "Now we wait. But Toddy Pete Steffen came, *ran* down to the stage, I kid you not, said he loved me for *Streetcar* and other shows, too. Just like we planned it when we were kids, took forever but—" My toes point; maybe I'll pirouette. "Sarah and I are leaving for the gospel brunch at the Park Grill—our own little watch party. Call me. Please come, I mean it. Okay? I want you to be there when we win." I flip shut and keep grinning at Sarah.

Sarah says, "Blanche and Arleen should pack for the talk-show circuit. You two may have just outgrown this town."

"No, no, no. Chicago makes it soooo much better. None of the Brennans will *ever* have to take the bus anymore. We *will,* but we won't have to. We'll buy a bakery; everybody I know gets crumble muffins!"

A long black limo stops at the curb. The driver exits and opens the passenger door on his side. Out pops a youngish woman in a sensible suit, large purse in one hand, a cell phone pressed to her ear. On my left, the doors to the Shubert pop open. Anne Johns rushes toward the limo with both arms outstretched. Behind Anne, her assistant trails with a phone to her ear. The limo hasn't emptied all its passengers. Perfect legs cross as they swing out of the passenger door; the rest of Tharien Thompson unbends into our director's waiting embrace.

Anne Johns grins into Tharien's face. "My God, girl, you look fabulous!"

They hug tight but air-kiss to protect Tharien's professional makeup. She's wearing a fitted postwar, flower-print dress, nylons, and low heels. She's from South Africa like Charlize Theron, but today she's stepping off a train from Biloxi in 1947, doesn't have to speak to say "fragile, pretentious Southern belle." Ten months ago Tharien won an Emmy for *Tarantula Rose* on HBO. Last Thursday she was nominated again.

Sarah says, "Hello, Tharien." I just stare.

Tharien raises her chin, as if to offer us a beau dollah to please retrieve her travel case, so in character I want to cry or applaud. She's whisked inside. Sarah and I are left to appreciate her limo. I ask her driver, "Was that the eight fifteen from Biloxi?"

Sarah reformats her agent's smile and pats my shoulder. "The French critics hated her in *Tarantula Rose.* Suggested she return to her cameras."

"Back to Africa would be better." Envy, fear, more envy. "Have to admit she was a good photographer."

Sarah throws her arm around my shoulders. "Not today, today and *Streetcar* belong to Arleen Brennan." Sarah's arm pulls me toward our brunch celebration. Our first step east is through a lingering wisp of magnolia perfume.

Frown. Tharien thought of everything that I didn't; just *too* perfect, and ten years younger. My bare shoulders tighten under Sarah's arm and I begin to see it coming, to recognize I will be the actress who *didn't* get it. You have to be that close—down to the final two, down to visualizing the dressing room, your wardrobe lady, hair and makeup, the preshow bus ride in from home every night, the new family who loves you, who depends on you. You have to be that close to be the actress who *didn't* get the part.

SUNDAY, 1:15 PM

Brunch is no longer the answer. Sarah grins at me across our plates of French Whatever; the French hated Tharien so Sarah thought haute cuisine was appropriate. She's talking, telling me not to worry. I stare out at the city in summer. Across Pearson Street, in Water Tower Square, a man and a woman throw popcorn to a flock of pigeons. The pigeons scatter and return as each pedestrian passes. The man wears a seersucker jacket on a hundred-degree day and doesn't look at us sitting under our table's umbrella. The woman is Asian, long black hair, sun hat, sunglasses, and sits with space between her and the man. Two policemen, both blocky, walk through the pigeons, but the man pays them no mind. The woman dips her head as if to hide. The man is Ruben Vargas.

Ruben Vargas places the popcorn on his bench next to the Asian woman, then reaches for a cell phone and dials. The woman looks across the square at Sarah and me.

Sarah's phone rings. She answers, smiling, "Detective Vargas." Sarah winks and pats my hand. "Yes. Sure, thank you. She's right here." Sarah hands me the phone. "Wants to wish you good luck. I'm going to the girls' room."

I accept the phone, smile at Sarah as she slices between tables, then stare at Ruben and his woman. Ruben removes his toothpick and says, "Tharien Thompson, huh? I still like your chances. Me, Robbie, Anne Johns, Sarah—you got a lot of folks on your side."

"I doubt you and Robbie are speaking much. What do you want?"

"Time to go, *chica.* Get you ready for the trade with the Japanese ladies."

"Bye."

Ruben pauses, then says, "Santa Monica, California. The pier, ten years ago last month."

The phone fumbles in my hand. Heat gushes my face. I smother the phone shut. Don't want to hear that again. Across Pearson Street, Ruben is standing.

The phone rings again. Ruben keeps calling until I answer. He says, "*Had* your audition, *chica.* Kept my word and will on the rest of our business. Robbie will get his share, so will the Koreans. No reason to blow up your Shubert run if you're good enough to get it—and from what I hear you are. No reason for any cops to go back to California, either." Pause. "But what I can't do is wait any longer to deal with the Japanese."

The phone trembles against my ear.

"Tell my friend Sarah Hellman *adiós.* We'll all party tonight when you get the part. Now, take a cab to the Sunday Market on Canal. I'll meet you on the west sidewalk at Fourteenth Street." Ruben picks up his popcorn and hands it to the Asian woman. "I *don't* see you at the curb in ten minutes, I make the call to Santa Monica. And don't think about bringing my little brother. Get him involved any deeper and it'll kill both of you."

Ruben clicks off. He and the Asian woman disappear into the throng of tourists and Michigan Avenue's well-heeled shoppers mingling with this afternoon's 10K runners, partiers, and concertgoers. Furukawa and Toddy Pete save Chicago. Chicago saves the Shubert Theater Company. I get *Streetcar.* All good. Then I help Robbie and Ruben blow up Furukawa. The Olympics go to Tokyo. Chicago goes broke. The Shubert closes. One big happy family.

Could you dig the hole deeper, Arleen?

Sure you can. With people like Ruben and Robbie, the hole always gets deeper. And now Ruben has another hole, from ten years ago, the night I ran from Santa Monica to New York and eventually back to Chicago. My pixie-dust plan won't hold together with the Santa

Monica pier in it. Not if Ruben somehow has proof. I'll always be one cop-to-cop phone call away from L.A. County jail and the *State of California vs. Arleen Brennan.*

A hand covers mine. I squeeze. Sarah yelps sliding into her chair. I let go, say, "Sorry," hand over her phone, and scramble for my purse.

Sarah grabs my wrist. "Wait. What's wrong? Are you all right?"

"I have to go."

"Where? Why?"

I stare at her not sure if I'll cry or scream. "I'll be okay. Have to be, right? This afternoon you'll tell me I got the part." Sarah doesn't let go. She stares at the bruises my makeup may no longer be covering, bruises from Ruben Vargas. "I have to go. But . . . don't call me if I don't get it, okay?"

Sarah lets go of my wrist and I grab my purse with the loaded 9-millimeter in it.

"Forget that. Call me either way. It'll settle a lot of things."

SUNDAY, 1:30 PM

A smudged Plexiglas partition separates me from the cabdriver. I'm alone in his backseat crossing the Roosevelt Road Bridge, but I'm not alone-alone. The nightmare man on the pier whispers what I already know, that my pixie-dust plan is over; my *Streetcar* future is gone unless the 9-millimeter in my purse is in my hand when I meet Ruben. *Just pull the trigger* is now, and always has been, the only solution. The nightmare man whispers, Like you did before. *Just pull the trigger . . . be a good girl.*

I gag, then choke. My hand covers my mouth. I force a swallow, then gasp. I'll call Bobby. Ask him what to do. The voice says, *No, you'll not need a Mexican's permission to do what has to be done. Chicago must have the Olympics and the Brennan sisters must have the Shubert Theater. Be a good girl. That's it, you know what to do.*

"Shut up!" My hands slam my ears. The cabdriver stares from his mirror. I fumble into my purse for my phone. The 9-millimeter stops me. Bobby is Ruben's brother; you can't call him. My fingers slide under and around the 9-millimeter's grips. The panic fades. What did

Ruben mean "get Bobby involved any deeper and it'll kill both of you"? That's the second time he's threatened Bobby.

The cab changes lanes as we climb above my father's river, twenty-nine years later still the demarcation between the haves and have-nots. We reach the bridge's apex on the west side of the river above an oily, half-mile-wide switching yard clogged with thirty or forty dormant trains. Just beyond their rust and decay, the Sunday Market sprawls ten blocks north and south on Canal. Twenty thousand Mexicans. A one-day foreign country. And Ruben Vargas, their *patrón del barrio.*

Chicago's immigrants come here for a taste of home, to buy from the rows of homemade tents and hawkers, to wade through the burlap sacks of chilies, first communion dresses, radial tires, cowboy boots, piles of used tools, and fresh-cooked goats. Even in the dead of winter this market is border-town Mexico, the same food frying, the same musicians playing.

My father hated Mexicans. Hated their food, their language, the soap they used. *Scabin' bastards, workin' my river for a day's pay niggers wouldn't take free.* Coleen and I hated our father right back, as much as any two nine-year-olds could.

On Sundays Ruben's a king here. That's why he picked this place to meet. The market is considered the "Mexican door" to the Four Corners; if you're Hispanic, the safest way home. My hand pats the gun. But Ruben isn't going home. And neither am I.

The cabdriver ekes through a break in the throng at the market's middle intersection. At the first opportunity he turns left, drives south to Fourteenth Street, and drops me ten blocks from where the Brennan sisters and the Vargas brothers grew up. I stand at the corner, anonymous in the overflow of buyers and sellers. Why get in Ruben's car? Why come here if you're *not* getting in the car? Two hours ago I shared the stage with Jude Law; now I'm about to share a car and a murder weapon with Ruben Vargas.

Call Bobby. Run away.

Or listen to the voice, walk east toward the market, put two in Ruben's chest, call it self-defense, for me, the city, the Shubert Theater Company.

Ruben's Crown Victoria is double-parked at Canal facing me, windows up, engine running. Last chance to call Bobby. If I get in Ruben's car, there's no turning back—either I use the 9-millimeter in my purse or front Ruben's blackmail on Furukawa. Anything else is a bet on the daytime-TV fantasy that three different prosecutors and the Korean mafia will believe I'm innocent enough to be left alone.

Is the 9-millimeter's safety off or on? Ruben's shape is bleary in the glare of his windshield. And the stage at the Shubert is very, very far away. Bump from behind; I jerk away; a Mexican man with his daughter stares as he passes. Ruben pops his door but doesn't get out. His door closes and he honks the horn.

Decide.

I reach in and thumb-off the safety. Kill Ruben, or don't. Believe him and blackmail Furukawa, or don't. You can't run and you can't hide. Do murder now, or— Or don't do it and call Bobby. I glance the buildings and dead-end streets, and the one absolute fact the Four Corners carves into your guts, true when Coleen and I were hugging each other in the shower, true when I was thirty-two on that pier in Santa Monica, and true now—happy endings require a girl believe in miracles; and to make it that far she better be able to pull the trigger.

I walk to Ruben's car, bend to see in the backseat, then get in the front. Ruben has a bandage above his eye and a fat lower lip that the distance at the Shubert and Pearson Street hid. His attention stays straight ahead, intent on something, toothpick moving between his teeth.

Decide. My heart begins to pound.

Ruben turns to me, watches me inspect his face as my fingers creep to the gun. He says, "There'll be two of 'em, the Japs I told you tried to cap my partner before she brought in me and Robbie. Dr. Ota thought he could rob her instead of pay. Now she's got me, and so do you." Ruben nods over his seat. "I'm giving you something to hand them. After you do, say, 'Open it.' " Ruben stares hard at me. "Understand?"

The *something* I'm to give them rests on the backseat, a six-inch tube of Pillsbury biscuits taped over at the top.

"Then you say, 'The 10K or the concert after.' Got it?"

"What?"

Ruben glares. "Repeat it, Arleen. 'The 10K or the concert after.' "

"10K or the concert after."

Ruben points into his mirror. "They'll be at the corner in ten minutes." He reaches over the seat, grabs the biscuit tube, and shoves it toward me. "Don't fuck this up and you're halfway home. Do anything other than what I tell you and you won't live long enough to stand trial in Illinois or California."

"I want out, Ruben. Now." My fingers reach the 9-millimeter's grip. "I mean it."

"Me, too." He backhands me into the window, jerks my purse away, and removes the 9-millimeter. Ruben drops in a tiny electronic device and throws the purse back. "This ain't my first day out here. Remember that. And you don't know shit about how things work—out here or at the courthouse. Illinois doesn't plea bargain murder for extortion, even to get a cop, no matter what they fucking promise. And California doesn't care about heroics in Illinois. And the feds cut bait, always trading up for bigger fish. Follow the script. Be an actress. Prove Tharien Thompson should go home and she will."

Blanche's scarf lies on my knees. I'm not strong enough to kill Ruben with a scarf. "What's in my purse?"

"I wanna know what they say." Ruben puts a device in his right ear and winces.

I chin at his bandage and lip. "Somebody finally whip your ass?"

"Remember this, *chica*. Fuck with me and I better die. If I don't, you will. My brother, too, if he's with you."

I grab the scarf and Ruben's biscuit tube, then exit the car. The tube's heavier than it should be. I walk east to the busy corner. Maybe Dr. Ota's women will shoot me and get it over with. Five minutes pass; no Japanese women. On the other side of the center-stall line, an Asian woman is out of place, surrounded by Hispanics. She has long black hair and the same sun hat as Ruben's woman in Water Tower Square. Is she Ruben's partner? Robbie's Vietcong bitch? If she is, would she get this close to the two Japanese women who tried to kill her? Can I use that? Somehow?

Bump. A woman in black has her back to me. Bump. I turn to another woman, this one facing me. Japanese. Almond eyes tight in mine. "Hello, Ms. Brennan."

"How'd you know my name?"

"Do you have something for me?"

"Are you—"

"Yes, I am." She extends her hand.

I hand her the biscuit tube. "I was told to say, 'Open it.' "

She accepts the tube, but doesn't open it. "Anything else you were told to say?"

"The 10K or the concert after."

The Japanese woman nods. "That doesn't allow much time. Where are your partners?"

"No, no, not partners. I'm being coerced into this. Just want to go home."

"We all do. Please inform your partners we will analyze the vial you have provided. Should it be what you represent, we are pleased to do business. Unfortunately, the analysis cannot be completed by four o'clock. Possibly, by concert time."

I don't understand the meaning, but nod that I understand the message. "Not by four o'clock, but possibly by seven. And they're not my partners, okay? Understand?"

She nods, but doesn't believe me. "Your telephone number, please."

"No."

My purse is jerked off my shoulder. The first woman in black who bumped me pulls out my cell phone, flips it open, reads the number, puts my phone back, and hands me my purse. She doesn't see Ruben's gadget. She is Japanese as well.

Behind me, the woman with Ruben's Pillsbury tube says, "If you have the Hokkaido package, we will do business. Should you disperse a particle prior to the ransom being paid, or speak of it publicly after the payment, we will kill your families and your friends. All of them. And all of you—Ruben Vargas, Robbie Steffen, Lý Thi Loan, and Arleen Brennan."

"No. Listen, I'm not—"

She's already gone. I turn for the woman who had my purse; she's gone. The Asian woman in the stalls is gone as well. Just Arleen Brennan on the corner, turning in a slow circle. My phone vibrates in my purse. Sarah! I got the lead. This nightmare's over—

Ruben says, "Walk west on the south side of Fourteenth Street. Keep walking till I pick you up."

Downtown and the Shubert are the other direction. Tharien Thompson's audition ended an hour ago. Producer, director, and backers have met. They've picked their actress. Ruben's call should've been Sarah. Sarah should call me, right now. Everyone loved me; I'm part of the family.

Ruben's voice: "Move, *chica*."

I do, but not toward Ruben's car. On Roosevelt I flag for a cab. Ruben pulls to the curb. "Get in."

I backtrack. Ruben rolls in reverse, talking to me through the passenger window. "Hey, c'mon, you did fine. We're cool." He pops the passenger door. "C'mon. We'll go see Sarah."

I jump around his front fender, slide through traffic to the north curb and wave at a taxi that passes. Ruben flips a U, pops his siren, and the open door almost knocks me down. "Get in, I'm not fuckin' around."

A squad car slows and pulls in behind Ruben, the driver eyeing me. Need a plan B; have to kill Ruben and Santa Monica. Think. Decide—

"Arleen. In the car."

Running away won't work. I slide into Ruben's car. He flips another U, hand out his window, giving the squad an air-pat/no-problem, then wheels us eastbound on Roosevelt. "We've got a surprise for the master race. One more step—"

"Not me. I'm done." I turn to check the squad car through Ruben's back window. The squad car hasn't moved. "Let me out at the next light."

Ruben pops his siren and doesn't slow down. "Want the Shubert? That you probably won?" He glances at me. "You're done when I say so, not before. Open that brown bag."

The bag is on his console where I leave it. Maybe the bag is plan B. "What'd that woman mean, 'disperse a particle'?"

"Wanna be a big star? The faster we finish, the faster you walk away. Open the bag and do what I tell you."

I don't. Ruben cocks his hand. "Open it."

Plan B. If the bag's heavy enough, I'll smash him across the nose with it. Take his gun and blow his stomach into the door. Bet he'll let me out then.

The bag is light. All it contains is an empty, old-style test tube and an odd-looking green rubber cap. Ruben tells me to put the cap on the tube and the tube in my pocket. "I'll drop you at Michigan and Congress. The reviewing stand is across Michigan in the Congress divider. Get up close now. At 3:55, five minutes *before* they fire the gun to start the 10K, toss that up on the stand at Dr. Ota."

I shake my head at him. "Not getting shot impersonating Sirhan Sirhan."

"There's nothing in the test tube, Arleen. No commotion, no cops chasing you. Only the good Dr. Ota will know what it means."

"Find another actress. I'm booked for the Shubert." I reach for the door handle. Locked. I turn to Ruben and he bangs me across the face.

"Don't make me bust up your moneymaker. And don't forget who's your pier buddy in Santa Monica. And don't forget Robbie and the Koreans—they gotta get paid *with Dr. Ota's money* or you're dead, twice." Ruben tosses me a Kleenex. "Wipe your nose before you bleed on your pretty dress."

21

OFFICER BOBBY VARGAS

SUNDAY, 1:45 PM

Mercy's emergency waiting room is loud, sweaty, and tense. I wipe the tears off my cheeks, ease through frightened parents and spouses to a hallway, then left to the T junction that leads to ICU.

The ICU waiting room can't hold all the men and women in black body armor and T-shirts—TAC and gang-crimes cops who aren't on duty and six or seven who are. Buff and Jewboy are two of the best-liked cops in 12; Buff may be the best-liked cop on the entire West Side.

In the white linoleum hallway, the grim faces above the armor and pistols describe Buff's chances. Heads are turning—guys with guns who want answers about Bobby Vargas and little girls, and federal judges, and dead friends.

I hear "Motherfucker," turn, and a punch lands high on my temple. "Fuckin' spic mother—" Another punch lands. I spin, duck, and bang into the wall. Buff's nephew jams a finger at my face. "Coleen Brennan! Fuckin' Ruben and you killed her." Jason jumps in and grabs the nephew. The nephew slams an elbow into Jason, gets loose, and dives at me. Jason headlocks him and jerks him back. The nephew screams: "Fuckin' Vargas brothers killed Coleen Brennan. Goddamn spic reprisals kill Terry Rourke and his daughter. And now Buff—" Jason chokes Buff's nephew to bright red, drops him to his knees, and lets go.

"Jesus Christ." I step back from the crowd-wall surging behind Jason and wipe at blood on my forehead. "Do I look Asian? Jason said an Asian shot Buff and Jewboy."

Jason keeps one hand on Buff's nephew. "Tracy Moens was just in here. Said Jewboy's dead and Buff's in ICU 'cause of you, Ruben, Robbie Steffen, and the Brennan sisters."

"And you believe Moens?" I wipe at the blood again. "A reporter stirring the pot?"

"Ruben, Jewboy, and Buff throw down at breakfast, now Jewboy's dead and Buff's here. Two hours before that, you're up here with Robbie. Somebody shot him, too, didn't they? Ruben's your brother. Half the kids in Chicago say you're fucking them in the ass. You didn't pass the polygraph—"

"The hell I didn't."

"The operator says Buff covered for you."

I fix on Jason, then the crowd behind him, everyone waiting for my answer, for me to *convince* them. It takes effort to make my lips move. "I did not give up the Toyota. I didn't kill Coleen Brennan."

Our new commander, the Hispanic highflier from the North Side, bumps through the crowd to Jason and me. She says, "Talk. Right now. That's an order," then grabs my arm and leads me forty feet away. "What were your brother and Sergeant Anderson fighting about?"

I blink at her, then past her, focusing on my team, *my family*. Glaring at me, seeing a child killer, child molester who's been alone with their kids.

"Officer Vargas."

I cut back. "What?"

"How is the Mesrow/Anderson shooting connected to Coleen Brennan and your brother?"

"Connected?"

She stares piercing brown eyes and stiffens to full height in her uniform and graduate degree from Northwestern. "Answer the question."

"I just came from the morgue. Maybe you can give me a minute—"

"We don't have a minute. We want the shooters of officers Mesrow and Anderson, even if you don't. And if that's connected to the Coleen Brennan rape/murder, so be it."

I lean back, stunned. "Coleen and my brother? Is that what you said?"

"Answer the question, Officer Vargas. I can't stop these men behind me if they decide—"

"I'm here to see Buff." I push past my commander to the ICU door and the nurse guarding it. "Buff wants to see me. Really important to him, life-or-death important."

The nurse says, "No one can see Sergeant Anderson."

"Let me stand at the window, just for a second. Buff has to know I'm here."

"I'll tell him." She turns to leave and I grab her arm.

"He has to see me. I won't say a word. Promise."

The nurse extricates her arm, turns again, but stops, eyes the armed, angry crowd behind me, and says, "C'mon, it'll help calm everyone down." She leads me through double doors into the ICU. Standing at the nurses' station is U.S. Attorney Jo Ann Merica and two FBI agents. All three are on their phones. One touches Merica's shoulder and points at me.

The window to Buff's room frames his wife, Sandy, and their three daughters at his bed. The nurse allows me to stand in the doorway, then turns to Merica and tells all three to quit their phones. Eight feet from me, Buff is motionless, swollen and bruised. Tubes are taped to his neck, down his nose, in his mouth. The white hair is wilted against pasty gray skin. All but one arm is tight under a sheet and thin blanket. Monitors blip. His eyes are open and don't blink, he and death's door are having their conversation. Buff's daughter Sasha, the one with MD, sniffles at her father's feet, rubbing his blanket, asking God to let her daddy come back home.

Sandy sees me, shields her eldest girl, and walks to the doorway. Sandy's eyes are red, she's shaking. "No, Bobby. You can't come in here."

Behind Sandy, the three girls watch us, searching our eyes and body language for clues, anything that will explain their father's chances. "I didn't do any of it, Sandy."

Anger bleeds through her fear. "Buff said your brother's dirty. Did Ruben shoot my husband? Is that why you're here?"

"No. Ruben didn't— And that's not why I'm here. I love Buff; he's mistaken."

"Is he?" Sandy points. "Who's on that bed fighting for his life? Not you. Not Ruben."

I bite back the anger. "I love your husband, no matter what he said or what he thinks."

The monitors blip. Sandy steps to the bed, a wife and mother on the vigil she's dreaded every night for thirty-plus years. I step past Sandy to the bed, telling my friend and his daughters, "Your dad will be okay because he's Buff Anderson. He survived being shot in Vietnam; he'll walk out of Mercy." I look at each daughter and tap my heart. "I know it right here."

The nurse reaches in for my arm. "Officer."

I turn to Sandy. "Did Buff ever mention a girl from Vietnam, Lý Thi Loan or White Flower Lý?"

Sandy leans back. "Why?"

I grab her arm. "What'd she want? What'd she say?"

Sandy pulls her arm away. "A woman called early this morning, woke us up. Buff said he knew her in Vietnam when she was a girl, hadn't heard from her in forever, but he didn't say her name."

"What'd she want?"

"She was in some kind of trouble. Bob called Jewboy, said they'd make a pass on 'Tu Do Street,' then go find you."

"Me?"

Sandy wipes at swollen eyes, not looking at me. "Bob said the girl/woman was with a nun from the Four Corners."

"A nun?"

"The nun ran an orphanage or something during the war, in Saigon on Tu Do Street. Bob helped the nun get out when Saigon fell. Seven or eight years later the nun and Bob helped the girl come over."

The nurse grips my arm and pulls. I jerk it free, glare her back on her heel, then turn back to Buff's wife. Tu Do Street I've never heard of. But if Buff's nun was from the Four Corners, she had to be at St. Dom's. Where the Brennan sisters went. "What's the nun's name?"

"Bob didn't say."

"Did he say where she was now? The nun?"

"No."

The nurse slides in front of Sandy, pushes me off-balance out of the room, then blocks the door. Jo Ann Merica steps up. "We're running out of time to get you on the right side, Officer Vargas. I'm sure Tania Hahn has detailed the potential severity."

"Hahn told me a story; put Robbie Steffen in it, then tried to put Buff in and my brother. For all I know you're in it, too."

Merica blinks the thirty-two-degree eyes. "Hahn's 'story' is surrounded by a mounting level of violence, serious conditions that could lead to—"

"*Serious conditions?* Like Jewboy being dead? And Buff in there dying? That what you mean?"

"My condolences. But the stakes are far higher than the current casualties."

"Can't get any higher for me."

"Unfortunately for all of us, I'm afraid they can." Pause. "Internal Affairs will be questioning you tomorrow morning *under oath* regarding *multiple* child molestation complaints. Undoubtedly, this will include questions concerning Coleen Brennan, while your brother is being deposed *under oath* at the Federal Building regarding *Coleen Brennan.* Once you two begin publicly convicting yourselves, my help will no longer be sufficient."

"If you want help, tell me Hahn's 'story,' if you know it. The whole thing."

She straightens. "That's not how it works."

"Then pardon me when you're governor." I step around the U.S. attorney and through the doors. Jason jumps out of the waiting-room crowd, grabs my arm, and pushes us up to the first intersection.

"I want answers, Bobby. I want 'em now. Don't give a fuck how mad it makes you."

I jerk free.

Jason grabs me with both hands. "Did your brother's business get Jewboy and Buff shot? Is this Coleen Brennan? Tomorrow's depositions?"

I spit in his face. "Fuck you."

Jason slams me into the wall. "No more disappearing, not till we hear what the fuck's up."

"I have to find Ruben."

"Fuck Ruben. If he's part of Buff and Jewboy, I shoot his ass with your gun."

My eyes narrow. "Whatever he is, Ruben's my brother. Hurt him and you better kill me."

Jason pushes Jewboy's badge into my face. "We can do that."

I back away from Jason until I can bolt through the emergency room crowd. Tania Hahn's outside, engine running in a '03 Ford Taurus, door open. I dive in and she slams the gas. "Got an address on White Flower Lý. Think your brother's with her." Hahn's no longer interested in me wearing a wire. "Bad news is the Koreans may have finally pegged her, too."

My feet brace into the floorboard. Ruben would be hard for the Koreans to corner, to trap. Hahn changes lanes, missing the fifth bumper by inches. Her near-death jerks and weaves mash into a familiar metal blur, the precontact rush to the destination, situations that nine times out of ten will end the same way. Sun glares the windshield blind. She tells her phone, "Car one en route. Bag the Koreans if they're on the apartment." Hahn asks me, "What'd Anderson say?"

"What's 'bag the Koreans' mean?"

"*Shoot them.* What'd Anderson say?"

"Buff's in a coma."

Hahn brakes hard facing an oncoming semi and veers westbound out of Michigan Avenue's southbound lanes onto Thirty-first. Cars line both sides of the residential street. We center-line way too fast to not kill a kid or a dog.

"Slow down."

Hahn doesn't slow until she turns south at Morgan and we enter the 3400 block. I don't see Koreans. Or Ruben's car. My brother. The Hokkaido package. Blackmail. Murder. We loop the block north, then south—no Ruben, no Koreans—then back to Lý's building, and park in her alley. Hahn tells her phone, "We're here." She listens through an earpiece, says, "Cover the front. We're going in." Hahn nods me out and we run for Lý's six-flat, guns drawn.

Lý's shotgun apartment is on the bottom floor, door open. The three rooms have been torn apart. We clear a wrecked living room–bedroom and kitchen for threat, then the bathroom. No sign Ruben's been here. Glaring among the shambles is an expensive, undamaged dresser. Carefully arranged on the dresser are china bowls, fruit, candles, and petite sepia photographs in expensive frames. Not uncommon in the Four Corners and all over Chinatown.

I hear myself say, "Ancestor altar, Spirit House."

Hahn begins to pick through the rubble. "Look for broken vials or green rubberized seals. If you see 'em, we're already dead."

We sift through Lý's belongings but find no vials or green rubberized seals. Hahn quits searching and steps up to the ancestor altar. She looks at me, then points at three brass shell casings. "Japanese 7.7s . . . from World War II." Her expression isn't comforting. Hahn does a slow three-sixty of the apartment.

I add Hahn's expression and the World War II reference to the damage all around us, try to see the room being torn apart. Maybe Lý's apartment wasn't searched. Maybe we're surrounded in *rage.* I say what Hahn is thinking: "These altars are for veneration . . . Veneration doesn't include your enemies, mass murderers who slaughtered your ancestors."

"Nope. And veneration doesn't include one dollar of blackmail money." Hahn stares at the 7.7 shells. "We're in a zero-sum game. Money isn't the answer. What Lý's ancestors want is *revenge.*"

I three-sixty again. "But why all the theater? Just shoot Dr. Ota on today's reviewing stand, spend the next ten years lecturing the media from Stateville."

Hahn nods, eyes still on the altar. "Unless you actually *had* something bigger than a gun; something with *scale*; something with *irony.* 'Cause, God bless 'em, Asians love irony."

"Nah. That'd mean White Flower Lý is running a game on . . . her partners—"

"On *Ruben.* Get used to saying his name. Game or not, *Ruben*'s our bad guy."

"'Cause you assholes never make a mistake, right?"

Hahn stares. "Who shot Jewboy and your sergeant? I hear a new witness ID'd a second perp to the feds—an average-size *male* driver. One male and one *Asian* female. Smell like any duo we know?"

I have to step back not to hit her. No way possible my brother shot Jewboy.

"What'd you hear at the hospital? Bona fide good-guy Buff Anderson confess before he stairwayed to heaven?"

My fist balls. "His wife said a woman called early this morning. Buff got dressed, said he was making a pass on 'Tu Do Street.' But no way

Buff takes Jewboy if Buff's committing felonies. Buff must've figured something, scared somebody. The call was a setup—"

"Tu Do Street was Saigon's R&R playground during the war. Our mystery nun's orphanage was at the bottom by the river. Lý Thi Loan—aka White Flower Lý—worked up the street out of the Continental Palace Hotel." Hahn nods at the altar. "Hundred percent this woman shot Jewboy and your sergeant."

"Then she's dead."

"No, she's with your brother—"

I swing. Hahn ducks, steps back, and flashes a military fighting knife. "Can't shoot you, Bobby, not yet. But you're not putting your hands on me."

I take a breath, then another. "And you're not shooting my brother."

Hahn shows me the knife. "Winner goes to the hospital. That'll be me."

"Hurt Ruben"—I point at her forehead—"9-millimeter between your eyes."

"How about we sift this debris one more time?" Hahn twists the knife behind her forearm. "So we can find White Flower and . . . her partner."

I jab a finger at her. "Buff and Jewboy aren't guilty."

"Whatever you say, Bob."

Six minutes of searching yields no evidence that Ruben, Buff, or the Hokkaido package has ever been here. It does yield two two-by-three yellowed photos, one a close-up of a brick building, the other of a nun. The building seems familiar, the nun doesn't but her habit does. I show the nun to Hahn. "Sisters of Providence—they're a teaching order based in Indiana, ran St. Dom's until it closed."

Hahn grabs the picture, turns it over, and back. I give her the other photo. She does the same, then looks at me. "What happened to the nuns at St. Dom's after it closed?"

I point north toward Twenty-second Street in the Four Corners. "Some might have gone to Cristo Rey, a church, school, and convent. It's in my district."

Hahn examines the building photo again. "Is this Cristo Rey?"

I take the photo back, try to see it different. "Not Cristo Rey. Could be St. Dom's. The shadows make it look funny, might be the south corner." Something clicks. "Buff's wife said the nun Buff helped in Vietnam . . . came to the Four Corners."

"The nun was here?"

"And you said Buff and 'his nun' helped White Flower Lý get out in—"

"—1982." Hahn stares at the two photos. "The year Coleen Brennan was murdered. But my nun wasn't Sisters of Providence; mine was a Carmelite. Or we thought she was."

"'Cause you assholes never make a mistake."

Hahn blinks, adding and subtracting. "Okay, Anderson gets the Sisters of Providence nun out as Saigon falls. Maybe he knew her before he shipped over. Hell, maybe the nun was from Chicago. And Anderson could've met White Flower in Saigon, 'cause that's White Flower's job. After the war, nun and cop get child hooker into the USA." Hahn points at the building photo.

"White Flower gets room and board where the Sisters of Providence live."

Hahn nods. "St. Dom's. Where the Brennan sisters are."

I don't like where this is going.

Hahn steps back, the knife blade visible again. "White Flower moves in a block from you and Ruben. *Twenty-nine years later* White Flower Lý hooks up with your brother to blackmail Furukawa. Ruben's an honest cop, right? Why approach him for blackmail help? Ruben the Saint arrests her on the spot. Right?"

I don't have an explanation, but neither does Hahn. That may prove Ruben's innocent or at least has extenuating circumstances. Something. Hahn waits for me to join her. I don't. She says, "Bobby, they must've known each other back then, in the Four Corners. Maybe White Flower and Ruben kept in touch. He could've helped her out of . . . a jam—"

"I lived there, too. I never heard Lý Thi Loan or White Flower Lý."

"Be a cop, Bobby, not a relative. There's something connected here and you know it."

"Where? I don't see your Hokkaido package. Two pictures of the old neighborhood don't mean anything."

"Ruben knew her. She was at St. Dom's . . . when Coleen Brennan died."

"Don't. Go. There. I warned you. Don't throw rape and murder at Ruben and me. I'm done defending that."

"Your brother's a gangster. I'm tired of proving that to you. Ruben's blackmailing Furukawa with a woman he knows. I'm showing you that connection, the rest of the JonBenet shit you just said is sewer you're thinking, not me." Stare. "'Cause I told you already, I don't care who raped Coleen Brennan. And I don't care who killed her."

"I do."

"Good. Solve that crime after we stop this one. 'Cause this one could get ugly, world-class ugly, if it's not a hoax." Hahn points to the altar. "I think Lý has it. The Hokkaido package. I honest to God think she does."

"Then we call the cops, the CDC, somebody. Explain—"

"No. If Lý thinks she's cornered before we can blindside her and Ruben, who knows what she'll do." Hahn's waits, then adds: "Your brother will let you close, closer than anyone else can get. We need a precision strike, not an army, not news leaks and families packing for the mountains. Panic and publicity guarantees Chicago loses their Olympic sponsor and Olympic salvation . . . and maybe way worse."

If Ruben's guilty, she's right. I'm the only one who could get close to him.

Hahn and I exit the apartment. Thunder hammers from the east. She keeps her Glock in hand, eyes fanning Morgan Street, and tells her phone, "Car two?" She listens, then: "Package isn't there, but I think we're finally looking at the goods. Gotta recover all thirty if we want to collect, not twenty-nine and a couple of hundred funerals." Hahn glances me, listens, then answers. "Roger that. We do it right now or we fold the contract, bump eight years' worth of work upstairs just when the payday's coming."

Hahn listens while walking us fast toward the curb. Mid-sidewalk she stops and tells her phone, "Like I'm not pissed, too? But it's getting outta hand. We don't put every ounce to bed in the next few hours—I say screw the contract. This girl wouldn't get within a mile of Lý or Furukawa's 10K without a Tyvek suit."

I stop her mid-step. "What do you mean 'payday'?"

Hahn pulls her phone away from her mouth, "Need to know," then sidesteps me toward her car.

I block her. "I know what a Tyvek suit is. I need to know why 'payday' and 'collect' are suddenly part of our vocabulary."

She tells her phone: "Follow me," drops it into her pocket and stares. "I told you about the Secret Service, chasing leads—counterfeiters, presidential assassins. Lots of leads, lots of threats—all have to be *looked at,* vetted. One in a thousand pan out. Takes lots of resources. Terrorist threats—and that includes my specialty, BW—same situation, okay?"

She ducks to pass. I don't let her. "You're hunting the Hokkaido package, Lý, and my brother for *money*?"

"Think of me as a bounty hunter, independent but sanctioned, like the private contractors fighting the war in Iraq and Afghanistan."

"You don't work for the CIA?"

"I do, we just get paid different, and our rules of engagement are deniable."

"You're a *bounty hunter*?"

Hahn's eyes harden. "Don't go stupid on me, Bobby. The Hokkaido package is too big, too real, and I think we're close this time. I smell it."

I stare at Hahn: profiteer, CIA-sanctioned bounty hunter. At the end of her 'payday' my brother will die, collateral damage whether he deserves it or not. My phone rings. I answer thinking it's Ruben.

Jason says, "Commander just signed off on a citywide for you. Thought you oughta know."

"For what?" I let Hahn listen so she knows it isn't Ruben.

"Murder one. For Danny Vacco."

Hahn turns to watch a white SUV pass.

I ask Jason, "How they figure me for Vacco?"

"A Mrs Baird's driver ID'd you running from a Pontiac by Ricobene's, wrote down the tag. Danny V turns up in the same Pontiac with two in his chest. You told three people, including me, you were capping him. Case makes itself."

"Except I didn't do it. Or molest any goddamn children."

"Reindeer can fly. My *friend* Bobby won't tell me shit about anything, runs out of the hospital. Why not believe it?"

I walk ten feet of street, glaring at a car as it passes. The children in the backseat shrink below their window. "I need help and so does Buff."

"Help? You got a *federal* judge for a playmate. Wanna explain that?

We got feds in our gang team and this judge gets you PR'd out on a child-rape complaint like it's a parking ticket. Wanna explain that? I pick you up out front of the L7 yesterday. You're with Arleen Brennan—the twin sister of a child rape/murder victim—the same day the *Herald* says you and Ruben are the little girl's killers. The day before Buff and your brother are to go to the depositions, Buff, Jewboy, and Ruben have a fistfight, then Buff and Jewboy go down via some Asian bitch—"

"How's Buff?"

Silence. "Dying."

Tania Hahn reaches me, but her eyes are fixed over my shoulder. She hides her Glock tight to her thigh and tells her phone, "Car two? Cadillac Escalade at the corner. Tinted windows. Second time it's passed. If it's the Koreans, they'll move on me. The Escalade is yours. I repeat, the Escalade is yours."

The Escalade begins a left turn away from us. I tell Jason, "I'm into something messy. Buff called it 'Shadowland.' Nothing's what it seems, but it's all bad."

"And you're not telling me, us? What the fuck is that about?"

"Survival. Yours and mine. Some kind of CIA maze. Can't tell the good guys from the bad. Hell, they're all bad." I turn away from Hahn and the Escalade's taillights. "Tania Hahn framed me, forced me to help her find a package that left Japan in the 1940s. We don't have much time. The package may be in Chicago to blackmail Furukawa and I need your help before—"

"Sorry. Fresh out of suicide."

"—someone can use it tonight."

Jason balks. *"Use it?"*

Hahn knocks the phone out of my hand. "Want panic in the streets, Officer Vargas?" She cuts to the Escalade's taillights, then back. "How many will a stampede kill? Everyone you tell has a family."

Lightning cracks the eastern sky. The Escalade does a U to face us, not the left turn it started. I draw my .38. Hahn steps back, thinking the .38's for her. I shove her sideways and two-hand at the Escalade's windshield. Jason's faint voice yells from the sidewalk. The Escalade stops hard a hundred and fifty feet up the block.

Hahn stiff-arms her Glock at the windshield. The Escalade doesn't charge or retreat.

Hahn bends her elbow, easing the Glock to her shoulder. "Koreans don't play tag. They'd already have us on the ground and their skill saws out." She thinks about it and frowns. "Gotta be Furukawa. And if Furukawa's here hunting White Flower, then the good Dr. Ota doesn't plan to pay your brother and White Flower when the package is exchanged. Somehow, Ota's gonna flash money, isolate Ruben and Lý, and smoke them both."

I lower my .38, eyes on the Escalade, and scoop my phone. Jason's disconnected.

Hahn taps her watch. "The Furukawa 10K starts in less than an hour. We bait the Escalade away from here, lose it fast, then hit Cristo Rey. If the nun's there she could still be Lý's friend or patron. Keep calling Ruben, my guys will go through Lý's apartment, find her job address. C'mon. You drive."

Hahn tells car two the new plan. I jump in her car, lay on the horn, and gun us south seven blocks on Morgan into the old stockyards. The Escalade stays in the mirror. I didn't tell Jason that Hahn wouldn't get within a mile of Furukawa's 10K without a Tyvek suit. What if Jason does? Hahn bends over the seat, Glock between the headrests at the back window.

My phone's in my lap; so's my .38. I'm doing eighty, weaving, hoping no uniform cars interdict us. We fly past citizens who pull cell phones to complain. This kind of driving won't dodge the uniforms for long. "Hold on." I brake hard, veer into an ungated warehouse lot, gun it to the next lot, jump the curb, veer into the open gate, gun it to a street, then back north. My phone rings.

Hahn grabs it from my lap. "Ruben, this is Tania Hahn."

22

ARLEEN BRENNAN

SUNDAY, 3:35 PM

"Repeat it back to me."

The homeless guy says, "When they introduce Dr. Ota, I turn around and throw the test tube."

I pat the shoulder of his bright yellow 2016 Chicago Olympics 10K T-shirt. "Good. Then what?"

"Stand there and let them jump me. Tell them you—the lady from Vietnam—paid me two hundred dollars to throw it."

I hand him five twenties, then tear five more in half, and hand five of the halves to him. "The rest tomorrow, back at the mission, okay? Got it?"

"Back at the mission. Tomorrow."

"Go up to the stand now. Get as close as you can to the middle. When all the people are up there, you look over here for me." I point to the northeast corner of Michigan and Congress. "When I wave this umbrella, you turn around and throw the test tube at Dr. Ota, the Japanese man at the microphone."

"They won't hurt me?"

"Not if you just stand there. They want to know where I am." I pat his shoulder again. "And you tell them everything you can remember."

SUNDAY, 3:50 PM

Ten thousand runners cram Michigan Avenue waiting for the starter's pistol. The river of summer Mardi Gras is eight lanes wide and stretches back six city blocks, an equal number in running shorts, Halloween costumes, and all manner of Chicago regalia. I call Sarah a fifth time and hang up before her voice mail answers.

Furukawa's reviewing stand is set up at the Congress Parkway divider on the Grant Park side of Michigan Avenue and covered in bunting. Dr. Ota and his fellow luminaries are thirty yards from me. Toddy Pete Steffen is up there next to the mayor. Security cameras rotate atop tall poles, scanning the crowd for people like me.

Presidential assassin.

For $124 cash at Filene's Basement, I bought a long black wig, an umbrella, sunglasses, and a Hawaiian-print muumuu that covers my Blanche DuBois dress. After my man throws the test tube I'll dive into the crowd and start running. That's plan B: nobody gets hurt; my part's done; I get the lead in *Streetcar.*

Lone gunman.

Theater, Arleen, a show, nothing more. Except it feels like we're throwing the grenade at Anwar Sadat. And it should. Dr. Ota won't know it's a warning until after the test tube scares the shit out of him in public. His bodyguards won't know it's a warning, either. No telling what they'll do, what the cops will do, or the runners, if people on the viewing stand stampede.

The PA buzzes: "TESTING, ONE, TWO. TESTING."

My guy's not as close as he should be. Dr. Ota is stage center, but back several feet. Someone will introduce him to the crowd; that's when Ruben said to throw the test tube. The test tube and Dr. Ota have to be connected, questioned, wondered about. If I can cause that, Ruben will let me go. Uh-huh, Ruben says he'll let me go, but he won't. There'll be another meeting, probably at seven or so when the Japanese women call my phone. By then I'll have *Streetcar*; I'll be able to go to Toddy Pete, tell him Ruben is sabotaging his Olympics.

"TESTING, ONE, TWO. TESTING."

I can threaten Ruben with Toddy Pete—tell Ruben he can have his blackmail money if he leaves me alone and pays all the people he says he'll pay. If Ruben won't leave me alone, Toddy Pete gets a full report on Ruben and Furukawa. That could work; it could. I'll have *Streetcar.* Ruben will either have his money or he'll have Toddy Pete and all the muscle in this city at his throat.

My stomach cramps. I blot out other outcomes. Plan B will work. I'll make it work.

"LADIES AND GENTLEMEN . . . YOUR ATTENTION, PLEASE."

Toddy Pete, Dr. Ota, and the mayor meet behind a grinning announcer holding the mic like a 1940s crooner in one hand, a red starter pistol in the other. Behind them, the reviewing stand is jammed with Chicago sports legends, politicians, black reverends, business titans, and every TV/film/stage actor and actress who claims Chicago as home. My man is up front, mixed in the crowd with other revelers, security men, and police.

"LET ME INTRODUCE DR. HITOSHI OTA, CEO OF FURUKAWA INDUSTRIES, OUR WONDERFUL SPONSOR . . ."

My man looks at me. *Theater, Arleen, that's all the test tube is.* I wave the umbrella. The crowd raises their arms to applaud. My man turns as Dr. Ota accepts the mic and starter pistol. The test tube arcs high and slow toward the stage, glinting as it reaches the top of its arc. Necks bend to watch. The test tube lands at Dr. Ota's feet and shatters. Dr. Ota lurches backward into his aides. One covers his mouth and points into the crowd. Security men rush toward the center. Toddy Pete grabs the red starter pistol, raises it, and fires. The runners behind me surge forward and I jump into the Mardi Gras river. Police shout at the reviewing stand. I'm crammed in with the runners, barely moving. The crowd at the reviewing stand surges back; police yell into radios. My man is grabbed—he's pointing, blurting my description. I try to run faster but can't. Shoulders and hips bump me. I forgot to put on the scarf.

I duck and fight left to filter toward the curb. We're moving so slow the police could walk faster on the sides. Lots of police on the corners, on the sidewalks, radios to their faces—

It takes two blocks to filter eight lanes of Michigan Avenue to the curb. At the first break in the bystanders I jump through, head down, and walk past two cops, reach an alley, and run halfway in to a Dumpster. The cops don't follow. Behind the Dumpster, I shed the muumuu, lose the wig and sunglasses, then watch the Mardi Gras throng passing the alley. Sirens wail. No cops in my alley; no Furukawa. I pat myself together, deep breath, and emerge a civilian in the Blanche dress and scarf.

Walking west, I act innocent, no idea how bad it's gotten at the reviewing stand. *Theater, that's all it was.* I call Sarah. No answer. Maybe they're all still at the Shubert, still deciding. It could happen like that. More sirens. It could. A squad car, lights flashing, roars up Madison at me. *The test tube was empty, wasn't it?* The cop's face in the driver's window cuts to me.

Ruben calls; Sarah doesn't.

I keep walking, scanning doorways for Japanese women, for Korean gangsters, for crooked cops, for Santa Monica. Stop it, this plan will work; feels like it won't; lot of amendments, but it will. Because it has to. It's what I have. I wait for the new plan's mild euphoria and get a huge rush of fight-or-flee. My phone vibrates. More sirens. *Sprint. Away.* To the Shubert! Run the last block to the Shubert; curl up out front; hug my knees; make a grown-up tell me my future. RUBEN vibrates on my phone. Pulse pounds in my head. This isn't a plan, it's a suicide attempt. I start to throw the phone—

It *is* a plan. Don't panic. Can't go to the Shubert; Ruben would figure the Shubert. I look east so fast I stumble, then west, then east, then west again. *Breathe. Exercise control.* We do not panic. We have self-esteem. Deep breath, then another.

YOU HAVE A PLAN.

Arleen the Poised takes another breath, then walks, not runs, west, away from the Shubert. I keep walking, head down, till I cross Wacker Drive, repeating the mantra: I have a plan. No more panic attacks. Not now, can't have them, won't have them.

At the river I quit concentrating on no panic and realize I've walked to the Furukawa Building. Ruben calls again. Be elsewhere; get a drink, drugs, something. Call Bobby? Sun glares off the river. *Like the lightning did on the Santa Monica pier.* I fumble my phone back into my purse, then pull it back out and read Bobby's text message wishing me luck for *Streetcar.* I put my phone on ring, won't have to read Ruben's name.

We do not panic. We have self-esteem.

I call Bobby and walk north, too jumpy to stay put anywhere. His phone rings. What do I say? Tickets to Farawayland? Make the Shubert call me? Your brother's a gangster who won't leave me alone? Can't we all just get along? Bobby's phone goes to voice mail.

We do not panic.

Drink, drugs, something. Coogan's Riverside is up ahead, but not far enough away from Furukawa. Coogan's is a neighborhood saloon that Sarah and many of the theater and opera crowd frequent. If Sarah's in Coogan's, I lost. My phone rings Sarah's ringtone. I squeeze my eyes shut. The phone keeps ringing. Please, God. Please. I'm too scared to answer.

Eyes shut, my thumb pushes the button . . . Sarah says, "They haven't decided. They want to see us tonight, eight o'clock at the theater."

Eyes open. "I didn't lose?" My back flattens on Coogan's door. "Sarah?"

"We're still in." Pause. "Great chance we win."

On my left, police lights flash onto South Wacker. Eight lanes of runners gush into the turn. "Why? Why 'great'?"

Silence on Sarah's end.

I turn my back to the police cars leading the runners. "Are you okay? Sarah?"

"Fine. Tharien may have a conflict—"

"Meaning they want her?"

"Arleen, I don't know. But I know Jude Law wants you. And Anne Johns wants Jude."

My entire life flashes in surround sound. "Oh, God. Should I go over?" The 10K front-runners charge at me, the huge pack bulging behind.

"No. No. You know better. I realize this is torture, but they'll decide when they decide. Trust me, I'll stay with it minute by minute. Just . . . keep the faith. It's your turn." Sarah clicks off. The river of runners floods into the gap. The Shubert marquee demands I fight through. Swim the river, kiss the dirty pavement. Maybe Toddy Pete is hosting an Olympic party in his office. I could go over there, beg, quick blow job, clean the furniture, help with the sushi canapés . . . Or if Dr. Ota didn't have a heart attack, I could tell him about Ruben. Then tell Toddy Pete about his son—

Don't even think that. We do not panic. We . . . we . . . I don't know what we do, but *don't* panic. Thousands of runners surge between me and my Shubert marquee. The grandly decorated Furukawa Building towers above us. I'm trapped; a new force of nature to contend with, to circumvent, to accommodate. A rush of anger bubbles in my stomach and throat. I focus hard on the runners, but the anger keeps coming. My eyes drift up to the Furukawa Building and the western skyline. The anger builds, flexing into my hands and back. Big phallic imposing monuments to the big phallic owners of all the stages in all the world . . . and if a girl aspires to be on one of those stages, she never stops chasing the stage owners' validation. Never stops hoping the stage owners will love you, won't hurt you . . . with their Big Swingin' Dicks.

Anger, good. Panic, bad.

Hard to be that stupid and out on your own. And yet, here you are. I stare at Furukawa, then down Monroe to the Shubert. The runners between us blur. Sarah's tone nags at me. Coogan's door opens into my back and I slide north along the wall. A bartender looks out. No, Sarah's fine, *Streetcar* is fine. I'm just exhausted, too adrenaline-fried to think straight. Get a drink or three, put the last forty-eight hours back in the bag. Be a good girl, like Da used to say.

I choke on my father and have to look up to swallow the bile. Furukawa is the skyline. Way out of your league, Arleen, dancing with the giants who never take you home, just out to the car. I turn away, but behind me is the river, my da's river. Always the giants. A river I ran from. Right to Hollywood's river, expecting it to be different. But they never are if you set yourself up as less than an equal. And now I've put Arleen in Ruben's river, and Furukawa's, and Toddy Pete Steffen's.

Ah, okay, maybe anger and history aren't the best answer to panic. Maybe stay closer to the now, keep the faith four more hours and—

Why? Why will these giants treat me different this time? Because I'm finally the lead in their drama, their future? The Furukawa Building covers the green water with its reflection, waiting for an answer. My phone rings in my hand. Ruben Vargas. I don't have to answer to hear Ruben threaten me with the Korean mafia, or hear Dr. Ota and Toddy Pete Steffen say, *C'mon, Arleen, you've been working for tips your whole life, the kindness of strangers.*

The phone quits ringing with me staring at the river. Then rings again.

Say it, Arleen: Please let me audition for your family. Please pay me for serving your meals. Please fuck me in the backseat of your rental car.

Eyes shut. Deep breath. You're tired, baby. Do not come apart. Imagine good things. Imagine playing once on level ground. Make that your future. Sit down with a boy like Bobby, gaze across a table, a lawn, a bed; talk about . . . anything. Touch his hands. Plan *that* future. One that doesn't require the grace of a theater or studio, the forgiveness of a multinational megacorporation, the head-pat of a critic after he came in your mouth, or the veracity of a crooked cop and his crooked police partners.

Actress. Actress. Actress. *Winning* actress.

My hand throbs, crushing the phone. Both eyes jam shut. Arleen's always hoping, always reaching, always . . . Since we were little, Coleen and I've been fighting to own our lives—they stole hers and I've always given mine away, hanging it on a silver thread and "the kindness of strangers." My right hand calls Bobby before the left hand can shove him back behind the giants. I hope he answers. My father's river says he won't.

23

OFFICER BOBBY VARGAS

SUNDAY, 5:00 PM

Cristo Rey's uniformed security guard is large, mid-sixties, and working a second or third part-time job instead of being retired. He limps on a trick knee back to his post at the far, far end the dark hallway, satisfied that Tania Hahn and I are the police. The blond back of Hahn's head is visible through the glass wall of the principal's office. She's talking to a white-haired woman. My phone rings, Arleen's name and number on the screen. I duck into a recessed doorway. "Hi. Hello, Arleen?"

Silence, then: "My knight in shining armor."

"Call me Lancelot. Did you get the part?"

"Not yet. Want to have that picnic anyway?"

"For real? You're . . . okay . . . with all the stuff they're saying?"

"We've all sinned, Bobby. Those aren't yours. And screw 'em anyway, you know? Been a tough weekend for all of us."

She sounds beat, like a prizefighter in the late rounds. "Absolutely—"

Hahn steps up, eyes narrow, and chins at my phone. "Who?"

I turn a shoulder. "Arleen."

"I'm here. Who was that? If you're busy—"

"No. Not busy. Someone I work with."

Hahn mouths, Arleen *Brennan*? I nod, holding my hand up and turn away. Hahn grabs my arm hard and shakes her head. "We have to find Ruben."

Arleen's voice adds pitch. "Bobby? Is Ruben there? With you?"

"No. That was the girl I work with. She's looking for him."

"Why?"

Odd question. I start to ask why Arleen cares, but don't. "Long story, and not particularly good."

Silence. Hahn fish-eyeing me and the phone.

"Arleen?"

"Yeah. Maybe we better not—"

"The stuff they're saying isn't true. None of it."

"What about Ruben?"

Blink. "What about him? Why does Ruben matter?"

Hahn grabs my arm again; puts a finger to her mouth.

Arleen says, "Who's the girl with you?"

Hahn nods, okay. I say, "Tania Hahn. She works for the CIA. Sort of."

"Sort of?"

Hahn grabs my phone. "This is Tania." She hits Speaker so I can hear. "If you know where Ruben is, it'll help a whole lot of people if you tell me."

"Put Bobby on."

I reach. "Gimme my phone."

Hahn bats my hand away. "Arleen, if you're in with Ruben, Robbie, and Lý, now is the time to come over with us. An hour or two from now there may not *be* a right side."

"I don't know what you're talking about. Put Bobby on."

"Yeah, you do." Hahn's voice ramps. "Was the vial empty? I have to know."

Click.

Hahn hits Redial. I grab the phone back. Arleen doesn't answer. I glare Hahn back two steps, then text Arleen: "Please call me."

Hahn points at my phone. "Bingo."

"Fuck you."

"Oh, yeah." Hahn nods big like she's reciting scripture. "Ruben wouldn't do Furukawa in person. Lý wouldn't, either. She tried that once and Dr. Ota's girls almost killed her. Someone has to do the exchange and Robbie's in the hospital."

Hahn floats her eyes like any cop would agree. I don't.

She holds up the photo of the nun we took from White Flower's apartment and points at the office behind her. "Sister Mary Margaret Fey just had a chat. She *resurrected* a Carmelite orphanage in Saigon during the war and ran it on her own. Taught math at St. Dom's until it closed and teaches math here at Cristo Rey. Degree from Cornell, two hearing aids, two knee surgeries, likes Fannie Mae candy, and is due to retire this year."

"So it's the nun, Sister Mary Margaret fronting the blackmail, not Arleen."

"The nun's crippled, Bobby. Can't walk. Guess who brings her Fannie May candy on her birthday? Arleen Brennan."

I scowl at my phone that's not ringing. The door to the office opens and a white-haired woman struggles out using a walker.

Hahn introduces us. "Sister Mary Margaret—Bobby Vargas, Chicago Police Department."

The nun smiles. "I remember you. From the neighborhood."

"Sorry. I don't remember . . ."

She smiles again. "Our habits; we all looked alike."

I point at Hahn. "She thinks Arleen Brennan is involved in a blackmail plot with my older brother Ruben. You remember Ruben, too?"

The smile fades. "Yes. The Four Corners was quite tough then, a premonition of what it is now."

Hahn taps her watch. "Sister, could you tell him what you told me."

Sister Mary Margaret straightens in the walker. "In 1975, Bob Anderson helped me escape Saigon. I had been young, impetuous, and political, and at odds with my order. We reconciled, the church and I, and sadly, I agreed to suppress my political activism in exchange for inner-city missions. Over the years, Bob assisted me in various government inquiries by forgetting my name."

"Hahn told you who we're hunting?"

"Lý Thi Loan. In 1982, Bob helped me bring her over from Vietnam. I had schooled her in the orphanage before the Korean mafia lured her away. Very bright, beautiful—thought to be the illegitimate daughter of a French missionary. Lý was my favorite. Bob knew her from the Caravelle Hotel and the Continental Palace as a prostitute with high-ranking customers on both sides of the war."

"Lý Thi Loan is White Flower Lý?"

"Yes. When White Flower arrived in the States there were issues with her documents." Sister Mary Margaret adjusts her weight in the walker. "White Flower was . . . unstable, damaged badly by her life in Vietnam since I had last seen her. Bob and I falsified her remaining paperwork and I gained her admittance to the convent at St. Dom's as a postulant. Almost immediately she had difficulty adjusting; there were arguments with students at the school. White Flower was expelled from the program and disappeared."

Hahn says, "She threatened you and St. Dom's."

"White Flower was quite angry. Understandable"—the nun focuses on me—"given the conditions at the time."

"What conditions?" I lean closer. "The Terry Rourke stuff?"

"The argument that resulted in White Flower's final expulsion was with the Brennan sisters."

"Brennan sisters" echoes in the dark hallway.

"White Flower was accused by the Brennans' father—a violent, frightening man—of physically threatening his twin daughters. Rumored as a former child prostitute and being from Vietnam exacerbated White Flower's guilt and the father's demands. He threatened the school with an investigation into White Flower's legitimate right to be in the United States. And, sadly again, we felt it best for all that White Flower leave the postulant program."

"And she did?"

"Yes."

I look at Hahn, then the nun. "What's that got to do with Ruben, other than we were all in the same neighborhood at the same time?"

The nun stares.

"What?"

"White Flower and Ruben were both questioned in the Coleen Brennan murder."

"So was I. So was everybody I knew."

Nod. "White Flower and Ruben were each other's alibi. They were together, sexually, specifically forbidden in the postulant program. White Flower had been admonished for a previous transgression with Ruben. St. Dom's saw the alibi as validation of her expulsion and that ended our association with her. I have not seen her since."

My phone rings—it's Arleen. I turn away from Hahn and the nun and an iron-clad connection between my brother and White Flower Lý. I ask Arleen, "Are you okay? Sorry, Hahn grabbed the phone—"

"Like I said, it's been a tough weekend."

"Maybe we skip the picnic, go straight to the Bushmills."

Arleen says, "Leave your girlfriend out. I'm ready now."

"I'm at Cristo Rey. Was about to tell you I was with your pal, Sister Mary Margaret. Hold on a second, she wants to say hi. Then it's you, me, and the hell with the rest of this." I bump Hahn away, hand the phone to Sister Mary Margaret, and stand between her and Hahn.

Hahn tries to get around me. "Gimme the phone. She has to talk to me."

The nun says, "Hi, it's Mary." The nun listens, her face tightening as she watches Hahn and me dancing. "No, I've never seen Ms. Hahn before." Pause. "No, I haven't discussed you other than to say—" Pause. "Child, if you're involved—" The nun stops, listens again, nods, and hands me the phone.

I walk down the hall, phone to my ear. Arleen says, "Why are you at Cristo Rey?"

"Looking for Ruben, like I said—"

"I'll meet you, but not your friend."

Hahn motions for the phone, walks alongside me as I tell Arleen, "I don't know what's going on, but I can help. And I can stop Ruben without him getting killed. I'll meet you wherever you want, alone, I promise. Let's just you and me talk, okay? You and me. If it feels weird, we walk away. If not . . . if not, we *fly* away. Just like we always planned."

Silence, then: "North end of the Michigan Avenue Bridge. I'm running out of reasons to believe, Bobby. Be alone, don't break my heart."

"Never happen." I fold the phone shut when Hahn grabs for it.

Hahn glares. "What do we know?"

"You're right, Ruben's using Arleen."

"She fronting the blackmail?"

"Don't know, but she's in, and she's scared."

"We can save her." Hahn stares hard at me. "I'm not kidding."

"Yeah. You're all about saving."

"I am. Your problem's that I don't have your brother and his pals at the top of my list."

"You think you're gonna kill Ruben, don't you?"

"'Cause he hung up on me a few minutes ago?"

"You're a bounty hunter. You hired Danny Vacco so you could shoot him. Ruben alive is the same kinda problem."

Hahn stares. "Your brother is one dangerous career criminal in a cop suit. But I don't care if he shot Jesus. And even if I did, there's a whole bunch of folks in line ahead of me."

"He's going to prison. You aren't killing him."

Hahn shrugs agreement, then points back at the Cristo Rey office. "CNN was on in there. An hour ago, a woman who matches Arleen's description paid a homeless guy to toss an 'empty vial with a green rubber cap' at the 10K reviewing stand. Shattered—that means it *broke*—at Dr. Ota's feet."

"*It broke?* How do we know it was empty?"

Hahn grits her teeth. "We don't."

SUNDAY, 5:30 PM

The sidewalks on both sides of Michigan Avenue are jammed with concertgoers streaming south. Furukawa's party in Millennium Park is expected to draw thousands. I call Ruben; his phone picks up but he doesn't speak. "Ruben, you can't do Furukawa—"

Thirty feet ahead, two cops scan the crowd and focus my way. I duck into the street and the stalled traffic. "I know all about it, Ruben: the Hokkaido package, White Flower Lý. I've been to her apartment, to Cristo Rey. She has an altar—somebody tore the place apart, probably her." My voice breaks. "She shot Jewboy, Ruben. Killed him dead. Buff's dying in ICU. You gotta give her to me; give yourself up. Call Barlow. I'll help you, but you gotta stop."

Silence.

"Ruben? These people are innocent—" Ruben's connection quits. The two uniforms stop a group with open beers. Behind them in the middle of the intersection, two more uniforms argue with a dented red Toyota they're forcing onto Illinois with the rest of the traffic. I make the west curb, ease into the crowd, and use my phone to block my face. The red Toyota turns in front of me; Ruben's number blinks in my hand . . . the combination hits me like a train.

I stumble into the glass of Walgreen's storefront. I didn't pass the polygraph because I *did* mention the Toyota—to Ruben, after dinner at the Levee Grill. From day one Ruben and Lý knew why Hahn and Lopez were in town. Ruben gave up the Toyota. My stomach heaves and I curl my face into the glass. *My brother* murdered Hahn's girlfriend.

The horror rush won't stop. White Flower had a male accomplice when she shot Buff and Jewboy. Was it Ruben? My fucking brother? The undeniable possibility blurs my vision. Buff brought White Flower over; she called him the day after Ruben and Buff had a fistfight . . . she set Buff up to die. Her and Ruben.

My knees buckle. On hands and knees, I stare at the concrete. Shoes and legs surge around me. I try to stand and two men help me up, asking if I'm okay. I nod and stagger for balance. For half a block, the revelers on Michigan Avenue carry me with them. I slide into a doorway and call Ruben again. Ruben's phone picks up, but he doesn't speak. Neither do I.

In our silence I want to scream, want to cry, but do neither. Revelers stream past, loud and oblivious. I wait for Ruben to pull us back from the brink, to tell me something, anything that changes the facts. He doesn't. I flip my phone shut. The *click* is so loud it rattles my spine.

At the bridge I step out of the flow but not out of the crowd. I have a citywide out on me for murdering Danny Vacco. Add cop fears that one of their own may be a psycho child molester and standing at the north end of the Michigan Avenue bridge may get me shot. Adults and teenagers school past, some with samurai headbands, some with togas, some bare-chested, painted with Chicago and Olympic logos.

I pat the pistol under my shirt—White Flower dies for Jewboy and Buff. Ruben goes to prison . . . and if Hahn can't or won't work her magic, I probably do, too. Hard to imagine America, the universe, going this bad, this fast.

Arleen appears out of the crowd. Five foot seven wearing a '40s dress and fragile smile. The universe improves. We're ten feet apart. I saw her yesterday—one time in twenty-nine years that wasn't an old photograph—and now she's the only good thing I know. There's a reason we're back in each other's lives. I feel it like baptism.

Her eyes fan left of me, then right. She steps back. "Am I safe, Bobby?"

"Knight in shining armor, remember?"

She's not sure. "Might take a lot of armor." She looks spent but stunning—windblown blond hair, heroic green eyes. The girl you've been waiting all your life for, who could make you stupid and sappy and happy to tell your friends how it feels. I don't want to ask, but I have to.

"Was the vial empty?"

ARLEEN BRENNAN

I keep ten feet between us, stare at all the things that could go wrong, or right. Bobby's not Ruben, not in his posture or clothes, not smiling, hoping to get laid when he's done with dinner. He isn't promising an audition if I . . . Bobby's just looking at my eyes, waiting for a sign, trying to decide . . .

"The green cap was already off when he gave it to me."

Bobby exhales and begins a smile he's having trouble stopping.

Twenty-nine years and one yesterday later I hear me say: "I want to kiss you once before . . . whatever happens, happens. Okay? I know it's stupid, but that's what I want."

He blinks but doesn't move, then steps through the crowd between us, slides his hands into my hair, and kisses me on the lips. Not a movie kiss, not overwhelming passion, but a strong man who means it. My arms slow-circle the strength of his shoulders because that's what I want them to do, then his neck as I press up from my toes. Our lips part and it's . . . so strong I shiver and squeeze against him to hold on. He does the same. His chest and my breasts are a thin layer of '40s fabric apart. I shiver again. If we were alone I'd want to be naked, or crying, or both.

SIREN.

Bobby doesn't let go. I press harder against him and don't let go, either. It *is* a movie kiss, the best of my career. His eyes are wet; my eyes are wet. My lips brush his cheek. Four of my fingers slide into his belt. I breathe shallow and say, "Um, hi?"

His left hand stays in my hair. "Hi."

We stay like that, feeling each other's hearts beat, the heat of our skin, the trembles that— He kisses me again. I don't startle or step back or care who's watching.

Bobby gently presses me to arm's length, holding my shoulders, then bends his knees so our eyes are level. He says, "I know Ruben's dirty. I know he's going to prison. You're not; I'll protect you from him and his crew. Promise."

Tears dribble my cheeks. Bobby hugs me to him. The tears don't stop, may never stop. He brushes them away, kisses me again, and hugs tighter. His heart is strong against my chest. He tells my ear, "We're gonna be okay. You're not in trouble. Nobody steals your dream. Not gonna happen."

I can smell the river at the bridge and semi-whisper, "Think I better sit down."

OFFICER BOBBY VARGAS

I slip us around the Wrigley Building's south half onto the Water Street promenade. A strip of shade runs underneath the sky bridge and that's where we sit with our backs to the wall. I hold both her hands and wait. Our legs touch from hip to knee. She trembles in the heat and doesn't speak.

"I have to find Ruben. If you can help me, I can stop him. Just help me find him before his scam gets any worse."

Arleen removes her hands from mine, wipes her eyes, and scans Water Street. "It's bad, Bobby."

"Yeah, it is. But Ruben's scam isn't how you and I finish. We're going to happy ever after. Got the script in my pocket."

Arleen almost smiles. She touches my face and watches my eyes, then takes a deep breath. "The Furukawa people don't think it's a scam."

"Why? What do you know?"

"Ruben made me give them a sample of something. The woman I gave it to was very careful with it. She said they'd test it and if it was real, they'd pay Ruben and Robbie what they're asking."

"When."

"Tonight. By seven o'clock."

"And you . . . have to front the trade?"

She nods. "Ruben got me involved on a lie. The situation went bad in a hurry, and I was trapped. If I don't keep helping him, he turns me in . . ."

"For what?"

"It's bad."

"I don't care. Help me find Ruben before he can continue and I'll forgive you anything. So will Chicago, the feds, and anyone with sense."

Arleen stares at our shoes. "Friday, I was delivering a message for Ruben on Lawrence Avenue. It was part of the lie Ruben tricked me into. Robbie Steffen drove up and shot a man to death. That makes me an accessory to murder and a witness Robbie Steffen can't leave alive."

Unfortunately, she's right. The ASA will roll her to testify against Robbie. If she can prove Ruben tricked her, the ASA will promise to cut her loose after the trial. But Robbie won't.

"Ruben said he could square me with Robbie. I believed Ruben and went to Greektown yesterday. But it was setup to get Robbie and me killed, to pacify the Koreans." Arleen stands. I pull her back. She squeezes her temples. "I might've shot one of the Koreans."

"You? Do they know it was you?"

"The Korean shot Robbie, then tried to kill me. I think I shot him. Twice."

I grab her hands. They're trembling. "Self-defense—have to convince the ASA you weren't a willing participant, then testify against Ruben and Robbie. Not easy, but with right pub and a good lawyer you could walk."

"Maybe, but I won't walk from Toddy Pete. He won't let me put his son in prison. Forever."

I point at the crowds heading south to the concert. "Toddy Pete won't let Robbie torch the Olympic rebid, either. Way too much at stake." I squeeze her hands. "Arleen, look at me. Do the Koreans know it was you in the alley?"

"I don't think so, not yet. But I'm dead if Ruben tells them. And he will if I don't finish with Furukawa."

She tries to stand again and I hold her down.

"Bobby, all . . . all I want is the Shubert; even if I can't have it. I want to win *once,* for Coleen and me. Just once."

"And you can; we can spin this. I know we can; a hero actress who goes undercover and saves a city. The *Herald* will front-page it."

Arleen starts a smile that she stops. "Robbie and the Koreans won't let me—"

"I carried your picture for twelve years. I only stopped because it was wearing out." I squeeze her hands again. "No one hurts you while I'm alive. Not the Koreans, not Robbie. No one."

ARLEEN BRENNAN

I concentrate on Bobby's brown eyes; not a spec of bad in them, just boyish promise surrounded by a man's resolve. He means to save us. Who knows if he can, but he means to, and right now that's our happily ever after. I lean forward and kiss him on the lips. And that feels like happily ever after for real.

I dig out my phone and hit Redial on Ruben's number, dry swallow, then hold the phone so Bobby can hear.

Ruben answers. "*Niña,* a homeless man? Beautiful, I gotta say. Threw a strike."

Bobby winces at the voice. I shrug, *sorry,* and say, "I'm out, Ruben, leave me alone."

"Almost. Just one more errand and you can have your Shubert role. Everyone gets paid, all is forgiven."

"Can't. Have to be at the Shubert at eight o'clock—"

"Yeah, I talked to Sarah. No problem. We'll be all done by then."

"Leave Sarah alone. I mean it. And stay away from the Shubert. I'm out, Ruben. Over. Done."

"*Niña,* don't go stupid on me now, not this close to the finish. Santa Monica and Lawrence Avenue just a phone call away."

Bobby taps my knee and mouths *Santa Monica*?

I stammer, losing my place.

"We don't want that pier in Santa Monica coming back, ruining everything."

Chicago fades to Santa Monica, the vengeful nightmare apparition cornering me on the pier. Lightning behind me; nowhere to run; years of little-girl horror packaged into one final assault. I scream: "Get away from me!" An arm grabs my shoulder. A phone yells in my ear. I blink back to Chicago, to crowds, faces staring, to heat searing my skin and Ruben's voice in my ear. Bobby squeezes me to him. I tell the phone, "Money. I want part of the money."

Silence.

I hang up, embarrassed, flushed at all memories, thoughts of . . . Bobby stares deep in my eyes. Looking for the pier? The man on it? Bobby touches the heat in my face.

"I don't want a dime; don't know why I said that. I want the Shubert, then I want this to end."

"Me, too." Bobby half smiles, cracked and friendly, but crushed by his gangster-monster brother. "When Ruben calls back, fight for money—be an actress, play it like a part—but agree to whatever will put you and him together."

My phone rings.

Bobby finishes with "And I'll take it from there."

I answer the phone. Ruben says, "So, *chica,* we in business now? How much you think you need to outrun Santa Monica?"

I channel Lilly Dillon in *The Grifters.* "Threaten me one more time, Ruben, and I'm calling the U.S. attorney."

Silence. Then: "Why? How much of my money do you want?"

Bobby mouths, *Five million.*

My eyes go wide. Bobby nods. I say, "Five million."

"Don't think so, *chica.*"

"Then you and your partners get another front man. Or face the Japanese yourself."

"The Japs runnin' scared right now; little jumpy after that vial hit their man. But they're good with you. We'll give you a hundred K—fuck it, two-fifty, cash—"

"Make it two million or I hang up and call Toddy Pete, tell him you're behind his only son being shot, and you're the maniac screwing up the biggest move of T.P.'s career."

"No Shubert for you."

"*Like you'll let me have it?* You're a bottomless pit, Ruben. Pay me and

I disappear. Or in the next ten minutes I bury you with Toddy Pete. Period. End of offer." I hang up, quit playing Lilly Dillon, and semi-fall back into Bobby's shoulder.

Bobby's gone pale listening to his brother, but builds me a smile. "That was good. Ruben will believe you want the money."

"I want the Shubert. Ruben's not taking the Shubert unless he kills me."

Bobby grips my arm. "I love Ruben, but Ruben's going to prison. I'll make peace with that before we see him. And I'll make him kill me before he hurts you." Bobby swallows and pats my arm. "He won't do that. I'm his brother; he won't hurt me."

I stare, don't tell Bobby that I think Ruben is a sociopath who wouldn't think twice about killing his little brother and eating him. "What about Agent Hahn?"

"She's a problem. A wild card. But she has to be part of the solution . . . to be sure Furukawa's . . . mess is cleaned up."

I scan the crowd on Water Street. "Do we trust her?"

"No. Tania Hahn's a private contractor, a bounty hunter with CIA credentials. She and her folks are who were packaging me as a child molester."

I pull away, not sure I heard that.

Bobby says, "So she could leverage me. To get to Ruben and Robbie and my sergeant."

"We're betting our lives on someone who'd do that?"

Bobby nods. "Hahn has resources."

"So does the devil, but we wouldn't trust—"

"I can't let her kill Ruben, I don't care what he's done. And I think she suspects Ruben gave up the Toyota that killed her girlfriend."

I lean farther away and Bobby pulls me back.

"It's complicated, I know, but I think you and I can collapse the whole thing in on all of them." Bobby makes a test tube with his fingers. "Provided the bomb hasn't already gone off."

"The vial I— It was symbolic. Something Dr. Ota would know."

"Hope so." Bobby eases back to explain. "There are thirty vials like the sample you gave the Japanese. Hahn calls them the 'Hokkaido package.' By the end of World War II, Dr. Ota and his fellow scientists had created what they hoped was the equivalent of America's atom bomb—a live virus, a form of the plague that helped them kill thirty million Chinese."

"That's what Ruben's selling?"

Bobby nods. "If his partner hasn't changed her mind."

"Oh. My. God."

24

ARLEEN BRENNAN

SUNDAY, 6:00 PM

My reflection in the coffee-shop window looks scared and off-balance—like me, not Lilly Dillon from *The Grifters.* I'm waiting for Ruben Vargas, a sociopath willing to unleash live-virus plague in Chicago.

A man I'm going to help. My phone rings next to my coffee.

Be Lilly Dillon. Be The Grifters. I inhale into a tough, streetwise character who spent much of her life outside the law, then tell my phone and Ruben Vargas: " 'Reckless' would be a compliment—"

"We have to talk right now," says Tracy Moens, "about your father. Before tomorrow's depositions."

"Bye."

"I know your father raped you. And Coleen . . . for years. Something happened that February night that was impossibly worse and your sister ran. You couldn't get away or didn't try, but Coleen did."

Moens keeps talking. My eyes squeeze shut—the *go-away* defense Coleen and I used. Before, during, and after—it didn't happen. She'd promise me; I'd promise her back—bad dreams, only bad dreams, hold each other under the shower till the bad dreams were gone.

"Your father lied to the police and the prosecutors during all three trials; stood by while one black teenager was imprisoned for life and Anton Dupree was executed. Your father knew *he* was the rapist, not Dupree. That's the same as murder." Pause. "Your mother knew. And you knew. But no one talked."

Coleen and I talked every night. She didn't stop screaming for years.

"That year you watched the echoes of that night slowly kill your mother, then ran away hoping to keep them from killing you. Nineteen years later a 'blond woman' shot and wounded your father on a pier in Santa Monica, and then let him drown . . . four days before you arrived in New York."

I hang up on Moens, drop the phone, and both hands wipe at my father on my skin. The air fouls with the taste of the Four Corners—the stockyards slaughter, and—

Ruben slides into my booth.

His hands and knees are inches from mine. Ruben looks at my hands, then me. His brown eyes are empty, chilling; my father's eyes. "One hour, you make the trade."

My phone rings again. Ruben barks, "Don't answer."

I force my father away. Lilly Dillon bites my jaw tight and stares at Ruben across the table. *I'm going to the Shubert, motherfucker. You're going to prison.*

Ruben's skin has blackened under the bandage that crosses his left eyebrow. His lower lip looks as swollen as three hours ago when he dropped me on South Michigan. With my empty vial of live-virus plague. That we hope was empty.

Ruben's clean jacket and shirt suggest he's been home, probably had a shower. Calm and cool, like a serial killer with a whole night ahead of him. Like killing your partners, robbing the Korean mafia, and risking mass murder for money is Lesson One in the sociopath manual.

He says, "My little brother and you find some time?"

Lilly Dillon: "Been kinda busy running your errands."

Ruben's coffee arrives. "Met his girlfriend yet, Tania Hahn?"

I don't blink or look away, or do anything Lilly Dillon wouldn't. "She your other partner? Robbie's mystery Vietcong bitch?"

Ruben smiles at another default admission I was in the alley, but he's focused on any tells, any hint that I intend to harm him or betray his plans. "In thirty minutes, you'll deliver a box to the Jap women who were at the Maxwell Market. That simple. We get a taste of the money, they get half their vials. Let the Japs inspect your box. They'll give you a bag that weighs twenty-two pounds. The bag and you drive back to me."

Lilly Dillon sips her coffee, wary but confident.

Ruben keeps watching me for tells. "Round one will be simple—half don't help 'em; they gotta recover one hundred percent of the package or Furukawa and Ota are front-page." Ruben stares. "Round two could be tougher."

Lilly Dillon: "My two million's paid out of the first trade or no deal."

Ruben leans his sociopath, serial-killer smile closer to me. "Or you're gonna call Toddy Pete and the U.S. attorney? From here? While I sit back and watch?"

I don't move or blink, because Lilly Dillon wouldn't. "I have a friend. My friend has a script and two phone numbers."

Ruben nods, then lays his oily hand on top of my coffee cup. Where my mouth was. His nails are long and perfect and way too close to me. "*Niña,* the Japs are only payin' one million up front, just a taste. We wanted more, thought we could get it, but old Dr. Ota's too smart for that. You get your money after round two. And save the lie that you don't care about the Shubert, okay? If that's the truth, then take a walk, make your next two million waitin' tables in a Koreatown basement."

Lilly Dillon adds up her limited options, demonstrating resolve not fear, then grabs her purse. "The very first lie I smell in the fifty lies you plan to tell me, I blow this up *for everyone.*"

"Don't need to hurt or rob you to get what I want."

Lilly stares. "Then let's go do it."

Ruben doesn't move. He peers out the window. "Your *friend* out there?"

"I'm not that stupid."

Ruben searches the street, the parked cars, the buildings, then says, "Catch a cab, take Ontario toward Greektown. I'll call you on this phone and tell you when to get out." He hands me a phone with no key pad.

"Big bad Ruben nervous?" I nod across Ohio Street where Bobby and Tania Hahn and her crew are supposed to be. "Maybe you'll have a heart attack. Die somewhere alone in the dark waiting for your life to catch up with you."

Smile. "Do this dance every day, *chica.*" He curls one finger at my purse. "Gimme your phone."

"No."

Ruben lowers his chin.

I pull my phone, flip it open, punch the Lock code, and hand it to him. "I want that back. And my 9-millimeter you stole at the market."

Ruben nods toward the door. "Wait five minutes, walk up to Ontario, catch a cab going west. Understand?"

Lilly nods, hiding bad thoughts she's thinking. Ruben drops a five on the booth table and leaves. Lilly watches him pass the window.

I exhale big and let go of Lilly, then slump back into the vinyl. The empty space where Ruben sat radiates scary. I dip my napkin in my water glass to wash Ruben's proximity off my hands and arms. Water was never enough to wash off my father.

More and more yellow Olympics T-shirts pass the window. There'll be a crowd at Furukawa's concert. Just what Ruben wants . . . My five minutes are up. I inhale a deep Actors Studio breath that remakes me Lilly Dillon, grab her purse, her cold resolve, and step outside.

Bobby and Hahn's crew are out here, but I don't see them. I walk up to Ontario and flag a westbound cab. Ruben or his partner are watching, tailing me to see if I'm followed. The cab that stops is a Yellow. Lilly opens the door, realizes the driver could already belong to Ruben, says, "Sorry, changed my mind," and shuts his door. He drives off without arguing. I wave down the next one, a gypsy, get in, hand him five twenties from my purse, and say, "Toward Greektown."

With the twenties is Bobby's number and a note that reads "Call this number now, leave your phone on, but don't raise it to your face." The driver sets his mirror to frame me. I smile. He shrugs, says, "Okay."

Lilly tells him to start singing. "Sing the name of the street we're on, your cab number, and the cross streets as we pass 'em."

He squints in his mirror.

"Go ahead, sing till I get out." He starts singing and I sit back, hoping Bobby can hear. Eight lights and hundreds of southbound yellow T-shirts later, Ruben's phone rings in my hand. Ruben says, "Left turn on LaSalle."

I lean forward to the hole in the Plexiglas, repeating Ruben's words to the driver and I hope Bobby listening on the driver's phone. We turn south, make almost five blocks. Ruben says, "Left on Kinzie." I tell the driver and he turns at the next light. Ruben says, "Get out at State Street. Walk to Rossi's, west side, 400 block at the alley. Stand out front."

I yell loud at the driver, "I'm going to Rossi's. Let me out at State."

OFFICER BOBBY VARGAS

SUNDAY, 6:45 PM

Arleen's gypsy cab is a block north. Hahn and I are running parallel. I pocket my phone. "Cab's dropping her at State and Kinzie."

Hahn loops into the oncoming lanes. She has an earpiece in her right ear and tells the mic bar at her mouth, "State and Kinzie. Stay well clear till she has the goods. Do you have visual?" Hahn listens, pushes her earpiece in tighter. "I say again, State and Kinzie. Do you have visual?" Hahn listens. "Car two, do you copy?"

HORN. Traffic jams behind two buses with Wisconsin plates. "Alley, alley." I point Hahn across traffic. "Go; I'll show you. Arleen's at a bar, Rossi's, west side of State Street." I brace into the dash. "Don't kill us or she's all alone."

Hahn skids into the alley, misses a row of trash cans, and tromps the gas. She says, "Car two, do you copy?"

ARLEEN BRENNAN

SUNDAY, 6:50 PM

The cab drops me at State and Kinzie. At the curb, I stare straight ahead in the heat. A bus passes so close Lilly and I can smell the dirt. Bobby said believe and that's what I'm doing. Lilly says, *I can beat this asshole.* We walk half a block north toward Rossi's faded green awning. I peek for Bobby or Hahn's crew.

Parked between Rossi's and me is a dented four-door white Mercury Marquis, engine running. Two young Hispanic men eye me from the backseat. Both wear T-shirts and bandannas instead of caps. One has the thin lines of a teenage mustache. The driver is older, no shirt, muscled and hard. He has Twenty-Trey tattoos on his neck. I haven't seen Twenty-Trey tattoos since I was a little girl, since my uncle Terry Rourke shot the little deaf boy and started the war.

I cross the alley and step under Rossi's awning. A late-model Chevrolet backs out of the Self Park entrance across State and straight into the alley. The tinted window drops. Ruben Vargas says, "Get in."

I back up, trying to kill time for the cavalry to get here. "Why? Where are we going?"

Ruben points my 9-millimeter at me from just above his window. "Get in or die."

Just as I get in, a green SUV veers into the corner to our left, screeching a tire. Ruben jerks to the noise. The SUV slows too fast and stops. Ruben tells his phone in Spanish, "Green SUV Ford Explorer, northbound. Two males." He glares at me and jams the 9-millimeter hard in my ribs. "I warned you."

The white Marquis with the Twenty-Treys eases from the curb, heading south toward the SUV, riding State Street's center line. The green SUV can't move. *No, don't—* The Marquis pulls broadside—driver to driver. The Hispanic boy on the passenger side stretches half out his window and over the roof with a short-barreled machine gun. The other boy extends a similar gun from behind the driver. Both open fire. Glass explodes into the street. Brass casings ribbon-arc in the flames and roar. The Twenty-Trey driver pumps a sawed-off shotgun point-blank. The SUV rocks on its tires.

Ruben wheels us out of the alley northbound and pounds the gas, the 9-millimeter stays jammed in my ribs. Over the seat I wide-eye the pocked and smoking SUV a block back. "You're a goddamn monster . . . you just murdered—"

"Your friends. That's what happens, *chica.* Fuck with me, people die." Ruben jams hard with the 9-millimeter. "Who'd you sell us to? Robbie? The Koreans? Tania Hahn?" Ruben jams harder. "Who?"

No SUV. Bobby wasn't in it. Be Lilly Dillon.

"I'm getting two million from you, right? So I'm gonna cheat you then hope my new 'friends' don't rob or kill me? Robbie wants me dead to stay out of prison; the Koreans want me dead; and I've never heard of Tania Whoever. You're an idiot lowrider who just shot a carload of choirboys."

Ruben backs off the gas, finishes seven blocks at the speed limit, then pulls into the parking lot across from Holy Name Cathedral. He eases the 9-millimeter out of my ribs but keeps it pointed at me. "Who was in the SUV? You're gonna tell me."

I make the fear spike a glare.

"*Chica,* I can smell gunfighters on you, not 'friends with scripts and phone numbers.' Could smell 'em when we were having coffee. I don't know who, but I know you got gunfighters." Ruben nods at the street. "If there's any left, best you send 'em home or all of you die today."

Lilly Dillon nods gangster to piker. "Okay. I'm caught. It was your little brother in the SUV. Batman, Bobby, and me; we're a three-way. You just killed him."

Ruben's eyes jump to his mirror—something he sees that I don't. He jams the 9-millimeter in my ribs again and says, "When the back door opens, keep your face forward."

I twist to see and he jams the 9-millimeter harder. The door opens behind me. Someone gets in. I smell oleander and glance at Ruben without moving my head. His eyes are in the mirror. He asks whoever he's looking at, "We good?"

Silence.

Ruben stares at the mirror. His tension screws the 9-millimeter deeper in my ribs. The back door opens. I hear a rush of movement, the door closes, and the oleander is gone. The side mirror flashes a grayish shape before the sun glare obliterates the reflection.

Ruben eyes his mirror for twenty seconds, then thumbs-down the hammer on my 9-millimeter, belts it, and points west. "Drive this car to the lot across from Harry Caray's. I have people in the lot to cover you. Find a space with an empty on your right. I'll call the phone I gave you." He points to the dash. "Put the phone up here and leave it on. Dr. Ota's Japs will find you. They'll want to inspect the package in the backseat." Ruben tilts his head to the backseat. "Don't let them in this car; Japs are tricky and might try to LoJack it. Take the package to their car, get in, let the Japs take a look. They give you our taste; you get back in this car, then I'll tell you where to go next to finish up."

Sweat runs down my sides. I know what's inside the box but Bobby wants to be positive Ruben does. "What's in there?"

"Your friends didn't say?"

"If I had friends who did this kind of thing, I'd have them kill you. And Robbie."

Ruben blinks once. "Drive this Chevy, *chica.* Don't drop the box. And don't make any new friends."

I inhale to answer. Ruben backhands me into the window, then grabs my dress and twists it to choke me. "Wanna fuck my brother before you die? Assuming you weren't ridin' his cock back in the day?" Ruben twists tighter and I fight at his hands. His face is dead calm but his eyes are molten. "Fuck with me and everything you care about dies." Ruben slams me back and lets go. "Drive, you make money. Fuck it up, I do shit to your life you can't imagine."

OFFICER BOBBY VARGAS

SUNDAY, 6:50 PM

White Flower dies; I trap my brother and he goes to prison; Arleen becomes a star; and I go to Jewboy's funeral. And maybe Buff's, if my friends will let me in. For the first time, I'm glad my parents are dead. Hahn wheels onto State, brakes hard, and stops half a block short of Rossi's.

Arleen's not out front.

Ruben's car isn't there; no Crown Vic, either.

Arleen wasn't supposed to get in *any* car. Not until she knew we were here. Hahn points at the south corner. Her crew's green SUV is mid-street, windows shot out, driver's door open, part of one man flopped out in the street.

Customers peek out Rossi's door. I stare at the Self Park across the street. No Arleen. Then check Magnum's Restaurant behind us on the corner. No Arleen. I pop the passenger door. Hahn grabs my shirt. I jerk out, gun in hand, loop between parked cars, and sprint sidewalk to Rossi's.

ARLEEN BRENNAN

SUNDAY, 6:55 PM

The box of mass murder in my backseat has no odor, but I can smell it and feel it. Fifteen vials of plague. Every pothole on the nine-block drive puts my heart in my throat.

The lot across from Harry Caray's isn't full of concertgoers willing to walk a mile, but they're beginning to pull in. The box on my seat has stains at the bottom. Never thought I'd die like this. A white Cadillac Escalade pulls in fast. I tell Ruben's phone, "Cadillac SUV."

The driver's tinted window drops to half. The Japanese woman from the Maxwell Market studies me without expression. She's wearing a mic and headset. "My associate will get in your car. I have a pistol pointed at you. Do not move or speak."

I shake my head. "No. Doors are locked."

Her passenger exits the SUV anyway, reaches to open the door to my backseat but can't. The driver says, "Unlock the door."

Headshake. "Can't. I have to bring the box to you."

The driver speaks Japanese to her mic and the woman passenger at my door returns to the SUV. The driver says, "Bring the box to the door behind me. Open, *get in,* shut the door."

The box of mass murder an oleander ghost placed in my backseat is UPS brown, twelve inches square, and sealed at the top with one piece of flimsy tape. I slide out and extract the box. The Escalade's back door opens. I place the box in the middle of the bench seat next to a Japanese man of middle age. He wears a helmet-less Tyvek suit; a thick pad covers his knees and legs. The driver says, "Get in. Close the door."

I climb in and close the door. Immediately, she and the other woman in the front seat exit the vehicle and shut their doors. The man says nothing and dons a Tyvek helmet over his mic and headset. I jerk the Escalade's door handle but it's locked. "Don't open that box while I'm in here."

His bio suit sealed, he opens the UPS box. From the box he pulls a large can of Crisco, carefully pops the lid, and one at a time, lifts fifteen green-topped vials halfway out of the thick white shortening. I hug my door, holding my breath. He stares at each top, uses a sanitized tissue to clean each seal and inspects them again, this time with an odd suction-cup instrument he places over each seal, possibly designed to show any escaping gas or particles.

I can't hold my breath any longer and gasp.

Next he uses another sanitized tissue to clean the exposed sides of each vial, then holds the Crisco can at eye level to locate something inside each partially exposed vial. Satisfied, he eases the vials back into the Crisco, closes the lid, and removes another instrument from the seatback pocket at his knees. He places the gauge in the air between us, waits, then removes his mask, and speaks Japanese to his headset.

The driver reenters the SUV and tells me, "The Yoshida Kaban on the deck behind you is yours."

I reach over the seat back and pull up an expensive black soft-side bag that weighs close to twenty pounds. My hand's trembling.

"Your vehicle has not been tampered with. We will not follow. In thirty minutes we will meet to complete the transaction."

"Can I use your phone?"

She stares, wondering why, then shakes her head slowly, no.

I exit the Escalade. The other Japanese woman is between our cars and stares me into mine. I toss the black soft-side bag on the seat, swallow two shallow breaths, turn the key, and drive toward the exit. The attendant moves the cones, I exit onto Clark Street, and Ruben's voice barks in the phone.

"Arleen?"

I scour for him. For Bobby. For Hahn. "Yeah. Yeah."

"Cut over to Dearborn, and head north."

OFFICER BOBBY VARGAS

SUNDAY, 7:00 PM

Smoke surrounds Hahn at the green SUV. Glass shards and brass casings litter the pavement. Hahn runs back up State Street toward her car. I run sidewalk from Rossi's and reach the car when she does. She jumps in; through bit teeth she says, "Both dead," drops her Taurus in gear, and screeches backward. Sirens wail inbound. Hahn pounds the brake and flips us north as the first squad veers to race past. For nineteen years sirens have been my friends; now I'm wanted for Danny

Vacco's murder and duck in the seat. I tell Hahn, "A guy in Rossi's said there was a good-lookin' blonde out front in a dress when he walked in. Gotta be Arleen. Bartender said he thought the shooters were bangers, might've been a gunship parked up the block."

Hahn jerks toward the curb to avoid another inbound squad.

Over the sirens I yell, "Shouldn't have been bangers anywhere near here today. Every cop in the city would've been told to burn 'em back a mile in every direction."

Hahn mashes the gas. "Unless they were connected. Had a friend on the force."

ARLEEN BRENNAN

SUNDAY, 7:25 PM

Ruben's voice: "Stay on Dearborn. Turn in to the parking garage just ahead past the corner."

At the drive I pull in to the gate. The machine pushes out a parking ticket.

Ruben's voice: "Drive to the top floor. Double-park at the elevator, leave the engine running. Take the elevator to the ground floor and stay in the lobby till I call. Don't go outside."

Lilly Dillon says, "I'm keeping the money."

"Probably has transmitters buried in the bills or sewn into the bag. Maybe worse. Might not want to handle the bag till we can be sure. Do it my way and you'll get yours."

"When?"

"Tiring me out, *chica*." The voice is hard, cruel. "I ain't in the mood to be tired."

I take the parking ticket and the bar rises. I stay on the brake.

"Move, *chica*."

Rearview mirror. No Bobby, no Hahn. Only Ruben, staring through his windshield. The Twenty-Trey shooters in the white Marquis pull in behind Ruben and block the entrance. The Japs won't be following us inside. Neither will Bobby or Hahn.

I drive switchback ramps to the top, park the Chevrolet, leave the engine running, then take the elevator to the ground floor. The lobby is stark, mildewy. One of the elevators is dropping. Is this where Arleen's supposed to die? I pop the fire-exit door and hold it open. The elevator blinks floors: 5-4-3-2-1. Ruben doesn't call. The elevator opens; I ease into the fire-stair. Two college boys exit in yellow Olympics T-shirts, laughing, smelling like reefer. One leers at my legs, then higher and smiles.

Purse, where's my purse? Ruben's phone isn't ringing because it's in my purse. Front seat. I left my purse in the car. Ruben's unloading the money from the Chevrolet, loading in the . . . package. No, Ruben won't get near the package, not after what I just saw in the Escalade.

I jump in the elevator as the doors close, punch the top floor, and ride silent.

The door opens. I turn the corner and the drive aisle's empty; the Chevrolet's gone.

No, it's parked in the shadows halfway down the descending aisle, trunk lid up, a woman bending in with her back to me. She turns just her head, sees me, and straightens. Long black hair. Not Japanese. Same clothes as the half-hidden Asian woman from the Maxwell Market; maybe the same as the oleander ghost who put the box in the Chevrolet's backseat. A pistol appears at her leg, a long silencer screwed into the barrel. I bend to run. She jerks the pistol to my chest: "No," and waves me to her.

I stop at twenty feet. Behind the gun, she stares a long inspection. Her posture is unbalanced, scary, a mental patient's forced calm. She seems to vibrate, but her pistol doesn't waver; the hole in the silencer is large and black. My heart begins to beat faster. Sweat beads on my neck.

Her free hand closes the Chevrolet's trunk. She slides up the fender to the Chevrolet's rear passenger door and pops it open. In the adjacent space is a ratty Corvair. Keeping the gun aimed at my chest, she backs to the Corvair's trunk and pops the rusted lid. Her free hand waves me to her. Each step I take closer, she matches with a step back. I stop at the Corvair's open trunk.

Her voice is monotone, the accent Vietnamese. "With care, remove the box. Place the box in the backseat of the Chevrolet." Her eyes are feverish. Beneath them, she smiles a disconnected, paste-on smile of bluish lipstick. Surgical gloves cover her hands. She gestures with the gun, pointing me to the Corvair's trunk.

I get a very bad vibe and step back. Her smile flattens into a frozen blue line. She gestures again.

My feet hesitate, then creep forward.

Up close, the Corvair smells of old dust; cheap, heavy oleander; and July heat. The backseat is full, covered in a blanket. Two women's shoes extend from the pile like the witch's feet did in *The Wizard of Oz.* The shoes are expensive and seem strangely familiar—

"Remove"—I jolt to her voice and the feverish eyes inspecting me again, all of me—"the box."

Alone in the trunk is a green-black metal box, a foot square and ten inches deep. Japanese characters are stenciled on the top. Sort of military looking. I step back. "Don't think so. I know what's in there."

"Does *Arleen Brennan* wish her share of Furukawa's payment?"

Her voice changed cadence when she used my name.

Prozac-mental-patient-ax-murderer Ted Bundy. Lilly Dillon whispers, *Get out of here, Arleen.*

"Does *Arleen Brennan* wish her money?"

"Ah . . . if she can spend it."

The woman points her pistol at the Chevrolet. "Sit in the front seat, hands on the wheel. Do not start the car. I will bring your money."

She'll be behind me. My neck exposed above the seat.

"Go. Now."

OFFICER BOBBY VARGAS

SUNDAY, 7:35 PM

"Arleen's with Ruben, *somewhere*—" Hahn runs the yellow light, then swerves to avoid a church crowd spilling off the sidewalk. "Where? Where would Ruben take her?"

I flash on the photo from Lý's apartment. "Cristo Rey."

Hahn cuts to me.

"Lý's altar had the Jap 7.7s, right? And the photos of the nun and St. Dom's. Maybe Lý puts all three together, organizes her and Ruben's payoff at St. Dom's or Cristo Rey."

Hahn blinks twice. "Feels right." She brakes hard, wheels west, and tromps the gas. Then swerves to miss a CTA bus.

And I see the billboard we've been missing since the beginning. "Lý's been planning each of these steps from jump street. This whole thing is about her. Lý's mad at the Koreans for whoring her—bunch of them are dead. Lý's mad at the Japanese—they're about to spend a ton of money and probably get front-paged anyway."

Storm clouds block the sunset and Chicago goes early dark. Hahn veers into headlights popping on. "Lý's not stopping at the front page."

I glance at Hahn and imagine the twenty-year-old betrayed by her benefactors, festering in that tiny apartment, aging, praying, waiting. "Buff brings Lý over, her life falls apart here—so Lý shoots him. The nun kicks her out—so Sister Mary Margaret's gotta die." *Swallow.* "Jesus. Row of dominoes, all the players in Lý's life from the beginning, wraps 'em all up in one big, irony-laced payback."

Hahn roars down the center line, jerking the wheel left, then right. "The nun kicked Lý out because of the Brennan sisters. And there's one Brennan left. Add your brother and the Twenty-Trey Gangsters and Lý's reassembled the whole cast of 1982."

I flash on the rage torn into the tiny apartment, the ancestor altar, the orphan girl whored at age eight, allowed to suffer and ferment by a number of societies that didn't see her as sufficiently valuable to save or threatening enough to kill.

White Flower Lý got Jewboy. Maybe Buff. And in a few minutes, she'll kill Arleen and my brother. Every person alive who matters to me. She is the plague. And I've never even seen her.

ARLEEN BRENNAN

SUNDAY, 7:40 PM

The backseat's full of live-virus mass murder. My hands are slick on the steering wheel. The car's humid, windows down in the hundred-degree heat. Ruben trails me thirty feet back. I'm driving a bomb set by his partner. Her breath on my neck ten minutes ago was— She brushed me with her lips, like she was . . . sniffing my skin. *Shiver. Sweat wipe.* Where does Ruben find these freaks?

Headlights pop on and flash across the windshield. *C'mon, Bobby, where are you?* It'll be full dark soon. Mirror glance—ten blocks and Ruben's phone is silent on the seat.

Man, that Corvair woman was creepy. And so was my reaction, like I've heard her voice before but was too shook to place it. *Swallow.* Mirror glance. Could've been an actress I worked with, or a flashback from my runaway years in sunny California, or a real mental patient from my teenage week at Tinley Park. When Coleen died.

Do not go there, not now.

The woman's voice was practiced, seductive, but Ted Bundy/Charles Manson behind it all. Ruben's phone rings. "Next block, turn right."

My eyes blur. I feel sick and pull to the curb.

Ruben yells: "Don't— What are you doing?"

Lilly Dillon tells Ruben, "Counting my money."

"No. Get movin'—"

I drop Ruben's voice onto the seat next to the *Herald* that claims Ruben and Bobby Vargas murdered Coleen, then heft the red gym bag Ruben's partner reached over and dropped onto my passenger seat. Fifty packs of hundreds, each an inch thick. Weighs about ten pounds. Half a million, not two million dollars. I grab the phone. Lilly Dillon says, "Where's the rest?"

"Move, or—"

"Threaten somebody else. My backseat's full of you and your psycho's future; fit perfect in the river." Pause. "I want the rest of my money now, or I take your box to Furukawa's building and give it to the doorman."

"The taste was one million, I told you that. We gave you half; will pop for another 1.5 when we're *all* done. Icing is the Shubert and my little brother. Arleen Brennan finally hits the lottery. That's worth followin' the script."

I scour the street for Bobby, and mumble, "Lottery my ass."

Ruben gives me directions that will head me and the mass-murder box due south. I have to find a way to tell Bobby where I am. Once Ruben has me where he wants me—

"Move, *chica.*"

"So we're clear, Ruben, if I'm not at the Shubert by eight tonight, my papers will be at your depositions tomorrow."

"Drop you myself. Sarah and I are your biggest fans."

Clark Street glance. No Bobby.

"Move, *chica,* or kiss the Shubert goodbye. Koreans get your name.

Spend the rest of your life explaining Lawrence Avenue, Greektown, and Santa Monica to prison guards and hit men."

I crush the phone. It's like being trapped in bed with a snake that bites you every time you move. If I had a gun, I could shoot Ruben, if I could get close enough. *Yeah, good, kill a third person.* Headlights blink to brights behind me. The box is still in the backseat. Lilly Dillon whispers, *Whatever it takes.*

Whatever it takes. Deep breath and I pull into traffic.

Ruben changes directions, winding me west under ten lanes of Dan Ryan viaduct. We're back near the Maxwell Market. The old streets are bumpy. Even driving slow, the box shakes on the seat. At each corner I hope for Bobby, see him there ready to save us.

My knight in shining armor doesn't miraculously appear. Ruben tells me to turn south through the switching yards, then past the tenement tear-downs of Union Avenue leveled for urban renewal when the city still had money to trade history for future.

Higher in the distance is the dullish glint of St. Dominick's steeple—the Irish anchor of the old Four Corners. Coleen and I and Bobby, the three of us one day would climb up there to the patinaed Gaelic cross, Tinker Bell would sprinkle us, and we'd fly away . . . Peter Pan, Wendy, and her sister. That was the promise, never see our father again. Coleen didn't.

But I did, on the pier in Santa Monica, the far far end, my father's brogue drifting toward me in the dark, him singing "Bold Belfast Shoemaker," the rest of him appearing out of the mist, mean drunk and sugary like he used to get, licking his lips, one thumb hooked in his belt, four fingers tapping at his jeans. Sixteen years after Coleen died and I'd run away . . . and there was my father, circling me again, telling me it was all my fault, me lying about that Vietnam hoor, how it killed my sister, his favorite little girl. Then me desertin' him, payin' his needs no mind at all.

Da was ugly and worn from the drink; worn from living with his awful self, but every bit as terrifying as before. His eyes were holes, burning with that cloying fever men save for *special times* with their little girls. Coleen and I hated that look and Ma never seemed to be around to make him stop. We were on our own when Da was like that.

Then Coleen was dead, and I *was* on my own. The last thing Da said to me was from five feet away.

"G'wan with ya then. If ya got the stones. Just pull the trigger."

And that's just what I did. Watched my bullets blow him into the Santa Monica Bay; watched his hands and arms reaching for me as he slowly sank under the pier, his face twisted into that same *special time* grimace.

Brights glare my mirror. Ruben's voice says, "The fence gate at St. Dom's is unlocked. Push the gate open with your bumper, drive in behind the convent."

I drive eight blocks of our old neighborhood. One streetlight is lit. St. Dom's is on my left, partially boarded up, and Gothic to the tall steeple and cross. At the gate, a Tim Rosinski FOR SALE sign is wired into the chain-link fence and spray-painted red with a five-point Latin King crown. Fresh blue TTG covers the crown and drips to the pavement.

More Twenty-Trey Gangsters. Coming back to life.

I left this place twenty-nine years ago. I knew it then, and I know it now: Something very bad will happen here.

25

OFFICER BOBBY VARGAS

SUNDAY, 7:45 PM

The hot, dark corridor echoes our footsteps. Cristo Rey is humid with blood and the stink of fouled clothing. The shape facing us from the shadows is the security guard, slumped to the floor. Blood fans the wall above and behind what remains of his head. I hear myself whisper, "Jesus." We search the office—no blood, but Sister Mary Margaret is gone and so is her walker.

Hahn and I guessed wrong; White Flower Lý's ancestor finale is at St. Dom's. It should've been here, electricity, nun who can't walk, except, except—it hits me with absolute certainty: "Lý's gotta kill *the building,* too."

Hahn stares.

"Lý's murdering her past. She's gonna let the plague go."

We run for the car. Hahn fires the engine, wheels from Twenty-second Place to Cermak, and guns us east. "When did St. Dom's close?"

"Ten years, twelve." I brace into the dash, imagine Arleen trapped inside with the plague. "Jesuits tried to use it as an outreach center for prostitutes and addicts. City and some of the neighbors shut 'em down."

Hahn pulls her second gun. "Grab the wheel."

"I promised I wouldn't let anyone hurt her. I fucking promised."

"Grab the goddamn wheel."

I do. Hahn checks the gun, then belts it. "Arleen knows my guys are dead; knows we lost her. She'll telegraph us, do something."

"I fucking promised."

Hahn knocks my hand off the wheel. "She agreed, Bobby. You didn't put her in here, your brother did."

I glare at Hahn, bounty hunter, acid queen. "If Arleen's not already dead, she's not dying for your money. And you aren't killing Ruben. Shoot him, I'll blow you're head off."

Hahn guns it through the red light at Ashland. "I'm here for the money and the plague. Your sainted brother is all yours."

My phone rings. "Arleen!" Thunder cracks in my ear, followed by crowd noise and static. "Hello? Arleen?"

Over the crowd noise Jason Cowin says, "Little Paul came in, recanted. So did the two debs who ID'd you. Everyone says Danny V made 'em."

Hahn brakes hard, bounces me into the door, and passes on the right. "And his mom, she alive?"

"Changed her story, too. ASA charged her and put the kid in Child Services. The Irish broad in your building hasn't folded yet, but we're all betting she will. When she does, maybe we talk to the Mrs Baird's driver and he changes his mind—nobody places you at Danny's death scene, no murder weapon, all is forgiven."

Something akin to relief pumps into the adrenaline. If I don't die in the next ten minutes, I'll only have to explain I'm innocent to half the people I meet. I don't tell Jason how I feel about being "forgiven," hit Disconnect, and re-brace into the dash. "Little Paul saw the light."

Hahn slips lanes doing ninety, loops across the center line into oncoming headlights, slides back in, and cuts off a van slowing to turn right. "I told you I took care of it." The van lays on his horn. Lightning cracks sideways across the sky.

I tell myself and the windshield, "Arleen and Ruben could be alive. White Flower's gotta have her show first, before she lets the plague go."

Hahn tells the traffic coming at us, "Show's already started."

ARLEEN BRENNAN

SUNDAY, 7:50 PM

Leaves and shadows brush at my ankles, then disappear into the dark of a long-dead playground. Above me, all around me, looms the Gothic roofline of St. Dom's. Sporadic lightning flashes the spire, painting the playground in stark, ominous shadows. Coleen and I played here as little girls. I see us in the harsh black-and-white flashes, our simple uniforms, the lies only partially hidden on our faces.

A dog barks twice. I blink, then stare out to St. Dominick's fence. Beyond the fence are the ruptured sidewalks and dented cars that fill the shadows. And out there, beyond the shadows, is the real horror of this place. I breathe short, taste the inner city and decay, and *will* Bobby to come here where we started.

A car approaches without headlights. Ruben, not Bobby, stops at the gate my bumper pushed open a moment ago. Ruben doesn't turn in. His phone rings in my hand. "*Niña,* take the box in the lunchroom door. The chain's cut."

I turn to the lunchroom doors. Doors I used till I was thirteen. Beyond them, the nuns ran a world very different from the one Coleen and I lived in a block away. Why pick this place of all the places?

"*Niña,* take the box inside. We're done and you can go."

My palms are sweating. My feet don't move.

"Now, *chica.* Or be late for the Shubert."

I stare at the red bricks around the doors, the old wood windows; a school, a convent with more ambition than money. More ambition than talent. I hold my breath, grab the box of plague, and walk to the doors. At the doors, I lower the box to the pavement, prop open the door with my foot, take another breath, slowly two-hand the box to my chest, and walk in.

Dark. Dusty. Mildew. Silent. My eyes slowly adjust. Lightning flashes the windows behind me and silhouetted shapes at a table at the far side of the lunchroom. I shuffle through the dark with my box of mass murder, careful not to bump or stumble. More lightning.

Up close, my favorite nun, Sister Mary Margaret Fey, is wide-eyed and gagged in her chair. She's wearing the Sisters of Providence habit she hasn't worn in twenty years. Down the table, the Japanese woman driver sits next to the male scientist from the Escalade—both wear Tyvek suits, gloves, and helmets that I don't. I place the box in front of them and wince at Sister Mary Margaret. "What . . . Why're you here?"

The Corvair mental-patient voice echoes from the dark. "You will sit."

"Can't." I back up toward the playground doors. "Have to go."

The man in the Tyvek suit lights a penlight and opens the box.

Behind me: "We are not done." The mental-patient voice blocks the playground doors. "Go back."

"No. I did my part—"

Ruben's voice barks, "Sit the fuck down."

I'm shoved forward by an unseen hand. Then shoved again and stumble to the table. The Japanese man steadies the box, glaring at me to stabilize. I sit across from Sister Mary Margaret. Her eyes are trying to explain, cutting toward the mental-patient voice.

Ruben's voice: "Inspect the package. Get on with it."

The Japanese man extracts the metal box I saw in the Corvair, sets the box on the table, steadies himself, then proceeds with his examination. When complete, he reexamines four vials, speaks Japanese to the woman in the Tyvek suit, and replaces the lid to the box.

The woman places both hands on the table. "We are pleased this is the Hokkaido package. We are not pleased that four vials are missing."

Ruben's voice: "Show us the money."

"We must have the vials first."

Ruben: "Guess we don't have a deal. White Flower goes to the *Herald.* Could stop by the concert along the way. With luck, Dr. Ota will escape, use the same pals bin Laden's family did."

The woman says, "This is a great sum of money to not have."

Ruben: "If I was lookin' at it, I'd believe you."

"Your gunmen are here." She gestures at the dark. "This is your place of choice."

A cloud of oleander makes me cough and the mental patient from the Corvair glides out of the dark. She places three vials on the metal box, hesitates, looking at Sister Mary Margaret, then me, then steps back into the dark. Sister Mary Margaret's eyes are full and desperate.

The Japanese man examines the three vials with great care, then the seals, then places the vials inside the metal container with the others. He tests the air at the table, then speaks Japanese to the woman, who in turn speaks Japanese to a phone she holds outside her helmet speaker.

She lowers the phone and says, "All but three million will be brought in. When we have the last vial, you will have your last three million."

Four minutes pass. I pat Sister Mary Margaret's hands, try to read her eyes but can't. Hinges creak somewhere in the distant dark. A baggage trolley materializes stacked with six large suitcases. A smallish figure in a wrinkled Tyvek suit pushes the trolley to the table and stops. The Tyvek suit speaks Japanese, probably the other Furukawa woman from the Escalade.

The seated woman says, "Three million per case. Please produce the last vial."

Ruben steps to the trolley, hip-checks the Tyvek suit away, and pulls on the heavy trolley. The smallish Tyvek suit jams a machine pistol in Ruben's ribs. Ruben stops. The woman at the table says, "The last vial, please."

Ruben says, "After I look at the money."

The woman speaks Japanese. The Tyvek suit with the machine pistol in Ruben's ribs lowers the gun. Ruben flattens one case atop the others, opens it, and shines a flashlight on stacks of hundred-dollar bills. Ruben uses a pen to mark bills in several stacks, closes the case, then repeats the process on another. Satisfied he says, "I have five machine guns pointed at you. I have two more at the door the money came through. Tell your associate next to me to go get my other three million and I'll ask White Flower to give you the last vial."

"The vial first."

"No, the money first, then the vial. That's how White Flower wants it, that's how it has to be."

The seated woman speaks Japanese. The smallish Tyvek suit next to Ruben disappears into the dark. We sit silent. I hold Sister Mary Margaret's hands. They're trembling but squeeze mine. I don't know a kinder woman. *Streetcar* was going to be my big surprise to her: limousine, front row, opening night.

Ruben glances his watch.

The Japanese woman and man sit motionless with their fourteen vials of plague.

Ruben speaks Spanish to the dark. I hear movement I can't see.

A moment passes. The second Japanese woman in the Tyvek suit reappears with another case. Except—blink, lightning flash—she's bent, rolling the case, but seems taller? Her Tyvek suit no longer has the wrinkles at the knees. *Squint.* And her gun's different? Following behind her is a Hispanic gangster, the Twenty-Trey muscled-up driver of the Marquis.

Ruben waits until the Twenty-Trey steps between him and the Tyvek suit, then flattens the case, opens it, and test marks the money. Satisfied, Ruben says, "Okay. Let's give 'em the last vial. Move on down the road."

Oleander sours the air. Ruben's partner steps out of the dark and stops at my end of the table. Her left hand is clamped around a green topped vial; her right hand holds the pistol with the long silencer I saw in the garage. She taps the silencer in front of Sister Mary Margaret and speaks Vietnamese. Sister Mary Margaret shakes her head an inch, eyes wide at the woman, then me. The woman leans in to me, the cheap oleander overpowering. Her mental-patient voice cracks on my name. "Arleen Brennan. But you do not know me? I do not matter, even now."

Blink. Stare. She's Asian, fifties, Vietnamese accent . . .

She says, "White Flower Lý? Lý Thi Loan? Tracy Moens knows. She search for me after Dupree lawsuit is filed."

The cheap oleander, the drinking fountain, Coleen— I push back in my chair, try to see better. Lightning flashes the windows. The face is the bad makeup from the garage, but smeared into—

Oh my God. *White Flower.* The winter of eighth grade, February 1982. White Flower had only been there a week. She and Coleen had an argument at the drinking fountain—White Flower was a postulant, no vows yet, but "living in the community," living at the convent to see if she wanted to become a novice. Like all the other girls, Coleen and I could become postulants, too, when we were older. My head begins to throb. It always throbbed when I thought about that year. So I stopped.

I see Sister Mary Margaret, then White Flower. It's 1982, we're all back together again.

Coleen and White Flower are at the drinking fountain, arguing, bitter, bitter. Sister Mary Margaret separates them, White Flower goes silent, but Coleen won't stop. White Flower's eyes are scary. Sister Mark, our prin-

cipal, steps into the hall and silences everyone. She calls us to her office; I don't want to go; Coleen doesn't want to go; we'll be in trouble with our da. We avoid trouble with our da at all costs. In the principal's office, Coleen accuses White Flower of things . . . things the girl didn't do. White Flower is very mad. Sister Mark is very mad—mad at White Flower, mad at Sister Mary Margaret. I know Coleen is lying but I stay quiet.

My head throbs. I shut my eyes. Coleen was sorry she lied, but she just didn't want our father to be mad, to be . . . involved. But he was.

Coleen and I sit as small as possible in our uniforms. Our da is on his way to St. Dominick's. Da will miss work on the river and be soooo mad. We wait a silent hour, holding each other's hands, knowing we will wet our pants when he begins to yell. He spanks us hard when we wet our pants. His work boots echo in the hall before he bursts through Sister Mark's door, the whole school can hear him yelling, "Hoorin' git Viet Communist messin' with my girls! And this being God's house, ain't that a damn lie!"

In the hall, Sister Mary Margaret leads White Flower past the door. Da leaps to the doorway screaming, "Aye, deport the hoor, ya should. Thievin' hoors got no business in a saint's school."

Coleen wets her pants and hides into my shoulder. Our parish priest appears at the door, "Francis Patrick Brennan, that'll be enough."

Da pays Father Crosby no mind. "Both you get home. It's a job and the belt you're needin', not a hoor's school."

Father Crosby steps between us and Da. "Your girls will be in the church, praying Hail Marys. I'll see 'em home when it's time."

"The hell you say." Da gives us the glare; we run all the way home.

Coleen and I never saw White Flower again. After Coleen died, I asked Sister Mary Margaret about White Flower. She shook her head, eyes on her hands, and said, "A sorrowful, sorrowful thing." Sometimes I thought it was me who was in the argument with White Flower, but I can't remember. Didn't want to remember.

Cold metal taps my cheek. My eyes jolt open. White Flower says, "Do you see? How all things end at the beginning? Same week as Moens began to search for me, Dr. Ota appeared on TV for the new Olympic bid. I've not see him since Saigon." White Flower raises the barrel at Sister Mary Margaret. "And while I watch Dr. Ota, now rich and powerful, forty years later, I knew what to do." White Flower shoots Sister Mary Margaret in the face. My nun catapults backward. Her knees hit the bottom of the table; she jerks back and slams face-first into the tabletop.

I jolt out of my chair, catch a foot, and splatter on the floor. Ruben mumbles, *"Chingada madre,"* and jumps behind the cases of money. I roll to stand, choking on blood mist and roar.

White Flower motions with her gun. "To the table. Everyone at the table."

None of me moves.

Lý aims at my chest. "Or I must kill you."

Nobody speaks. Blood drips off the table. Cordite mixes with copper air and adrenaline rushes. I climb into the chair, scrape it sideways but not closer to the table.

White Flower stares. "The Brennans age well." She taps the table with her vial.

"No. No." I shrink from the vial. "Don't do that."

Behind me, Ruben says, "Yeah, don't do that." His voice is sharp, parental. "Give the vial to our friends and let's be on our way."

White Flower looks past me to Ruben. "Do you wish to tell her?"

Silence, then Ruben says, "No kiddin' now; give the vial to the nice Japanese people and quit jerking around. This isn't the nail salon. You're rich. Act like it."

"I will tell her then." White Flower points her gun at my face. "Your sister died because of you, because you and she lied about me. Because your father fucked you, you afraid. You lied about me, and my life in America is over before it starts."

Ruben barks, "That's enough. Give them the vial."

Lý uses two fingertips to hold the vial four feet above the floor. "I will give them the vial. I give it to everyone."

Ruben: "Don't do that—"

"Then you must tell. Make pretty Arleen Brennan happy like she made me."

Silence. Ruben says, "Dupree may have raped your sister but he didn't kill her."

I turn my head to Ruben's voice. White Flower says, "Yes, Dupree raped her, or tried—he and his friend. But he did not kill Coleen. She was alive when we scared them off. We tell her we can help her. She was very scared. Very scared. Like you now."

I turn back to Lý's mental-patient voice. She's still dangling the vial, still aiming the pistol at my face. "You killed Coleen?"

Lý smiles the smeary Baby Jane paste-on smile.

"Did you?"

Ruben's voice: "If you're gonna shoot her, shoot her."

"I helped pretty Coleen into a better purpose. Where she can make apology for her lies. Ruben assist me. Remember? Ruben and I are alibi for each other. We stayed with Coleen until winter freeze and her wounds kill her—she was very, very hurt; very, very scared—then Ruben took credit with the Twenty-Treys. He is initiated. All good for everyone."

I lunge for the vial. White Flower fires. The bullet twists me sideways and the vial flutters between us. I land on the floor. Ruben fires across me and White Flower jolts off her feet. Ruben steps over me and shoots White Flower again. I palm the vial off my stomach and roll fetal.

Hurts bad to breathe. My ribs burn; blood soaks my dress; pumps on my arms. Ruben straddles my hips and aims at my head.

"Sorry, *niña*. Nothing personal, but . . . no Shubert after all."

The Tyvek suit to Ruben's right yells a muffled, "No!" I roll away from Ruben's gun; he fires. Concrete explodes by my head. The Tyvek shoots Ruben twice, spins, jams the pistol into the Twenty-Trey behind Ruben and fires twice. Machine guns roar. I crawl over Ruben and past White Flower. Starburst flames light up the dark. The vial is slippery in my hand. At the playground doors, I reach to push one open. The door and glass shatter above me. I push hard, wedge through at the bottom, and crawl out into pounding thunder.

Lightning rips through the black. Alone in the sky, St. Dom's Gothic spire is backlit in the storm and towers above me. I jolt away. Lightning and thunder pound again. The Chevrolet's front bumper flashes twenty feet ahead. *The Shubert.* I can still make the Shubert. Hurry.

I stagger to standing, lurch to the Chevrolet's fender, land hard but don't break the vial. My blood helps my hip slide fender to the door. I fight the driver's door open and crawl into the seat. The windows of

St. Dom's are flash and roar. My key twists in the ignition. The spire's jagged shadow swallows the car. No! I can get to my audition. Coleen and I will be stars; we'll be the girls who made it out of the Four Corners.

OFFICER BOBBY VARGAS

SUNDAY, 7:55 PM

Machine-gun bullets rip linoleum and plaster. My brother and his banger are sprawled at my feet. Hahn fires at a flame signature on my left; the Japanese woman fires at it from the table. Her man covers the package with his chest. One machine gun is down, another sprays the lunchroom until his clip empties. Hahn arcs left toward the shooter; I arc right, both of us invisible without the muzzle flashes. No other machine guns fire. On the playground side, Hahn stumbles or falls. The machine gun fires at her. I empty my pistol twelve-inches right of the flame. The flame jerks up into the ceiling and quits.

I rip off the Tyvek helmet, still can't hear, then creep darkness one hand in front, toward where the last flame signature was. Lightning cracks outside and flashes the floor thirty feet in front of me. A shape is prone, not moving. My pistol's empty. I extend it anyway, wait for a lightning flash, see the machine gun, kick it away, jump on the figure and smash his head with my forearm. He's short, Hispanic, and dead.

I yell for Hahn. "Shooter's down."

My echo answers.

I grab the machine gun, dump the clip, feel bullets, but no idea how many, slam the clip back and creep darkness back toward the trolley. No one fires. Ruben's gunmen are dead, out of bullets, or gone. I make the trolley and duck behind it.

Lightning flashes—my brother on his back. I drop to both knees. "Ruben. It's me."

Nothing, motionless.

I rip off a Tyvek glove and squeeze his wrist for pulse, then his neck.

"C'mon, Ruben, help me." I press hard on his chest, then harder and harder. Ruben's blood covers my hand. He doesn't breathe. He doesn't do anything.

"Ruben!" Tears well through the adrenaline. I hug Ruben to me hard as I can. Lightning flashes his face cradled against my chest, his brown eyes staring up at me. "Ruben!"

My brother Ruben is dead. I killed him.

Voices.

A penlight is lit on the other side of the trolley. Hahn and the Japanese woman face each other, pistol to pistol across the table. The woman's Tyvek suit has two bullet holes. Hahn's neck is bloody and gripped by her left hand. Hahn says, "I'm taking the money."

Japanese woman: "No. One vial is missing. Arleen Brennan must give it."

I scan for Arleen, wipe at the tears and smooth Ruben's hair. "It's okay, *carnal.* The vial didn't break."

The Japanese woman glances to my voice. Hahn shoots her twice, jumps left, and jams her pistol into the Japanese man covering the Hokkaido package. Hahn says, "I'm taking the package."

The man doesn't move. He has one bullet hole in the back of his helmet and a screen full of blood. Hahn gingerly pulls him back to sitting and he slumps in the chair. The package is intact. Hahn glances at me cradling my brother on the floor and levels her pistol at my chest. Instead of finishing her mission, she says, "Those cases have $18 million. The Koreans believe it's theirs and they know Arleen's name. I'll give you three mil. Take one case, find your girlfriend before the Koreans do, and bury your brother." Pause. "Or start shooting."

My finger tightens on the trigger.

So does Hahn's.

ARLEEN BRENNAN

SUNDAY, 8:15 PM

Dizzy. Rain pounds in sheets.

My Chevrolet's front wheel is on the sidewalk under the Shubert's marquee. The doors to the theater are locked. I pound the glass and yell: "Hello? Hello?" Cough. Swallow. "Out here. Hello?" The lobby's dark and no one answers. *But I'm in time.* I'm not too late. I use both hands to peer; the glass smears red. Sarah's not here. Having trouble keeping my breath. I wipe at the blood smears on the glass. My knees begin to give. I swivel my shoulders to the doors and slump to a pile. Breathe deep. *Pro-ject.* I try to stand but can't. But I'm here, under the marquee lights, in time. Swallow. When the director comes and Jude Law and Toddy Pete . . . I'll be here ready to go on.

I reach for my phone. No purse. I want to call Bobby, tell him to come watch me win. We'll go out after. Be great. Pizza and Guinness. I touch my dress. Lotta blood. Blanche will have to wear a sweater.

Where is everyone? They should all be here; this is important.

Lightning crashes through the rain. A car screeches to the curb behind mine and up onto the sidewalk. Sarah! No, it's Bobby Vargas. Bobby made it. He kneels, eyes glisteny, and touches my shoulders.

"C'mon. The Koreans know your name; they'll be looking here. We gotta get you to a hospital."

I wince back. "No. My audition. Right now."

He blinks, looks up at the marquee, then stares at me, touches my dress, then my arm. His voice is a whisper. "I didn't know what Ruben did to Coleen. I didn't. I'm so sorry. I just didn't."

Ruben? Ruben's not in *Streetcar.* I finger at the spacesuit Bobby's wearing, the blood splattered on it. "Why are you wearing a spacesuit?"

"That was me at St. Dom's, at the end. C'mon, you're hurt."

He lifts at me. "Oughh! Stop; I have to stay. To meet Sarah."

"No, honey, listen. Sarah's not coming."

"Yes, she is! She is. She has to—"

"No, honey. They found Sarah in the backseat of a Corvair. Your number was the last one she called."

Blink. Swallow. "She'll be here. Eight o'clock."

Bobby puts both hands on my face. "They postponed the audition for an hour so you can clean up, give it your best shot. Okay? Let's get you cleaned up so you can win."

"I can win, Bobby, I can. Coleen and I will win this time. Ruben can't stop us."

Sirens wail; lightning flashes like cameras. I made it. I'm under the Shubert's grand marquee on opening night; finally the right place, the right time. Coleen and I get our chance.

Bobby helps me to my feet. In the rain, the brilliant lights of the Shubert's grand marquee are reflected in the glass building across Monroe Street.

Just Signed!
Jude Law & Tharien Thompson
A STREETCAR NAMED DESIRE

26 RITA BLANCA NATIONAL GRASSLANDS

Oklahoma–Texas Border, Two Days Later

OFFICER BOBBY VARGAS

TUESDAY, 3:00 PM

I've had forty-three hours to justify killing my brother, the brother who taught me everything I know about being the police; the brother who raised me after my father died, who protected my mom and a neighborhood of people the system failed or outright abused. I shot him twice, not once. One, he might have survived. And that wouldn't be right.

I stopped crying in southern Iowa—for him and for Coleen—then slept in fits at a rest area when my eyes couldn't take any more headlights. Mostly I've driven parched, dusty back roads by day and anonymous, dark interstates by night. Fifteen hundred miles of blurred America while Arleen cried in her sleep or stared blank-eyed at her window. We've made four stops for gas, plastic-wrapped food, and maps. I've stolen license plates in Iowa, Oklahoma, and Texas, and against all reasonable odds, Arleen and I are still free.

The Chicago Doc-in-a-Box visit cost us ten thousand, but he patched Arleen's side and gave me a bottle of painkillers to keep her calm. I don't know if I've ever wanted a dope vacation more, but someone had to drive. I wouldn't say we've been the best company. And I wouldn't say that the pixie dust I hoped for has been anything but dust.

We cross into Texas in the Rita Blanca and the radio plays Joe Ely's "Row of Dominoes." Arleen pushes back in her seat, winces at the hole in her side, and looks at me. Her green eyes show age that wasn't there two days ago, clouded with what she knows and what the drugs cover.

She motions for the water bottle on my lap, takes a sip, blinking at a vast prairie that could be another planet. She scoots to mid-seat, leans her head gently on my shoulder, says, "All things considered, you may be Peter Pan after all," and goes back to sleep.

27 U.S.-MEXICAN BORDER

Santa Elena, Texas

OFFICER BOBBY VARGAS

WEDNESDAY, 1:00 AM

Texas is low and hot and withered where it meets the Chihuahuan Desert. *Meets* is the wrong word; *collides* is what the two nations actually do. At the western tip of the Big Bend, Mexico isn't twitch-eyed and subservient. Here the favored destination of most U.S. fugitives on a budget is a massive fourteen-hundred-foot, raw-limestone escarpment cleaved by a narrow canyon river. The river empties into our southern border, the oddly named Rio Grande—a thick, bubbly trickle of mostly fertilizer washed down from the desert above. The river separates third world from first. It has a certain smell a Chicago kid would recognize; our river's like that, too, flows backward so what we put in it doesn't come back to poison us.

Same as a lot of things.

In the moonlight, Arleen sits the same heavy wooden bench as me, leaning her bandaged back against a chalk-stained adobe wall that's supported many a weary traveler in its two hundred years. Her knees are pulled to her chest. She sips a Shiner beer and balances the bottle on her knees. There's an awful lot of dark between us. In us. All around us.

Arleen nods toward the border. "Think we'll make it?"

I stare at the only girl I ever really wanted, dreamed about her so hard she came back to life. "You mean us? Arleen and Bobby?"

She sips the Shiner again.

"Do you want to?"

Arleen nods. "Think so. Could be the drugs, though."

I squint at my watch, try not to grin. "If we're gonna beat the posse, my boys have to get here before sunup."

Arleen searches the vast starlit horizon for the riders coming to hunt us down. "How much money do Bobby and Arleen have for happily ever after?"

I show her six fingers.

"Six *what*? My purse had my wallet; the red bag's in the Chevy. I'll need clothes for our first date."

"Million. Hahn wanted to give me three, but I explained you'd need money to build a theater."

The beer drops out of her hand. "You have six *million*?"

"*We*. Arleen and Bobby." I nod at our car. "In there."

Arleen blinks, exhales, and almost smiles. "Hadn't thought of building my own theater. And you could have the blues club next door."

"Yep. Plan to buy a studio soundboard; Ed Cherney will visit; show me how to use it. We'll be the new Buena Vista, like in Havana." I sit up straight. "Call it the Seven Spanish Angels."

Arleen's eyes add a bit of sparkle, war-torn but it's there. "If you were nice, I might wait tables for you, teach your crew how to run it."

"But you'd still open the theater. You have to."

Arleen shrugs. "Those days may be past me."

"No. No. You believed in you for twenty years. I believe in you now. We'll build the theater first; I'll run the bar at halftime."

"Intermission."

"Yeah. See, we're already halfway through opening night."

She actually laughs, then winces. "*Jesus*. Don't want to get shot again." She inspects her side. "Will I be all right?"

I smile twenty-nine years at her. "Already are."

She reaches to the floor, wincing again, grabs a handful of sandy dirt, kisses it, and throws it across the hood of our car. "Pixie dust. Everyone believes in something, might as well be us."

I kiss her on the mouth; start to tell her— She puts a finger gently on my lips.

"Don't talk. Show me."

WEDNESDAY, 6:00 AM

Maybe Masters and Johnson could describe it as sex. But I can't. I've never experienced the absolute electric shock of book-and-movie passion before; the five-senses, all-consuming, drown-yourself-in-happiness epiphany. If that was sex, there'd be no time for eating or drinking. It's all anyone would do. They'd be here in the moonlight, on the border, on the run with Arleen Brennan, the Rosetta stone of delirious, skin-on-skin, don't-ever-let-go, first-time, prom-night, best-girl-ever loves me *and* wants to prove it. Bobby Vargas stands corrected, there is a God. And she's a woman. No guy could put that together.

Arleen nuzzles against me on our bench. Her bandaged back rests on my stomach, her strawberry blond hair and its scent on my chest, both of us watching the ceiling fan's slow rotation. She listens to my iPod. I'm planning our dazzling future once we're smuggled out of the United States.

Any minute, with a last bit of luck, we'll be headed to the state of Michoacán, the city of Villamar, and my mother's family. I never met my mother's family and I never met Mexico, the land of my ancestors. Mexico and Mexicans will save us—no irony in that. The family doesn't don't know I shot Ruben, just that their favorite nephew is dead.

My phone rings; the number is Tracy Moens. I answer, not sure why, maybe because she's called fifty times in the last three days and her "life/death" text messages deserve at least one comment before this phone goes in the river. I pat Arleen's strawberry blond hair, say, "Our taxi," loud to her earphones, then button green.

Moens says, "Don't hang up. First, thanks for the vial, the Hokkaido package tip, and the warning. Made quite an impression."

"Thought you'd see a story there somewhere. Spell Jewboy's name right."

"I will. Bad news is, so will the U.S. attorney. In nine hours, Jo Ann Merica says she will charge and prosecute *someone* for terrorism under the Patriot Act—nationwide, hell, *worldwide* media coverage of a major World Trade Center attack that she and a federal undercover agent kept from happening."

"Merica wants to be governor. Wish her luck."

"Yes, she does, maybe president when she also rights the wrongs of the Coleen Brennan murder and Dupree execution."

"Like I said, wish her luck."

"She needs someone to charge, Bobby. And it won't be Robbie Steffen. Two Koreans shot him yesterday. He died this morning." Pause. "That leaves you and Arleen Brennan."

Eyes shut. The dark never stops. Eyes open. "Two things that might matter: we don't live in America anymore, and the facts don't fit."

"They fit well enough. Ask Dupree. Add Robbie to the eight dead at St. Dominick's and Chicago's chances of being selected the 2016 Olympic City dim to candle power. Lot of angry movers and shakers, including the mayor and the superintendent. Someone has to hang and it's not going to be them."

"How about the actual bad guys?"

"All dead, other than Dr. Ota—Chicago's esteemed benefactor. Merica and the feds will cleanse Furukawa's CEO as a quid pro quo to the mayor's political weight in D.C. and Furukawa's Wall Street bankers—both carry a lot of water on Pennsylvania Avenue. Merica will cast Dr. Hitoshi Ota as the victim/target of a 'racist lie and blackmail plot' perpetrated by rogue Chicago cops and serial child molesters/murderers long involved with the Twenty-Trey Gangsters. Merica intends to make you her centerpiece in the crime, partners from the beginning with your brother, Robbie Steffen, and the Twenty-Treys."

I don't answer. Thinking instead about my parents, immigrants Vargas and Ruiz who loved America every day they were alive. Now their names and Ruben's, and mine, will be one comma from Gacy and Speck.

Moens says, "Coleen Brennan was exhumed yesterday morning. In the casket was a diary written by her and Arleen. Other than the parts about you, the entries I've seen aren't pretty." Pause. "The U.S. attorney will leak her 'interpretation' to garner maximum public support pretrial, and by the time the public understands what Arleen and Coleen really meant, they'll have lynched you as a serial child molester/murderer who also planned to turn the plague loose in the city."

"Does Arleen get a part in . . . this?" Arleen bends her neck to look at me. I wink *No problem.*

"If you surrender, Merica will not indict, nor arrest, Arleen Brennan. And as a bonus, Merica will drop your gang team from any federal investigation."

"Buff, my sergeant?"

"He made it out of ICU, beyond that I don't know. I *do* know that if you *don't* surrender today, *now*, U.S. Attorney Merica will immediately initiate a worldwide manhunt for terrorists Arleen Brennan and Roberto Vargas. By lunchtime a federal grand jury will indict Arleen and you as coconspirators on the terrorism charge and anything else CPD can dig up. Merica also promises to use her federal budget to go after everyone in Gang Team 1269 whether she and her undercover agent can put them at St. Dominick's or not—charging them with terrorism and/or conspiracy to commit. All anyone on your team had to do was help you once in the last six days and they're in Marion or Leavenworth for life."

"Merica making me the devil doesn't mean I know anything about St. Dom's other than the address."

Silence, then: "Odd mix, Bobby, even for the Four Corners—a cop, three newly minted Twenty-Trey gangsters, a Vietnamese woman missing since 1982, a nun, and three employees of Furukawa Industries, two of them in Tyvek suits."

"What's that to me?"

"The cop was your brother."

"Yeah." Exhale. "So I hear."

"Tania Hahn says you were inside St. Dom's and heard it all."

"She's mistaken."

"Hahn says she'll do what she told you she would do if you leave her out of it."

"You and Tania pals now?"

"She has her reasons." Pause. "I can help you—*I think.* It'll be risky as hell, but you have to come back, turn yourself in, and stand trial, maybe trials." Pause. "I have some of the story of the Brennan sisters and the Vargas brothers—you give me the rest on the record. Then you tell me everything you know about the Hokkaido package and the massacre at St. Dom's—on the record. I'll make sure Jo Ann can't spin you into a noose or convict you without a trial."

"Geez, that's all? Helluva deal."

Moens says, "I think we can beat her heads up, win an acquittal, but there'll be no bond and it'll take a while." Moens lays out a plan that three days ago I would've laughed at. But three days ago I wasn't a fugitive, wanted for murder and child molestation, and about to be charged with terrorism under the Patriot Act. I tighten my hold Arleen. She won't do well in jail.

Moens closes with "If you come back, Merica and CPD will leave Arleen alone. I can get that in writing in the form of full immunity— that's how bad Merica wants you to stand trial for your brother's . . . enterprise." Pause. "Carve this last advice in stone: If you don't surrender, there is absolutely nowhere either of you can hide from a terrorism charge in the age of 9/11. Period. Unless you're Osama bin Laden . . . and they probably know where he is anyway."

"Call you back." I flip my phone shut.

Arleen pops out her earphones. "We okay? Everything set?"

"Pixie-dust express is on the way. Had to clear up a few things."

My hand and pistol rest on Arleen's flat stomach. She snuggles her shoulders into my chest. "I was thinking two hundred seats, but maybe one-fifty is better. Three sections, no center aisle, a balcony—"

"Duh? How else would they throw the roses?"

She cants her head up and cuts those green eyes toward mine. "You've never been in a theater, have you?"

"A drive-in. And, ah—"

She rolls back to flat. "We'll let you usher, work security. In no time at all, you'll be crew, then who knows, a bit part, the chorus . . ."

"Don't I own part of the theater?"

"Yes." She pats at my hand, avoiding the pistol. "But where we're headed, it's talent and effort only. No plastic surgeons or *American Idol* auditions. The Lost Boys Theater Company is the province of hopes and dreams, not crocodiles."

"Thespians . . . I'll be next door at the Seven Spanish Angels. Build three or four apartments; play the blues with the old guys rap doesn't care about. You can come over after the show."

Arleen turns all the way over, mouth tight against the pain, and pulls herself up to my face. She flutters eyes that would stop traffic in Ireland, then kisses me just once. "I'd whore to keep you in microphones." She kisses me again, this time with her hands in my hair. "We'll build your bar first. I'll train the waitresses."

"Who trains the owner?"

"Is he handsome? Does he have a *really* big thing for me?"

I stare, soaking it in for as long as I can. "Yeah, he does. Always has."

She smiles like she has for twenty-nine years on those nights I'd let it go that far, like Jenny did in *Forrest Gump* when she finally came home for good.

Car engine. We both roll off. I stand with my pistol. Arleen steps back. The headlights cut; it's a pickup truck, old but sturdy. Two men exit, tanned or brown, sweat-stained, rancher hats and T-shirts. They see my gun and me, but not Arleen. The drivers says, "*Hola,*" then continues in Spanish.

"English. This is America."

The driver blinks, confused, then looks across the fender to the other man. He chins at me, asking, "Roberto Vargas Ruiz?"

My mother's family name is Ruiz. I nod, hand tightening on the Glock Hahn gave me. "You are?"

In Spanish he says, "Not a man who wishes to be insulted."

He has workingman's hands and today is a workday. I ask his name. "*Cómo se llama?*"

"Renaldo Ruiz Peña." In Spanish he adds, "We flew a thousand kilometers from Guadalajara, then drove three hundred from Ciudad Acuña to be here. To do your mother's memory this favor."

I belt the Glock and offer my hand. In Spanish I say, "My apologies, *señor.* Thank you for coming. And thank you for honoring my mother."

He nods. "The family knew your brother, but not you. We understand being away from us is your choosing." He shakes my hand anyway. His passenger steps around the fender and does the same. The driver says, "We must go, the sun rises early for the farmers and the border patrol." He points west in the darkness.

"My Spanish isn't so good. Can we speak English?"

He nods.

"Only one of us is going. Take her to Villamar like we agreed, okay?"

He glances past me.

"Get her settled, talk to the pilots at Concepción de Buenos Aires, you go with her when she flies to—"

A hand jerks my shoulder. "I'm not going anywhere *alone.*"

Arleen glares. I wince at Renaldo Ruiz Peña. *"Con permiso, señor."* Arleen follows me twenty feet back under the lean-to roof. She stops at the two suitcases, shoulders back. "Doesn't matter what you know that I don't, you and I are driving, walking, or swimming across that border. You're the first man I've ever slept with because I wanted to. Think about that. I was just happy for five whole hours. I'm not ready to quit and neither are you."

I show her the phone.

"I knew it was Moens. I don't care what she said, promised, or threatened. To hell with the Korean mafia, the Japanese—"

"It's not Moens, it's the U.S. attorney. If I surrender, Merica leaves 1269 and . . . everyone else out of her 'terrorism' run for governor."

"No." Arleen shakes her head. "You're not going back. We'll find another way. We have money; we'll buy your friends a way out. They can come live with us on our island, in Cuba, South Africa, wherever."

"I fit too well. My friends are just accomplices."

"Señor Vargas?"

I hold up my hand again. *"Un momento, señor."*

Arleen shifts so she's between Renaldo Ruiz Peña and me. "No, Bobby. No way. You're not going."

I try to hug her; she shoves me back. "No."

"Jason and Buff are my family. If I'd let them hang, then I'd let you hang." Gray light hints on the distant horizon. "You've seen an awful lot of promises go bad, and so have I. You'd wonder about me, about us. This way, if I make it back, you'll never have to wonder. Every night, for the rest of your life, you'll be safe." I wait for her agreement. "C'mon. That's worth the risk, isn't it?"

"No." She glares, a lioness rising to protect a cub. "Hundred percent they'll bury you in some version of Guantánamo Bay for the rest of our lives. This will be it, Bobby—*three days, five hours*—and a goodbye at the border." Headshake. "No. Absolutely not."

I try to clutch her shoulders and she knocks my hands away.

"Arleen, c'mon, you think I *want* to go back? Where could we go after a U.S. attorney classifies me or you as a terrorist? Our part of the world doesn't have Pakistan and Afghanistan. The CIA or the FBI will have me, us, in a month. My gang team still gets jammed, everyone loses but the bad guys."

"It's not your turn, Bobby. The Brennans and the Vargases have paid enough dues. We get more than three days."

"Señor Vargas, the sunrise, we must go."

"Lo siento. Un momento mas." I turn to Arleen. "Here's the plan—"

"I know the plan, I listened to you put it together in Iowa and Oklahoma—we get in the truck with these gentlemen. They sneak us across the river, then drive us twelve hundred kilometers south into the Michoacán mountains. From your mother's hometown we fly private across Mexico's southern border into Panama where we buy a case of champagne and sunblock, hide in Casco Viejo, sort ourselves out for Africa or some uncharted island paradise, hire a boat to sail there, and live happily ever after."

"Going back is just an interim stop."

"Yep. For somebody else."

"Señor Vargas—"

Arleen grabs me, and walks us toward him. "We're coming."

I stop and she spins into my face.

"Do you love me, Bobby? You love the *concept* of us? Twenty-nine years later we make it out of the Four Corners; we beat the system, the odds, the goddamn horror memories of Eighteenth and Laflin. Tell me you love me, us, *the goddamn concept* enough to let us win one goddamn time."

"Will you listen? Stop being *a star* for one minute?"

Glare.

I touch her shoulder. "Sorry; I didn't mean that. Listen, okay? All the vials have been recovered, so there's no current threat. Furukawa and all the politicians they've bought over the years don't want publicity. Chicago wants the Olympics—when all the negotiating is done, Merica wants to be governor, the CIA's deal with Hahn and her ilk isn't something Langley wants to talk about, and no one wants me defending myself daily in the media—"

"Double-cross the U.S. attorney, Wall Street, and the biggest fundraisers of both political parties . . . screw them over and win? That's the Moens plan?"

"Spin, that's all. You're in the movies. Think *Taxi Driver*—the guy's a nutcase who circumstance casts as the hero instead of the presidential assassin he is. This spin's no different, and it saves the *Herald* if they push it. Moens already has most of our story in the Four Corners for her 'MONSTER' exposé, and now she has a worldwide scoop on a second World Trade Center attack that she'll say *you and I stopped.* If I come back, Hahn will anonymously help Moens and me if we don't name her in my testimony and the articles."

Arleen steps back, doesn't want to hear any of it.

"It's a long shot, but it could work. We win, forever, not just a couple more days till they find us. Neverland, Arleen, where we swing on the porch hammock, not hide in the basement. And I can do it."

I grab one bag of money and toss it in the truck. Arleen watches. Then I pay my uncle for the trip and promise a substantial bonus when Arleen calls me from Panama. My uncle and I shake hands; he slides in behind the wheel, fires the engine, and his friend jumps in the pickup's bed.

The passenger door hangs open, me next to it, Arleen Crista Brennan ten feet away. "Arleen, if you don't go now, our chances are zero." I chin at the sunrise coming in a few minutes.

Arleen stares for ten long seconds, then shuts her eyes in submission and pushes strawberry blond hair behind her ear. "Bye, Bobby."

"No. I'll do this, I will."

Her shoulders relax, both hands rest limp on her hips.

"I will. I'll be there."

Arleen nods small. "I forgot that three days ago I was bleeding to death under a marquee with someone else's name on it, forgot that when we drove away I quit begging people to want me and my dreams. But I guess I begged so many and for so long it's hard to stop." She walks past me and pats my hip as she does, slides into the truck, and closes the door. "Wendy had to leave, had to grow up—that's the part we never talked about."

My uncle drops the truck in gear, and that fast, after twenty-nine years, three nights, and five hours, Arleen Crista Brennan is gone.

EPILOGUE

ARLEEN CRISTA BRENNAN

I come here once a year. At exactly this time. And lay the unbound pages on this table. I come here thinking I'll write the ending to *The Four Corners,* but I haven't.

Beyond the iron railing, the sun drops slow into an icy South Atlantic; the harbor's saltwater air and today's catch of rock cod drift upland in the wood-fire smoke. Gusts ruffle my hair and the yellowwood trees. A winter gale's coming, but then there's always a gale coming at the Cape—took me two winters to get used to wearing sweaters in July, to having the seasons backward. Becoming someone else wasn't as difficult; except for a few hours five years ago on the Mexican border, I've always been someone else.

Thunder rumbles behind Hout Bay's Constantia Mountains. And who's to say which plans work out and which don't? Some plans are fairy tales from the beginning, the only thing they can do is fall apart.

Was being a valued, successful actress a fairy tale? Was for me, is for most of us aspirants, more of a Pentecostal walk through the fire than a career. If you're still alive after the fire walk, you don't exit *cleansed,* just charred; but if you're willful to a fault, and tough, and lucky to have options other than old photographs and an apron, you find another dream when the actress dream dies, another dream that can save you.

You shoot for happiness instead of bright lights and marquees, however happiness might come. And then when some form of happiness is so close you can actually believe it's your turn—it crashes at the Mexican border. Then you come here—out of hiding twice a year, stand on this high, seafront patio with two bodyguards from Pretoria, and wait. It's risky and childish and melodramatic, but it's what you have, what Norma Desmond had.

Because on any given day—ten thousand miles across that stormy ocean—Bobby Vargas could walk out of a special U.S. military prison and into a federal courtroom that frees him and forces a trial. Political winds change; Japanese campaign contributions fall out of favor. Fear of all things dark stops winning elections, selling NRA memberships, and anointing TV demigods.

If that day comes, and relentless Korean mob bosses magically quit believing we have their $20 million, Bobby Vargas will walk between these empty, windblown tables, Fender guitar case in hand. And I'll be here. It could happen—he was sitting in the L7 after twenty-nine years. What are the odds of that? Forrest and Jenny found each other in the thousands at the Lincoln Memorial.

For more nights on my pillow than I'd care to admit, I've watched Bobby walk across this patio. I blink, not believing it's finally him—the boy who promised to save me from the Four Corners and did—I run into his arms, his lips on mine, his hands in my hair, the same kind, beautiful hands that drew on my stoop. It's good, better than what Tennessee Williams could write.

Sometimes it's the night after, Bobby and I are smiling like little kids, sharing one of these cliff-side two-tops, the candle barricaded from the wind, our hands gripped soft under the table. Just us out here, the whole world our vista. We sip Castle beers that taste sweet like his mouth, talk about Cape Town and Hout Bay while the South Atlantic's twenty-foot waves crash below us, talk about how our dreams ended up so far away in Africa.

But they are *our* dreams and we finally have them; that's how I've written it, how J. M. Barrie would've written it had he known about Bobby Vargas, Coleen, and me. J.M. would write that Coleen was Wendy, the girl who went back long ago to grow up and show us the way here, then Bobby and I flew and flew and flew till we found each other again, found our Neverland at the far end of the world.

When I cleared customs into Namibia's Restricted Area, the first thing I bought was the case of champagne and sunblock. Call them a talisman; I was angry and hurt and bought them anyway. Both are stored upstairs in the small apartment I keep over the bar. The Seven Spanish Angels. A handsome Afrikaner runs it for me, a rugged gentleman I shared a bed with briefly last year, before he and I realized that my heart and head were elsewhere, or gone altogether. I keep Tharien Thompson's photo on the wall as well; a rave review in the *Cape Times* for her performance in *Streetcar.* Like Julie McCoy's famous faces and their photos in the L7, Tharien stumbled into the Seven Spanish Angels once and signed hers. They love her here.

Watch check. Low clouds top the mountain and spill toward the bay. Might want to go inside and tell the staff I'm in town. With the time difference, in three minutes it will be five years since I got in that dusty pickup with Bobby's extended family. That part of the plan worked—not perfect, and not without a few scary moments, but it worked. Made me think hard about family, why some people have it and many don't. Other than Coleen, the families I built were wastelands. Bobby has two sets, neither one a wasteland—the Mexicans who saved me, and the gang cops and city he saved. Some people are like that; they look for the light until it finds them.

I wonder if there's light in Bobby's cell, what it's like to be a hero, the price you pay when the crimes of a brother can't go unrepented. I didn't know it then, but I do now—Bobby went back to save me, to buy the Brennan sisters a pass at a life we'd never had. Just like he promised he would.

My fingertips trace the play I've written—we've written, using my hand.

An Alfa sedan passes slower than it should and I reset the SIG Sauer under my jacket. The Korean mafia is a world organization with a strong element in Nigeria and South Africa, but I had connections here via the ex-military couple who kept me at the L.A. youth home. All alone in Panama, they seemed like my best option—hell, my only option. Carel Roos of CTC Security eyes the Alpha, hand inside his jacket. Carel and one of his Afrikaners travel with me when I come down here through Port Nolloth from the Restricted Area. Out in the open I'm a much easier target. I've heard Bobby and I are both worth mid-six digits, but it has to be alive.

Thunder rumbles closer behind me, one of the daily storms that batter the end of the African continent. More than anything, I wanted Bobby and I and Coleen to win one time. I wanted to deserve the light, wanted to hold hands with it, with a man who wasn't my father or a director or a casting agent. Just a man who loved me, a boy in a window whose promise that we would fly away kept me alive through a lifetime of dark.

Carel Roos nods not to worry about the Alfa, then steps back to his spot on the stairway wall. His shoulders flatten against the cut granite, as does the sole of one shoe. He turns to the Seven Spanish Angels' arched front door and a black girl exiting toward me. Stephanie smiles at him, then hands me an envelope. "From America." She points inside at the bartender opening up. "Étienne thinks it might be for you."

The envelope's addressed to Blanche DuBois, c/o the Seven Spanish Angels Bar, Hout Bay, South Africa; then the postmark—Michoacán, Villamar, Mexico. The Ruiz-Peñas know the Seven Spanish Angels and the name Blanche DuBois should there ever be a reason . . . I check Carel, then Chapman's Peak Drive, heart adding beats, fear of contact, the price on my head. I draw the SIG Sauer. Carel stiffens, eyes on me, the patio, the road. He draws his pistol, sends his man back inside the bar, then up into the apartment.

Nothing. No Korean kidnap team.

Exhale. Swallow. Bobby Vargas is dead: that's what is inside this envelope.

I belt my pistol and open the envelope, all the emotion I thought was dead rushing at me. Inside is a newspaper clipping from the *Chicago Herald* dated six weeks ago and nothing else. The clipping recounts the successful business dealings of Furukawa Industries and its CEO, Dr. Hitoshi Ota. The last paragraph mentions a Chicago ex-policeman, Roberto "Bobby" Vargas. Concern has been expressed by a spokesman for Furukawa because the terrorism charges against Bobby Vargas have been dropped, and pending a trial for the murder of Danny Vacco, Bobby Vargas has been released but did not appear at his pretrial hearing.

Wind flutters the clipping; I grab it back before I lose it to the South Atlantic. On the back is an outline . . . a heart, like the chalk ones we drew on my stoop. Inside the heart, tiny letters read: Forrest & Jenny.

Stephanie says, "Hand delivered," and points across the road.

DEDICATION

SIMON LIPSKAR–JASON KAUFMAN

Publishing is a tough business, not densely populated by individuals on whom it pays to rely, especially if you intend to say what you mean and cash a second check. Simon Lipskar has stood with me through one fire after another and never done anything other than exactly what he said. This novel is at Doubleday, the top of the mountain, for one reason: Simon Lipskar. The reason it stayed there is Jason Kaufman.

Jason Kaufman knows the commercial market the way you and I know the way home. Yet he bought a novel of "devastating violence" and didn't suggest I add a warm puppy or a vampire, or match a national retailer's color scheme. Instead, Jason focused his editorial participation on rebalancing character and plot, a difficult, artful undertaking that requires a deep understanding of the form, the message, and the author's limitations. Win or lose, I buy his drinks forever.

AND . . .

To the angel of Andre Libre—although you weren't—we promised to tell your story one day. Should you be at peace with it, these two fellows are who you thank.